SONS AND DAUGHTERS

Love, tragedy and excitement in the lives of the Adams family

By the year 1949 life in Walworth has almost returned to normal and Sammy and Boots, now in a highly successful partnership, are rebuilding the family firm. An old enemy resurfaces who seems determined to ruin the various branches of the growing business and it takes all the well-known Adams ingenuity to outwit his thugs. Meanwhile, an attractive blonde woman has caught Boots's eye, stirring the worst of memories for Boots from the darkest days of the war. On a happier note, there is some surprising news for Chinese Lady, which will affect the whole of the Adams family.

1857

SONS AND DAUGHTERS

SONS AND DAUGHTERS

by

Mary Jane Staples

Magna Large Print Books
Long Preston, North Yorkshire,
BD23 4ND, England.

British Library Cataloguing in Publication Data.

Staples, Mary Jane
    Sons and daughters.

    A catalogue record of this book is
    available from the British Library

ISBN   0-7505-1944-4

First published in Great Britain 2002 by Bantam Press
a division of Transworld Publishers

Copyright © Mary Jane Staples 2002

Cover illustration © Nigel Chamberlain by arrangement with
Transworld Publishers, a division of The Random House Group
Ltd.

The right of Mary Jane Staples to be identified as the author of
this work has been asserted in accordance with sections 77 and
78 of the Copyright, Designs and Patents Act, 1988

Published in Large Print 2002 by arrangement with
Transworld Publishers

Magna Large Print is an imprint of Library Magna Books Ltd.

Printed and bound in Great Britain by
T.J. (International) Ltd., Cornwall, PL28 8RW

THE ADAMS FAMILY

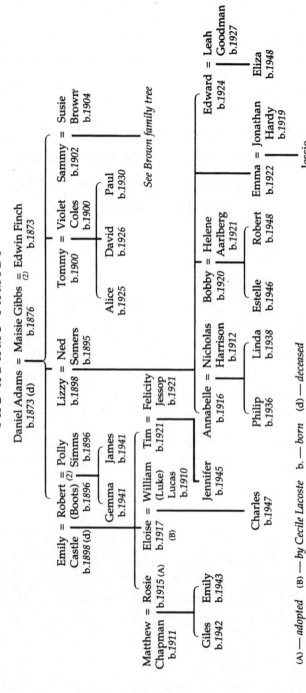

(A) — *adopted* (B) — *by Cecile Lacoste* b. — *born* (d) — *deceased*

THE BROWN FAMILY

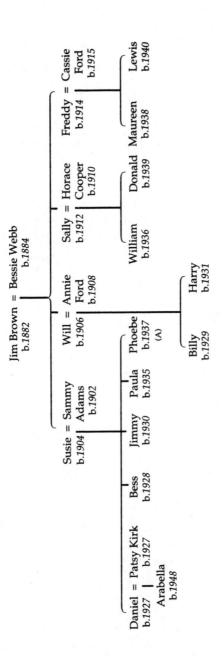

Prologue

1949

Millions of people displaced by man's inhumanity to man during the Second World War had managed, under the aegis of the Allies, to return or be returned to their countries of origin. Stalin's armies had secured the release of two million Russian prisoners of war, most of whom his police had arrested, tortured and either murdered or despatched to Siberia to die of starvation and freezing cold, on the grounds that they should never have surrendered in the first place.

Jewish and other survivors of the death camps had been resettled in Palestine, or returned home according to their wishes, while the whole world tried to take in unbelievable accounts relating to the purpose and use of Nazi gas chambers and crematoria.

Slave labourers from every country invaded and occupied by the Germans had perished by the thousands in the appalling conditions forced on them by the sadists of Hitler's war factories. Those who survived had gradually found their way home.

Many Nazi war criminals of the SS had avoided capture and used a prearranged escape route to reach safety in South America or anti-Semitic Middle East states. Or elsewhere.

In the UK, a number of men and women who had served in General Sikorski's Free Polish Army refused to be returned to Poland, since it was now one of Stalin's post-war puppet states. These particular Poles applied for permanent residence in Britain, and received it. And, surprisingly, so did some German prisoners of war, mostly of the staunch anti-Nazi calibre, who were disgusted by all that they had come to know of Himmler's atrocious SS and its murderous ideology.

These Poles and Germans settled down to life in Britain. So, it was rumoured, did a few undetected war criminals.

With the return home of the men and women of the Armed Forces, the people of the UK seized the chance to rebuild their lives. Families split and unsettled by the demands and circumstances of the war made the effort to resume normal life.

The families relating to Mrs Maisie Finch went about the pleasure of reunion with typical enthusiasm. Marriages that had been blessed by the arrival of children during the war were followed by postwar marriages and births. In the third year of the war, Boots and Polly had become the parents of twins, Gemma and James. And in 1945, Felicity, the blind wife of Tim, had had a baby girl, Jennifer.

Post-war, a girl, Estelle, and a boy, Robert, had been born to Bobby and Helene Somers. Bobby's brother Edward and wife Leah had brought forth a girl, Eliza. Sammy Adams's son Daniel, married to Patsy from America, was presented with a girl, Arabella. Boots's French daughter, Eloise, and her husband, Colonel Lucas, had a boy, Charles. And Emma and Jonathan had a girl, Jessie.

With the advent of 1949, life was in full swing for Mrs Maisie Finch and her extensive family.

Chapter One

Late July, 1949

The day was breezy, the sky above London a pattern of swirling white clouds against the canopy of blue. The cockneys might have admired the picturesque look of such a sky if they hadn't known July clouds could turn as spiteful as April's and drop heavy showers on them.

It was midday Saturday, and in Walworth's East Street market a flowing tide of shoppers surged around the stalls. The war had been over for four years, and while some foods were still rationed, home-grown produce was up to the mark in quality and quantity, and imported fruit was beginning to add colour and choice to laden stalls.

A well-dressed man, whose stylish grey trilby was worn at a dashing angle, was moving from stall to stall, pausing to say hello to stallholders he had come to know years ago. The responses were of a typical cockney kind.

'Well, if it ain't Mister Bleedin' Sammy Adams 'imself in a Sunday suit. How yer doing, Sammy?'

'Still standing up,' said Sammy.

From another stallholder, 'Blimey O'Reilly, ain't seen you in years, Sammy old cock. Thought Hitler had got yer with his bombs.'

'Well, he tried, believe me he did,' said Sammy. 'He dropped one straight through the roof of the family castle, and it fell down. Fortunately, no-one was in it at the time, including me.'

It was an excursion into the old and familiar for Sammy, who had left his office early to visit the market. He was now forty-seven, but still a fine figure of a bloke with electric blue eyes that could make some ladies feel he could see more than was good for him. Sharp as a needle, but with an unfailing sense of humour, his exchanges were lively with the men and women he had known since he himself had been a stallholder. Sammy had a long memory for good turns done and friends made in true and hearty cockney fashion during his struggling years. Although some faces were missing, he liked the fact that those who'd survived the war had kept their stalls going. They were all older than he was, but still sturdy on their feet, still offering bargains to the people of Walworth and the kind of competition that made Walworth Road shop prices look a bit over the top.

Down near the middle of the market was a stall that specialized in quality fruit and vegetables, the prices always a little more per pound than elsewhere, but the quality guaranteed. The woman running it looked up into the face of her next customer. She blinked.

'Well, bless me old plates of meat,' she said, 'is that you, Boots?'

Robert Adams, known as Boots, smiled. Just fifty-three, he was a distinctive figure in his Norfolk jacket, light grey trousers and tweed hat. He had served in both world wars, but neither had soured him. His whimsical nature, his interest in life and people, and his love for his family were always evident. If age could not weary those who had fallen, neither did it yet sit tiredly on survivors like Boots. His wife Polly, who thought him the best of men, also thought it was time he showed his age, since she was sure she herself showed her own. Actually, that was not the case.

'Hello, Ma,' said Boots, 'how are your best pippins?'

One could have said he wasn't referring to her apples, for Ma Earnshaw was decidedly overflowing and always had been. Still, everyone who knew her agreed that even at her advanced age she made up for the beanpole look of her old man, a retired railway porter who was talking about going to live by the seaside at Southend. Some hopes, said Ma Earnshaw, I'm living and dying at me Walworth stall.

'Now then, Boots,' she said, 'none of yer sauce, I used to get all I needed from yer brother Sammy. How are yer, love, and how's that Sammy?'

'He's around,' said Boots, 'he'll be along to say hello.'

'I felt for yer fam'ly when the bombs started dropping,' said Ma Earnshaw. 'It got around, Boots, that you lost Em'ly.'

'Damned dark day, Ma, for all of us,' said Boots.

'I felt real sad for you, Boots,' said Ma. 'Them 'orrible bombs did for others like Em'ly. Mind, I heard from someone that you'd got married again– Here, wait a bit, is that lot yourn?'

'This lot?' Boots turned and looked down at three girls and a boy. 'Well, they're all family. The two small ones are mine.

Gemma and James. Twins by my second wife. The larger ones are Sammy's, Paula and Phoebe. Say hello to Mrs Earnshaw, young 'uns, she's an old friend.'

'Hello.' The three girls and a boy responded in chorus.

'Well, ain't you all a sight for sore eyes?' smiled Ma, her weathered face creasing benignly.

Paula, fourteen, was fair, slim and skittish. Phoebe, twelve, was dark-haired, dainty, winsome and adopted. The twins were seven but hardly identical, for Gemma owned the dark sienna hair and piquant looks of her mother, while James had his father's deep grey eyes, dark brown hair and firm features. Each was a bundle of energy, even if at the moment they were shyly quiet under the motherly gaze of Ma Earnshaw.

'I think they'd all like some oranges,' said Boots.

'Well, bless 'em,' said Ma Earnshaw, 'and for old times' sake they can 'ave two each and I couldn't say fairer.'

'You could if you'd include two each for their parents,' said Boots, 'and two for the girls' brother Jimmy.'

'I don't know I was ever able to say no to you, Boots,' said Ma. A natural gent, that was how she saw Boots, a credit to his mother and his Walworth roots. 'Mind, they're tuppence ha'penny each, five for a bob. Penny oranges, well, they're like Queen Victoria, gone for good.'

'There are compensations,' smiled Boots, 'such as the happy fact that you're still with us. Now,' he said to the children, 'who's got the shopping bag?'

'Me,' said Paula. 'I,' she said correctively. Not being certain, however, she retracted. 'Me,' she said.

'Eyes right,' said Boots. At least, that was what the children thought he said, and so they all turned their heads, perhaps in anticipation of seeing an organ-grinder and his monkey. Organ-grinders and their performing monkeys were a disappearing feature of London's streets. Kids, accordingly, didn't like to miss the chance of spotting one of these popular combinations.

What these Adams children saw, however, was an advancing blonde lady of pleasant looks and fulsome figure. She was comfortably dressed in a blouse and skirt, and wore a close-fitting hat. She came to a startled halt at suddenly finding herself under the survey of four staring children. Her fine blue eyes blinked. However, since she was only one more woman among the many in the market, the three girls and a boy turned their eyes back to Boots after a mere second or so.

'Uncle Boots,' whispered Paula, 'why did we have to look at her?'

'Yes, why did you?' asked Boots.

'Because you said "Eyes right",' whispered Paula.

'No, I said, "I's right",' explained Boots.

'Yes, eyes right,' said James.

'Well, never mind now,' smiled Boots. He glanced at the woman, noting her looks. She was now awaiting her turn at the stall, while keeping her distance. 'Open up the shopping bag, Paula, my poppet.'

Paula did so, and Ma Earnshaw put eighteen shining oranges inside it. The fruit was from Israel, the independent post-war homeland of the Jews, including many of those who had managed to survive the concentration camps.

'That's three and sevenpence ha'penny,' she said. 'It's a shocking price for oranges, Boots, and I can't say it ain't, but it's what winning the war's done for us. Like it did last time, in 1918. Makes a body wonder if we'd be better off losing the next one. See what I mean?' she went on as Boots offered four silver shillings and a smile. 'All that much for eighteen oranges. It hurts me customers and me as well.'

'Cheer up, Ma,' said Boots, 'the kids won't feel any pain, and you can give the change to your grandson. So long now.'

'Been grand seeing yer, Boots,' said Ma, and off he went with the girls and the boy, the well-built blonde lady watching him with interest before advancing to the stall.

'Oh, hello, Mrs Kloytski,' said Ma Earnshaw. 'How's yerself and Mr Kloytski?'

'Ah, him?' said the blonde lady in thickly accented English. 'He is very good. Yes, all the time. "I am very good," he always says.'

'He means in good 'ealth, I expect,' said Ma. 'Well, it's nice you're both settling down, like all the Polish people that's living in London these days.'

'Better than in Communist Poland, yes?' said Mrs Kloytski. 'Ah, who was that man with the girls and a boy?'

'Oh, that was Mr Adams that used to live off Browning Street,' said Ma. 'His fam'ly was always reg'lar customers of mine.' She cast a knowing smile. 'If you fancy him, ducky, well, so 'ave a lot of ladies in their time.'

'No, no,' said Mrs Kloytski, 'it is only that

I thought I might have seen him somewhere. Somewhere in London, I think.'

'Well, London's where he lives,' said Ma.
'Now, what can I serve yer with?'

'Ah, yes. Two pounds of your best apples,
please, four pounds of potatoes, one red
cabbage and one white cabbage.'

'My, you and Mr Kloytski do like your
cabbage, eh?' said Ma amiably, and began
weighing up the apples.

'Was he in the British Army?' asked Mrs
Kloytski.

'What, Mr Adams? Well,' said Ma, 'he
wasn't in any French or German Army, it
was our Army all right, where he got to be
an officer. Very high-ranking, me old man
said.' Ma weighed potatoes, then selected
two large crisp cabbages, one red and one
white. 'There y'ar, Mrs Kloytski, two
pounds of me best apples, four pounds of
spuds and the cabbages. That's two shillings
and eightpence.'

'Oh, I am obliged, Mrs Earnshaw, yes,'
said Mrs Kloytski. She paid up and left,
walking very brisk and graceful, Ma Earnshaw thought.

Boots took his twins and Sammy's two
girls to a stall selling knick-knacks and toys
at bargain prices. There, he invited them to

select a toy each. Paula chose a girls' annual, Phoebe chose a painting book, and Gemma and James indulged themselves by taking their time.

'Crikey,' said Phoebe after a while, 'are we going to be here all day instead of getting home in time for lunch?'

'Looks like it,' said Paula, and glanced around. 'Bless me, Uncle Boots, there's that lady again.'

Boots turned his head and saw the fulsome blonde woman on the other side of the market. Their glances met, and again he noted her looks. Curiosity surfaced as she turned away, moving to examine a stall selling jellied eels, still a favourite with many of Walworth's cockneys. Something stirred Boots's memory, but it was too faint to pull any image into being, and Sammy joined them at that moment.

'What's going on?' he asked.

'Oh, only Gemma and James taking all day to choose a toy each,' said Paula. 'Daddy, Uncle Boots is treating us. I've got an annual and Phoebe's got a painting book.'

'And who's got a bagful of oranges?' asked Sammy. 'Ma Earnshaw said she'd sold you eighteen of the best.'

'Me,' said Paula. She looked up at Boots. 'I mean I've got them, don't I, Uncle Boots?'

'Quite right,' said Boots, 'so you have.' He gave her a smile. He had an easy affection for young people, especially those of the Adams family. 'I's right, Paula,' he said.

'Oh, now I see what you mean,' said Paula.

Gemma and James made up their minds then. Gemma chose a pack of bright crayons, and James a tin box of paints. Boots settled, and they all went on their way. The eyes of Mrs Kloytski followed them.

Chapter Two

Mr and Mrs Kloytski lived in a house in Wansey Street, off Walworth Road. Wansey Street's well-built terraced houses had always had a superior look, and still did, for they'd escaped any bomb damage. The Kloytskis had very friendly near neighbours in Mr and Mrs Hobday, and Cassie and Freddy Brown.

Mr Kloytski was about to say goodbye to a visitor. Mr Kloytski, a handsome man in his thirties, looked pleased with life. His visitor, a soberly dressed man in his forties, looked as if he had known better days than this one.

'No, I'm afraid I cannot let you have the negatives as well as the photographs, only my promise to keep them securely locked away,' said Kloytski. His English was excellent, but there was an accent identifying him as no native of England.

'Existing on a promise of yours isn't my idea of how to be happy,' said the visitor, scholarly features expressing disgust and disillusion. 'You're a swine, you know, and your wife, quite frankly, is a bitch.'

'Come, come, my friend, is that the way to talk about a woman who has given you sweet pleasure?' said Kloytski.

'That sweet pleasure has turned humiliatingly sour.'

'We needed you and what you could do for us,' said Kloytski, 'and since your feelings and inclinations are sympathetic, a decision was made to take advantage of your – ah – sexual urges. Surely your times with my wife were preferable to your times with women you picked up in Soho, yes?'

'My infatuation with your scheming wife is costing me far more than all the women of Soho.'

'Your pride, you mean?' Kloytski's smile did not reach his eyes. It rarely did. 'Or your integrity? Oh, you'll adjust, I'm sure, and as soon as you have any information for us, let me know through the agreed channels. Then either my wife or I will arrange to collect it.'

'Damn you for your blackmail.'

'Sometimes it happens,' said Kloytski. 'As this is a beginning for you, I'll give you a month to make your first delivery. We can now part as friends and comrades?'

'That's a bad joke.'

'Perhaps it is at the moment,' said Kloytski. 'Ah, yes, and by the way, remember you will be known to us only as Victor.'

'So you said ten minutes ago, an even worse joke,' remarked 'Victor' acidly. 'Idiot would have been a more suitable code name.' He departed in an angry but resigned mood. What he was about to become was not altogether against his political convictions, but he felt furious and humiliated at the way his recruitment had been contrived. His weakness for women willing to perform unconventionally had been his undoing.

Approaching the corner of Wansey Street, he saw a woman turning in from Walworth

Road. She was carrying a shopping bag. They glanced at each other and stopped. Victor bit his lip, and a slight flush tinted his cheeks.

'Ah, hello, good morning,' said Mrs Kloytski.

'Allow me to inform you you're a reincarnation of Jezebel,' said Victor.

'But everything is now arranged?' smiled Mrs Kloytski. 'We are now all in the same ship?'

'Boat,' said Victor curtly. He eyed her fulsome figure as a man who had come to know it intimately. 'If I had my way I'd throw you overboard.'

'Tck, tck,' chided Mrs Kloytski, 'after such happy times together?'

'With a hidden camera keeping us company?' said Victor in disgust. 'Goodbye, madam.'

'Goodbye,' responded Mrs Kloytski. 'Victor,' she added, with another smile, and they went their separate ways. Mrs Cassie Brown, coming out of her house with her son Lewis and her daughter Maureen, received Mrs Kloytski's next smile. It was of the kind disillusioned Victor would have called glutinous. Certainly, it parted Mrs Kloytski's full lips wide and revealed shining white teeth. It could make susceptible men think of sweet sugar. 'Ah, hello, Cassie, hello, childer.' She meant children.

'Hello, Mrs Kloyst,' said eleven-year-old Maureen, known as Muffin. Kloyst was as much as her young tongue could manage.

'Nice to see you,' said Cassie, as exuberant at thirty-four as she had always been. Life was still well worth living to Cassie. If gloom happened to be lurking about, she vanquished it. She sometimes thought about vanquishing this Polish woman. Mrs Kloytski was inclined to get too close to Freddy, much as if she had illegal designs on his person. Not to Cassie's liking, that, no, not a bit. Freddy's person was personal to her alone. He'd served with distinction in the hellhole of Burma, making sergeant and turning himself into the kind of man who, at thirty-four, could catch the eye of busty blondes like Mrs Kloytski. At the moment he was at his work. Saturdays were full days for him.

'Your little ones are so sweet,' said the fulsome lady. 'And Freddy, how is Freddy?'

'Safe at work,' said Cassie.

'Safe?'

'Oh, from – from–' Cassie thought of a phrase she'd come across in a novel of dark

29

doings. 'From the forces of evil.'

'The forces of evil?' Mrs Kloytski looked astonished. 'They are here, in our community?'

Cassie went all melodramatic. She looked around, here and there, and whispered, 'Pssst, Mrs K., they're everywhere.'

'No, no, I cannot believe you,' said Mrs Kloytski, and laughed.

'Oh, they're not easy to spot,' said Cassie, 'especially when they're wearing a smile.'

'Oh, come on, Mum,' said nine-year-old Lewis. Except for his happy mum and his playful dad, grown-ups didn't count much with Lewis. Well, they were old and a bit bossy, like the teachers at St John's Church School. Crumbs, he said to his dad once, them teachers are more old and bossy than anyone.

'Got to go, Mrs K.,' said Cassie, 'I promised Muffin and Lewis I'd take them to the park to fly their new kites now that we've had our lunch. Goodbye.'

'Goodbye, Cassie,' said Mrs Kloytski, and walked on to her home. When she reached it, Mr Kloytski greeted her with a matter-of-fact statement.

'He has joined us.'

'Yes, I saw him,' said Mrs Kloytski. They

30

spoke in their own language. 'He was very abusive. I'm afraid he no longer likes me.'

'Natural, yes, in a man who has just seen photographs of himself on a bed with you,' said Kloytski. 'But as I pointed out to him, it was his reluctance to be recruited that compelled us to use the camera. Our friends will be pleased he's now one of us.'

'Our friends, yes. Good,' said Mrs Kloytski. They were referring to people who had helped them during the immediate post-war upheaval in conflict-torn Europe, when Germany's liberated slave labourers of many different nationalities were crowding the roads in all directions, and so were refugees and Jewish survivors of concentration camps. Murder could happen over possession of a shabby coat, and summary executions could take place when Russians or the Allies shot suspected war criminals out of hand.

'He'll accept his role with grace soon enough,' said Kloytski. 'It fits his sympathies.'

'Yes, but let me speak of something else,' said Mrs Kloytski. 'I saw someone in the market I think we both know.' She went into details about the man who had three girls and a boy in tow, and she spoke of where and how they had originally encountered him.

'God Almighty, that swine?' said Kloytski. 'Are you sure?'

'Yes, I'm sure,' said Mrs Kloytski. 'He said something to the children, and they all turned to look at me.'

'You think he recognized you?'

'If he didn't, why would he have said something to the children that made them look at me?'

'No, no, he'd have done more than mention you to his children,' said Kloytski, 'he'd have confronted you. Perhaps he only thought he'd met you somewhere, perhaps that was all he said to the children.'

'Yes, and perhaps he'll begin to think of exactly where,' said Mrs Kloytski, 'and if he remembers, he'll try to trace me, and if he succeeds in that, he'll find you as well. Then the confrontation will happen, a serious confrontation.'

'It's a possibility, I suppose,' murmured Kloytski. 'But where, I wonder, would he begin his search for you?'

'He'll return to that market stall and ask Mrs Earnshaw about me,' said Mrs Kloytski.

'That peasant? Our supplier of fine cabbages?'

'Yes, and because she's a chatterer, she'll tell him about both of us as a Polish couple,' said Mrs Kloytski. 'Listen, when I asked her who he was, she said his name was Adams, and that he'd been a high-ranking officer in the British Army.'

'So? Adams, you say?' Kloytski mused on the name. 'Adams, yes. Well, if he does ask questions about you, we'll have to consider how to deal with his curiosity and his memory.'

'Meaning how to silence him?'

'If he really is the swine in question, and any confrontation becomes as serious as you suspect, it'll be a pleasure to silence him permanently,' said Kloytski.

'You and I will share that pleasure,' said Mrs Kloytski, the reincarnation of Jezebel in the eyes of the man called Victor.

Sammy arrived home at his house on Denmark Hill. It had been built following the end of the war, on the site of the house completely destroyed by a bomb.

He spoke to his wife Susie in their well-appointed kitchen.

'Susie, before we head off to Cornwall for our holiday next Saturday, I've got to find time to go to a warehouse in Edmonton. It's in North London–'

'Pardon me,' said Susie, fronting a working top on which she was mixing a bowl of salad. Close to forty-five, she was admirably well-preserved. Like Boots's wife Polly, she was fighting the good fight against the little spoiling devils of middle age. 'Is that you talking to the back of my head, Sammy Adams?'

'Yes, it's me, Susie, just back from the outing to the old Walworth market, and–'

'Excuse me,' said Susie, turning, 'but would you mind saying hello to your wife?'

'Eh?' said Sammy. 'Oh, right, yes, hello, Susie, how's your Saturday bib and tucker?'

'Never mind my apron,' said Susie, 'you've been out all morning at the office and the market, and you're not supposed when you come in to talk to the back of my head about going somewhere else.'

'Susie, I like the back of your head, I'm genuine admiring of it–'

'No soft soap,' said Susie, so Sammy gave her a kiss as a peace offering. Susie smiled. She always enjoyed keeping Sammy in order. Sammy, energetically involved with business, was inclined to live in leaps and bounds. 'Where are the girls?' she asked.

'Outside, talking to friends they bumped

into,' said Sammy. 'They'll be here in a tick. Look, about going up to this place Edmonton–'

'Never been there,' said Susie, 'so tell me what it's got that Camberwell hasn't.'

'A warehouse, Susie, which a business friend I happened to bump into says is chockful of bales of nylon, which is that man-made material that could be considerably valuable for our garments factory, especially if Eli Greenberg can point me at a stocking-making machine that's not doing anything–'

'It's black market,' said Susie.

'Well, a new one might be,' said Sammy, 'but with Eli's help I'll settle for a reconditioned one.'

'I'm suspicious about the stocking-making machine, the warehouse and the nylon,' said Susie, 'and I bet the business friend you bumped into is a spiv.'

'On me honour, Susie.'

'You sure about that?' said Susie.

'No spiv, Susie, give you my word,' said Sammy. 'Mind, the info about the warehouse is sort of confidential.'

'Meaning black market,' said Susie.

'No, just confidential,' said Sammy, 'and listen, Ben Ford, the Fat Man, has risen from the dead and I hear he means to give me the kind of competition I can do without.'

'That's a fib,' said Susie.

'Eh?'

'Sammy, you've left the Fat Man far behind,' said Susie. 'You've got Adams Enterprises and its garments factory, you've got Adams Fashions and all its shops, you've got the thriving property company with its houses, block of flats and still some bomb sites ready to be sold for development, you've got the new store in Walworth and happy bank balances for each company. And what has the Fat Man got? His one grotty shop in Camberwell New Road, an oversized paunch and some loose change.'

'Susie, that's what I call a handsome inventory of our assets,' said Sammy, 'but what's the Fat Man going to do with his loose change? He's going to carry it up to Edmonton with crafty ideas of outbidding me. It's against me strictest business principles, Susie, to let anyone outbid me, especially the Fat Man. D'you know, I think I've still got bruises from what his heavies did to me when they once jumped me.'

'Show me,' said Susie.

'Eh?'

'The bruises, Sammy. Show me.' Susie shook her head at him. 'You daft ha'porth, that must have been over twenty years ago.'

'Well, I won't say it wasn't, Susie, but I will say that whenever I hear mention of his monicker, I can still feel painful twinges in various places all at once.'

Susie laughed. There was always something comically likeable about Sammy and what was known as his own kind of wordage.

'You'll do, Sammy,' she said. 'Go up to Edmonton, then, and sit on the Fat Man.'

'I think I'll go first thing Monday with Eli Greenberg, and be there to catch the start of the auction at ten,' said Sammy.

'Take Jimmy with you as well as Mr Greenberg, why don't you?' said Susie. 'You'll have useful company then, and you can all sit on the Fat Man together.'

Jimmy, their younger son, was nineteen and worked at Sammy's new Walworth store as assistant to the manager, Freddy Brown, Susie's younger brother.

'Good idea,' said Sammy. 'It'll be another step on learning him what business is all about. What we've got to do, Susie, is some kind of wangle that'll stop him being conscripted for his National Service stint next year.'

'Sammy, I don't do wangling,' said Susie. 'Now bring the girls in and we'll have lunch.'

Chapter Three

Sammy's Walworth store, where his son Jimmy worked, was a large replica of his original shop at Camberwell Green. It sold Army, Navy and Air Force surplus, as well as reconditioned domestic appliances and kitchenware. Jimmy was taking ten minutes off to eat his lunchtime sandwiches, while manager Freddy Brown and his other assistant, Mrs Ruby Turner, attended to the customers.

Jimmy, like all the Adams males, was long-limbed and personable. It made his notable grandmother, called Chinese Lady, feel quite proud that her sons and grandsons had all inherited the physical traits of her handsome first husband, Corporal Daniel Adams of the Royal West Kent Regiment. She didn't show too proud, however, because too much pride was a sort of vanity, and the Bible was against vanity.

Ruby popped into the little room used as a staff retreat. Thirty-six, she was a rosy, round-faced, plump and jolly woman, looking more like a Devonshire farmer's wife than a female cockney of smoky old Walworth. Her husband was a postman, and she'd taken the job as a store assistant so that they could better themselves. Neighbours asked them what they wanted to better themselves for. Well, for a garden, like, instead of a backyard, they said. Daft, said their neighbours, what's wrong with your back yard? Well, for one thing, Ruby said, we still keep finding bits of shrapnel in it, and for another me hubby says an unexploded bomb might pop up one night and go off bang. 'Crikey, the customers we've 'ad today,' she said to Jimmy, 'but it's gone a bit quiet now. Enjoying your sandwiches, are you? I'll 'ave mine when your break's up. What kind of sandwiches you eating?' Ruby liked to collect information, a typical hobby of Walworth housewives.

'My sandwiches,' said Jimmy, 'are constituted of pulverized boiled egg and delicately sliced cucumber.'

'You don't half use big words,' said Ruby, 'you must've been born with a dictionary in your north and south.'

'True, I was,' said Jimmy, 'and my dear mother informed me years later that it would have choked me if the midwife hadn't taken it out.'

'Your dear mother?' Ruby let a plump smile show. 'Why can't you just say your mum?'

'Why?' said Jimmy, munching. 'Because my mother has always been dear to me.'

'Oh, me tonsils,' said Ruby, 'you slay me, you do.'

'Shout if it hurts,' said Jimmy, 'and I'll call an ambulance. Might I ask what kind of sandwiches you've got?'

'No sandwiches,' said Ruby, sighing, 'just a couple of lettuce leaves and a slice of bread with a smear of marge.'

'Who's being hard on you?' asked Jimmy, still munching.

'Me hubby. He says if I don't lose a bit of weight, he'll bounce me up and down on the pavement all the way along the Old Kent Road every Sunday. That'll do the trick, he says.'

'Well, watch how you rebound,' said Jimmy, 'or you'll disappear over the wall of Marshall's freight yard.'

'That ain't funny,' said Ruby, but she laughed, all the same.

'Ruby, service!' called Freddy Brown.

'Oh, that's me demanding manager,' said Ruby.

'I'll go,' said Jimmy. 'You take your own break. Enjoy your lettuce.' He disappeared to attend to the wants of a chatty young housewife who was after a mincer. It had to be a good one, mind, no bit of old rubbish. Don't stock old rubbish, said Jimmy, and went to work on her. By the time he'd successfully extolled the merits of a re-conditioned model, she looked as if she fancied him more than her purchase. Or even her husband, perhaps. Well, Jimmy was already decidedly masculine. Further, he had a good baritone, like his brother Daniel. Still, on account of her marriage vows, no doubt, the chatty lady left without inviting him to meet her at the witching hour for a surreptitious tryst.

Then, with Ruby back from her frugal repast, it was Freddy's turn to take a break. Saturday afternoon shoppers began to arrive, and Jimmy and Ruby were kept busy. Jimmy sold six pairs of RAF socks to a bloke who only wanted a couple. Look ahead, said Jimmy, you've got years in front of you, and wrapped up six pairs while the bloke was scratching his head. Jimmy, as a salesman, was a chip off the old block.

When Freddy returned from his break the influx of customers had increased. It was a fact that civilian clothes, generally, were suffering from the limitations of post-war austerity. Prime Minister Attlee's Labour government was having a tough time trying to improve Britain's balance of payments. The country, well and truly broke at the end of the war, was still in a parlous economic state. While Germany and Japan were rebuilding their industries with generously massive American help, Britain's factories were having to make do with machinery rapidly becoming out of date. Garment manufacturers were beginning to order man-made materials, treading on each other to obtain what they could of limited supplies. Hence, good business for Sammy's Walworth store, since there were always people ready to opt for surplus military wear. The stocks and the bargains were Sammy's way of offsetting shortages, much as his original shop had been after the First World War. Both profitable, of course, and he had a long-term view in mind for the Walworth Road place, that of turning it into a quality store once austerity had been given the boot. Wages, after all, were much better than pre-war, and the people of Walworth were never hoarders. They liked having money to spend. Sammy felt everyone ought to be prosperous. Prosperous people were very good for business.

Jimmy was aware that his job as assistant to Freddy Brown meant his dad was starting him at the bottom of the ladder, but he knew his dad, and accordingly he knew he had prospects. His brother Daniel and his cousin Tim managed the firm's property company under Sammy's eye, and their prospects were firmly on the positive side by now.

A peach of a girl, entering the store on crisp, clicking heels, made straight for Jimmy as he said goodbye to a customer.

'Hello, are you serving?' she asked.

'Well, yes, I won't get paid if I don't,' said Jimmy, noting her stylish dress, her stunning looks and her auburn hair. Auburn hair struck a chord with the family, mainly because his late and well-remembered Aunt Emily had owned a wealth of it, and cousin David's wife Kate owned the same kind. 'Can I help you, miss?'

'You'll disappoint me if you can't,' said the girl, her voice belonging to the well-bred. 'I want two RAF shirts.'

'For your dad?' said Jimmy.

'Don't be funny,' said the girl.

'Your boyfriend, then?'

'My friends of the male gender can all shop for their own shirts,' said the girl. 'These are for me.'

'Pardon?' said Jimmy.

'For me,' said the girl. 'You're not deaf, are you?'

'No, surprised,' said Jimmy, who felt certain she was slumming it, since her dress looked like an unusually rich post-war Mayfair creation. 'Unless you mean women's shirts. The Waafs?'

'Men's, the RAF, so get a move on,' she said.

'At once, miss,' said Jimmy. 'What size?'

'My size.'

'Ah,' said Jimmy, and took a look at her height, which was about five feet eight, and her figure, which was proud. She went haughty.

'D'you mind?' she said.

'Um – men's 36, I think,' said Jimmy, and led the way to the stocks of boxed RAF shirts.

'If you must know, I want them for my Cornish holiday,' said the girl. 'For the beach. I also want them because an uncle of mine was a Battle of Britain pilot. So it's a matter of beachwear and family pride. I adore the pilots of the RAF.'

'One in particular?' said Jimmy, extracting a box of shirts.

'You're interested in my personal life?' said the girl, about eighteen, he thought.

'The fact is,' he said, taking out one shirt, 'the management here insists on promoting a happy relationship with our customers.'

'Yuk,' said the girl.

'Will this suit your ladyship?' asked Jimmy, offering the shirt. She didn't take it, she gave him a look.

'Are you related to Max Miller?' she asked. 'If so, you're not as funny as he is.'

'Oh, I'll go along with that,' said Jimmy. 'I'm chiefly related to my parents and I'm not aiming to be a comic all my life.'

'Really? How ducky.' The girl took the shirt. 'Where can I try it on?'

Jimmy showed her. She disappeared. Ruby sidled up.

'Bless me corsets, Jimmy,' she said, 'you've found a looker. Getting off with her, are you?'

'Well, frankly, no, I'm not, Ruby, being fairly sure that if I tried it on I'd carry a black eye home with me.'

45

'Your dear ma wouldn't like that,' said Ruby.

'Nor would I,' said Jimmy, and Ruby answered a call for help from Freddy, whose female customer was insisting she wouldn't be served by no-one except a lady assistant on account of what she wanted. ATS and WAAF surplus was plentiful. If Sammy had been present, he'd have been reliving his days in his original shop at Camberwell Green.

Out came the posh Mayfair-style girl, the unfolded shirt over her arm.

'How'd it go?' asked Jimmy.

'Over my shoulders,' she said. 'You can wrap it up, with another of the same size. How much?'

'Three bob a shirt, madam, five and elevenpence for two,' said Jimmy.

'Cut the madam stuff,' she said. 'But the price doesn't offend me and the shirts will make history.'

'History?'

'Yes, Cornish history,' she said. 'I'll be the only woman making a landing on the beach wearing an RAF shirt.'

Woman? She was promoting herself, thought Jimmy.

'Well, if that's going to make history,' he

46

said, refolding the shirt, 'I'm rapturous for you.'

'You're what?' The girl looked as if she'd encountered a freak.

'Yes, best of luck,' said Jimmy, placing another shirt on top of the refolded one.

'Rapturous, you said? You're killing me.'

'Sell you an aspirin for free,' said Jimmy, wrapping the shirts on the counter next to the till. The store was still busy, Ruby buzzing about. 'By the way, I'm off to Cornwall myself next Saturday for my fortnight's holiday.'

'Really? I'm thrilled.' The girl dug into her pretty white handbag, found a ten-bob note and handed it to Jimmy in exchange for the parcel.

'Much obliged,' said Jimmy.

'You're welcome, put the change in that charity box,' said the girl, and off she went, heels crisply clicking again. Jimmy was left gawping at the airy way she chucked her money about. Then his grin surfaced, and he put the change from the till into the collecting box for War Orphans. What a caution. In a verbal duel with her, even his Uncle Boots would have trouble coming out on top.

What a stunner. Pity about her haughty nose.

Chapter Four

In a handsome house on Red Post Hill, off
Denmark Hill in south-east London, Mr
Edwin Finch addressed his wife, known to
her extensive family as Chinese Lady. The
reasons for this went back a long way, to her
years of struggle, when she often had her
Monday washing collected and done by Mr
Wong Fu of the local Chinese laundry.
Further, she had an almond tint to her
brown eyes.

'Maisie,' said Mr Finch, 'would you like a
daily to help with the housework?'

'D'you mean a servant?' asked Chinese
Lady. She was seventy-two, and still upright, but her dark brown hair was liberally
streaked with grey.

'Yes, I do mean a servant,' said Mr Finch,
seventy-five and silver-haired. His distinguished looks hadn't yet departed, however.
'The house, my dear, is large and you aren't
getting any younger.'

'Well, I'm still not old,' said Chinese Lady.
'At least, I don't feel I am, and we're not

going to move, not while the family still visits. We wouldn't know where to put everybody if we bought some poky place.'

Mr Finch smiled. That was her chief reason for living, her family. There seemed to be members by the dozen, beginning with her three sons, Boots, Tommy and Sammy, her daughter Lizzy, and their spouses. There were innumerable grand-children and great-grandchildren. And she always seemed to know what any of them were up to at any given moment, even Alice, Tommy and Vi's daughter, and Bess, Sammy and Susie's eldest daughter. Alice, having graduated from Bristol University, was now secretary to the bursar, and Bess was an undergraduate there.

Much to Maisie's pleasure, her favourite granddaughter Rosie, with her husband Matthew and children Giles and Emily, had moved from Dorset to run a large chicken farm in Surrey. In partnership with Rosie and Matthew were Lizzy's younger daugh-ter Emma and Emma's husband, Sussex-born Jonathan. In these post-war years of austerity, the farm was prospering in its sales of eggs and laying hens. Everyone wanted eggs after a war that had reduced the supply to about one per person per week. And many people wanted to keep chickens that would lay daily for them. One didn't feel austerity was knocking holes in the stomach if one could tuck into fried or scrambled eggs on toast for breakfast every morning. Also, a nice soft-boiled egg with Sunday tea was a traditional treat for many people.

'Very well, Maisie, only if the housework should begin to be a little too much for you will we think about a daily help,' said Mr Finch, knowing that Boots and Polly employed a daily, and so did Sammy and Susie.

Chinese Lady gave him one of her rare smiles. Edwin was a good man, a gentleman, and a comforting, providing husband. Retired from his job with the Government, he enjoyed a generous pension and what she called a respectable bank balance, which was something she had only read about during her years of penury in Walworth. She was comfortable with a respectable balance, because it meant she and Edwin weren't vulgarly rich, like war profiteers were. She had a warm, enduring affection for her man, and whenever she was out and about with him she could rightly be proud of his distinguished appearance. Boots took a whimsical view of such outings, since he was pretty sure his indomitable Victorian mother liked to let people see she wasn't married to someone who could be rated insignificant.

'Well, all right, Edwin,' she said, 'I'll think about a daily if the housework gets too much for me. Mind, as we live on the ground floor, I don't have to worry about most of the upstairs rooms unless some of the family come to stay for a night or two.'

'But you do a fair amount of dusting all over,' said Mr Finch, whose own daily labours were mainly devoted to keeping the garden in order. The front doorbell rang at that moment. 'I think that's Peregrine Winters, Maisie. I'll entertain him in the study, and perhaps you'd make us some coffee in about ten minutes, would you?'

'But it's afternoon, Edwin, it's nearly teatime.'

'Mr Winters dislikes tea—'

'Not like tea? It's not natural.'

'He prefers coffee at all times.'

'What a funny man, but all right, Edwin,' said Chinese Lady as he went to answer the ring. She knew he'd favour her using their latest kitchen item, a percolator. One more new-fangled contraption, that was what a percolator was. Still, it never threatened to

51

electrocute her, like the blessed telephone used to. Full of those kind of threats, that thing had been until it became friendly towards the end of the war.

She hoped her husband's visitor, a man from the Government, wasn't going to ask him to come out of retirement and return to his job, not at his age.

Mr Finch, opening the front door, said good morning to the caller, Peregrine Winters, an ex-colleague now in his fifties. The visit had been arranged over the phone.

'Happy to see you again, Edwin old man,' said Mr Winters, 'hope you don't mind sparing me five minutes or so on a Saturday afternoon?'

'A pleasure,' said Mr Finch. 'Come in.'

The visit actually lasted an hour, for after Mr Winters had explained the purpose of his call they enjoyed some very entertaining reminiscences over the percolated coffee. They had both served British Intelligence for many years. When Mr Finch was finally saying goodbye to his ex-colleague at the front door, he said, 'I'm not sure how my wife is going to react to what's on offer.'

'Most women are unpredictable,' said Mr Winters, 'but I don't imagine Mrs Finch will actually – um – fall down. A delightfully resolute lady, your wife, Edwin. Goodbye now, it's been a great pleasure to see you again and to chat over old times. We're both lucky to have survived intact.'

Following all that, Mr Finch rejoined Chinese Lady who, of course, asked the leading question. Was the Government going to make him return to work? Mr Finch assured her no, not at all. So she wanted to know why Mr Winters had called. Mr Finch coughed, fiddled with his tie, gave her a smile and told her.

True, she didn't fall down, but she did quiver all over and turn pale.

'Oh, dear Lord,' she said faintly, 'where's my smelling salts?'

Mr Finch called on Boots and Polly at their Dulwich home later that afternoon. Their daily maid, Flossie Cuthbert of Peckham, opened the door to him.

'Oh, hello, Mr Finch,' she said in bright welcome. Flossie was a typical Peckham cockney, perky, cheerful and resilient. With her parents she had endured and survived countless German air raids, raids that had shattered much of Peckham, and reduced many of its older inhabitants to nervous wrecks.

'Good afternoon, Flossie,' smiled Mr Finch. It was a daily help like Flossie he had in mind for Chinese Lady.

'Come in, sir,' said Flossie, a smile lighting up her prettiness. 'Mr and Mrs Adams are expecting you, except they're in the garden just now, teaching the twins 'ow to play cricket, and them little angels only seven, would you believe.'

'Cricket at the age of seven is hard going, even for little angels, I suppose,' said Mr Finch.

'Not half, sir, specially as Gemma can 'ardly keep hold of the bat,' said Flossie, and led the way through the house to the garden. There, Boots and Polly were engaged with the twins in the rudiments of how to guard three stumps and two bails with a bat. Gemma and James were willing pupils, although helpful hints and sound advice to Gemma went into one ear and straight out of the other. Well, everything was a scream or a giggle to Gemma, born to regard nothing very seriously, except earthquakes.

'Am I interrupting?' called Mr Finch.

'Well, some interruptions are welcome, old thing,' said Polly, advancing to meet him. She was fifty-two and still elegant, her body slim, her dress a classical achievement from the gifted hands of brother-in-law Sammy's designer. Sammy wasn't keen on any of his close female relatives appearing in the austerity fashions of these post-war years, especially Polly, whom he regarded as a high-class aristocratic advertisement for his best designs.

'How are the cricket lessons coming on?' asked Mr Finch.

'Chaotically,' said Polly, accepting a kiss on her cheek from her father-in-law. 'But you know, of course, that our ungovernable pair live on the closest terms with chaos.'

The twins arrived in a rush then, determined to bring a little chaos into the life of their grandfather by trying, apparently, to knock him down in the energetic enthusiasm of their greeting.

'Steady, monkeys,' said Boots, coming up.

Mr Finch, staying on his feet, knew there was one certain way of disentangling himself. He gave the twins sixpence each for their money boxes, and away they went, dashing into the house to safely bank the silver coins. Flossie, fearless in the face of their rush, took charge of them.

'Can you spare ten minutes for a chat?' asked Mr Finch of Boots and Polly.

'I suspected from your phone call that there was something on your mind,' said Boots, and they all sat down at the garden table in the sunshine of the afternoon. Boots, in a white cricket shirt and camel-coloured slacks, looked untroubled by his years, his features firmly masculine, his dark brown hair still thick. No more than Polly did he wear the mantle of middle age, although Polly was fighting faint crow's feet that were trying to establish themselves at the corners of her eyes.

'Is this going to be serious?' she asked.

'Only in one respect,' said Mr Finch.

'Which is?' said Boots.

'That off and on since early this afternoon, your inimitable mother has been in need of her smelling salts,' said Mr Finch.

'Her smelling salts?' said Polly. 'I'm to believe that?'

'You can believe the bottle is the one she's had for many years,' said Mr Finch, 'and it's still effective.'

'But why is she in need?' asked Boots. 'Is she having fainting fits?'

'No, she's simply in shock,' said Mr Finch.

Boots, noting that his stepfather was showing neither worry nor alarm, said, 'Out with it, Edwin, what's the reason?'

'The reason, Boots,' said Mr Finch, 'is that an ex-colleague of mine called to notify me well in advance that my name is going forward for inclusion in the New Year's honours list. I'm to be offered a knighthood for services rendered.'

Boots said warmly, 'My sincere congratulations, Edwin, and I'm not surprised.'

Polly looked tickled. She knew by now that her father-in-law had served with British Intelligence for many years. She had suspected so, and Boots had at last confirmed her suspicions, while asking her to keep the information to herself. Other facts relating to the life of his stepfather he still held close to his chest.

'Edwin, old thing,' said Polly, 'I'm delighted for you, I really am.'

'Thank you, Polly,' said Mr Finch. 'But it means, of course, that by this time next year your mother, Boots, will be known to her family and friends as Lady Finch. The prospect is alarming her. She's in shock. Hence her recourse to her smelling salts.'

'What can one say?' said Polly, rolling her eyes, while Boots expressed his own reaction by throwing his head back and roaring with laughter.

'I'm glad you're amused, Boots,' said Mr

Finch, a smile showing.

'He's a philistine,' said Polly.

'Lady Finch?' said Boots, and laughed again. 'My dear old mother? Lady Finch? No wonder she's in shock. I imagine she's been telling you she wasn't brought up to be a lady, that a title would be an embarrassment to her.'

'And make people talk about her?' murmured Polly, who knew that to Boots's old-fashioned mother being talked about meant one's respectability was suspect. 'Very embarrassing.'

'Indeed,' said Mr Finch, 'and so she's been asking if I have to accept the honour, if I'm compelled to. I can turn it down, of course—'

'Edwin, no, you mustn't,' said Polly.

Mr Finch mused, then said, 'Maisie is seriously set on not becoming Lady Finch, so I've come to talk it over with you two.'

'Talk it over with Polly,' said Boots. 'I'll drive round and talk to my mother.'

'Yes, famous idea, don't you know,' said Polly, still given on occasions to using the idiom of the Twenties. 'Off you go, old scout, do your good deed and wean her off her smelling salts.'

When Boots arrived, Chinese Lady tottered

into the living room with him, sank into an armchair, sniffed at her ancient bottle of smelling salts and said that what Edwin had been offered was the fault of the Government, the Labour Party, and that she hadn't had a more embarrassing shock like this in all her life, not even when the family found out her only oldest son was the unmarried father of a French daughter. Boots said well, old girl, you got over the shock of that misdemeanour of mine in no time at all. You'll get over this new shock as soon as you realize our respected monarch thinks this highly of Edwin.'

'Beg pardon?' said Chinese Lady faintly.

Boots, knowing she considered King George a sure shield against any possible advent of what she called the Bolsheviks, and that Conservatives were staunch upholders of respectability, said, 'Yes, forget the Labour Party, it's the King who will personally conduct the investiture, and Winston Churchill who'll give Edwin a pat on the shoulder.'

'Well, of course, I've always been admiring of Mr Churchill, but Edwin didn't make any mention of the King doing the honour himself,' said Chinese Lady.

'Oh, the King will, old girl, I assure you,'

said Boots, 'and you'll be invited to the Palace to watch the ceremony.'

'Oh, Lord help us, Buckingham Palace, Boots, I just don't know if I could fit into that,' said Chinese Lady. 'Would it upset the King if I didn't go?'

Boots said no, it wouldn't upset His Majesty, but it would be a pity to miss all the pomp and circumstance. Chinese Lady said she was fond of pomp and circumstance, like in 'Land of Hope and Glory'. Boots said he knew she was. Yes, she said, but not close to in Buckingham Palace.

'There'll be other wives to keep you company,' said Boots, 'you won't be alone. Edwin won't be the only man to receive a knighthood.'

'I can't think what he's specially done to be honoured,' said Chinese Lady. But she was recovering, she was beginning to sit up straight. 'I mean, he's only ever worked in one of the Government's offices.'

Boots suspected, rightly, that his step-father's secret work in the field during Hitler's rise to power had been primarily responsible for so notable an honour as a knighthood.

'But you can understand he'd have been excellent at his job,' he said, 'and invaluable during the war. Mr Churchill himself probably noticed him.'

Chinese Lady, not as daft as all that, said, 'Now don't tell me no fairy stories, Boots. Mr Churchill would of been far too busy to go round government offices noticing who was who. Mind, I can't think Edwin was a sort of nobody, no-one could ever say he was that. I was always able to ask him to talk to the Government about some things, like when Sammy's son Daniel was in trouble in Palestine. But me being called Lady Finch? Oh, lor', I just don't know what the neighbours will say, or my old friends in Walworth.'

Boots said she could tell her neighbours and her old friends that to them she was simply Mrs Finch, as heretofore. Chinese Lady, of course, at once said her day was upsetting enough without having to listen to words like that. Still, she said, perhaps she needn't tell her neighbours and old friends about being Lady Finch. That's it, said Boots, keep it under your Sunday hat. But what about the family, they'd soon know, she, said.

'All the family will be delighted,' said Boots, 'and no-one will have to address you as Lady Finch.'

'I should hope not,' said Chinese Lady. 'Lizzy calling me Lady Finch when I've been her mother all her life? The very idea.' Then, sure that her eldest son knew a lot more than anyone else in the family, she asked, 'Would you know what Princess Elizabeth and Princess Margaret call the Queen?'

'Mum, probably,' said Boots, and Chinese Lady gave him one of her looks. Knowledgeable he might be, but sometimes a body still wasn't sure that what he said was what he meant. And you couldn't always trust that smile of his.

'Even if the Princesses are both her daughters, I don't know I can believe they call her Mum,' she said suspiciously.

'Well, not in public, of course,' said Boots, 'only in private, at teatime, say. Look, old girl, to all your family you're always going to be yourself, whether you're Lady Finch or the Duchess of Bermondsey.'

'But Lady Finch, me?' said Chinese Lady. 'If I'd been born middle class, well, that would be different, but I wasn't, I've been an ordinary woman all my life.'

'Ordinary?' Boots shook his head. 'Not you, old girl, nor Sammy or others of your family. Listen.' He talked encouragingly to her, pointing out that a knighthood was a great honour for Edwin, and for her too, come to that. A supportive wife was just as worthy as her husband. Further, she was the kind of woman who could adjust to her exalted status.

'My what?' said Chinese Lady. 'Boots, d'you have to use French at a trying time like this?'

Boots said it wasn't French, it was a conviction that she could get used to her title, and be able to look everyone in the eye. He could have said the honour was something that must have touched Edwin deeply, since he'd been a German citizen who became a naturalized British subject out of affection for the United Kingdom. That was something known only to Boots and British Intelligence.

Chinese Lady ventured to say it perhaps wouldn't be right to ask Edwin to refuse the title, especially if the King was going to do the honours. She said she'd do her best to put up with the embarrassment, as long as no-one in the family made jokes about it. Boots said he'd guarantee that no-one would.

'But if I've got to go to Buckingham Palace with Edwin,' she said, 'I just don't know what I'd wear.'

'Edwin will look after that,' said Boots, 'he'll buy you a suitable new outfit.'

'Where from, Bond Street?' gasped Chinese Lady faintly. 'But I've never been in any posh ladies' shop, only in Gamages, where Lizzy used to work when she was young.'

'Any Bond Street shop will welcome you when you're about to become Lady Finch,' said Boots.

'Oh, lor',' sighed Chinese Lady, but Boots had won the day, and was able to tell his stepfather he could accept the honour. Further, the family could be advised, but not until tomorrow, Sunday. Chinese Lady needed all of twenty-four hours to put her smelling salts aside and to be able to receive any of the family.

Chapter Five

Chinese Lady's daughter, Mrs Lizzy Somers, was getting buxom. Her husband Ned didn't mind, not a bit. Comely, that's what you are, Eliza, he told her.

'Wait a minute,' said Lizzy, 'comely doesn't mean fat, does it? It had better not, Ned Somers, or you'll be in trouble.'

'It means you've got pleasing looks and a good figure,' said Ned.

'Well, thanks, but you sure?' said Lizzy. 'I always thought it meant sort of plump and countrified.'

'Like a fattish dairymaid?' said Ned. 'Well, you're not that, Eliza, you're comely.'

Which Lizzy was, which was pretty nice going for a woman of fifty-one. Not that her years worried her. She was more equable about being middle-aged than her sisters-in-law, Polly and Susie. Polly and Susie cultivated a well-preserved look. Lizzy, with the aid of expensive lightweight corsets, simply kept herself looking well put-together. She felt life had been as kind to her as it could be. Her daughters, Annabelle and Emma, and her sons, Bobby and Edward, were all happily married. Well, they all seemed to be. None of them complained. And imagine, Bobby had a French wife, Helene, and Edward a Jewish one in Leah, the younger daughter of an old family friend, widowed Rachel Goodman.

Lizzy, as a contented wife, mother and grandmother, could put up with getting

65

buxom, although it puzzled Chinese Lady. She was slim herself and always had been, and none of her three sons had ever been overweight, nor had their father, her late first husband. I just don't know why Lizzy's getting a bit plump, she remarked to son Tommy, it's not something that runs in the family.

'Beats me too,' said Tommy, 'unless it's her liking for roast potatoes and Yorkshire pudding. Tell her to eat more salads.'

'Oh, I couldn't interfere like that,' said Chinese Lady.

'Nor me,' said Tommy, 'and if Ned don't mind, why should we worry?'

About midday on Sunday morning, after church, Lizzy received a phone call from Boots. It wasn't about her diet, it was a piece of news that nearly made her drop the instrument.

'What?' she said faintly.

'It's a fact,' said Boots.

'If you're having me on–'

'Not on a Sunday,' said Boots.

'Are you telling me that my mum and stepdad are going to be Sir and Lady?' asked Lizzy, quivering.

'Yes,' said Boots, 'so if you and Ned want to call on them this evening, arrive in style.'

'What d'you mean, in style?' asked Lizzy, still fighting a dizzy feeling.

'With a bottle of champagne from Ned's cellar,' said Boots. Ned was still in the wine trade.

'I'll be lucky if I manage to get there,' said Lizzy, 'I'll still be near to fainting. Our stepdad's going to be Sir Edwin Finch, and our mum's going to be Lady Finch? I can't believe it. Boots, you sure you're not having me on?'

'I'm sure,' said Boots.

'Lord, I'm having palpitations,' breathed Lizzy.

'Try some hot tea,' said Boots. 'Lizzy old girl, let's all accept it's a great tribute to our stepdad, even if it has knocked Chinese Lady off her feet.'

'Yes, and me off mine,' said Lizzy. But she was capable of adding, 'Don't call me old girl, not till I'm eighty.'

'Eighty? Right, Lizzy,' said Boots, and she heard him laugh as he rang off. Then she made compulsive use of her wavering legs to stagger to Ned and tell him the astonishing news, on receipt of which he gave a shout of disbelief before opening a bottle of wine. After a heady glass, Lizzy began to phone her sons and daughters.

Meanwhile, Boots put a call through to Tommy.

'What?' said Tommy. 'What?'

'You can believe it,' said Boots, 'and you and Vi can toddle round this evening and congratulate the happy pair. But don't be surprised if Chinese Lady isn't her usual self.'

'Listen,' said Tommy, 'don't give me that kind of old Walworth codswallop. I'm too old for it.' He was forty-nine. 'And you're too old to hand it out, unless you've been on the bottle. Our stepdad getting a knighthood? What for?'

'Years of service to the Government,' said Boots. 'And to King and country.'

'Stone all the crows,' said Tommy, 'it's gospel?'

'It's a fact,' said Boots, and after another exchange of words Tommy hung up, found Vi, told her the news and asked her to fan him. Vi failed to oblige. She fell about instead, and took fifteen minutes to recover. She then made phone calls to her daughter Alice and her son David. Paul, her younger son, was out at a gathering for Young Socialists, all of whom were in favour of liberty, equality and reducing rich toffs to rags and patches.

Sammy was next to hear from Boots.

He took a deep breath and said, 'I don't think I'm hard of hearing, not yet I'm not, but could you repeat that?'

Boots repeated the news and said, 'Does it grab you, Sammy?'

'You kidding?' said Sammy. 'What I heard I don't believe. Don't hand me comical porkies, I'm not in the mood. There's all this fantastical nylon up for auction, and like I mentioned to Susie, I'm having to face competition from Ben Ford, the Fat Man. He's bobbed up out of nowhere. Probably spent the war under a palm tree eating dates.'

'I know all about that,' said Boots, 'and it's irrelevant at the moment. Your stepdad's getting a knighthood, and your mother's still trying to work out how to cope with being Lady Finch.'

'Lady Finch? Holy Joe,' said Sammy, 'what a turn-up for the Book of Solomon – no, wait a bit, if it's true I could stock up with new business cards. I quote. "Sammy Adams, Managing Director of Adams Enterprises Ltd, close relative of Sir Edwin and Lady Finch." Now that does grab me. Does it grab you, Boots?'

'By my shirt tails,' said Boots, and heard Susie's voice in the background.

'Sammy, is that Boots you're talking to?'

'You could say Lord Boots, Susie,' said Sammy.

'What d'you mean?' asked Susie.

'Hold the line for a bit, Boots, while I explain to me trouble and strife,' said Sammy. Boots, smiling, held on. Susie's voice arrived in his ear eventually.

'Boots lovey, you're not joking, are you?'

'I've had trouble getting Lizzy and Tommy to believe it,' said Boots. 'It's no joke, Susie.'

'Wow,' said Susie, 'I'm going to be the daughter-in-law of Lord and Lady Finch?'

'Sammy upped the status when he explained to you, did he?' said Boots. 'It's a knighthood, not a seat in the House of Lords.'

'I'm still flabbergasted,' said Susie, 'but happy, of course. Boots, how did your step-dad come to be offered such an honour?'

'Probably by being chummy with Church-ill during the war,' said Boots.

'Now you are joking,' said Susie.

'Let's opt for services rendered to the Government, Susie. I'll look forward to see-ing you and Sammy, and the others, at the Red Post Hill house this evening.'

'Shall I wear something special?' asked Susie.

'Your best Sunday hat?' suggested Boots.

'I was thinking of my best Sunday dress,' said Susie.

'Yes, good idea, that as well,' said Boots.

Susie passed the news to daughters Paula and Phoebe, to son Jimmy, and by phone to son Daniel and his American wife, Patsy. It was Patsy who answered the phone, and on being told the reason for the call, she shrieked.

'Oh, my stars, Mother-in-law, are we all joining the English nobility?'

'Daniel's grandfather and grandmother are,' said Susie, 'the rest of us will still be common.'

'Common?' said Patsy.

'Well, Daniel's dad will be,' said Susie. 'By way of celebration, he's thinking about buying a coat with a fur collar to it. He'll look like a spiv, and you can't get more common than that, so I'm going to stick pins in him.'

'Mother-in-law, you're cute,' said Patsy.

'Patsy, you don't have to call me Mother-in-law. Mum will do.'

'OK, Mum,' said Patsy, 'you're still cute.'

Polly took over from Boots to give him a break from the phone. She rang his son

71

Tim, his French daughter Eloise, and his adopted daughter Rosie. Tim said bloody marvellous, and that he'd always felt Grandpa Finch was a bit of a VIP. VIP was new, an abbreviation of Very Important Person. Tim's wife Felicity, blinded during an air raid, came on the line and asked Polly to confirm the news. When Polly did so, Felicity asked if it meant Tim's grandmother would be entitled to wear a coronet. Polly said no. Bloody swizzle for Grandma, then, said Felicity, but say hooray to Grandpa for us. Felicity made good use of her sense of humour to prevent people feeling sorry for her.

Eloise, living near Aldershot, where her husband, Colonel Lucas, a regular Army officer, was a regimental commander, despite the loss of an arm, received Polly's call. She immediately expressed herself in typically exaggerated style, declaring how enthralled she was at such amazing news and how excessively proud she was of her English family.

Rosie took the news in cryptic fashion.

'I knew it,' she said.

'You knew?' said Polly.

'Only that something like this was bound to happen,' said Rosie.

'Meaning?' said Polly.

'It's that kind of family,' said Rosie.

'Enlighten me, Rosie old sport.'

'It's a family specializing in the extra-ordinary,' said Rosie. 'Do you and I know anyone quite like Grandma Finch or Sammy?'

'Or Boots?' said Polly.

'Boots of all people,' said Rosie.

'Can we leave out Edwin for a worthwhile mention?' murmured Polly.

'Oh, he's the unassuming kingpin, of course,' said Rosie. 'I now have a feeling we'll all end up being invited to take tea with their Majesties.'

'I can't wait, ducky,' said Polly, 'but Boots will have to put a stop on Sammy or he'll embarrass all of us by trying to sell the freehold of Buckingham Palace to King and Queenie.'

'Isn't he more likely to try to buy it from them for his property company?' said Rosie.

'Well, sweetie,' said Polly, 'don't even suggest it, or he'll give it his best go.'

Rosie laughed.

'What a family,' she said.

Paul, Tommy and Vi's younger son, was back home from his political meeting in time for Sunday dinner. He had a sturdy resemblance to his dad, but, unlike him, and very unlike his Uncle Sammy, he was against capitalism. At the Young Socialists' meeting he'd enjoyed discussion and argument concerning the advantages of an Act depriving the rich of the best part of their ill-gotten oof and redistributing it to the poor and needy. Tommy, a director of Adams Enterprises and efficient manager of its garments factory, and accordingly a practising capitalist, had pointed out more than once that if that came about all the riches would disappear overnight, most of it in pubs. Paul always responded by saying no, of course not, the poor and needy weren't daft, they would use it to improve their lot. When Tommy asked how many people were poor and needy, Paul said a couple of million at least. Well, say they each received a hundred quid, said Tommy, how much improvement would that give?

Paul said a hundred quid was peanuts. A thousand was the minimum requirement. Well, count up how many people are filthy rich, said Tommy, and then try working it out.

'Did you have a nice meeting, lovey?' asked Vi, laying the dinner table. Homely

74

and affectionate, Vi was the most equable of the Adams wives. Although not in the least interested in politics herself, which she was pleased to leave to men, who were born argumentative, anyway, she always referred to Paul's meetings as nice.

'Well, we enjoyed some meaningful discussions,' said Paul, accepting a glass of brown ale from his dad.

'I get you,' said Tommy. 'You mean rowdy.'

'Enthusiastic,' said Paul.

'How much bawling?' grinned Tommy.

'I refute bawling, Dad,' said Paul.

'Hollering, then?' said Tommy.

'I grant you, sometimes someone has to make sure his point is heard,' said Paul, 'but it's all civilized.'

'I see,' said Tommy, the family stalwart. 'Who got hurt?'

'I'll have you know, Dad, that Socialism's not a joke,' said Paul. 'Its purpose is to free the workers of the world from the crushing bonds of capitalism.'

'Well, seeing we've got a Socialist government, are you talking about communism?' asked Tommy.

'Lor', I hope you're not, Paul,' said Vi, 'it would make Grandma Finch think you supported what she calls the Bolsheviks, which would really upset her. Especially now.'

'Why especially now?' asked Paul.

'Well,' said Vi, then, 'Tommy, you tell him.'

'Paul,' said Tommy, 'your grandpa's going to get a knighthood for services to the country, and your grandma's going to be Lady Finch.'

'Eh? What?' said Paul.

'Yes, it surprised us too,' said Vi, 'but isn't it lovely?'

'Lovely?' Paul staggered about. 'It's a shocker. I'll never live it down. I'll get chucked out, me, the full-time paid secretary and chief speaker of the Young Socialists. I'll have to go underground and do my work for the starving poor on a clandestine basis.'

'Clandestine?' Vi giggled. 'Clandestine?'

'Never heard of it meself,' said Tommy.

'Will someone tell me it's not true?' implored Paul.

'I'll bring the dinner in,' said Vi, 'then we can all have a nice talk about Grandpa being Sir Edwin over the roast lamb, even if it's only a small joint.' Out to the kitchen she went, leaving Paul groaning theatrically.

'Your mum and me are going round to pay our compliments to Grandma and Grandpa this evening,' said Tommy, his grin a yard

76

wide. 'You coming with us, sunshine?'

'I won't be able to,' said Paul. 'On account of being related to titled members of the Establishment, I'll be spending the evening committing suicide.'

'Well, I'll stay home to see you don't,' said Tommy.

'Thanks, Dad, glad you care,' said Paul, 'but it won't help the fact that my political career's up the spout.'

'Yes, rotten hard luck, me lad,' said Tommy. 'Still, your Uncle Sammy will always find you a job.'

'Yes, I know,' said Paul, 'but much as I like him, he's a capitalist and it's against my convictions to work for any capitalist.'

'Oh, well, cheer up,' said Tommy. Vi reappeared, pushing the laden dinner trolley. 'Your mum will make sure you don't get to be one of the starving poor.'

That evening, Chinese Lady's weekend of disbelief and smelling salts was favoured by the arrival of her sons, her daughter and their spouses, together with the twins and Jimmy, Paula and Phoebe. Boots and Polly, Lizzy and Ned, Tommy and Vi, and Sammy and Susie all offered the right kind of congratulations to Mr Finch, with Chinese

Lady's expression daring any of them to make jokes.

However, Jimmy presented himself to his grandma by bowing to her.

'Grandma, Your Ladyship,' he said, 'I'm–'

'None of that, you saucy boy,' said Chinese Lady.

'Well, of course, I know it hasn't come to pass yet,' said Jimmy, straightfaced, 'but out of respect for what's forthcoming, my mother – that lady's my mother – she said I was to–'

'No, I didn't,' said Susie.

'Didn't you say I was to bow?' asked Jimmy.

'No,' said Susie, 'I told you to honour your grandma and grandpa.'

'Oh, right,' said Jimmy. 'Well, Grandma and Grandpa, Your Honours, I'm chuffed about Grandpa's–'

'Jimmy Adams, d'you want your ears boxed?' said Chinese Lady.

'Not much, Grandma, no,' said Jimmy, 'I just want to say you're a wonder, and so are you, Grandpa. Many congrats.'

'Thank you, Jimmy,' said Mr Finch.

'That Jimmy, can't he talk?' said Phoebe.

'Ever so unfortunately, yes,' said Paula.

Paul turned up later, nursing a political

78

headache, but saying not a word to Mr Finch or Chinese Lady about being against honours on principle. He let family affection guide him, which was a relief to Vi, who thought he might make a speech about what the working classes had to suffer from lords and ladies with high-sounding titles. But he didn't, he was very nice to his grandparents.

Other members of the family, such as Rosie and Matthew, Tim and Felicity, were going to call separately sometime during the coming week. This evening, a large crowd was avoided for the sake of not over-whelming Chinese Lady, and the relatively modest number present made the occasion a success, which further encouraged her to face up to the future embarrassment of a title.

Chapter Six

At the advent of twilight that evening, a ten-acre field near the village of Woldingham in Surrey was under observation. Matthew Chapman and Jonathan Hardy lay flat on their stomachs in a fold in the ground close to a hedge. The field was their chicken farm, the land with its cottage owned by Matthew and his wife Rosie. The farm was run by them and their partners, Jonathan and his wife Emma.

The field was the haven of a multitude of chickens and a dozen sheep. The sheep kept the grass cropped, which made it easier for the chickens to get at the worms. A neighbouring farmer brought a ram to the sheep in the autumn for a reasonable fee, and in the early spring when the lambs arrived, foxes prowled at night, and the ewes kept their little ones sheltered by their bodies.

There were lambs now, a few months old, gambolling bundles of soft creamy wool in the bright light of day, but nestling close to the ewes at the moment. Dusk was due, and night would be close on its heels. Dangerous night. Foxes had taken two lambs last night. The mothering ewes had no defence against foxes. The ram would have charged, and the foxes would have scattered, but there was no ram. Its autumn visits lasted only a few days.

The chickens and cockerels were roosting, the henhouses full of happy egg-layers dreaming of tasty earthworms. Matthew and Jonathan, armed for a confrontation, were waiting in the hope that the foxes would reappear before darkness fell. Their rifles, old but reliable ex-Army Lee Enfields, were at the ready, fingers around triggers, eyes glued to the mounted telescopic sights, watching the hedge opposite them at a distance of one hundred and twenty yards. The fox trail in the adjacent field, also owned by Rosie and Matthew, led to that hedge. Matthew and Jonathan were concentrating on a certain spot, scented by the foxes. They were silent, vigilant, hoping to put paid to the animals that preyed on the lambs and chickens. They devoured lambs, they slaughtered chickens. Some people thought them endearing. Matthew and Jonathan, rural men, thought otherwise.

So they were waiting. The distance of one hundred and twenty yards was no problem for the Lee Enfields, but would be for the eyes if darkness fell.

It was a ewe that first signalled the approach of the enemy. It came to its feet in agitation. Its recumbent lamb protested at the withdrawal of its mother's warm body. Other ewes rose to stand disturbed.

Baa, baa.

Matthew nudged Jonathan.

Dusk was beginning to turn the sky a deep grey as through the hedge slipped the dog fox, its vixen and their two large cubs. Burn my boots, the whole bloody family, thought Dorset-born Matthew. Durn my eyebrows, thought Sussex-born Jonathan, here's a chance to down all the sly buggers.

The dog fox and its vixen halted and sniffed the air in search of the scent of man. Their cubs, sizeable enough for their parents to tell them to push off and find their own patch, fidgeted. The sheep became distressed and the lambs bleated. As agreed in advance, Matthew lined up the dog fox, telescopic sight bringing the animal clear to the eye. Jonathan aimed for the vixen. Rifle butts bit deeper into shoulders. Each man had a cartridge up the spout.

The dog fox and its vixen had their heads lifted, stiff legs poised. They moved forward just as two rifles fired simultaneously. The parent foxes leapt and fell.

'Downed 'em!' breathed Jonathan.

Bolts were drawn back fast and rammed home, shunting new cartridges into the breeches. Telescopic sights searched for the cubs, which were whining around inert parents. At that point, the dog fox and its vixen rose up, turned tail and vanished through the hedge, the cubs whipping after them.

'Diddled us,' said Matthew, and softly swore.

'Diddled, dished and done,' said Jonathan.

'Did you note that forward shuffle at the moment we fired?' said Matthew.

'That I did,' said Jonathan, 'and nor did I miss 'em playing possum.'

'Jonathan, they were laughing at us,' said Matthew. 'They knew we were here.'

'Smelled us, I reckon,' said Jonathan.

'But they'll stay off limits now for a few nights,' said Matthew, and they walked to the cottage, Jonathan limping along. The war had left him with a tin kneecap.

Reaching the cottage, with its gabled upper windows and its annexe, they fortified themselves by sharing a bottle of beer. Beer, like spirits, was still in short supply, and a fair amount of under-the-counter tactics prevailed with one's local suppliers. Not everyone knew a black market alternative, to wit, a spiv. Spivs, of course, were all in favour of short supplies, much as Al Capone was in favour of no legal supplies at all during America's Prohibition years.

Fortified to some extent, Matthew and Jonathan informed Rosie and Emma exactly how the perishing foxes had diddled them.

'You mean you two old Army crackshots both scored misses?' said Emma.

'They ducked the moment we fired,' said Matthew. 'They scented us.'

'At that distance?' said Rosie.

'Ah, well,' said Matthew.

'Emma,' said Jonathan, 'you'd tell me, wouldn't you, if I had a high level of BO?'

'I'd divorce you,' said Emma. 'Listen, how d'you feel about letting those mangy lamb-eating foxes diddle you?'

'Fair mortified,' said Jonathan.

'Well, men, Emma and I will forgive you this time,' said Rosie, 'but don't make a habit of it. Lost lambs mean lost revenue.' A local butcher bought the lambs at the right time. 'Those foxes have got to pay the penalty.'

'Too right,' said Matthew, a lean and sinewy man of endurance and vigour at thirty-eight. 'And don't I know it.'

Rosie gave him a little pat of sympathy. The adopted and treasured daughter of Boots, at thirty-four she was still extraordinarily attractive, and still like Boots in finding the peccadilloes of people amusing rather than irritating. To Matthew, Rosie in line and form made everything in his immediate world look better than anything in the National Gallery. In fact, the National Gallery was overburdened with far too much plump flesh for his liking. He saw Rosie as a tribute to God's finer handiwork, and that went for her intelligence and disposition as well as her looks, although there were a few things she couldn't suffer gladly, such as badly behaved kids who bawled in public places. Crying babies, well, they were understandable, but bawling kids, no.

As for Emma and Jonathan, both in their late twenties, they had one child, little three-year-old Jessie, and a shared gift for funny repartee. Jonathan came of a Sussex family full of jokers from his parents downwards, and Emma came of Adams stock, noted for what Chinese Lady called its music-hall comedians.

Saying goodnight to Rosie and Matthew, Emma and Jonathan went through the kitchen to the annexe, their living quarters, where little Jessie lay sound asleep. Their own home, off Denmark Hill in south-east London, was occupied by a young couple who were renting it on a year-by-year lease.

'Is Emma expecting?' asked Matthew. He and Rosie knew their business partners wanted a brother or sister for Jessie.

'Not as far as I know,' said Rosie.

'Still no bun, then?' said Matthew.

'No conception.' Rosie smiled. 'Matthew Chapman, I object to bun.'

'Noted,' said Matthew. 'Jonathan looks healthy enough, but I wonder, would a Guinness a day help him if we could feed him oysters as well?'

'Phone the fishmonger tomorrow,' said Rosie, 'and if he can oblige, we'll feed Jonathan a Guinness and some oysters with his lunch.'

'Who's serious?' asked Matthew.

'I am,' said Rosie, 'and so are you. And so is Emma, I'm sure.'

'Oysters and Guinness for Emma too, then?' said Matthew.

'Don't go over the top, Dorset man,' said Rosie. 'I'm still trying to come to terms with Grandpa's promised knighthood.'

'That,' said Matthew, 'would be way over the top in my book if it weren't for the fact that my wife's the natural daughter of a baronet.'

'I'm happy you're able to live with it,' smiled Rosie, and went a little pensive. Sir Charles Armitage, her natural father, had been killed at Tobruk during the Middle

East campaign. Rosie had come to find him a completely likeable man, but had never been able to give him the kind of love she gave Boots.

Sometimes that love had had its dangerous moments. If no-one in the family had noticed, Polly had, and she experienced clear-cut relief when Rosie fell in love with her Dorset man, Matthew Chapman. Even then, Polly felt Matthew's initial attraction for Rosie was due to the fact that he was not unlike Boots in his dry humour, his tolerance and his naturalness.

'Penny for them, Rosie,' said Matthew, interrupting her musings.

'Oh, I'm thinking we must keep our promise to call on my grandparents one evening next week,' said Rosie.

'To congratulate them?' said Matthew.

'Well, we should, shouldn't we?' said Rosie.

'Personally, I'd like to,' said Matthew.

'Personally, so would I,' said Rosie, and Matthew put his hands on her shoulders and kissed her.

'You're a sweet woman, Rosie,' he said.

'Thank 'ee, m'dear,' said Rosie in West Country lingo.

Chapter Seven

Monday morning.

Sammy and Jimmy were motoring north to Edmonton, and Paul was at the desk of his poky office in the Labour Party's Walworth headquarters. His brow furrowed. It was no joke, it seriously wasn't, being related to a title. Here he was, coming up to a man's age of nineteen, secretary of the Young Socialists and a dynamic political career in front of him. But he could imagine some know-all heckler getting at him with a lot of heavy sarcasm about the titled toffs in his family, his grandparents. As it was, he already had problems on account of his Uncle Sammy being a bloated capitalist and his dad being a well-off one. Curses, there was something else too. Suppose someone who wanted his job as secretary found out that on top of his granddad getting a title, the father-in-law of Uncle Boots was General Sir Henry Simms? Working-class voters could sound off in shocking fashion about generals who were also titled toffs.

Paul, usually a brisk and bright young bloke, gloomed.

John Saunders, the local Member of Parliament, came in. There was a young lady with him.

'Morning, Paul, enjoy your weekend? That's something the Party never let up on, campaigning for the workers' right to a five-and-a-half-day week. Now we've got a five-day week in mind, to give 'em a full weekend of freedom from their labours. And freedom from their sweatshops and their bosses, eh? Come to that, who needs the general run of bosses? I hear certain Cabinet ministers are prepared to back nationalization of private business and getting the workers to run their own factories, but of course we can't do that sort of thing overnight, eh? We've done welfare, the health service and the mines, but the PM's treading water on other matters until after the recess. Bevan's rumbling and growling, of course. But you'd expect that of a man who embraced the compassion of the Labour Party from the day he was born. All that's given you something for some new leaflets, eh? Well now.' The MP, having automatically delivered a speech, made way for the young lady. 'Here's my daughter Lulu, your new assistant.'

'Pardon?' said Paul.

'As arranged,' said the MP, burly figure attired in a smart suit. He wore his cap and scarf only when meeting the workers during electioneering. 'Wake up, brother.'

'Oh, yes, right,' said Paul, remembering that his previous assistant had been upgraded to the post of secretary to the local constituency's agent. He looked up at the MP's daughter, dressed in long-skirted mauve. His notes told him she was eighteen. She looked twenty and a bit more. Her black glossy hair, parted down the middle, hung like straight curtains on either side of her face, and between the curtains dark eyes regarded him through the lenses of horn-rimmed spectacles. She wasn't bad-looking, she had a wide firm mouth and an unblemished skin, but against that, she also had the paleness of a student given to earnest study all day and half the night. 'Hello,' he said, rising to shake her hand, 'I'm Paul Adams, secretary of our group.'

'Yes, good-oh,' she said. 'Lulu Saunders. Miss. Pleased to meet you. Trust we'll get along. Can't always tell. Not at first sight. Still, here's hoping.' Her speech was clipped and staccato, putting Paul in mind of Mr Jingle making his mark in Dickens's novel *Pickwick Papers*.

'Well, I'll leave you to it,' said the MP, and ducked out, looking so happy to escape that Paul suspected the daughter made him nervous.

'Fill me in,' she said.

'For a start,' said Paul informatively, 'our chief work here is recruiting and propaganda.'

'Know that, don't I?' said the earnest young lady. 'Good at it, are you?'

Paul blinked.

'Good at it?' he said.

'No worries if you're not,' said Miss Saunders, 'I'm brilliant.'

'References?' said Paul.

'What?'

'References to confirm your brilliance,' said Paul.

'Give over. My father's my reference. Honest John. Not many like him in Parliament. But he'll never make Prime Minister. Not the right kind of brain. If he had mine, he'd stand a chance.'

'How'd you come by all that modesty?' asked Paul.

'Modesty?' Miss Saunders looked sorry

for him. 'Can't afford modesty. That's for shrinking violets. Gave all that bunk the heave-ho when I was nine. Knew by then life was a curse for shrinking violets. Earned myself a good education. Now I've got my foot on the ladder.'

'Tell me more,' said Paul.

'Nothing to tell. Apart from making a decision.'

'What decision?' asked Paul.

'Going to be a Member of Parliament by the time I'm thirty,' said Miss Saunders.

'Is that a fact?'

'A promise. Where do I sit?'

'Over there.' Paul indicated a desk opposite his own. There was a chair and a typewriter.

'Crummy,' said Miss Saunders. 'Listen, Adams. Let's understand each other. I do what's required of me, but I don't take orders.'

'Listen, Saunders,' said Paul, 'you'll do what's required and you'll take orders.'

'How old are you, bossy boots?' asked Miss Saunders.

'Fifty.'

'What's your real name, then? Peter Pan?'

'How would you like to be fired before you start?' asked Paul, thinking her name suited her. She was a Lulu all right, full stop.

'That's it, make me laugh,' she said. 'Suppose we get down to biz? Don't like wasting time. What's the schedule?'

'Delivery of leaflets,' said Paul. There was a large parcel on his desk, brown wrapping paper ripped open. 'Five hundred. They came to us from the printers Saturday morning. See that satchel?'

Miss Saunders saw it, hanging on the door peg.

'Well?' she said.

'You carry the leaflets in that,' said Paul, 'and you spend the day knocking on doors, talking to tenants and leaving a leaflet at every house. Whenever you get no answer, slip a leaflet through the letter box.'

'Listen, Adams–'

'That's all, Saunders,' said Paul. 'There's a General Election coming early next year, and these are pre-election leaflets, spelling out the dangers of the Conservatives getting back in if we take victory for granted.'

'Now you're talking,' said Miss Saunders. 'Don't want that bloody lot back in. Nor that warmonger, Churchill. Upper-class drunk. Wouldn't surprise me if the Establishment made him Lord Churchill. Probably give him his own distillery too.'

'Some of our voters like the old boy, even if they'd never vote Tory,' said Paul. He fidgeted. 'Forget upper class and titles.'

'Forget 'em? Why?' Between her shining black curtains, Lulu Saunders peered suspiciously at him. 'That's what we're fighting, aren't we?'

'Don't ask the converted,' said Paul, 'just talk to the people of Walworth about the points detailed in the leaflet.'

'Wait a minute,' said Lulu. 'Didn't take this job on to deliver leaflets, did I?'

'Consider it a pleasant surprise,' said Paul. 'Off you go. You can take all day. Tomorrow you can do some typing for me.'

'I've got a feeling,' said Lulu.

'What feeling?'

'That we're not going to get on. You're playing the superior male.'

'How about that?' said Paul. 'Just when I was thinking what a superior female you are. Nice to have you with us.'

'Someone here needs sorting out,' said Lulu, 'and it's not me. Right, Adams, let's have the bloody leaflets, then. But watch your back.' Her spectacles looked threatening. 'I'm a killer.'

'Enjoy your day,' said Paul.

He felt better after she'd gone. After all,

with luck, no-one need find out in due course that Sir Edwin Finch was any relative of his. And if anyone did, well, he could ride the upper-class stigma as an incorruptible Young Socialist.

Miss Saunders. Why the long, ankle-length dress? Was she, one, a bluestocking? Two, a frump? Three, bow-legged? Not three, he hoped. If one or two, well, a bloke could forgive a girl for either if she had good stilts.

Paul's politics did not limit his interest in the opposite sex. As a young man, he naturally subscribed to the belief that politics exercised a bloke's social awareness, and girls exercised his imagination.

Sammy, Jimmy and Mr Greenberg arrived at the specified warehouse in Edmonton. Brick-built, with dusty skylights in its roof, it seemed old enough and grimy enough to date back to Roman times. There was a tough-looking geezer about four feet wide at the door.

'Morning,' said Sammy.

'Name?' growled Toughie.

'Adams, Sammy Adams.'

Toughie consulted a well-thumbed note-book.

'Ain't got no Adams,' he said, 'and if I ain't got yer monicker, you ain't getting in.'

'Have another look,' said Sammy, and Toughie did another scrutiny, thumbing pages.

'Oh, I got yer,' he said, 'Jammy Adams. But hold on, who's he and who's him?'

'Him's my son and he's my business consultant,' said Sammy. It was black market all right, and only authorized dealers were going to be admitted. Well, he needn't tell Susie.

Toughie scrutinized Jimmy, then eyed Mr Greenberg. Mr Greenberg's white-peppered beard advertised he was heading towards old age. His round rusty black hat was already there. But he still loved business and still pursued his rag-and-bone rounds in South London. He was also known north of the river.

Toughie, grinning, addressed him.

'Watcher, Eli, how yer doing, you old pirate? Nice to see yer.'

'My pleasure, ain't it?' said Mr Greenberg.

'Didn't spot it was you at first,' said Toughie. 'Jammy Adams was in the way. All right, in yer go, you've got time to look at the apples and oranges before you place yer bids.'

They entered the warehouse. Tiers of stout shelving on either side contained bales of material, and plain wooden stairs led up to the top tiers. Dealers, some furtive and some brazen, were making inspections of the wares. At the far end two men sat at a desk, observing the scene.

Sammy was after bales of nylon, one of the modern man-made materials beginning to replace natural yarns. All bales were marked with a number.

'So vhat do you think, Sammy?' Eli's whisper murmured through his beard.

Sammy, noting a dealer talking to the men at the desk, said, 'I think, Eli old cock, that that's where we place our bids.'

'Vell, Sammy,' said Mr Greenberg, who had never lost his own kind of pronounced English, 'it's done that vay in some vare-houses.'

'Warehouses that don't advertise?' said Jimmy.

'We won't tell your mother,' said Sammy.

'Hello, hello,' wheezed a squeezed set of tonsils, 'who's slumming it?'

They turned to find an enormously fat man regarding them out of eyes set in blubber. Beside him was a large lump recognizable to Sammy as a bodyguard.

'Well, well,' Sammy said, 'I think I know you, don't I? You're still putting on weight, y'know. How d'you manage it, seeing the rest of us are living on this austerity diet?'

'Always the second-class funny bugger, are you?' wheezed Ben Ford, the Fat Man. He turned to his large lump. 'Ask him what he's after.'

'Mr Ford wants to know what you're after,' said Large Lump, his jaw looking like old concrete. 'Tell him.'

Dealers sidled around them as Sammy said, 'Oh, bits and pieces, y'know.'

'Tell him to lay off the nylon,' wheezed the Fat Man.

'Mr Ford says lay off the nylon,' said Large Lump.

'If I might put in a vord,' said Mr Greenberg, 'Mr Adams don't take kindly to being told vhat he can and can't do.'

'That's true, I don't, normally,' said Sammy amiably. 'Still, they're a lot bigger than we are, Eli, and I can make exceptions.'

'We've come a long way to make exceptions, Dad,' said Jimmy.

'Tiny, tell the runt to shut his cakehole,' wheezed the Fat Man.

'Button your bleedin' lip,' said Large Lump to Jimmy.

'That's not friendly,' said Jimmy.

'It's what Mr Ford wants,' said Large Lump.

'Oh, well,' said Sammy, 'let's go looking for allowable stuff, Jimmy. Come on, Eli.'

They went looking. The bales of nylon were all on the bottom tier of shelving, together with rayon and very poor quality cotton. Sammy told Jimmy to pencil in certain numbers, and Jimmy did so, using a notebook. The Fat Man moved ponderously around, his wheezy breathing audible among the noise of dealers conferring with each other up above and down below. You bid for those, I'll bid for these. That sort of thing.

Large Lump was nowhere to be seen, but from the top tier of shelving a bale of rayon, all of a hundredweight, lost its place and came bounding down. Mr Greenberg, a wily old bird who always kept an eye on what he considered suspect, gave Sammy a hefty shove, and the bale thudded to the concrete floor well short of Sammy's feet.

Sammy controlled reactive shakes and said, 'Well, who did that, I wonder?'

'An accident, Sammy, ain't it?' said Mr Greenberg.

'It would've been, if it had landed on my

loaf of bread,' said Sammy.

Dealers were looking on with startled eyes. The Fat Man was breathing heavily. Up rushed one of the men from the desk.

'What the bloody hell happened?' he bawled, as Large Lump materialized beside the Fat Man.

'That bale fell off the shelf,' said Jimmy.

'Ah, vas it falling or vas it pushed?' murmured Mr Greenberg.

The bloke from the desk, muttering, inspected the bale, then looked upwards at the top tier. There was an empty hole where the bale had rested, but that was all.

'Don't make sense,' he muttered. 'Still, no damage to the goods, gents, and by the way, all bids in before two o'clock.' He returned to the desk.

Sammy looked at the number on the fallen bale of rayon.

'Twenty-seven, Jimmy,' he said.

'Eh?' said Jimmy.

'Twenty-seven,' repeated Sammy very clearly.

'Oh, right, got you, Dad,' said Jimmy, and made a note of the number. The Fat Man and his Large Lump looked on from the other side of the shed.

Dealers milled. Sammy, Jimmy and Mr

Greenberg slowly traversed the place in a tour of inspection, Jimmy with his notebook at the ready. Now and again, it looked as if Sammy was quoting a rayon bale number.

'Eli old cock,' he murmured after a while, 'accept my gratitude for saving me from going home flat.'

'My pleasure, vasn't it?' said Mr Greenberg.

'I think someone's declared war,' said Jimmy.

'Well, Jimmy,' said Sammy, 'that kind of war happened before we got clouted by Hitler, and somehow the Fat Man was always close by. Now that he's risen up from what I thought was the welcome departed, watch the Walworth store in case a Molotov cockroach comes flying in.'

'Cocktail, Dad,' said Jimmy.

'Not for me, Jimmy, and they don't sell 'em here,' said Sammy.

'I mean Molotov cocktail,' said Jimmy.

'Same thing,' said Sammy, 'they're both 'orrible. And God bless Eli for saving me from a Molotov hundredweight.'

'Ah, Sammy,' said Mr Greenberg, 'but vhere vas God vhen Himmler vas gassing and burning my people in his murder camps?'

'Ask me another,' said Sammy.

'Weeping with His angels?' suggested Jimmy.

'I'll go along with that,' said Sammy, 'and put down number forty-one, Jimmy.' Reaching the end of their floor-level inspection, he added, 'I don't think we'll go upstairs in case we fall through a trapdoor. We've got all the numbers I'm willing to bid for.' He took the notebook from Jimmy, consulted it, whispered numbers to Mr Greenberg, slipped something into his hand, then said, 'So will you have a word, Eli?'

'So I vill, Sammy, von't I?' said Mr Greenberg.

'At the usual commission,' said Sammy.

'My pleasure again, ain't it?' said Mr Greenberg, and he made his way through wandering dealers to the men at the desk, where he quoted certain numbers, but not twenty-seven, then made a proposition and, on reaching immediate agreement, handed over a large cash deposit. He then rejoined Sammy and Jimmy, and they all left.

Chapter Eight

'Fill me in, Eli,' said Sammy, as they walked to his parked car.

'Your deposit, Sammy, vas happily received on account of how much it vas. I vill go back at three, vhen the highest bids vill be honoured.'

'Honoured?' said Jimmy. 'Is there honour in the black market, then?'

'Ah, there is some, Jimmy my boy, you may be sure,' said Mr Greenberg, 'or – ah – accidents happen.'

'I think I know about accidents,' said Jimmy.

'Vhen I go back at three, I vill, of course, find out vhat are the average highest bids for nylon bales.'

'Won't they be announced?' asked Jimmy. His dad and Mr Greenberg looked at him. 'Silly question,' he said.

'But I vill find out.' Mr Greenberg's little chuckle emerged but lost itself in his beard. 'That vay your papa von't be cheated, and vill add ten per cent to the highest bids made on the bales he vants, vhich the gentlemen at the desk vill make known to me. Then I vill have to pay any balance. In cash, Sammy.'

'Which I'm confident I can supply from my wallet,' said Sammy.

'I presume,' said Jimmy, 'these kind of transactions are always in cash.'

'Granted, a supply of the readies is always necessary,' said Sammy, 'but your mother needn't know.'

Jimmy grinned. He was beginning to understand that business was business whatever.

'The bales must be collected tomorrow, vhich collection I vill do for you, Sammy, vith the help of my two sons.' His stepsons, actually. But he was a fond father to them. There had been three until the eldest, serving with the Royal Navy, had been drowned when his ship, torpedoed in the Atlantic, blew up and sank. 'I vill also deliver to your factory, Sammy, von't I?'

'Not in your open cart, Eli old cock, or the bales might get nicked by Dick Turpin,' said Sammy. 'Now let's find a cafe and see if they'll do us a light lunch of ham and eggs, except no ham for you, Eli. Kosher bangers instead?'

'Vhat cafe will do kosher, Sammy?'

'No idea,' said Sammy. 'I'm a foreigner here. So let's go looking.'

'Vell, Sammy, I think I know just the place,' said Mr Greenberg. 'In Lower Fore Street.'

'Take note, Jimmy,' said Sammy, 'that if you want to know anything about London that you don't know, our old friend Eli will supply you with the works.'

'That's a kind reference, Sammy, ain't it?' said Mr Greenberg, who sometimes woke up in the night and said a grateful prayer for never having been in danger of finding himself in a Nazi concentration camp.

'By the way,' said Sammy, as they reached the car, 'cost of commission, collection and delivery, might I ask how much?'

'Sammy, Sammy, vould I ask more than vhat you think is fair?' said Mr Greenberg.

'Half the shirt off my back, that's fair,' said Sammy, happy to have six bales of nylon for his factory, plus Mr Greenberg's promise of pointing him at a reconditioned stocking-making machine.

'Yes?' said the woman on answering a knock on the front door of her house in Manor Place, Walworth.

'Good afternoon,' said Miss Lulu Saunders, who felt this must be the five hundredth house she'd called at, but knew it couldn't be because she still had a large number of leaflets in the satchel. 'You're a Labour Party voter, of course? Good, I–'

'What d'yer mean, good?' said the woman.

'Your husband's a worker?'

'So am I, I've got four kids and they're all terrors.'

'You're a prime worker,' said Lulu. 'You're all benefiting from our Labour government. Want that to continue, don't you?'

'Leave off, I'm still doing me week's washing,' said the woman. 'Kindly hoppit.' She shut the door. Lulu stuffed a leaflet through the letter box.

Her day so far hadn't been joyful. Only a relatively few people had cared to discuss politics with her. Most didn't want to discuss anything except something like why was meat still rationed considering there was plenty of live beef plodding about in the countryside. And others weren't at home.

She knocked at the next house. The door was opened by a rugged-looking bloke in trousers, shirt and braces. He had a half-eaten slice of cake in his hand.

'Afternoon,' said Lulu.

He looked her over.

'Afternoon,' he said, 'what can I do for you?'

'You're a Labour Party voter?'

'I'm nobody's voter. I hate politicians.'

'Such as the Tories?' said Lulu.

'All of 'em.'

'You need talking to about the Labour Party,' said Lulu, favouring the possibility of converting the bloke.

'Right,' he said, 'come in and have a cup of char and a slice of cake, and I'll lend you my ear.'

That was the first time Lulu had encountered a real welcome.

'Pleasure,' she said.

Ten minutes later she was on her way out. What had been on offer was not just tea, cake and a willing ear, but also his bedroom, and the pleasure of rolling in the hay with him, since he had a thing about females in glasses. But he made it clear that her mauve dress didn't suit her, so let's get rid of it, you sexpot. Lulu floored him at the moment when he had her dress nearly up to her knickers, the saucy cowboy. She used the satchel, heavy with leaflets. She left him on the floor, seeing double.

Sammy, Jimmy and Mr Greenberg were on their way home, the transaction having been completed over an exchange of whispers and the inaudible rustle of a sheaf of the readies. If whispers were synonymous with the black market, the readies were what kept it going. Sammy had principles, of course, but could stretch them for the sake of his business.

What was pleasing as much as anything was the way good old Eli had handled the transaction, thereby doing the Fat Man in the eye without Sammy himself being present at the final exchanges, and accordingly avoiding being trodden on by Large Lump.

The lady customers of his various shops were going to be made very happy when nylon stockings became available to them. Lady customers were nearly fanatical about nylon stockings, and most wouldn't even ask how much they were.

'Eli, my old mate,' he said, 'I'm totally admiring of your valuability.'

'My pleasure, Sammy, ain't it?' said Mr Greenberg.

Jimmy smiled.

Miss Lulu Saunders was back at Paul's office before four, dumping the satchel on the floor and plonking her bottom on the edge of her desk.

'You're early,' said Paul.

'You're lucky I'm still alive,' she said. 'Had doors slammed in my face. Nearly had my nose flattened once or twice. And some oversexed bloke nearly had my dress off.'

'While you were on his doorstep?' enquired Paul.

'While I was in his kitchen,' said Lulu.

'By invitation?'

'Said he'd lend an ear to my politics. Over tea and cake. What a swine. He had bed in mind. Had to knock him blind with the satchel. Hope he's still hurting.'

'Next time you get an invitation from a bloke to step inside,' said Paul, 'sum up your prospects before you accept.'

'Don't worry, I will,' said Lulu. 'Listen, what's the point of my preaching to the converted? Walworth is eighty per cent Socialist.'

'Any leaflets left?' asked Paul.

'Bags of 'em,' said Lulu.

'Try going farther afield tomorrow,' said Paul. 'Get yourself among the lower middle class and see if you can convert them. Take a bus, and we'll pay any fares out of the petty cash.'

'Now you're talking,' said Lulu. 'Making converts is more my style. Especially middle-class converts. Any tea going?'

'The kitchen's along the corridor,' said Paul. 'There's sugar and milk. Make a pot for two and I'll have a cup with you.'

'You'll be lucky,' said Lulu. 'Dead lucky. I'm nobody's skivvy.'

'All right,' said Paul, getting up from his desk, 'I'll make it myself. I'm thirsty.'

'I'm worn out,' said Lulu.

'D'you take sugar?'

'No sugar. Ta.'

Paul, going to the kitchen, thought about the oversexed bloke trying to get her dress off. That was no laughing matter, no, not a bit.

All the same, he was grinning as he filled the kettle.

That evening, Boots was doing one or two jobs on his old but still reliable Riley car. With Saturday's journey to Cornwall in mind, he had the sparking plugs out and was cleaning them, much to the fascination of James. Gemma, however, thought nothing of soppy things like plugs, and much more about sandy beaches.

'Daddy, are we going to have buckets and

spades for sandcastles?' she asked, hovering close.

'Going to?' said Boots. 'You've got them.'

'Daddy, mine's got a rusty bottom,' said Gemma.

'Rusty bottom?' Boots, using a little wire brush on a plug, smiled. 'Sounds painful.'

'Yes, and it'll fall out, I should think,' said Gemma.

'Well, I'll have a look at it, and if its condition is serious, we'll buy you a new one when we get there,' said Boots.

'Crumbs, you're a sport, Daddy,' said Gemma, piquant features shining with pleasure.

'And he knows about cars, don't you, Daddy?' said James, rag in his hand and ready to give each cleaned plug a finishing wipe.

'A little,' said Boots.

'I'm going to drive racing cars when I'm old enough,' said James.

'So am I, then,' said Gemma.

'You're a girl,' said James.

'Yes, and I'm nice too,' said Gemma. 'Aren't I, Daddy?'

'You're a poppet,' said Boots, handing a plug to James.

'Girls don't drive racing cars,' said James,

wiping the plug with the rag and with serious concentration.

'But I won't be a girl for ever,' said Gemma, 'not when I'm grown-up.'

'She's daft,' said James, but not without a hint of affection. He and Gemma had their arguments and their yelling moments, but woe betide any misguided kid who upset James's twin sister in one way or another. He would wade in, fists flying in defence of her.

'But I won't be a girl for ever, will I, Daddy?' said Gemma.

'Not when you're eighty,' said Boots, handing another plug to James.

'Crumbs, I don't want to be eighty,' said Gemma, 'well, not yet I don't.'

'What do you want to be?' asked Boots.

'Like Mummy,' said Gemma.

'I see,' said Boots gravely, 'a woman.'

'Yes, and with nice frocks like Mummy's,' said Gemma.

'You can't drive a racing car in a frock,' said James.

'Course I can, when I'm a growed woman,' said Gemma.

The woman who wore nice frocks and was a growed woman was standing behind the window of the lounge, watching her husband and children, a little smile on her face.

In the years gone by, Polly would never have believed she would end up as a suburban housewife and mother, and content to be so. But there they were, the man, the girl and the boy who belonged to her, and she asked for nothing different, nothing more sophisticated. Boots had done that to her, made a wife and mother of her, the old darling. The twins loved him, although not in the same kind of way she did. If she was less passionate now in her demands on him, she still bristled at the way some women looked at him, and crept up on him. It was absurd that at fifty-three he was still uncommonly attractive. One woman had boldly said to her, 'My God, Polly, your husband's got frightening sex appeal.' 'Well, buzz off, ducky, before I have to chop your head off,' said Polly.

She opened the window and called.

'Supper on the table in five minutes. But Flossie won't stand for any of you having filthy hands. Wash yours, James, and you too, Boots.'

'Mine aren't filthy,' said James. 'Well, not much.'

'You'll still have to wash them, and I'll have to wash mine,' said Boots. He winked at Gemma. 'That's what comes of your mother being a growed woman, poppet.'

Gemma giggled. Polly called again.

'I heard that, you bounder.'

It had been many years since Boots had suffered nightmarish dreams about the hideous trenches of France and Flanders during the First World War. Since the end of the conflict against Nazi Germany, he had had the occasional restless dreams of the ferocious campaign in Normandy, when the roaring guns blew men to bits. And there had been the horrendous dreams of Belsen concentration camp, of dead and dying inmates, and of faces, brutalized SS faces, uncaring faces and cold blue eyes that still mirrored a belief in the sickening ideologies of Hitler.

This night the dream woke him up. The faces, the cold eyes, the corruption. Reminders, reminders. But of what, apart from the stinking foulness of the camp and its guards? Something was ticking away in his mind, but it struck no bell.

Beside him Polly lay in the warmth of sleep. Polly. A growed woman. Witty, amusing and unfailing. A friend, a wife and a lover, as necessary to him as Emily had been.

He relaxed and drifted back to sleep.

Chapter Nine

'So the factory's going to turn out nylon stockings,' said Susie over breakfast the next morning.

'So it is, Susie, so it is,' said Sammy.

'And the material wasn't black market stuff?' said Susie.

'What brought that up?' asked Sammy.

'Yes, what did?' said Paula.

'Beats me,' said Sammy.

'I think Mum's got suspicions,' said Paula.

'Oh, lor',' said Phoebe. 'Crikey, suspicions,' she said.

'I've been thinking since yesterday evening,' said Susie.

'Crikey, thinking,' said Jimmy, 'that's on a par with suspicions.'

'Mum's got principles,' said Paula.

'Principles?' said Phoebe. 'Oh dear, what's Dad got, then?'

'Twice as many as anybody else,' said Jimmy, 'on account of twice as many being necessary to a businessman who's always having to fight competition.'

'I've been thinking,' said Susie, 'that you didn't look me in the eye, Sammy, when you were telling me yesterday evening about the auction and the Fat Man.'

'Ah,' said Sammy.

'Ah-aah-ah-aaah,' sang Paula through a mouthful of toast.

'I think Dad's in trouble,' said Phoebe.

'Sammy, what I really want to know is did you really sit on the Fat Man?' said Susie, looking charming in a button-through flower-patterned housecoat.

'Believe me, Susie, we really did,' said Sammy. 'Well, he was trying to do a black market deal on the crafty quiet, so we upped our bid fair and square.'

'We flattened him,' said Jimmy. 'Mr Greenberg added his weight, the good old codger. So there you are, Mum, six walloping great bales of nylon for the factory. Thousands of nylon stockings.'

'I'm looking at you, Jimmy,' said Susie.

'Crikey, looking,' said Paula.

'Is that special?' asked Phoebe.

'It is when Mum does the looking,' said Paula.

'Believe me, Mum, it was a fine bit of business done fair and square, as mentioned by Dad,' said Jimmy.

'Thousands of pairs of nylon stockings?' said Susie.

'Thousands, goodness me,' said Paula.

'Sammy, reserve six pairs for me,' said Susie.

'And me, and me,' yelled Paula.

'Then there's Lizzy, Vi and Polly,' said Susie.

'And Rosie, Emma, Annabelle, Felicity and Auntie Tom Cobleigh and all,' said Jimmy.

'Well, as it wasn't black market,' said Susie, 'the family can benefit with a clear conscience.'

'Well, of course, Susie, and at a family discount,' said Sammy, and looked her in the eye. Susie's Pacific-blue left optic closed in a slow wink.

'Crikey, now what's happening?' asked Phoebe.

'Dad's gone potty,' said Paula.

Sammy was shouting with laughter.

Miss Lulu Saunders alighted from a bus at Herne Hill railway station at nine thirty. She looked around. This is it, lower middle class vintage, she told herself. The Party's fixed enemy. Shame, really, that Socialism frightens them. Right, let's storm their privet hedges. If I only make one convert, I'll be a magician. Is magician masculine? Bound to be. What's the feminine? Magicienne, I suppose. Here goes.

She began her round, the satchel containing about two hundred leaflets.

At the end of an hour, she'd had some quite interesting conversations with housewives who didn't mind a chat, and some brusque invitations to go back home to Trotsky. She'd as good as made one convert, of a lady whose war-disabled husband had been awarded what she thought was a criminally rotten pension in 1944.

'Churchill's wartime government did that,' said Lulu, and expounded on the infamy of Conservative attitudes towards soldiers and workers, and the benevolent generosity of the Labour Party towards one and all. It impressed the lady, and she received a leaflet with pleasure.

Lulu carried on.

At eleven, Chinese Lady answered the doorbell.

'Good morning,' said Lulu.

Chinese Lady surveyed the caller, a young woman in a black beret, long purple dress, pale face and dark eyes framed by spectacles.

'Good morning,' she said.

'May I take up a few minutes of your time?' said Lulu.

'Not if you're going to try and sell me something,' said Chinese Lady.

'Sell you something?' said Lulu. 'Not I. Not likely. Don't go in for making a living on people's doorsteps. That's for plodders. Like the man from the Pru. No, I'd just like to ask if you're a supporter of the Labour Party.'

Chinese Lady, with her fondness for respectability, considered the Labour Party a bit loud and vulgar.

'D'you mean Socialism?' she said.

'The compassionate system of government,' said Lulu.

'What's that mean, might I ask?'

'Caring,' said Lulu. 'Caring for the poor and needy. And the sick. And the downtrodden workers.'

'Well, I'm sorry for anyone that's downtrodden,' said Chinese Lady. 'I've been downtrodden myself in my time, and you look as if you are a bit. Yes, a bit like the poor and needy.'

'Excuse me,' said Lulu, 'I'm not–'

'Of course, it could be a touch of anaemia,' said Chinese Lady sympathetically. She didn't like to see young ladies looking a bit pale and lacking. And she didn't like to close the door on this one, especially as her fondness for a doorstep chat had stayed with her all the way from her years in Walworth, where such sociable moments of gossip had always been enjoyable. 'Have you tried lightly cooked liver? Lamb's liver's nice, and you don't need ration coupons for it.'

'Excuse me,' said Lulu again, 'but I'm not anaemic. Or poor and needy–'

'Well, about this Socialism,' said Chinese Lady, 'you're not a Bolshevik, are you? Lor', the times I've worried what would happen to my family if Lenin and his Bolsheviks came and took over.'

'Lenin's dead, Mrs – er–'

'I don't know anyone's ever told me he was,' said Chinese Lady, 'or if he'd stopped throwing bombs. Now, if you're not a Bolshevik, would you like to come in? I'll make some tea and a nice sandwich for you.'

'Pardon?' Lulu gaped.

'Well, if you don't mind me saying so, you look as if you'd like a nice sandwich, and you can meet my husband. He used to work for the Government, and can tell you a lot about what them politicians get up to, and what Mr Churchill thinks of Lenin. My family's very admiring of Mr Churchill.'

'Because of his record as our wartime leader?' said Lulu. 'But he's a back number now. Just as well–'

'D'you mean like last week's Sunday papers?' said Chinese Lady.

'You could put it like that,' said Lulu. 'Out of date, you know. Still a Victorian. And a bit of a blimp. Good thing the country got rid of him. Hope he–'

'Lor', I never heard the like,' said Chinese Lady, 'and I don't like listening to it at my own front door, it's downright scandalous. You sure you're not a Bolshevik?'

'I'm a modern Socialist,' said Lulu, 'and I–'

'What's a modern Socialist, might I ask?'

'One dedicated to practical help for the downtrodden–'

'I don't know any downtrodden,' said Chinese Lady. 'I used to know a lot, but wages being a lot better now, no-one ought to be downtrodden.'

'It's the capitalistic bosses who–'

'I suppose you work for one like that,' said Chinese Lady. 'No wonder you look a bit starved and chronic. Still, you're young yet, and I expect you can get a better job.'

Lulu, getting a bit steamed up about being pitied, said, 'I'm a volunteer worker for the Young Socialists. We're–'

'I don't know I like young people getting mixed up with Bolsheviks,' said Chinese Lady, frowning.

Silly old cow, thought Lulu, she's barmy.

'Nothing to do with Bolsheviks,' she said. 'The Bolshevist Party became the Communist Party. Massacred Hitler's Nazis. Relieved the world of them. What the Labour Party–'

'Me and my family wouldn't want anything to do with them Communists,' said Chinese Lady, just about ready now to bid the caller goodbye.

'I'm getting nowhere,' said Lulu, just about ready herself now to file this barmy old biddy as a lost cause. 'You're not hearing what I'm saying. What the Labour Party in this country would like to do, is make sure you, me and everyone else get a fair deal. To start with, relieving it of the bosses who still think they're God Almighty.'

'Well, I never did,' said Chinese Lady, 'if I wasn't standing in the way like I am, that blasphemy would of jumped straight through my open door and gone all over my house. I'd best close the door right away. Good morning, young lady.'

The door closed. Lulu, beefed up, gave herself the satisfaction of shoving not one, but three leaflets through the letter box before striding off.

In the kitchen, Mr Finch, who had come in from a stint in the garden and was making coffee, said, 'Who was that, Maisie, someone interesting?'

'Oh, just some poor starved girl who liked the Labour Party, but had some funny ideas about the Bolsheviks,' said Chinese Lady.

'Ah, the Bolsheviks,' said Mr Finch and smiled. 'Very interesting.'

'Upsetting, more like,' said Chinese Lady.

'Well, how did you make out today?' asked Paul when Lulu arrived back at five o'clock.

'I think I made three middle-class converts,' said Lulu, dumping the empty satchel.

'That all? Just three in a day?'

'Three middle-class converts in a day I count as a triumph,' said Lulu. 'I lost out badly on one silly old has-been. Kept asking me if I was a Bolshevik. Bolshevik, would you mind. In this day and age. Still, give her her due. She stuck to her guns. Stayed on her barmy level from start to finish.'

'You get characters, even among middle-class women,' said Paul, 'and barmy is more interesting than boring.'

'I haven't asked,' said Lulu, 'but what's your background?'

'Respectable,' said Paul.

'Hard luck, mate, I had some of that,' said Lulu. 'All the time my mother was alive. By the way, you owe me one and tuppence for bus fares.'

'Right,' said Paul, and settled up from the petty-cash box. 'By the way, the satchel belongs on the doorpeg, not on the floor.'

'Who's a bloody fusspot?' asked Lulu.

'Me,' said Paul.

'That grin on your face labels you,' said Lulu, 'as a male who kids himself he's superior.'

'Still, we're in the groove, you and me,' said Paul, 'we're on an equal footing.'

'Is that a fact? Fill me in,' said Lulu.

'You're as superior as I am,' said Paul.

'You're killing me,' said Lulu, and chucked the satchel at him.

Chapter Ten

Before that day was out, the bales of nylon were safely lodged in the stockroom at Sammy's factory at Belsize Park, north-west London. Gertie Roper, chargehand and faithful servant before the Second World War, all through the war and now post-war, was getting on a bit, but jumped about like a two-year-old at the prospect of the factory turning out nylon stockings.

'But we got to have a machine first,' she said to Tommy, factory manager.

'All in hand, Gertie,' said Tommy.

'Vell, Gertie my dear, ain't I pointed Sammy at vhat is just the job?' said Mr Greenberg, whose stepsons had cheerfully borne the burden of hefting the bales into the factory from the 'Greenberg & Sons' furniture van, once in ancient times an LGOC omnibus. 'As Tommy says, all in hand, ain't it?'

'And ain't I now a happy woman?' said Gertie, whose husband Bert was assistant manager and maintenance man. 'How did we get hold of such large bales, Mister Tommy?'

'Fair and square, wasn't it, Eli?' said Tommy.

'Sammy's exact vords,' said Mr Greenberg.

'Well, who's going to ask questions?' said Gertie. 'Not me. What about the girls, Mister Tommy?' She was referring to the machinists and seamstresses.

'They'll all want the nylon stockings?' said Tommy.

'Most will, specially the younger ones,' said Gertie.

'Well, as long as their legs qualify,' said Tommy. 'Tell 'em I'll make a leg inspection last thing Friday afternoon.'

'Don't say things like that, Mister Tommy,' said Gertie, 'or you'll find 'em all in your office last thing Friday afternoon, with their skirts up on account of your man appeal, like. So I 'ope you're joking.'

'I'm joking,' said Tommy hastily. 'Take orders from the girls, Gertie. Eli, that's a bad cough you've got.'

'Vell, so I have just now, Tommy, so I have,' said Mr Greenberg, and put his cough away. A throaty chuckle took its place.

'Stay for a cup of tea, Eli, and your sons,'

said Tommy.

'Ah, ain't I had a thousand kind cups of tea from you and your family?' said Mr Greenberg.

'Have one more,' said Tommy.

Over the tea in Tommy's office, with Mr Greenberg's dark, curly-haired stepsons present, the long-established rag-and-bone merchant mentioned that he, his wife and their sons, Michal and Jacob, were going to Israel next spring to see what their people had made of their independent state, and to allow Michal and Jacob to work at a kibbutz for a year.

'You'll think about staying, you and your family?' said Tommy.

'Michal and Jacob, they vill please themselves,' said Mr Greenberg. The young men, sturdy and muscular, smiled. 'But my good Hannah and me, vhy, ain't our home here among the people of London? No, no, Tommy, London is our home and alvays vill be. Vhat vould I do in Israel if I could not be on business call for Sammy or say shalom to you and Gertie from time to time?'

'This country's still broke,' said Tommy.

'So the Government don't have money in the bank? Is that something to make us veep?' Mr Greenberg shook his head. 'Ve should all be proud, Tommy, that it spent its last farthing to fight the Devil and his black angels along with the people of the vun they call Uncle Sam. But it is still the same country to vhich my thinking father brought his family many years ago from the pogroms of Russia. I kiss his memory for that, don't I? Your people are my people, Tommy, and I don't ask for more. Except a kind refill from the pot?'

'After that speech, Father, you should toast yourself in vodka,' said Michal.

'No vodka,' smiled Tommy.

'He should worry?' said Jacob. 'Tea will do, won't it?'

Gertie's voice was heard in the passage.

'Here, what d'yer think you're doing of, nearly walking over me? What d'yer want? Here, leave off– Oh, yer saucy sod.'

The office door flew back, and in the doorway stood Large Lump.

'Where's Jammy Adams?' he growled.

'Next time, knock before you enter,' said Tommy.

'Who the bleedin' fanackapan are you?'

'I'm Tommy Adams.'

'Brother, are yer?' said Large Lump, making the office look half its normal size.

'I am,' said Tommy. 'What's your business?'

'Mr Ford wants his bales back.'

'We don't have any bales belonging to Mr Ford,' said Tommy, who knew from Sammy what had happened at Edmonton. 'So long, mate. Close the door after you.'

'Don't make trouble, faceache, or yer factory might fall down,' said Large Lump, indifferent to whether Mr Greenberg and his sons were present or not. 'Just come quiet and talk to Mr Ford.'

'Shove off,' said Tommy.

'Gawdblimey O'Reilly, the trouble some people give me,' said Large Lump. 'Listen, if you don't come and talk to Mr Ford, things'll get noisy and there'll be blood-stains.'

'Sounds messy,' said Tommy, and got up. 'Stay there, Eli, I'll only be a tick.'

'Vell, all right, Tommy,' said Mr Greenberg. Tommy left with Large Lump. 'Sons of your mother,' said Mr Greenberg, 'out you go.'

'We should get our heads split?' said Michal.

'Hurtful, ain't it?' said Jacob, and exited with his brother.

Tommy, out on the factory forecourt with Large Lump on his heels, saw a van and a car parked inside the high wire perimeter.

At the open gates stood the Fat Man.

'Who's this specimen?' wheezed Fat Man.

'Jammy Adams's brother,' said Large Lump.

'Tell him to bring out my bales of nylon.'

'Bring 'em out,' said Large Lump to Tommy.

'Bloody hell,' said Tommy, with Michal and Jacob looking on from the factory entrance, 'what makes you think I was born yesterday?'

'You're trouble,' said Large Lump, looking disgusted. 'I knew it first time you opened yer cakehole. Mr Ford, he's trouble.'

'Tell him I'll do him and his bleedin' brother a favour,' said Fat Man, looking like a dressed-up balloon on short legs. 'Tell him I'll give him a fiver each for the bales. That'll take care of his trouble.'

'Mr Ford says–'

'I heard,' said Tommy caustically, 'and if I did hand the bales over – if – I'd want fifty quid each for them.'

'Let him see my back-up,' wheezed Fat Man.

Large Lump cracked a thumb and forefinger, and out of the car stepped the back-up, comprised of three more heavies.

'That's real trouble,' said Tommy.

'Tell this squirt we'll help ourselves to my bales of nylon,' said Fat Man.

'See here, squirt,' said Large Lump, 'like Mr Ford says, we're coming in. Shift yer pins or you'll get run over.'

Tommy turned his head. Michal and Jacob were still at the entrance, and behind them were Gertie and a crowd of machinists. Mr Greenberg's stepsons looked sturdy enough, and Gertie and her girls formed a barrier, but Tommy knew he didn't want mayhem and bloodletting.

'You mean to commit daylight robbery?' he said to Fat Man. 'I ain't in favour, so oblige me by floating off to your balloon shed.'

'Dear, dear,' sighed Fat Man, and gave Large Lump a nod.

'Right, guv,' said Large Lump, and advanced with the three heavies. Michal looked at Jacob, Jacob looked at Michal.

'We should worry?' said Michal.

'No worry,' said Jacob, and they moved forward to meet Large Lump and his heavies. Tommy's eyes opened wide at the sudden vision of flying bodies and kicking feet. Gertie and her girls shrieked. Large Lump, bawling, was flat on his back from a kick in his stomach. A heavy was rolling about, hollering blue murder. Michal and Jacob were whirling, leaping and kicking. Down went another heavy, gasping, and down went the last one, his ribs painfully bruised.

Large Lump came up, still bawling. He rushed at Michal. Michal effected a swift, dancing sidestep, spun round, took off and delivered the sole of his right shoe to the small of Large Lump's back. Large Lump pitched forward, howling. He's cross, thought Tommy, and his heavies don't like it, either. I think I'm watching a performance. What is it, judo or something? Don't think I'll interfere.

The heavies, unable to get to grips with Mr Greenberg's fast-moving stepsons, were pitching, staggering, falling. To give them their due, they kept coming back for more, and so did Large Lump, to show how they earned their tax-free handouts from the Fat Man, who was looking on, his blubber quivering with outrage.

Mr Greenberg joined Gertie and her open-mouthed machinists.

'What's happening?' asked Gertie.

'Vell, Gertie my dear,' said Mr Greenberg, 'it's vhat some people call karate.'

'What's that?'

'Vell, you might say punishing,' smiled Mr Greenberg.

'Oh, me 'appy heart,' gasped Gertie joyfully, 'I never seen nothing I liked better.'

With flying kicks and fist-thumping body blows, Michal and Jacob finally laid the opposition low. Large Lump and the heavies lay groaning and twitching. Fat Man's red face was purple, and Gertie was sure the balloon was going to burst.

'Thanks, lads,' said Tommy.

'Pleasure, Mister Tommy,' said Michal.

'No blood, I notice,' said Tommy.

'You would like to see some?' offered Jacob.

'Not on your nelly,' said Tommy, 'I like things just as they are.'

Large Lump lurched to his feet, and his battered heavies came up one by one.

The Fat Man said from the back of his outraged tonsils, 'You useless fairies, now see what you've done, cost me my nylon. I hate the bloody lot of you, and you too, Tommy Adams.'

'Stay there,' called Tommy, and turned to Michal and Jacob. 'I've got a feeling he wants to meet you.'

'He's big, Mister Tommy,' said Michal.

'So?' said Jacob.

'Sure thing, let's go meet him,' said Michal.

The Fat Man waddled in frantic haste to the car. Large Lump, spitting iron filings, followed on with the heavies, one of whom climbed into the driving seat of the van. Large Lump and the other two joined Fat Man in the car.

Van and car, grinding through the open gates onto the road, disappeared in what Tommy later told Vi was a cloud of the Fat Man's steam.

'They're not staying for tea?' said Jacob.

'Pity,' said Michal.

'Where did you two learn to fight like that?' asked Tommy.

'In the Army, from an instructor in a Commando unit,' said Michal.

'What is it, judo?' asked Tommy.

'Karate,' said Jacob.

'Well, good on yer, lads, I like it,' said Tommy, and went back into the factory with Eli's stepsons, where Gertie and her girls received them like heroes, and the younger ones asked if they could feel their muscles.

'Would they like some more tea, Mister Tommy?' asked Gertie. 'With a slice of cake?'

'If I might speak for them, yes,' said Mr

Greenberg. 'A celebration, ain't it?'

Tommy phoned the Camberwell office after Mr Greenberg and his stepsons had left. He spoke to Sammy, giving him details of the incident. Sammy listened with a happy ear to Tommy's description of how Michal and Jacob had dealt with the opposition.

'I'm admiring of that kind of talent, Tommy.'

'I liked it meself,' said Tommy, 'but don't let's start laughing yet. Just in case.'

'Got you,' said Sammy. 'Just in case the Fat Man thinks of something different.'

'Right,' said Tommy, 'so talk to Boots.'

'Listen, I can handle problems,' said Sammy.

'Not like Boots can,' said Tommy. 'Talk to him.'

'Now listen–'

'Talk to Boots.'

Sammy put the phone down, sat back and rubbed his chin. Enter, a lush-looking lady with magnificent black hair, melting brown eyes and what some poetical wallahs would have called a form divine.

'Sammy?' said Mrs Rachel Goodman, a wartime widow and the mother-in-law of Lizzy and Ned's younger son Edward. She was also the company secretary. 'Deep in thought, are we?'

'It's like this, Rachel,' said Sammy, giving her a thoughtful glance and noting that, at forty-six, she was still a fine figure of a female woman. 'The Fat Man's bounced back again.'

'Yes, Sammy, I know,' said Rachel. 'You told me this morning what happened at Edmonton yesterday.'

'I'm talking about today,' said Sammy, and quoted from what Tommy had told him over the phone. Rachel laughed.

'Mr Greenberg's boys saw them off, and the Fat Man too?' she said. 'And they used what?'

'Tommy said feet and fists, and they called it katari,' said Sammy.

'I think you mean karate,' said Rachel.

'No difference,' said Sammy. A grin showed. 'Well, not to Fat Man's gorillas. Point is, is he going to try again?'

'Not if Michal and Jacob are close by,' said Rachel.

'I think I'll talk to Boots,' said Sammy.

'Yes, do that, Sammy.'

'Of course, I could handle it myself,' said Sammy.

'Still, it won't hurt to talk to Boots,' said

Rachel, 'especially as he knows about yesterday.'

'What we need is an answer for tomorrow,' said Sammy, and went to see Boots.

Boots listened, and his smile, that still seemed to be permanently lurking, came to broad life at hearing how Michal and Jacob Greenberg had performed, and how they'd acquired their punishing expertise.

'Did any of us know they were in a Commando unit, Sammy?'

'I didn't know meself,' said Sammy, 'but there you are, nobody ever tells me anything.'

Boots laughed.

'Watch out, Sammy,' he said, 'you're sounding like Chinese Lady.'

'Who's laughing about that?' asked Sammy. 'I'm not, I'm fond of our dear old ma and her sayings.'

'Join the club,' said Boots.

Sammy fidgeted, but there it was, you couldn't shake Boots, he took everything in his stride, good news, awkward news and serious news. The Fat Man could get spitefully serious, and he'd be boiling and steaming after watching Michal and Jacob wipe the floor with his heavies.

'Come on, Boots, what's the right answer?'

he asked.

'Talk to Eli,' said Boots. 'Find out if he can release Michal and Jacob. If so, take them on. It'll be the factory the Fat Man will go for.'

'Blind Amy,' said Sammy, 'he did that years ago to our original factory. He torched it.'

'It'll be a night job again,' said Boots, 'but my old Great War West Kents are past active service now. Providing Eli agrees, see if Michal and Jacob will stand factory guard at nights. If they will, pay handsomely.'

'Handsomely means adding considerable to overheads,' said Sammy.

'Worth every penny, Sammy. It'll see the Fat Man off for good if his torch-bearers get flattened again. Or you could, of course, alert the local police.'

'Nothing doing,' said Sammy. 'They'll ask questions, and you know I like to keep our business problems confidential.'

'Talk to Eli, then,' said Boots.

Which Sammy did over the phone, quoting Boots and his suggestions, and his old business acquaintance said, 'Vhy ain't Boots ever been our Prime Minister?'

'Not being fond of politics, he ducked it,' said Sammy.

'But vhat a pity, ain't it, Sammy?'

'Listen, Eli old cock, like I've mentioned before, Boots has been the family's Lord-I-Am ever since he started his grammar school education,' said Sammy. 'Do we want him to be God-I-Am, which he would be as Prime Minister? We'd all have to make appointments to see him. Me, Sammy Adams, making appointments to see me own brother? My importance as a business-man would hit the bottom of the Serpentine, and the kids would row boats over it. Besides, I had the same idea about Michal and Jacob in mind myself. At least, I think I did. Well, I'd have come round to it. Anyway, what about the specific proposition?'

'Consider it done, Sammy,' said Eli.

'Boots and me, and our families will be going to Cornwall for our fortnight's holiday on Saturday,' said Sammy, 'so I'll talk to him and you can confer with him, eh?'

'Of course, Sammy,' said Mr Greenberg, 'and I vill tell my sons to come and see you tomorrow morning, and I vill also tell them to do as Boots commands.'

'Here, hold on,' said Sammy, 'I do the commanding of staff.'

'Vell, so you do, Sammy, so you do,' said

Eli. 'I vill tell them that. But give Boots my regards, von't you?'

'I don't know how it happens,' said Sammy, 'but every so often I get a feeling I'm not Sammy Adams, I'm Billy Muggins, the office boy.'

'Not you, Sammy,' said Eli, chuckling as he rang off.

'Well, sod me,' said Sammy to the silent phone, 'he's laughing at me. All right, from now on me business cards will be in the name of Daft Dick.'

It was at this time that the Mayfair-style girl who had bought RAF shirts from Sammy's Walworth store arrived in Cornwall with her family. She was the daughter of a rich City stockbroker, a member of Lloyd's.

Chapter Eleven

With the twins in bed that evening, Polly and Boots were relaxing in their living room, waiting to switch on the television for BBC's nine o'clock news. BBC had pioneered this visual medium, the first of its kind in the world, but had suspended it all through the war. Pre-war, the images had lacked sharpness. The post-war reintroduction produced welcome clarity.

Boots had told Polly of the incident at the Belsize Park factory, and Polly now brought the subject up again.

'Boots, about this Ben Ford, the Fat Man,' she said. Her slim body was curled up in a deep and wide armchair of velvety maroon, her knees peeping below the hem of her navy blue skirt, slender legs sheathed in dark blue fully fashioned stockings. Nylons. Supplied by Sammy to many of his female relatives by way of a furtive geezer he happened to know. A spiv, of course.

'What about the gent?' asked Boots.

'I don't think you ever mentioned him before now,' said Polly.

'Before was a long time ago,' said Boots, 'back in the Twenties.'

'Well, you dear old thing,' said Polly, 'I like to know everything about your life.'

'The Fat Man came suddenly into my life as a pain in the neck,' said Boots, 'and disappeared just as suddenly. He gave Sammy some unwanted trouble.'

'What made him disappear?' asked Polly.

'Rough-house action on the part of some of my old Great War comrades,' said Boots.

'They beat him up American-style?' said Polly.

'They knocked the stuffing out of his bruisers a couple of times,' said Boots.

'And today, Mr Greenberg's stepsons did a similar job?' said Polly.

'Apparently,' said Boots.

'Isn't it time the Fat Man himself took a hiding?'

'Probably,' said Boots.

'You old darling,' said Polly. 'Whatever worries Sammy and Tommy might be suffering about what will happen next, you're not worrying at all.'

'Sammy and Tommy won't be worrying,' said Boots. 'Tommy can take a knock or two without running for cover, and Sammy can take several knocks as long as they don't add ruinously to the overheads. Incidentally, do you know your legs are still as good-looking as they were in your days as a flapper?'

'Yes, I do know,' said Polly, 'but it's more important to me that you know too. Is Sammy now going to be able to let Susie and me have nylon stockings on demand instead of a pair here and there from his spiv sources? You'd say my legs deserve to know there's a regular supply available, wouldn't you?'

'I'd say so,' said Boots.

142

'Well, then?'

'Sammy will meet the requirements of all the family's female legs, and at a discount,' smiled Boots.

'Oh, jolly good show,' said Polly. 'Sammy does have his priorities in the right order. And I accept your exciting compliments about my legs.'

'Is a compliment exciting?' asked Boots.

'From you, it's uplifting,' said Polly.

'You're very welcome,' said Boots.

'Oh, those gorgeous flapper dresses,' sighed Polly. 'Silk stockings and sexy garters, sometimes with little bells on them so that we chimed when dancing the Charleston. Mad days. And sad days too, because of out-of-work old soldiers. And lovely days too, because of meeting you.'

'Stop the conversation and switch the news on,' said Boots.

Polly smiled.

'Love you, dear old thing, you do know that, don't you?' she said.

'You can accept it's mutual,' said Boots, getting up and switching the television set on himself.

'What an old-fashioned pair we are,' said Polly.

The image of the newscaster appeared at

that point, and they settled down to absorb the news, much of which was devoted to the Labour government's continuing efforts to boost the economy, which Boots, along with Mr Finch, suspected would amount to very little, mainly because of its high taxation policies. Government spending was never as stimulating as consumer spending. Its main effect was to increase the Civil Service empires.

Later, when they were about to retire, Polly said she'd been thinking that it was time Boots and his brothers, and some of the family's young people, stopped calling his mother Chinese Lady. It was disgraceful, and not on.

'Polly old girl,' said Boots, 'in her struggling days she made regular use of Walworth's Chinese laundry, and came to respect the proprietor, Mr Wong Fu, and all his Chinese helpers. So we began to call her Chinese Lady. She thought it a great compliment, and still does.'

'That story's got white whiskers on it,' said Polly. 'It won't do, and I'm not sure I've ever believed it.'

'Well, we're all stuck with it now,' said Boots.

'I'm going to work on you and all the

others until you're unstuck,' said Polly. 'Chinese Lady my eye, it's a fantasy.'

'Is this something to do with her future elevation to Lady Finch?' asked Boots.

'Shame on you for even thinking I'd ever be influenced by something like that,' said Polly.

'My mistake,' said Boots, but his smile crept into his eyes, and Polly wondered, not for the first time, how it managed to reach his almost blind left one.

'By the way,' she said, 'how do you know the Fat Man will attack the factory and not the Camberwell offices?'

'I don't know,' said Boots.

'Well, you're probably right that it'll be the factory,' said Polly, 'especially as the nylon bales are stored there. I suppose he'll either try to purloin them or ruin them. Now, let's go up, shall we, and you can have a thrilling inspection of my fully fashioneds.' That was what nylon stockings were called.

Boots laughed.

'Polly, you're always an entertainment,' he said.

'Delighted you think so,' said Polly, and they turned out the lights and went up.

Boots had another dream that night, not of

Belsen, but of Elsie Chivers and Emily, both gone and both of whom he had loved. They were out shopping together, and he, desperate to make contact, was trying to catch them up. They turned, saw him, laughed and ran. He chased after them, but while they were quick and agile, he was leaden-legged. Further, people got in his way. As in slow motion, he cannoned into a bulky figure. The Fat Man. He rebounded from the collision and slowly fell backwards. The Fat Man laughed at him. Emily and Elsie appeared, smiling and beckoning as he sank into a roaring black pit and woke up.

Now what the devil, he thought, is the meaning of a dream like that?

He might have searched for a reason at least, but he was asleep again in less than two minutes, relieved of the dream.

Wednesday morning.

Miss Lulu Saunders was typing out suggestions and notes made by Paul for next month's propaganda leaflet.

'Listen,' she said.

Paul was reading the morning's mail, mostly letters of enquiry from potential

146

recruits or of abuse from non-Labour voters. He looked up. There she was, with her curtains of black hair and her earnest spectacles. At least, they seemed earnest. And she was wearing a grey blouse and a long dark grey skirt. Pity she didn't know attractive clothes had been invented. Or perhaps she wore what she did wear to discourage any advances. And perhaps she did so in order to concentrate single-mindedly on a political career. But it hadn't discouraged the oversexed bloke from trying to defrock her.

'Can I help?' he asked.

'Your handwriting's lousy, d'you know that?' she said.

'I admit I scrawl down my thoughts and suggestions.'

'Scrawl's too flattering. It looks like a spider's left its eight-feet tracks. Didn't you attend school?'

'Grammar school,' said Paul.

'Well, it looks as if you didn't pay attention,' said Lulu. 'Ought to go back and ask for a handwriting refresher. You're smiling.' That was an accusation. 'Nothing to smile about, you know.'

'I'm smiling at your sauce,' said Paul.

'It's honest frankness,' said Lulu. 'Look, come here and tell me what this word is.'

'Bring it over,' said Paul.

'Don't get me ratty,' said Lulu. Paul humoured her. He crossed to her desk, and stood beside her chair while she pointed to some scribble. 'What's that word, for God's sake?' she demanded.

Paul leaned and took a look, noting with automatic male interest that however drab her blouse was, it at least obviously housed the kind of development that the butler liked to see through Lady Lovelace's bed-room keyhole.

Concentrating on that which Lulu's finger was touching, he translated his scrawl.

'Practical measures,' he said.

'That's two words. That's joined-up writing gone pathetic. Still can't decipher it. Looks like paralisationers.'

'Bunkum,' said Paul.

'Bunkum? All that long scrawl is supposed to be bunkum? You just said–'

'No, what you said is bunkum. There's no such word as paralisationers.'

'I know that,' said Lulu. 'But it's what it looks like.'

'I repeat, it's practical measures.'

'Oh, jolly good and hooray,' said Lulu, and flipped a curtain of hair away from her glasses.

'Tie it behind your neck with a ribbon,' said Paul, going back to his desk.

'What?' said Lulu.

'Your hair. Use a ribbon.'

'Mother O'Grady,' said Lulu, 'which age are you living in? Hair ribbons went out with Hitler.'

'Arm in arm?' said Paul.

'What?'

'Arm in arm with Hitler into the fiery sunset of Berlin?'

'God, you're rubbish,' said Lulu. 'Listen, I make out here that you say practical measures should be taken to rebuild the Tower of London. Crazy.'

'The East End of London,' said Paul.

'Anyone who makes East End read like tower is an illiterate,' said Lulu. 'Anyway, rebuilding's already taking place in the East End.'

'I side with the few Labour MPs who don't like what's going up, enormous blocks of flats.'

'If you favour practical measures,' said Lulu, 'then blocks of flats are very practical. Don't need acres of ground space.'

'Wait till the people of the East End find themselves living twelve floors up,' said Paul. 'They won't like it, they won't have a street door and a decent doorstep.'

'What do you know about street doors and decent doorsteps?' asked Lulu.

'My paternal grandma could tell you,' said Paul. 'She lived for years in a terraced house not all that far from here. To her, a doorstep is a place where you enjoy gossiping with neighbours.'

'Sounds a nice old lady,' said Lulu. 'How'd she come to have a grandson with rubbishy handwriting?'

'How would you like your bottom smacked?' said Paul.

'That's it. Give me hysterics. What are you, a born-again Victorian reactionary?'

'You're supposed to be typing my notes,' said Paul. 'Get on with it, then prepare to type letters.'

'From your handwriting?'

'It'll be clearer.'

'Better be, I tell you,' said Lulu.

'You can make the morning coffee in five minutes,' said Paul.

'Oh, I'll iron your shirts as well, won't I?' said Lulu.

Paul grinned. What a character. He thought of Aunt Lizzie, Aunt Vi, Aunt Polly, of cousins Emma, Annabelle, Rosie, Bess and Patsy, the American one by marriage.

Lulu Saunders wasn't a bit like any of them. What was she like? Well, as his Uncle Sammy would have said, she wasn't a female woman. Uncle Sammy meant feminine, of course. Lulu was a Lulu all right.

But she made the coffee, although she did insist they took turns at the chore.

'As the boss, I'm not sure I should say yes,' said Paul.

'The boss?' Lulu gave him a pitying look. 'You're out of your tiny mind. We take turns. Right?'

'I've got a problem,' said Paul.

'What problem?'

'You,' said Paul.

'Ha ha,' said Lulu.

In sunny Cornwall the City stockbroker's daughter, clad in brief white shorts and an RAF shirt, was crossing from the little sailing resort of Rock to Padstow by the ferry. With her were several friends.

'That shirt, where'd you get it?' asked one of the girls.

'Where?' The shirt was tied by its tails, and had its top buttons undone, revealing some very nice cleavage. 'In a shop.'

'Which shop? I'd like that swanky kind of shirt myself.'

'Sorry, Fiona, not telling. The shop's exclusive to me, and so are the shirts.'

'Spoilsport.'

'That's life. Eureka, here we go.' The ferry was docking by the harbour wall of Padstow, the young people on their feet.

The quaint fishing port of Padstow received the sightseers with balmy indulgence.

Chapter Twelve

Thursday.

Large Lump, having been informed by the Fat Man that something still had to be done to Sammy Adams, made a suggestion out of the top of his head.

'We could do a clever job on his new Walworth store.'

'Clever?' wheezed the Fat Man, obese bulk squashed into the necessarily strong ramifications of his padded office chair. 'Clever?'

'Yus, guv, clever being doing it quick, like,' said Large Lump, practically standing to attention on account of the Fat Man's evil dislike of sloppiness. 'The four of us could smash up every window in the place and pee all over the stock in no more'n five minutes.'

'Eh?'

'Having had a few pints first in the local boozer,' said Large Lump.

'Shut up,' growled Fat Man.

'Right, guv.'

'Clever my bleedin' elbow,' said Fat Man. 'There's flatfeet on the beat all over Walworth, like shiploads of sailors searching night and day for who swiped their rum. You think they're going to look on and sing, "Clap hands, there's old Charlie", do you? They'll cop you as soon as you throw the first brick. So listen.'

'All ears, guv.'

'I can bloody well see that, can't I?' said Fat Man. 'Get 'em trimmed. Now, I know the Adams family. Thick as Ali Baba's forty thieves.'

'Who's he, guv?'

'One of Sammy Adams's ancestors.'

'That a fact, guv?'

'Shut up and listen,' said Fat Man, whose every word was squeezed out on account of his neck blubber. 'The Adams family. The men are all ponces, the females all do what they're told, and they all love each other.'

'Strike a ruddy light, ain't that incestry, guv?' said Large Lump.

'Only at bedtime,' said Fat Man.

'I tell yer, I'm having a bad time believing that,' said Large Lump.

'I'm having a bleedin' worse time knowing you do, you brainless tadpole,' said Fat Man. 'Now, what I also know comes from Poky Prodnose who did some work for me yesterday.' Poky Prodnose was a shifty private investigator. 'Sammy Adams has got a married niece, name of Rosie Chapman. She's a favourite of his. I knew that. I've now been informed by Poky that she and her husband, and another niece of Sammy Adams, run a very profitable chicken and egg farm. I want it smashed up, torn to pieces and every chicken turned into a bit of ruined poultry. And you can scramble any eggs you find. Get the idea?'

'Yus, guv, smash it all up, chop the chickens and jump on the eggs.'

'The idea, you berk, is to hurt Mister Bleedin' Sammy Adams through his poncy family,' said Fat Man. 'When that job's done, I'll get Poky to find out which of his other relatives Sammy Adams cries over at Christmas.'

'Well, guv, all right, if that's what you want,' said Large Lump, 'but might I be so bold as to mention it ain't going to hurt his business?'

'It's going to hurt him and his bleedin' lovey-dovey family,' said Fat Man. 'After which, I'll think about his business. Now then, about this chicken farm and how to get there. Listen again.'

'I'm still all ears, guv.'

'Well, don't wag 'em, or you'll take off,' said Fat Man.

'Boots old love,' said Polly that night, 'with you and Sammy away in Cornwall for two weeks, are you sure Tommy can manage if trouble arrives?'

'Trouble from the Fat Man, you mean?' said Boots.

'Yes, I do mean him,' said Polly. 'From all you've told me he's a dyed-in-the-wool crook.'

'He'll make it a night job for certain,' said Boots, 'and Tommy, I hope, will be safely asleep at home. It's Eli Greenberg's stepsons who'll do the managing. They're already on night duty at the Belsize Park factory.'

'You're confident they can cope with a spot of midnight villainy?' said Polly.

'I'm confident that Eli Greenberg knows precisely what Michal and Jacob can cope with,' said Boots.

'Did you say that with your fingers crossed?' asked Polly with a smile.

'Did I?' said Boots.

'Did you?'

'Yup,' said Boots.

'You old darling,' said Polly.

'What brought that on?' asked Boots.

'Your ability to look a possible crisis in the eye without biting your lip, scratching your ear or losing your head,' said Polly.

'What's on the surface can be deceptive,' said Boots.

'Your surface is true,' said Polly. For the umpteenth time she thought how relaxed he always was, and so content with life, dispensing goodwill to all and sundry, awkward or stupid people included. She knew it was his survival from the war of the trenches that had made him treasure life and framed his attitude of tolerance and understanding, although there were, of course, the certain moments when his hidden steel showed. That could excite her, the surfacing of the Viking.

'Look here, old sport, are you certain the Fat Man won't blow up the shop and offices, and not the factory?'

'No, I'm not certain,' said Boots, 'so I've made arrangements.'

'Well, tell,' said Polly.

'You know Mitch, our van driver, one of my corporals during the war against the Kaiser, and a sergeant in the Home Guard during the war against the Nazi lunatic,' said Boots. 'He and an old West Kent comrade are also on night duty. In the Camberwell shop.'

'But he must be well over fifty,' said Polly, 'and so must his old comrade.'

'No problem,' said Boots. 'The moment any villains arrive, they'll fix bayonets and charge.'

Polly had hysterics.

'Oh, my God,' she said, 'are you real?'

'Alive and well, Polly.'

'Fix bayonets and charge?'

'In a manner of speaking.'

'Your manner of speaking is sending me dotty.'

'Fascinating,' said Boots.

'Fascinating?'

'Yes, dotty Polly,' said Boots.

'Dear man, come to bed,' said Polly.

'Now?' said Boots. 'It's not ten yet.'

'Can't help that,' said Polly, 'I'm sexy.'

'You're what?'

'Sexy,' said Polly. 'Isn't it bitter that so many people think you shouldn't have sex when you're over fifty?'

'It's even more bitter when so many people think you can't,' said Boots.

Polly had another bout of enjoyable hysterics.

'I can't cap that,' she said.

'Did I say something?' asked Boots.

'Everything,' said Polly, rising from her armchair. She took a few sinuous steps, bent her head and kissed him. 'Boots old soldier, you're dear to me,' she said.

'Since it's mutual,' said Boots, 'let's go up to bed, then.'

'Yes, let's show 'em,' said Polly.

'No, let's keep it to ourselves,' said Boots. 'That kind of thing is strictly private. The day it becomes public will be the day when it'll be on a par with shopping.'

In the living room of a house in Kestrel Avenue, Mrs Patsy Adams, formerly Patsy Kirk of Boston, USA, was thumping husband Daniel with a cushion. Daniel, seated in an armchair, was taking the blows like a man. He was, in fact, shouting with laughter.

'Take that!' said Patsy. Thump. 'And that!'

Wallop. Then she chucked the cushion at him. Daniel caught it and cuddled it.

'Nice when it leaves off,' he said.

'Daniel Adams, I hate you,' said Patsy, dark hair ruffled, hazel eyes full of sparks. She was twenty-two, a few months younger than Daniel, and a credit to the land of her birth in her looks and her outgoing nature. 'You were letting Betty flirt with you. Worse, you were ogling her.'

'Patsy, I honestly beg to differ,' said Daniel. They had been entertaining friends, a young married couple like themselves, and the visitors had only just left. 'I mean, ogling?'

'Ogling for sure, when she was sitting on the arm of your chair and showing her skinny legs,' said Patsy.

'Believe me, Patsy,' said Daniel, 'I reserve my ogling just for you. I can say with a fair amount of sincerity that I didn't notice whether Betty's legs were skinny or fat, or even if she had one leg or two. What I did notice was her scent, something like minty garden peas.'

'You're not fooling me,' said Patsy.

'Come here,' said Daniel, and he dropped the cushion, leaned forward, grabbed her and sat her on his lap. Patsy let it happen. 'Now listen, Patsy, you're definitely what the doctor ordered for me.'

'Well, I sure am glad I was specifically prescribed and not pulled out of a hat,' said Patsy. 'Daniel, d'you like being married?'

'I like being married to you,' said Daniel. 'I don't think I'd like being married to Betty. She gushes.'

'I'll say,' said Patsy, 'and all over you.'

'Well, if she's got a problem, I can't help,' said Daniel. 'You're my one and only, now and until I'm ninety.'

'What happens when you're ninety?' asked Patsy.

'I think that's when I'll need my own kind of help, to get myself pointed at you,' said Daniel. Patsy laughed then. So he kissed her, and her forgiving lips clung. Daniel was her fun guy, her very own fun guy, and she definitely objected to covetous outsiders. Come to that, Daniel could object very vigorously to any guy giving her the eye, which in a way was kind of thrilling. 'Well, now,' he said, 'I hope Dad's business worries will be solved by the time he gets back from his holiday.'

'That fat crook you told me about sounds like a hood,' said Patsy. 'Can't someone blow his head off?'

'It'll take a cannon shell to do that,' said Daniel, 'and there's not a lot of them about in this country.'

'Well, find one, buy it and use it,' said Patsy.

'That's all right in the Wild West,' said Daniel, 'but not here. I'd get executed at dawn.'

'Oh, gee whiz,' said Patsy, 'please don't get executed at dawn, or at sundown, Daniel.'

'Dad and Uncle Boots are leaving it all to Michal and Jacob Greenberg,' said Daniel. 'Hello, do I hear a real cry for help?'

'It's Arabella,' said Patsy, 'she's awake.'

Arabella was their infant daughter.

'I'll go up,' said Daniel.

'We'll both go,' said Patsy, 'she likes seeing both of us.'

'Right, start legging it to the apples and pears,' said Daniel, which Patsy knew was the cockney term for stairs.

Chapter Thirteen

Up in the Lake District, Sammy and Susie's eldest daughter, twenty-year-old Bess, was on a little copse-covered island in the middle of Lake Windermere. She had rowed herself there in a hired boat, while her friends and other visitors toured the expansive, shimmering lake in a large tourist motor-driven vessel. Some of her undergraduate friends had become noisy and irritating, and she felt like being by herself for a couple of hours. She had a lunch picnic of fresh rolls, cheese and ripe tomatoes with her, plus a flask of hot coffee.

She wandered in and out of the leafy copse, emerging to find a man sitting near the lapping waters, absorbed in the shining ripples. He turned his head as he heard her.

'Hi there,' he said, 'are you alone?'

'Oh, sorry if I disturbed you,' said Bess, fair-haired like Paula and her mum, and distinctly appealing. Once she had been noticeably plump, and Sammy had called her his little Plum Pudding. Blessedly, however, growing up had effected the demise of hitherto obstinate puppy fat. Now she had no quarrels with her figure.

'No, you're not disturbing me,' said the man, black hair glinting in the sunshine, strong-boned face brown, dark green sweater and well-worn oatmeal corduroys close-fitting. 'Unless you've brought a dozen friends with you.'

I think he's American, said Bess to herself.

At least, he sounds like one.

'Oh, I'm by myself,' she said, 'I was going to have a picnic here.'

'Search me for a surprise,' he said, 'I'm just about to have mine of Lancashire meat pie and cheese. You're welcome to join me. Where I'm sitting isn't exactly London's Hyde Park, but there's still room for one more.'

Bess hesitated. Compared to Paula and most of her cousins, she was a little reserved. But the day was fine, the lake lovely, the small copse quiet, and the man himself very natural in his friendliness.

'Oh, thanks,' she said, and sat down next to him. Her picnic was in a carrier bag.

'Jeremy Passmore,' he said with a smile, and put out his hand.

Bess took it and they shook hands.

'Bess Adams,' she said.

'Happy to meet you, Bess Adams,' he said.

'I think you're American,' said Bess as the waters lapped by.

'Sure,' he said. 'From Chicago. Enlisted in 1942, when I was twenty and thought I knew all I needed to. Had my baptism of fire in North Africa alongside Monty's Eighth Army, which sobered me down a little. No, more than a little. I was given a liaison posting later, as a lieutenant, with Monty's Second Army Group a few weeks prior to D-Day. Slightly wounded during that hell of a battle for Caen, badly wounded early in '45, hospitalized in England and stayed there when the war was over.'

'Stayed in hospital?' said Bess.

'No, in this little old island. I'll be going back to Chicago one day soon, I guess. That's my life story, which you probably noted didn't start for real until '42. Now tell me yours, or I'll hog our time together.'

'But what made you stay here?' asked Bess, hair travelling around her head in the breeze.

'Ancestry,' said Jeremy. 'My great-grand-parents emigrated from a small town name of Tenterden in your county of Kent. Would you know that, Bess?'

'I know of it,' said Bess, 'but I've never been there.'

'Try it one day, it's charming,' said Jeremy. 'I wonder sometimes, I sure do, why my ancestors ever left it for Chicago.'

'Most emigrants left because of the economic doldrums, didn't they?' said Bess.

'Economic doldrums?' Jeremy eyed her like a man tickled. 'I like that. Well, a few months after the war ended, I tracked my ancestors down and found I had aunts, uncles and cousins. I've been hitting it off with Aunt Amy and Uncle Dan for over a couple of years. They insisted.'

'You mean you live with them?'

'Bess, it's home from home, but I can't stay under their feet for ever, and as I said, I'll be sailing for the States soon.'

'Don't you have a job?' asked Bess.

'You're asking?' said Jeremy. 'So I'm telling. I've a work permit and have been earning my English dough as manager of a farm.'

'I think that's wonderful,' said Bess.

'Wonderful?' Jeremy looked tickled again. 'I think you're being English.'

'In what way?' asked Bess.

'The polite way.'

'No, really,' said Bess. The breeze plucked at the skirt of her dress and lifted it. Hastily, she adjusted it. Jeremy noted her slight blush.

'Your turn, Bess,' he said. 'Or shall we start taking in some calories first?'

'Well, I do feel a bit peckish,' said Bess, and they brought their food into being and began to eat.

'Now start talking,' said Jeremy.

So Bess, put at ease by his camaraderie,

told him about her family, particularly about how her dad became a self-made businessman.

'Yes, and would you believe, he started with capital banked in his old socks.'

'Banked where?' said Jeremy.

'Well,' said Bess, 'from the time when he was about seven he saved every coin he could and kept them in his old socks in a box under his bed. When he finally came to disgorge it, he had twenty full socks and what my Aunt Lizzy said was a small fortune.'

'A saving guy with an eye to his future?' said Jeremy.

'Oh, I think he had his eye to his future when he put his first farthings into a sock,' said Bess, and went on to detail some of Sammy's achievements. 'He and his brothers were all adventurous, they're all in the business, and might have taken off for dizzy heights if my grandma, Chinese Lady, hadn't kept them in order.' Bess laughed softly. 'And she still does, and everyone else in the family as well.'

'Chinese Lady?' said Jeremy. 'Come again?'

So Bess had to explain how her paternal grandmother came to be called Chinese

Lady. Jeremy laughed until he shook.

'Mind, that's only what I've been told by my dad and uncles,' said Bess.

'It's still a hoot,' said Jeremy, which made Bess think of brother Daniel's wife, Patsy. Patsy used that expression.

Encouraged, she talked some more for quite a while, and Jeremy listened, liking the sound of her English voice with its little musical lilts. Eventually, she thought of Patsy again.

'Oh, would you like to know I've an American sister-in-law?' she said.

'That's a fact?' said Jeremy, who had finished his Lancashire meat pie, and was making healthy inroads into a large wedge of cheese and some crusty bread.

'Yes, it's a fact,' said Bess. 'She comes from Boston and is married to my elder brother. She's really very nice.'

'Well, I sure wouldn't go for her giving the rest of us a bad name,' said Jeremy. 'So if she's pretty nice, send her my regards. Now carry on.'

'I'll probably get boring,' said Bess.

'I'll take a bet you won't,' said Jeremy.

So Bess told him about Bristol University, where she was reading French, maths and English Literature because she wanted to be a schoolteacher.

'Wow,' said Jeremy.

'Wow what?' asked Bess.

'Schoolteachers get headaches and take pills,' said Jeremy.

'That's ridiculous,' said Bess.

'My college fraternity took pills for breakfast and lunch.'

'Probably because the students were devilish,' said Bess.

'As a teacher, what would you do with your devilish students?' asked Jeremy.

'Point them to their natural home,' said Bess.

'Natural home?'

'Hell,' said Bess, all diffidence having slipped away.

Jeremy shouted with laughter.

'Bess, I sure am pleased to have met you,' he said.

'Thanks,' said Bess. Noting he had no flask, she asked if he'd like some coffee.

'I was thinking of calling at the hotel and ordering a beer at the bar,' he said.

'How are you going to get there?' she asked.

'Hail someone in a boat,' said Jeremy, 'it's how I landed here.'

'Well, you can share my coffee first, if you

like, and then I'll row you back in my hired boat.'

'You'll do that?'

'I'm game,' said Bess, 'and I have to join up with my friends in an hour, anyway.'

'We'll take an oar each,' said Jeremy.

Which they did some time later, seated side by side, Bess a surprised young lady at how comfortable she felt in company with this easy-going American. She thought that was probably how women felt in company with Uncle Boots, the most easy-going man she knew. Grandma Finch had once said her only oldest son would have been a danger to even the most respectable women if he hadn't been a properly brought-up family man who, being married, didn't go in for anything unlegal. Bess felt that many of the male undergraduates she knew were too noisy and callow to be a danger to any discriminating woman. Some of them had begun to get on her nerves soon after her arrival in the Lake District with a group of both sexes. Her closest friend in Bristol certainly wasn't a male undergraduate. It was Alice, Uncle Tommy and Aunt Vi's daughter, who worked for the bursar.

Out on the sparkling surface of the lake that had been born amid surrounding green hills, the boat zigzagged a bit. Jeremy suggested they weren't pulling together.

'Well, just look here,' said Bess, 'I'm pulling my share.'

'I'll call the tempo, shall I?' said Jeremy. 'Right, one – two, one – two–'

Bess caught a crab and fell backwards. Up went her legs, and her dress played about again. She shrieked. With laughter. And as Jeremy brought her upright again, she was still laughing, with not the faintest hint of a blush. She grabbed at the loose oar.

'Don't let me do that again,' she said.

'Fair and sweet young lady,' said Jeremy, 'the last thing I want is to have you fall overboard.'

Bess did blush then, just a little. Fair and sweet? Oh, help.

They rowed to the jetty, delivered the little craft to the boatman, and walked to the hotel, where Jeremy asked if she'd like to join him at the bar.

'Oh, thanks,' she said, 'but I really don't drink very much, and I'd better wait for my friends. They'll be back soon.'

'Let's sit,' said Jeremy, 'and I'll wait with you.' They sat together on a bench looking out over the long, shining lake. Other holidaymakers ambled contentedly around.

'What will you be doing after you've left the Lakes?' asked Jeremy.

'Oh, I'll be going home mid-August to spend the rest of my vacation with my family before I return to Bristol,' said Bess. In the distance she saw the motorized tourist vessel approaching. Oh, blow, she thought, that's a bit too soon.

'Well, tell me if I'm being pushy,' said Jeremy, 'but may I call on you at your home?'

'Pardon?'

'No go?' said Jeremy. 'You've got a feller?'

'Oh, no,' said Bess.

'Well, then?'

'I'll give you my address,' said Bess.

'I'm touched,' said Jeremy, 'since that's going to mean you'll be giving me a yes as well.'

Bess ripped a page from the back of her pocket diary, pulled out its pencil and wrote down her address. And, after a brief second, her phone number.

'There,' she said, handing the little page to Jeremy. Lord, she thought, what's the family going to think, Daniel with an American wife and me suddenly with an American friend, a feller from Chicago? Not wanting her noisy group to gallop up and spoil the moment for her, she said, 'D'you mind if I go and meet my friends at the jetty? If I don't, they'll come up and smother us.'

'Whatever you want, Bess,' said Jeremy. 'Just let me say I've known a few English girls–'

'I'm sure you have, since you've been in England since the end of the war,' said Bess.

'Right,' said Jeremy, 'and I'm now telling you I've played around with one or two.'

'I know about GIs and English girls,' said Bess, and thought again of Uncle Boots, and his brief time with a French farmer's daughter just before the first Battle of the Somme, which had resulted in the birth of Eloise. When she'd talked about it with her mum, her mum had said no-one with any understanding was going to say hard things about what the men of the trenches did with French girls, and that people ought to thank the French girls for giving the Tommies a bit of pleasure before they died. But Uncle Boots didn't die, said Bess. For which let's all say a happy Amen, said her mum.

'In '44, some months before our GIs and Brits sailed on that seasick trip to the Normandy beaches, I took a real shine to a redhead,' said Jeremy.

'I do understand,' said Bess, eyes on the

docking tourist boat.

'Serious shine,' said Jeremy, 'but by the time I came out of hospital late in '45, she'd skipped off to California as a GI bride of some other guy, taking a diamond engagement ring with her. The ring I'd slipped on her finger. I thought hard about that piece of chicanery and decided I was luckier than the other guy.'

'You were,' said Bess. 'What a hateful and shallow person she must have been.'

'Infatuation takes all common sense out of a man and makes a fool of him,' said Jeremy. 'It won't happen again. Bess, thanks for our time together today, and for the rowboat ride. I'll be in touch.'

'That's a promise?' said Bess, little flutters, hitherto unknown, happily attacking her.

'It's a promise,' said Jeremy. 'Now go and meet your friends. Goodbye, Bess. For a while.'

He touched her hand, that was all. Then he walked into the hotel, and Bess walked to meet her noisy, exuberant friends. For once their boisterousness didn't irritate her. Something very nice had happened, something that put brightness into her eyes and her smile.

Mrs Kloytski, returning from shopping in the market, saw one of her very appealing neighbours, Mrs Cassie Brown. Cassie was putting a shine on her iron doorknocker.

'Ah, you are the good housewife, Cassie,' said Mrs Kloytski.

'I'm not out here because of that,' said Cassie, 'I'm out here because it's bedlam inside. Listen to my terrors.'

From the interior of the house came yells, bangs, clangs and thumps.

'Heavens, what is happening?' asked Mrs Kloytski.

'Muffin and Lewis are playing at being a brass band,' said Cassie. 'Muffin's using Lewis's toy drum, and Lewis is using our dustbin lid and the kitchen poker. If you'd like to go in and watch them, you're welcome.'

'Oh, I think not,' said Mrs Kloytski.

Pity, thought Cassie, if she went in the noise alone could injure her. Cassie had begun to actively dislike the lady. She didn't trust her smile or her bold blue eyes, or the way she kind of sidled up on Freddy. Cassie treated herself to happy thoughts of waylaying the buxom Polack in the dark and spoiling her looks with the dustbin lid.

Clang went the makeshift cymbal. Bong

went the drum.

'School holidays, I don't know,' said Cassie.

'It is a youth organization they need,' said Mrs Kloytski, 'with good strong men in charge. Like sergeant majors, yes?'

'Not for my cherubs, thank you,' said Cassie.

'Ah, well, goodbye for today,' said Mrs Kloytski and walked on to her house where, once inside, Mr Kloytski put an immediate question to her.

'Any danger signals?'

'None,' said Mrs Kloytski. 'The woman at the stall–'

'The peasant?'

'Yes. No-one has asked her about me. I told her that if anyone did make enquiries, it would probably be someone who knew me and my family in Poland during the war and is trying to trace me. She said she'd be glad to let me know, and called me "ducks".'

Kloytski, thoughtful, said, 'It occurs to me that if the man you saw last Saturday did have suspicions about you, he'd have made enquiries before now. Therefore, he either had no suspicions or he could not place you in his memory.'

'Perhaps because he could not see me in

the atmosphere of a London market as he saw me at that first meeting,' said Mrs Kloytski.

'A very different set of circumstances,' said Kloytski. 'All the same, we'll take no chances. Open the door to no-one without first taking a look through the spyhole.' He had fitted that several days ago. 'If he should call, don't let him in.'

'I'm not a fool,' said Mrs Kloytski.

'After he's gone, go and see the peasant woman again,' said Kloytski. 'Tell her you are now sure you once knew the man and would like to call on him. Ask for his address.'

'She may not know his address.'

'Ask her,' said Kloytski.

Chapter Fourteen

Friday. Going-home time.

'Well, Saunders, I hope you can manage while I'm away,' said Paul. He was going to do a week's walking tour of the Yorkshire Dales with a Young Socialist friend.

'I'm confident you won't be missed,' said Lulu, wearing a long loose ankle-length brown dress, which Paul thought Noah's wife might have worn on the Ark, and which Noah, when the Flood receded, told her to put in a jumble sale.

'Watch out that you don't fall over your confidence and break a leg,' he said.

'I suppose you know women have to be twice as good as men if they want to be recognized,' said Lulu, cramming a black knitted pull-on hat over her twin curtains.

'Recognized as what?'

'Bloody marvels,' said Lulu.

'Tuppence in the box,' said Paul.

'What box?'

'The swear box. It's new and I've just put it on the window ledge. It's to discourage unwelcome language when visitors are present. Also, I'm against women speaking like that.'

'Why should it be exclusive to men?' demanded Lulu.

'Men are more uncivilized,' said Paul.

'And women are sweet, soppy and goody-goody?' said Lulu. 'Listen, Adams. There's been an earth-shaking war. It's changed things. Kicked conventions to bits. Made women look for independence.'

'Don't forget to answer every letter that arrives,' said Paul, 'and don't forget to sign them on behalf of Paul Adams, Secretary.'

'Do what?'

'It's an order,' said Paul.

'You're too young to give orders,' said Lulu. 'Wait till you're old and hairy.'

'Get your hair cut and styled,' said Paul. 'Make this office look a bit pretty. So long now.'

She followed him out.

'Grow a moustache,' she said as they parted company on the pavement. Paul went off grinning, she went off like Boadicea looking for her fiery chariot.

'They're back,' said Matthew over supper that evening.

'I know,' said Rosie, 'I heard the vixen caterwauling in the night.'

'I heard her too,' said seven-year-old Giles, a slim boy with an unruly mass of dark hair.

'Oh, was it the foxes?' asked Emily, only a week short of six. She was as golden-haired as her mother, with a quick smile already cheeky. She had been named after Rosie's late adoptive mother, Boots's first wife.

'It was, little chick,' said Matthew, 'but

178

they did no damage, apart from trying to dig their way under the chickens' wire fence. I suspect they'll have another go tonight.'

'Still, I like foxes, don't we, Daddy?' said Emily.

'You can't say I, then we,' said Giles.

'Mummy, I'm not,' protested Emily.

'I didn't mean wee,' said Giles. 'Soppy date.'

'Let's have some improved conversation, shall we?' said Rosie.

'Kids grow up with saucy ways, and give their parents worrying days,' said Matthew.

'Crikey, you made a rhyme, Dad,' said Giles.

'Just another piece of ancient Dorset doggerel,' said Rosie, 'but we'd feel deprived without it.'

'We'll be watching for the beasts tonight,' said Matthew.

'You and Jonathan?' said Rosie. Jonathan and Emma were enjoying their own supper in the annexe.

'Oh, can I watch with you, Dad?' begged Giles.

'Will you be awake, my lad?' asked Matthew.

'Yes, course I will,' said Giles.

'We'll see,' said Matthew.

Dusk was descending over the gentle hills of Surrey, and there was no sign of the foxes. Matthew and Jonathan were close to the wired-in henhouses. Giles was absent, having failed to stay awake, of course.

'I wonder,' whispered Jonathan, 'do those four-legged chicken-slayers know we're here?'

'I'm thinking about laying traps if we don't bag 'em soon,' murmured Matthew.

'That won't please everyone in the village, Matt.'

'Nor the four-legged enemy.'

Night followed dusk, but they stayed where they were. They were both handy-men, and Matthew's war years with REME had made him the complete electrician. With Jonathan's help he had fixed a floodlight to illuminate the wire-guarded henhouses and beyond. Close to his recumbent body was a remote control, and on this occasion he and Jonathan both had shotguns. They were armed to protect their livelihood.

Time went by. Eyes strained in attempts to penetrate the darkness. They were prepared to wait until midnight at least, when they would keep solo watch in three-hour shifts.

At eleven, they drank hot coffee from a flask, their movements as quiet as possible, their whispered exchanges the bare minimum. Bless my good old pa who used to put paid to foxes down in Sussex, thought Jonathan, these contrary Surrey foxes are lying low, and I've got an ache in every muscle.

Beside him, Matthew alerted. Jonathan whispered.

'You hearing something?'

'I'm hearing a vehicle in the lane,' whispered Matthew.

The lane ran past the bottom of the field. Jonathan listened. The noise of a motor engine reached his ears, the vehicle hidden by hedges. But they heard it stop. The lights and the engine were switched off.

'Visitors?' murmured Jonathan.

'RSPCA?' murmured Matthew.

'Someone's informed them we don't care too much for foxes?' murmured Jonathan.

In the deep quiet of the night, a creaking sound was audible.

'Well, blow my boots off,' said Matthew, 'whoever it is, Jonathan, is coming through the hedge gate.'

'I'd like to know who,' whispered Jonathan, 'but I can't see for looking.'

Down at the gate, Large Lump was doing some whispering himself.

'The sheep first, Rollo.'

'You sure there's sheep?' said Rollo, a heavy.

'Didn't Poky Prodnose inform the boss there was?' said Large Lump. 'And didn't Mr Ford inform me likewise? So get at 'em.'

'I ain't against taking one home,' said Rollo, 'me and the missus is partial to roast mutton.'

'Find 'em, and run 'em out through the gate,' said Large Lump.

'Find 'em?' said another heavy. 'In the dark?'

'We use our torches, you faggot,' said Large Lump, 'and don't forget Mr Ford wants 'em to keep running till they fetch up at Land's End.'

'Ain't that where the sea is?' asked one more heavy.

'Yus, and where they start swimming the Atlantic,' said Large Lump. 'Get moving.'

On went the torches. Startled sheep stood up. So did Matthew and Jonathan as they spotted four tiny beams of light in the distance.

'Ruddy cows,' breathed Jonathan, 'what's going on?'

'My guess is black market sheep rustlers,' said Matthew. Meat shortages had resulted in the emergence of more than a few such opportunists.

The sheep and their fat lambs were running, a frightened herd, but not towards the gate. They were heading for the area of the henhouses. The beams of light followed them.

'Well, sheriff?' said Jonathan.

'Let 'em come, cowboy,' said Matthew.

The running sheep were bawling, the lambs bleating.

'Sod me,' panted Large Lump, 'that Poky Prodnose didn't mention no noise, the bleeder, did he? I hate noise.'

The sheep and lambs scattered as they neared the wired enclosure. Booted feet thudded after them, torches piercing the darkness. Their bright beams, however, were suddenly lost in the totality of a dazzling floodlight.

''Ere, what's 'appening?' hollered Rollo.

'We're bleedin' nailed, that's what,' shouted Large Lump, and turned tail. He had enough savvy to know Mr Ford would get cross, very cross, if any of them landed in the arms of the law. So he bolted. So did the other three, the floodlight encompassing their going.

'Jonathan!' Matthew was urgent. 'I think the gate's open!'

'Christ,' said Jonathan, 'the sheep!'

They were running all ways, the ewes, their lambs bleating for their mothers. The shotguns stayed silent. To blast off would panic the already frightened animals. Matthew and Jonathan took off as fast as they could, Matthew's gammy ankle not as much of a handicap as Jonathan's tin knee.

The Fat Man's bruisers heard them coming at a thumping run.

'Bloody hell, it's got to be the cops!' panted Large Lump. 'This ain't what I like.'

He galloped over the ground. The other men picked up pace. They didn't like the prospect of letting the law catch up with them any more than he did. Cops weren't friendly. They had bad-tempered ideas about how a bloke earned his oof. You could never trust a flatfoot to mind his own business.

Torches lit the way for the four bruisers, although the beams wavered and shook in hands that moved to the tempo of each man's flight. At this stage of the sweating retreat the open gate seemed as far away as Land's End. Large Lump felt shocked at the growing suspicion that somehow some coppers' nark had listened at a door and used his squeaky cakehole to spill the beans. He plunged on, panting, and his heavies panted with him.

Matthew, legging it at a fast limping run, was yards in front of Jonathan, whose liability was slowing him down. Need Emma's legs, so I do, he thought. Best runners in the family, Emma's got. Her sister Annabelle would have queried that, so would Eloise and Helene. Rosie, who had unequalled stems, would have laughed and told Jonathan to keep going. He kept going anyway, conscious that the sheep, led by a robust if fearful ewe, were following.

Bleedin' elephants, thought Large Lump, where's the perishing gate? He was hot, wet with perspiration, and short of breath. Rollo reached the open gate first and bounded through the wide gap to pound for the van. After him lurched Large Lump and the other men. Matthew was coming up fast and, just as conscious as Jonathan of the following sheep, he slammed the gate shut. It shook and vibrated, and the metal connections rattled. He glimpsed what he thought were the black market rustlers, an active breed these days. He shouldered his shotgun and fired a burst high over their heads. High it might have been, but Large Lump felt something like a fiery needle prick his backside. He bawled. Two of his confederates were tumbling into the back of the van, which contained axes and fire-lighting items. The third man, Rollo, was climbing into the driving seat. Large Lump threw himself into the back, swearing about the fact that unless the redhot pain in his bum went away, he wasn't going to be able to sit next to Rollo. Nor sit at all. Lying on his broad stomach, he thumped on the partition.

'Get going!' he bawled.

The van jerked forward and motored off noisily. Jonathan, arriving at the closed gate, said, 'Damn all, they're away.'

'They won't come back,' said Matthew. 'How's the knee?'

'Complaining,' said Jonathan.

The sheep were all around them, nuzzling close to known bodies.

'I don't think the foxes will turn up now,' said Matthew, 'but we'll keep the floodlight on just in case. That'll keep them away from the henhouses. If they attack any of the lambs, I tell you, I'll set traps.'

'Those lambs are due for the market,' said Jonathan.

'I've let the butcher know,' said Matthew, 'and he's arranging collection on Tuesday.'

'What's he offered?' asked Jonathan, as they began their walk back.

'Top price,' said Matthew.

'My knee feels better,' said Jonathan.

Matthew clapped him on the shoulder.

'On my Sunday boots, Jonathan, I'm happy to be related to you.'

Well, he was married to Emma's cousin Rosie, and that was as good a relationship with Jonathan as he could get.

Saturday arrived. Boots and his family were up early, very early. So were Sammy and his family. The journey to Cornwall could take ten to twelve hours. They had to cover over two hundred and fifty miles, and with few town by-passes available on the route, they would be lucky to average twenty-five miles an hour.

So they were away from their respective houses just after six a.m., having arranged to meet for breakfast at the Hog's Back Hotel, a little way on from Guildford.

Large Lump, reporting to the Fat Man that afternoon, was complaining that failure to get the sheep running and to chop up the chickens was due to the fact that a squad of interfering rozzers had been waiting for them with a shotgun.

'You useless fairy,' wheezed Fat Man, 'rozzers with a shotgun?'

'I tell you, guv, I got potted in me exterior,' said Large Lump. 'Had to go to 'ospital this morning to have it dug out. Talk about painful, and there was blood as well. And it's still sore, it's interfering with me walking.'

'Are you telling me you're responsible for a washout?' growled Fat Man.

'Guv, we had to scarper bloody quick, like,' said Large Lump. 'If it wasn't the cops, it must've been Sammy Adams's whole bleedin' family.'

'You're making me spit,' said Fat Man evilly. 'Stop fidgeting, will you?'

'It's me sore backside.'

'Oh, is it?' said Fat Man. 'Take a seat.'

''Ere, have a heart, guv, I ain't going to be able to take a seat for a week and more.'

'I'm crying my eyes out, ain't I?' said Fat Man.

'Kind of yer, guv,' said Large Lump. 'Listen, I think we've got a nark in the firm, yer know, and that he's been listening at keyholes. Well, it's me honest belief that it was either the cops or Sammy Adams's family waiting for us.'

'Shut up,' said Fat Man. 'We're going to have to think again about Sammy Adams's business. I've still got his factory and all that nylon keeping me awake at night.'

'I can put a couple of bombs together,' said Large Lump.

'You'll blow up Belsize Park and Happy Hampstead as well,' said Fat Man. 'I want a fire job done, one that won't look like arson. So I need an expert. Someone like Sparky Dewdrop, known for his runny nose and his baptismal monicker of Cyril Juggins.'

'Jenkins, guv.'

'Shut up. You and the other wallies can take your orders from him.'

'Guv, ain't I done you some high-class jobs in me time?' said Large Lump, looking as if his pride was paining him as well as his rear end.

'I ain't disputing that,' said Fat Man, 'but your brain's falling about and you're slipping. Go and talk to Sparky Dewdrop and tell him I want to see him. Take a bus.'

'Right, guv,' said Large Lump, wincing. 'It'll have to be standing room only.'

In Tenterden, Kent, that evening, Jeremy

Passmore had returned from his relaxing and leisurely holiday in the Lake District. He brought with him a delightful oil painting of Lake Windermere for his English aunt and uncle, Amy and Dan Passmore, a middle-aged couple who were parents and grandparents, and had been good-natured and willing hosts to him for over two years. Jeremy had found it so easy and pleasant to lodge with them that he had, at their encouragement, extended his original stay of a few months, although he often said he really ought to find a place of his own or to think about going back to Chicago. Aunt Amy, who had acquired a motherly affection for her quiet-living American nephew, always responded to the effect that as long as he was happy with things as they were, he might as well stay until he did go home.

She and Uncle Dan were delighted with their gift, which she said was ever such a pretty picture and could be hung in the parlour.

Jeremy had also brought back a book of poems by William Wordsworth of Lake District fame. He put that in a drawer in his bedroom.

Aunt Amy said how well he looked, and

what a blessing it was that having made up his mind to go home at last to Chicago, he could sail there in the pink.

'Brown, I'd say,' said Uncle Dan, who had a well-kept iron-grey moustache and a bit of a twinkle.

'Brown?' said Aunt Amy, comfortably plump. 'No-one says you're in the brown. It's in the pink.'

'From where I am,' said Uncle Dan, observing Jeremy, 'I can't see any pink. You haven't been at your elderberry wine, have you, Amy?'

'Me?' said Aunt Amy. 'I just have one glass with Sunday dinners, that's all. Oh, you daft thing, you're talking about pink elephants, aren't you?'

'Just a thought,' said Uncle Dan, winking at Jeremy.

'Jeremy,' said Aunt Amy, 'have you made up your mind exactly when you'll sail?'

'Before you left for the Lakes, you mentioned you'd like to book a passage on the *Queen Mary* when you got back,' said Uncle Dan.

'From Southampton,' said Jeremy. 'That, at least, was the idea. I came over on that great old tub. With the *Queen Elizabeth* it was turned into a troopship for the GIs, and both ships could outrun the fastest U-boats. For sure, what a couple of game old girls.'

'Wait a bit,' said Uncle Dan, 'did you say something that meant you were changing your mind about going?'

'I'm thinking, after all, that I'll postpone my return,' said Jeremy.

'Oh, my goodness,' said Aunt Amy, 'we'd be the last ones to push you, but what's made you have second thoughts?'

'There's my employers,' said Jeremy. 'I know they'd like me to stay through to harvest time. I guess I will. It's that kind of summer.'

'Well, so it is,' said Uncle Dan, filling his briar pipe. He was fond of Jeremy. He wasn't loud or obtrusive, he had a very even temperament and a likeable personality, and he gave a hand with anything that needed a young man's technique. 'Now and again we get a summer like this.'

'I've also been thinking, how would you two like a return trip to America on one of the Queens?' said Jeremy. 'To Chicago, to meet some of your American Passmores? You could stay with–' He paused. No, not with his parents. His father was heavily in-volved in the booming packaging industry, his mother a bustling figure in charity work.

They were a couple committed to life outside their home. 'Sure, yes, you could stay with my sister and her husband. They'd be delighted to have you, fuss you and take you sightseeing. I'd say that idea is one of my best. I'll go to the agents in the High Street, and book you both for a sailing at a time that suits you best. It's all on me, naturally, just a little return for your heart-warming hospitality.'

Aunt Amy was open-mouthed, Uncle Dan searching for words. As a compositor in the printing shop of the local newspaper, he had a few pounds behind him and he owned his house, but the cost of a visit to America was out of his range.

'I'm not sure I know what to say,' he said.

'Oh, we couldn't let you pay for all that, Jeremy,' said Aunt Amy.

'You'll disappoint me if you turn me down,' said Jeremy, and began some very persuasive talk. His offer was a heartfelt and genuine attempt to repay these kind and affectionate English relatives for all they had done for him. His persuasiveness won the day, Aunt Amy almost misty-eyed with happy emotions. A trip to America, oh, my goodness, she said, wouldn't that be the trip of a lifetime?

She and Uncle Dan settled for next spring, if he could persuade the local newspaper owners to let him take a month off, the month including his regular two weeks summer holiday. He'd talk to the owners on Monday, he said.

'You get that fixed up, Dan,' said Jeremy, 'and then I'll book your passages and write to my sister.'

'Amy,' said Uncle Dan, 'help yourself to a glass of your elderberry wine, while I share a bottle of beer with Jeremy.'

'That's the kind of talk I like to hear,' said Jeremy.

Chapter Fifteen

Boots, Polly and their twins, together with Sammy, Susie, Jimmy, Paula and Phoebe, had arrived at their holiday destination, a white-stuccoed cottage roofed with colourful Delabole slates close to Daymer Bay in North Cornwall.

The cottage, large, had five bedrooms, a colourful living room, a spacious kitchen with a dining area, and all the amenities necessary to the holidaymakers who rented it, and were in the main regular visitors with their families. Boots and Polly, and Sammy and Susie, had become regulars.

Tired out, the twins were in bed, and by ten o'clock Paula and Phoebe had also retired. Now Boots and Sammy were relaxing over the bottle of whisky Boots had brought from home. Susie and Polly were each enjoying a gin and tonic.

Jimmy had just gone for a walk to take a look, he said, at the local talent. A Cornish holiday nearly always meant girls were in the mood to let acceptable blokes strike up a lively and entertaining, if brief, friendship with them.

'Jimmy's got an itch,' said Susie with a sweet smile.

'I note that smile,' said Sammy, 'it means you'll be watching what he finds. I might say that if he didn't have an itch at his age, I'd worry about him.'

'Tell about the itches you had, Sammy,' said Polly.

'I only had one itch,' said Sammy. 'Financial. Well, someone had to think about getting the family out of patched trousers and darned jerseys. Boots, of course, did what suited him best, lording it.

So I took it on myself to found the family business. I couldn't afford an itch for girls.'

'Not much,' said Susie. 'You've got a dark past, Sammy Adams.'

'What was her name?' asked Polly.

'Rachel Moses,' said Susie. 'Afterwards, Rachel Goodman.'

'Oh, Rachel,' said Polly, smiling.

'A beauty, even at sixteen,' said Boots.

'A young man's fancy?' said Polly.

'I'm not listening,' said Sammy.

'However, when Susie arrived in his life,' said Boots, 'he developed another itch, an incurable one.'

'Some hopes,' said Susie, 'he made me eat pie and mash every day for months, giving me the horrors about getting fat.'

'And they're living happily ever after,' murmured Polly, looking a little dreamy.

'I don't know how all this came about,' said Sammy.

'From a mention of Jimmy having an itch,' said Boots, deep in an armchair and long legs stretching.

'Which he's just taken for a nice walk,' said Susie.

Jimmy was standing at the open edge of the grass field that overlooked the beach of

Daymer Bay. He was taking in the soft Cornish night air, the indigo sky casting velvet darkness over the sea and sand. Brea Hill was a black bulk rising up from the sand and backing onto an unseen golf course. On the other side of the estuary were the twinkling lights of Padstow.

Jimmy, musing on his holiday prospects, turned and began his walk back to the cottage. Going up Daymer Lane, he heard voices ahead, voices of exuberant young people. He stood aside in the narrow lane to let them pass. They chorused, 'Happy holidays.'

'Same to you,' said Jimmy.

'We're going for a night runabout on the beach,' said a young man.

'I'd join you,' said Jimmy, now dog-tired, 'except I'm going to my bed for a good night's kip.'

They laughed and went on. Jimmy glimpsed the blur of white shorts and bare legs. One girl was wearing a tail-tied RAF shirt, unnoticed by Jimmy in the dark.

By the time he arrived back at the holiday cottage, Susie, Sammy, Polly and Boots were about to retire after their long day on the road. Susie, however, did ask Jimmy if he'd had time to sum up the local talent.

Jimmy said he thought there was a lot of it about, but it was all covered up by the dark.

'Oh, well, Jimmy,' said Polly, 'who knows what the light of day will uncover tomorrow?'

'Good question,' said Jimmy, 'and if it's all spoken for, I'll help the twins build their sandcastles.'

They all said their goodnights then, and a little later the warm velvety night enclosed them and drew them into healthy sleep.

Sunday.

The fine morning was nature's gift to holidaymakers. The twins, of course, could hardly wait to take their buckets and spades to the beach, and by ten o'clock there they were, making a huge sandcastle, watched over by Boots and Polly, who'd carried deckchairs down with them. Boots was wearing light tropical slacks and an unbuttoned shirt, his sandals off, his bare feet touching sand. Polly's slim but quite shapely frame was graced by the lightest of cream-coloured blouses with a knee-length pleated camel skirt, her uncovered toenails varnished pink.

Sammy and Susie, both lightly clothed, were at the edge of the lapping sea, watching Paula and Phoebe who, with other people, were swimming. Jimmy, in white shirt, blue shorts and sandals, was considering his annual climb to the top of Brea Hill, from where the view was always spectacular. In a group of several young people, a girl was berating a feller.

'You're a lost cause,' she said, 'it's all I can call somebody who sprains his ankle on only the third day of his holiday.'

'My hard luck,' said the lost cause, a large bandage around his ankle.

'Well, who's going to take your place?'

'None of us,' said three fellers together, 'Chloe, Fiona and Matilda won't let us.'

'Certainly not,' said Chloe, Fiona and Matilda.

'Otherwise one of us will be odd,' said Fiona, 'unless she takes on Barry and his sprained ankle.'

'There you are, odds are out,' said one of the fellers. 'Look for someone else. Try that lonesome ranger over there.'

The frustrated girl cast a glance. Well, she thought, he looks as if he could play. He's got the legs and the right kind of physique.

'Hey!' she called.

Jimmy turned. The girl walked towards him, lithely brisk. She was wearing brief white shorts that hugged the upper reaches of her firm thighs, and an RAF shirt that was tied by its tails around her lower ribs, its top buttons undone. Cleavage saucily peeped.

'Hello,' said Jimmy.

'Listen,' said the girl, dark springy hair kissed by the warm sea breezes, 'd'you play golf?'

'Cricket,' said Jimmy, recognizing her.

'That's no good. Come and try some golf. My partner Barry's a dope, he managed to sprain his ankle last night. I'm mad about golf myself. You're not doing anything, are you, except standing about?'

'I do my standing about in my father's Walworth store if there's a shortage of customers,' said Jimmy.

'What?' She blinked and stared. 'Well, I'm blessed, I know you, you're the bright spark who sold this shirt and another to me, and gave me some unwanted conversation.'

'Hello, hello,' said Jimmy, peering, 'it's you. I thought that shirt looked familiar. And I remember now, you mentioned Cornwall, but I didn't—'

'Never mind all that,' she said, 'come and

play some golf. Useless Eustace and I went to the clubhouse yesterday and booked a round for this morning, and the green fee's paid.'

'I've never even held a golf club, let alone used one,' said Jimmy.

'But you've got arms and legs, haven't you?' said the girl. 'Yes, of course you have, and I'll give you a few tips. It's no fun going round on one's own. Come on, we can get there from the beach, and you'll like the game.'

'I'll chance it,' said Jimmy, 'but hold on a tick while I let my family know where I am.'

He did a quick run to the nearest kin, Boots and Polly, and told them he'd be on the golf course until lunchtime, probably. Some girl needed a partner.

Polly smiled. She and Boots hadn't missed the advent of the girl in question.

'Off you go, Jimmy old sport,' she said, and he made quick tracks back to the girl.

'I don't think he's ever played any golf,' said Boots.

'That's hardly important, when the local talent has just shown up,' said Polly.

'Are you a matchmaker?' asked Boots, down on the sand now and helping the twins to make the sandcastle huger.

'Perish the thought,' said Polly.

Jimmy set out with the girl to make the slight ascent from the beach to the golf course and the clubhouse. Thirty minutes later they were on the first tee, each with a bag of clubs hired for a fee of seven and six and containing golf balls and tees. The morning round of enthusiasts was well under way by now, and the first fairway was clear.

'Watch closely,' said the girl. Having used some sand from a box to make a tee for her ball, she began to execute some practice swings with her driver. 'By the way, what's your name?'

'Jimmy Adams.'

'I'm Jenny Osborne.'

'How d'you do?'

'Don't talk,' said Jenny, taking her stance. Jimmy watched her, a lithe and stunning girl with gorgeous legs, her hands gripping the club firmly. Up it went, her arms lifting high, and down it came in a fast graceful swing. She cracked the ball away, high over the fairway. It descended, bounced and ran on.

'Good shot, was it?' said Jimmy.

'Well, I liked it,' said Jenny. 'Come on, try your luck. Don't use a driver, use an iron. An iron's easier for a beginner.'

'What's a driver and what's an iron?' asked Jimmy.

She selected a number 3 iron from his bag, gave it to him and watched as he made a sand tee and placed the ball on it. He then did some practice swings.

'Keep your legs and hips still,' said Jenny.

'Right,' said Jimmy. He squared up to the ball and delivered a thumping whack with the club. The ball remained on its sand tee.

'Air shot, you clumsy chump,' said Jenny. 'Try again, and keep your head still, eyes on the ball.'

Jimmy had another go. The clubhead just tickled the top of the ball and it fell limply off the little tee of sand.

'Who's a duffer?' he said.

'You are,' said Jenny. 'You lifted your head. Didn't I tell you to keep it still? Try again.' Jimmy teed up his ball and took a new stance. Jenny watched him keenly. 'You ought to be able to hit a ball,' she said, 'you're tall enough and you're not an old fogey yet.'

'Right now,' said Jimmy, 'I think I've got an inferiority complex.'

'Well, get rid of it and hit that ball,' said Jenny.

Jimmy concentrated with set teeth. He

swung the club and followed through with his hands and arms.

Crack!

In astonishment and experiencing a fair amount of rapture, he saw the ball flying high through the air and bounding along as it hit turf.

'Blimey,' he said, 'did I do that?'

'Good shot, Jimmy,' said Jenny, 'let's get going.'

They shouldered their bags and set off down the fairway, the links course a vista of green in front of them, the air warm and balmy, the sky an azure blue.

They played golf. Jenny hit crisply sweet shots, Jimmy sometimes hit a cracker and most other times had air shots or shocking shots. And on the greens, his putter behaved like a useless lump of old iron. Jenny kept berating him.

'Keep your head still, you dope, don't I keep telling you?'

'Listen, Jimmy Adams, whoever you are, that's a golf club you're using, not a pick-axe.'

'I don't know why you're so hopeless. You don't look hopeless, but you are.'

Sometimes, however, 'Oh, good shot, that's better.'

Jenny enjoyed her golf. She shook her head over his. Jimmy reckoned his round had given him a totally forgettable morning.

'Thank God,' he said at the end.

'What for?' asked Jenny, as they walked to the professional's shop.

'It's all over,' said Jimmy.

Jenny laughed.

'Cheer up,' she said, 'it didn't actually slay you.'

They delivered the clubs back to the professional, who asked if they'd enjoyed their round.

'Lovely,' said Jenny.

'I'm keeping quiet,' said Jimmy.

Leaving the shop, he looked at his watch. Five minutes past two.

'Do you have time for a drink?' he asked Jenny.

'Thanks, but no,' she said. 'I'm getting back to the beach. My friends have a picnic going.'

'Well, I ought to get back for lunch at our cottage,' said Jimmy. 'If there's any left.'

'Good luck,' said Jenny. 'Thanks for coming round with me. So long.'

They parted. On arriving back at the cottage, Jimmy found some lunch had been saved for him, and so had some questions.

'How'd you get on?' asked Sammy.

'Painfully,' said Jimmy.

'With the girl?' said Susie.

'With the golf,' said Jimmy.

'No good?' said Boots.

'Ask me another,' said Jimmy.

'How about the girl?' asked Polly.

'Hot stuff,' said Jimmy.

'Crikey,' said Paula, 'really hot stuff?'

'At golf,' said Jimmy.

'When do the two of you meet again?' asked Polly.

'Never on a golf course, I hope,' said Jimmy.

'What was he like?' asked Fiona.

'Hopeless,' said Jenny, helping herself to a sandwich and a tomato. The beach was near to golden under the bright sun, perfect for holidaymakers acquiring a tan.

'No sex appeal?' said Chloe.

'Who's talking about sex appeal?' said Jenny.

'There's plenty here,' said Barry of the bandaged ankle. 'Including mine.'

'Yours is sprained,' said Jenny, 'and who let sand get into the sandwiches?'

'She's complaining,' said Chloe. 'Is that a sign she's going to add her goofy golfer to our group?'

'She can't,' said Barry, 'we're eight, we're four and four. He'll be odd.'

'Oh, I don't think he's odd,' said Fiona, 'he looked a sweetie to me.'

'Shut up!' bawled the four fellers.

'Don't get an anxiety complex,' said Jenny, 'my round of golf with him wasn't meaningful.'

'Famous last words,' whispered Chloe to Matilda.

The sun beamed out of the blue sky. Children fished about with nets in little pools, adults strolled at the edge of the sea, parents relaxed and let cares float away, and the laughter and ribaldry marking the spot where Jenny and her friends were grouped was a clear indication of the joys of being young.

Chapter Sixteen

Jimmy enjoyed a rousing swim with Paula and Phoebe the following day. Phoebe was as smooth and agile as a fish in the water, as adept at the butterfly as at the crawl, and

Jimmy made a mental note to contact Surrey's swimming chiefs and let them know he had a young sister who could possibly be trained to become a county champ.

He let the girls go their way while he floated on his back. The sea was calm, the tide out, the sand of Daymer Bay a huge shining expanse in the light of another sunny day. He mused on his golf round with the stunning Jenny Osborne. Calamitous. Pity about that. He'd performed like a useless Charlie right in front of her eyes. Not just for a few minutes, but for three hours. Once or twice, when he'd nearly fallen flat on his face, she'd shrieked with laughter. Mostly, however, she'd either groaned or sighed, then delivered a verbal blow. True, she'd helped all she could with advice and instruction, but the perishing ball simply didn't like what he'd tried to do to it. Talk about disastrous.

He sat up then as he spotted two bathing beauties approaching the sea. One was in sleek blue, the other in white. Sun-kissed legs and thighs shone. He swam into shallow water, stood up and waded towards them.

'Hello,' said Aunt Polly, the one in white.

'We couldn't resist,' said Susie, the one in blue.

'Well, I'll go to the market with a camel,' said Jimmy. 'How'd you do it, considering one of you's my mum, and the other's my aunt?'

'Is that a compliment or what?' asked Susie.

'Don't explain or what,' said Polly.

Jimmy laughed. He wouldn't have been what he was if he hadn't felt proud of them. Their swimsuits were first-class in style and quality, and they both looked as if they'd been poured into them.

'Listen, my beauties,' he said, 'are you going in?'

'This beauty is,' said Polly, dark sienna hair styled in curling fashion around her head.

'So is this one,' said Susie, fair hair fairer in the sun. A group of young people on the far side of the beach went running and splashing into the sea, whooping with the bliss of being alive. Somehow, and for a brief moment of sadness, she thought of the millions of men, women and children taken from life in the gas chambers of the German concentration camps. Life in all its variations was a gift from God. How terrible for children to be brutally robbed of it. Boots had known a concentration camp, and had seen its remnants, the dead, the dying and the walking skeletons. Polly had said that for all his tolerance, he would always consider Himmler and the SS as totally unforgivable.

'Where are your bathing caps?' asked Jimmy.

'Jimmy old scout, I look hideous in a bathing cap,' said Polly.

'I look as if I'm bald,' said Susie, 'so we'll shampoo the salt out of our hair tonight.'

'In you go, then,' said Jimmy. 'The girls are out there somewhere, and Phoebe's after swimming the Channel. Her swimming's famous, but her geography's wonky. Who's looking after the belongings?'

'Your Uncle Boots and the twins,' said Susie. 'He and the twins have had their swim.'

'He's now helping them build the biggest sandcastle ever, with a moat,' said Polly. 'He's reliving his childhood. Happily, the old darling.'

'And Sammy's gone up to the village to buy some bottles of lemonade for our young ones, the sweetie,' said Susie. 'Come on, Polly, let's brave the sea. Last one in is a wimp.'

Jimmy watched them wade out until the water was deep enough for them to dive in.

His Aunt Polly was quickly away, using a long-armed easy crawl. His mum followed with a sedate breast stroke. There were cries of encouragement from Paula and Phoebe, way out with other young swimmers. The picture was a sun-splashed, sea-splashed sparkle so colourful that Jimmy decided to go in again. Wading out, he saw a girl approaching him on his left.

'Hello,' she said.

'Hi,' said Jimmy, swimming trunks plastering his hips, little beads of water dappling his fine, firm chest.

'I know you,' she said, 'you played golf with Jenny yesterday.'

'In all honesty, I've got to correct that,' said Jimmy. 'I went round with her and fell about all over the course. Not my game, I suppose.'

'Still, you're smiling about it,' said the girl.

'It's hiding my mortification,' said Jimmy.

'I'm Fiona. Who were those two dazzling women you were talking to?'

'My aunt and my mother.'

'My mother doesn't look like that in a swimsuit,' said Fiona, glowingly brunette. 'Still, she has lots of other assets – or do I mean virtues?'

'All mums have some virtues,' said Jimmy.

Up came a young feller, gleaming wet from the sea.

'Excuse me,' he said to Jimmy, 'but Fiona's got an appointment.'

'With her mum?' said Jimmy.

'With me. So long.' He took Fiona away, but not before she cast Jimmy a smile and a wink.

Jimmy waded on towards a bevy of bathers, girls, fellers and adults. The sea at Daymer Bay was devoid of the rollers that crashed in at Polzeath and Newquay, and the bathing was safe. Away to his left, he saw Jenny and her group turning the sea to foam around their splashing, moving bodies. He plunged in and struck out. Up popped Paula and Phoebe in front of him, streaming water.

'Wow, isn't it great?' spouted Paula.

'Fantastic,' said Jimmy.

'We saw you talking to a girl,' said Phoebe.

'She's got a feller,' said Jimmy, treading water.

'Hard luck,' said Paula.

Apart from the fact that Jimmy kept reliving his disastrous round of golf, the day was perfect.

So were following days, the weather set fair.

Sparky Dewdrop, a skinny bloke with a perpetual sniff, had a talent for dropping insurance companies into a heap of liabilities. He used arson that couldn't be proved as such. It was a happy little earner that kept him in unlimited groceries and the convenience of a battered old car. He had no trouble in acquiring petrol coupons. Or unlimited groceries.

Having been talked to by Large Lump, which wasn't the wittiest discourse to which his ears had ever been treated, he called on the Fat Man, knowing that if he didn't, something heavy would fall on him or his car or both.

The Fat Man acquainted him with what was required, grievous injury in some form or another to Sammy Adams's business. The factory at Belsize Park, for instance, or the shop and offices at Camberwell Green.

'Don't like the sound of Camberwell Green, y'know,' said Sparky, sniffing. 'It ain't quiet enough at night. It's a regular coppers' beat.'

'I had that problem with his store in the Walworth Road,' said Fat Man.

'Walworth Road?' Sparky shook his head and sniffed again. 'I tell yer, Mister Ford,

213

that's what some of us call no-man's-land.'

'Don't I know it?' said Fat Man.

'Belsize Park's better, it's full up with respectable people that don't give the cops trouble,' said Sparky, sniffing yet again.

'Do me a favour,' said Fat Man, 'blow your bloody nose.'

'Eh?' said Sparky.

'Blow it.'

'It ain't bothering me,' said Sparky.

'It's bothering me,' said Fat Man, who was fastidious himself about personal habits.

'Oh, right you are,' said Sparky, and searched for a handkerchief. He was lucky enough to find one up his sleeve. It wasn't exactly pristine, but it did the job. He blew hard, snorting.

'What's your suggestion for Belsize Park?' wheezed Fat Man.

'Well, you know me speciality,' said Sparky, 'and I ain't ever let a client down.'

'If there's going to be a first time, don't make it me,' said Fat Man, 'or you'll disappear into a large lump of wet concrete.'

'You're a hard man, Mister Ford,' said Sparky. He sniffed. The Fat Man rumbled with irritation.

'I ain't ungenerous for a successful job, you know that,' he said.

'I'm appreciative, appreciative,' said Sparky. 'When d'you want the job done?'

'Yesterday.'

'Eh.'

'That means immediately,' said Fat Man.

'Immediate being tomorrow night?' said Sparky.

'That'll do,' said Fat Man, 'but I've been thinking. Make it an obvious arson job, then bleedin' Sammy Adams won't get his insurance paid. Instead, he'll get investigated by the police for a fraudulent claim.'

'Well, I can see yer point, Mister Ford,' said Sparky. 'But I don't like the prospects of being investigated meself as well.'

'You've got no record,' said Fat Man.

'But I ask yer, do I want to start one?' said Sparky plaintively. 'It'll ruin me living.'

'Just don't leave any fingerprints,' said Fat Man. 'Or any footprints. D'you need any help?'

'Help?'

'I can let you have a back-up.'

'Ta very much,' said Sparky, 'just a bloke to keep watch. It'll take a bit of time to plant the necessary. I usually use Larry Larkins, but he fell over his feet doing a solo job at Epsom. Now, of course, he's a guest of the law at the Scrubs, where he don't like the food. All the way to Epsom for a few sparklers, I tell yer, he might as well have carried on till he reached Brighton Pier, where he could have fiddled a purseful of pennies out of the slot machines with no hard feelings.'

'You'll get your back-up,' said Fat Man. 'I'm now contracting you for the job. Tomorrow night.'

'Mister Ford, I ain't fond of that word. Contracting.'

'Get on with it,' said Fat Man.

'Well, a job's a job,' sighed Sparky. 'Arson, you said?'

'Obvious arson was what I said.'

'Might I ask the terms?'

'Four ponies,' said Fat Man. A hundred quid.

'Now that's what I am fond of,' said Sparky, sniffing.

'That's all, then,' said Fat Man, 'and blow your nose on the way out.'

Friday.

Jimmy was at the golf club, paying for a lesson from the professional. His failure to master the art of striking a ball cleanly had given him not only mortification, but the groans of a girl with stunning looks and high-class style. Since his sense of failure had, in a manner of speaking, followed him about, he had finally decided to have the friendly pro teach him the basics. That was purely in the hope of restoring some of his manly pride, not for making himself eligible for another round with Jenny. She and her group, sufficient unto themselves, appeared and reappeared on Daymer Beach without looking for other company.

Mind, she had spoken to him once, catching up with him in the sea.

'Oh, it's you,' she said.

'Well, hello, it's you,' said Jimmy. 'How's your golf?'

'I don't play a lot when I'm on holiday,' said Jenny, rising from the sea to present her shining wet swimsuit to his eyes. Its bodice clung without coyness around her healthy and interesting development. 'I'd get booed if I did. Who are you here with?'

'My family,' said Jimmy. 'Here, it consists of my parents and two of my sisters, an uncle and aunt and their twins. My other sister and my brother–'

'They're not here,' stated Jenny.

'No, my other sister's up in the Lake District.'

'Lovely,' said Jenny. 'By the way, sorry I

can't invite you to join our lot, but the ones in trousers say you'd be odd. We're four and four, you see.'

'That's all right,' said Jimmy, 'so tell the ones in trousers I don't hold it against them. Nobody likes to be odd, anyway.'

'On the other hand, Fiona thinks you're a sweetie,' said Jenny.

'I'm touched, and I think I've met Fiona,' said Jimmy.

'Fiona's evil,' said Jenny. 'She's livid about my RAF shirts, and she'll pinch one if she can.'

'Tell her to come to the store,' said Jimmy, 'and I'll sell her as many as she'd like.'

'You traitor,' said Jenny. Waist-high in the sea, she splashed him with some of it. 'Don't you dare do that. Those shirts are exclusive to me. Sell her Waaf shirts instead, if she ever gets there. But I'm not telling.'

'Your men's shirts suit you, I'll say that much,' said Jimmy.

'Thanks,' said Jenny, 'and I must say you're a better salesman than a golfer.'

'Listen, Miss Osborne,' said Jimmy, 'that was the first time I've ever tried the game, and if Fiona's evil, so was that golf ball.'

Jenny laughed.

'You're not a bad old joker,' she said.

'Well, so long, must get back to my loud lot.' Off she went to rejoin her group in the watery distance.

That, as well as the other reasons, put Jimmy on the practice green with the golf club's professional, who set about the task of helping him to acquire what was most important to any golfer, the right kind of swing. The pro's instructions were clear, given and repeated with the necessary patience. For half an hour, Jimmy didn't hit a ball. He wasn't asked to, he was simply required to first develop a satisfactory swing. That necessitated keeping his bonce still, and following all the way through with his arms.

'How does that look?' he asked once.

'As if you're tied up in knots,' said the pro, 'but you're coming along.'

'Thanks for the kind words,' said Jimmy.

Eventually, the pro said, 'I like it now.' And he teed up a ball for Jimmy. 'Hit it,' he said.

Jimmy took his time to address the little round white devil. Then he swung the club. The ball, smacked clean and hard, travelled into what Jimmy considered infinity.

'Well, how about that?' he said.

'Congratulations, but only a beginning,' said the pro. 'Hit another.'

For the rest of the hour's tuition, Jimmy swung at one ball after another. If some drives were patchy, others were exhilarating, and he had no air shots. The pro told him he had promise, but would have to play regularly or have regular practice lessons if he wanted to master the game. Jimmy told him what a good bloke he was, and they had a drink together, Jimmy standing treat.

'Are you going to take up golf, Jimmy?' asked Susie after supper that evening.

'I doubt it,' said Jimmy.

'Why the lesson today, then?' asked Polly.

'Just to find out if I could hit a ball,' said Jimmy.

'Ah,' said Sammy, sort of knowingly.

'Ah, well,' said Boots, tanned to a deep brown, which made Polly think in warlike terms about certain women who'd been giving him the eye on the beach.

'Nothing to do with the girl,' said Jimmy, 'just for my own satisfaction.'

'Yes, of course, Jimmy love,' said Susie.

'There's a lot of winking going on,' said Jimmy.

'Ah, well,' said Polly.

'I'm looking at you, Aunt Polly,' said Jimmy.

'I cherish your admiration, Jimmy old lad,' said Polly.

Later that night. Much later. Past one o'clock in the morning, in fact.

Belsize Park slumbered in the darkness. Sparky Dewdrop and Large Lump were wide awake, Large Lump keeping watch as Sparky went to work. The gates of the high wire perimeter were closed, a chain and padlock in place. Sparky fiddled with the padlock, using a stout darning needle. A little click signalled success. Carefully he removed the padlock and parted the chain. He cast cautious glances.

'All clear, Sparky mate,' whispered Large Lump.

'Stop shouting,' hissed Sparky.

'Shouting?' said Large Lump, affronted. 'Me?'

'Good as,' sniffed Sparky. The coast clear, he gently opened the left-hand gate. 'Right,' he breathed, taking his oversized carpet bag from Large Lump, 'come inside, close the gate and stand there. Don't want you looking untidy by standing outside. Keep yer mince pies peeled. Got it?'

'I ain't daft,' whispered Large Lump. He entered the forecourt with Sparky, and closed the gate silently. Sparky, rubber soles softly treading, made for the double doors of the factory. There were two Yale locks. His torch was in the carpet bag, and he left it there while he applied himself to springing the locks.

That took less than a minute. He opened one door, picked up the bag, and inserted himself soundlessly into the gap. He stood and listened. Not a sound. Good-oh. Interference on a job like this could damage his career which, after all, was only injurious to insurance companies loaded with the ready.

He closed the door, gently set the carpet bag on the floor, opened it and extracted his torch. Facing the wide passage, dark as the night, there were no windows at his back, and he switched on the torch. Its beam cut a bright hole in the darkness and illuminated a large sliding door on which was painted a notice.

'WORKSHOP AND STOCKROOM. NO UNAUTHORIZED ADMITTANCE.'

Very right and proper, thought Sparky, but I'm under contract.

Picking up his bag, he advanced, sniffing a bit, but otherwise in sound working order. A door opened on his right, a light flooded on, and a thunderbolt fell on the back of his neck.

Sparky dropped, out cold.

At the gate outside, Large Lump was suddenly aware that one of the factory's windows was showing light. Eh? Sparky wasn't noted for turning on lights when doing a job. It advertised the kind of thing that the law didn't like. The law was as interfering as the rozzers.

The factory entrance doors opened. Framed in the gap, with light behind him, was a broad-shouldered man, nothing like narrow-shouldered Sparky. He shouted a command.

'You there, stay where you are!'

'Flaming clappers, it's Scotland Yard in a suit,' hissed Large Lump to the night. The night offered no help, so he opened the gate and set off like a galumphing elephant with a scalded tail. He breathed bitter words about what his horoscope was doing to him lately.

He charged into the night.

Neither Michal Greenberg nor his brother Jacob followed. They were quite happy with having downed the man with the carpet bag.

'He's coming to,' said Jacob.

'Give him some of the coffee,' said Michal.

'His mouth isn't open yet,' said Jacob.

'Pour it over his head,' said Michal, 'then we'll ask him a few questions. If he turns out to be a Nazi as well as a threat to Tommy and Sammy Adams, we'll torture him.'

'I should do that?' said Jacob. 'I'm declining.'

'We'll only pour hot coffee over his assets,' said Michal.

'I ain't declining that,' said Jacob.

Chapter Seventeen

Saturday.

Tommy, having received a telephone call from Michal at seven, arrived at the factory some fifteen minutes ahead of Gertie and the machinists, who always travelled from the East End by the underground railway.

Michal and Jacob, a little heavy-eyed from their long night, introduced Tommy to the slick, skinny geezer whose monicker was Cyril Jenkins and who, under some direly threatening interrogation, had admitted to the nickname of Sparky Dewdrop, and to having been contracted by Mr Ben Ford to do an arson job on the factory.

'You lump of skinny meat, I've a good mind to tread your face in,' said Tommy. He was tall, sturdy and muscular enough, as well as grim enough, to make Sparky feel the messenger of death had arrived to do him a fatal injury. Gawd help us, he thought, that could kill me.

'Honest, guv,' he said, 'I know it don't look too good, but I got to earn an honest living. Well, it's honest use of me talents, and there's me missus and five kids – no, six – to keep.'

'What a barrowload of wet winkles,' said Tommy. 'You're an out-and-out crook, and your missus ought to run you through her mangle until you're flat all the way up and down, then slip you down a kerbside drain.'

'Mangle?' said Sparky, whose head was still aching from the chop he'd received on the back of his neck hours ago. 'She don't use one of them antiques, guv, she sends all the washing to the local laundry. Course, it costs a bit, which costs me a bit, and what with that and all the other expenses, you can see I got to make a name for meself at me profession.'

225

'By doing dirty jobs for ugly spivs like Ben Ford?' said Tommy, scowling.

'Well, I grant yer, guv, Mr Ford ain't exactly handsome,' said Sparky, 'and I promise yer, you give me permission to go on me way and I'll cross him off me list. On behalf of me missus and all me kids – oh, I nearly forgot, there's me old widowed mother and her wooden left leg as well–'

'Has he been like this all night?' asked Tommy of Michal and Jacob.

'He would've been if we hadn't stuffed his socks into his tonsils,' said Jacob.

'Guv, I ain't telling no lies,' said Sparky, sniffing. 'Me dear old mother lost her left leg when one of them 'orrible doodlebugs dropped in Kennington. It was there one minute, next to her right one, and a second later it was gone. She never found it, and had a terrible job getting to hospital. Still, they fixed her up with her wooden peg, and seeing she relies on me, like me missus does, and me kids, I'd appreciate it if you didn't mention me name to the cops. I've–'

'Shut your gob,' said Tommy. He heard the machinists arriving. 'Michal, on your way home, could you deliver this heap of no-good cabbage back to the Fat Man? With a message?'

'No sooner said than done, Mister Tommy,' said Michal. 'We'll use his car. It's parked a little way down.'

Sparky shook his head gloomily.

'Mr Ford ain't going to like it,' he said. 'Still, no cops, guv?'

'Next time there will be, you squirt,' said Tommy.

'You're a gent,' said Sparky, 'specially as these two coves give me a terrible night. Didn't sleep a wink – ouch!' Michal had kicked his thigh. ''Ere, what's that for?'

'For your old mother's wooden leg,' said Michal.

Breakfast over, and with Cornwall bathed in morning sunshine, Jimmy took a walk up Daymer Lane while everyone else made preparations for another day on the beach. Jimmy had holiday cards to post for himself and the two families. The little post office of Trebetherick that sold newspapers, tobacco, confectionery and gifts was at the top of the lane, and the walk was an exercise of the will for people who spent most of the year inhabiting the flat streets of inner London. Jimmy, however, living on Denmark Hill, made easy work of the climb.

He popped into the shop to buy penny

stamps for the cards, and who should be there but none other than gorgeous Jenny Osborne, and what a picture postcard she herself looked in the tail-tied RAF shirt and hip-hugging, thigh-hugging navy blue shorts.

'Oh, hello,' he said.

'Are you following me about?' she asked, face browned by the sun and the sea air.

'Definitely not,' said Jimmy. 'I've been brought up by a dad who believes in leading, not following. Leading means initiative and a bright future, and who gets anywhere by just following?'

'Well, you've got here, which isn't anywhere, it's suspicious,' said Jenny. 'What have you come for, anyway, if not to ask me for my home phone number?'

'I've come for stamps,' said Jimmy.

'Stamps?' said Jenny.

'Postage stamps for holiday cards,' said Jimmy. 'What've you come for?'

'Stamps,' said Jenny, and laughed. 'And a straw hat for the beach.'

'Here's one,' said Jimmy, lifting a round white creation with a wide brim from a shelf. 'Try it for yourself, it'll suit you better than it'll suit the beach. Do beaches wear hats?'

'You're killing me,' said Jenny, but she took the hat and plonked it on her head. Jimmy thought it made her look like the spirit of Mayfair in the summer. 'How's that?' she asked.

'Buy it,' said Jimmy, and watched as she took a mirror out of her handbag and studied her reflection.

'Love it,' she said, 'I will buy it. What led you to choose it?'

'Initiative,' said Jimmy.

'There's a clever boy.'

'I'm wearing trousers,' said Jimmy.

'Oh, very manly,' said Jenny, and she paid for the straw hat. 'Well, I must be off, Jimmy, me and my lot are going sailing off Rock today, with my father and his yacht.'

'Sounds breezy,' said Jimmy.

'Not too breezy, I hope,' said Jenny, 'or Barry will get seasick again. That and a sprained ankle, what a buffoon. So long – oh, d'you want to try a round of golf again tomorrow?'

Jimmy experienced a mental shudder, then thought about the hour he'd spent with the club professional and what he might be able to achieve in company with stunning Jenny.

'I'll chance it if you will,' he said.

'See you at the pro's shop at two tomorrow afternoon, then,' said Jenny.

'By the way, what's your home phone number?' asked Jimmy.

'I didn't hear that,' said Jenny, and off she went.

Jimmy bought his stamps and some more picture postcards for his mum and Aunt Polly, then returned to the cottage, where he found everyone ready for another day in Cornwall's balmy sea air.

He imparted the news of a second go at golf.

'Hello,' said Sammy, 'something's cooking.'

'Something is,' said Susie.

'So it should be,' said Polly.

'Crikey,' said Phoebe, 'is she getting keen on you, Jimmy?'

'I can truthfully say I'm doubtful,' said Jimmy.

'Ah,' said Sammy.

'Ah, well,' said Boots.

'Ah, my eye,' said Jimmy.

Large Lump was in another difficult position in trying to explain one more failure to Mr Ford. The Fat Man listened to details, including an assertion that Sparky Dewdrop, very unfortunate, had been copped by a bloke who looked like Scotland Yard in a suit. Large Lump also asserted that it all pointed very suspicious, like, at an interfering informer, as he'd mentioned before.

'I tell yer, guv, the plain clothes cops was waiting for us,' he said. 'Large as life. And seeing I couldn't do nothing for poor old Sparky, I scarpered double quick.'

'You half-baked rissole, you're giving me a pain in my posterior,' said Fat Man, and looked at his gold pocket watch. 'It's gone eleven. Why didn't you report at nine?'

'Have a heart, guv, I didn't get home till four in the morning,' said Large Lump. 'I ain't never felt more worn out. So I flopped, didn't I? I only woke up half an hour ago.'

'Listen, are you telling me the cops have got Sparky Dewdrop for definite?' asked Fat Man.

'I'm telling yer it's a fact, guv,' said Large Lump.

'Because you saw some geezer in a suit?'

'Well, it was dark and the light was behind him,' said Large Lump, 'but I could make out he was wearing a suit, and he hollered at me to stay where I was so he could finger me collar.'

'He said exactly that, did he?'

'Not exactly, guv, but sort of good as. Yus, "Stay where you are." That's what he said. Hollered it at me.'

'And you didn't think it might have been Tommy Adams, Sammy's 'orrible brother?'

'Eh?' Large Lump looked vague. He'd been a bit slow on the uptake since he'd been conked by a beer mug in a pub brawl. 'Eh?'

'Tommy Adams, I said, didn't I?' Fat Man's growl sounded like bacon frying.

'Well, it could've been, I suppose,' said Large Lump. His brain worked then. 'Mind, I got to point out that Sparky ain't showed up. So I ask yer, guv, why ain't he?'

At which precise moment, the door opened and the bruiser Rollo appeared.

'Someone to see yer, Mr Ford,' he said.

'Got an appointment, has he?' said Fat Man irritably.

The door was pushed wider open, and Sparky Dewdrop entered at a lurching stagger, having been shoved in. He was followed by Mr Greenberg's sturdy stepsons, Michal and Jacob, who made short work of Rollo's attempt to get in their way.

''Ere, I know you,' said Large Lump, twitching.

'Good morning, gents,' said Michal.

232

'Nice weather we're having, ain't we?' said Jacob.

'Get 'em out of here,' said Fat Man.

Rollo made another attempt to assert himself, this time by trying to eject Michal. Michal, with a flip of his hand, put him on his backside.

'That's assault and battery,' said Fat Man, solidly wedged in his chair. But, recognizing the intruders, he decided not to lift himself to his feet, anyway. 'I'll have the law on the pair of you. And what the hell happened to you?' he asked Sparky.

'Good question, I tell yer,' said Sparky, looking tired out. He sniffed forlornly. 'These geezers—'

'Copped him,' said Jacob.

'With a bag of fire-lighting naughties,' said Michal. 'Would you like to sign a receipt for his delivery? It'll let Mr Tommy Adams know he's now all yours.'

'Drop dead,' said Fat Man.

'There's a message from Mr Tommy Adams,' said Jacob.

'I hate Mr bleedin' Tommy Adams, and his brother Sammy,' wheezed Fat Man out of his purpling face, 'and I ain't listening to any message.'

'You'd better,' said Michal. 'Mister Tommy

says if you don't behave yourself you'll end up stuck on the spire of your Sunday church. He further says he'll get his brother, called Boots, to lift you off and shove you under a tram.'

The Fat Man's purple face swelled and darkened. Many years ago, Boots had threatened to wrap him up in barbed wire and roll him all the way down Brixton Hill.

'You dogs' dinners,' he howled, 'I hate that bleedin' Boots worse than I hate bleedin' Sammy, and I ain't taking messages like that from a pair of fleabags like you two.' He turned his glare on Large Lump and Rollo. 'Get rid of 'em.'

'We'd like to, guv, honest we would,' said Large Lump, 'but we need some back-up on account of that recent ding-dong at–'

'Shut up!' bawled Fat Man.

'I'd like to go home,' said Sparky, 'I'm all wore out.'

'Well, there you are, Mr Ford, the geezer's delivered back to you,' said Michal, 'and you've had the message.'

'Yup, that's all,' said Jacob. 'Good day, gents.'

He and Michal left.

In due course, they reported to Papa Eli at his Camberwell yard.

'My sons,' he said in Hebrew, 'for that I am proud of you, and so will your mama be. Always, since I first knew them, I have had fine and steadfast friendship from Boots, Tommy and Sammy, and their kin. True, in some business deals, Sammy has had the shirt off my back with his percentages not coinciding with mine, but friendship counts for more than a shirt or two, which is good to remember. In helping him and his brothers so well with their little problems, you have pleased me more than if you had sold that piano for twenty pounds, say, it being worth no more than five as it stands. Go home now and sleep, while your mama spends the day baking special cookies for you.'

That evening, a telegram was delivered to Boots in Cornwall, where he and all the others had acquired a handsome holiday tan.

'FAT MAN FOILED STOP ALL TAKEN CARE OF STOP NOW ENJOY YOURSELVES TOMMY.'

'The Fat Man done in the eye? Lovely,' said Susie.

'Better than a picture postcard,' said Polly, who had received one from her parents, presently sunning their ageing selves in the South of France.

'Mind, a telegram's expensive,' said Sammy, 'but the news was worth it, and I daresay Tommy will claim reimbursement out of the petty cash.'

'Will it hurt, I wonder?' said Boots.

'Hurt what?' asked Jimmy.

'The overheads,' said Boots, which created mirth.

'I don't know why everyone's having a fit,' said Sammy, 'overheads ain't funny.'

'But you are, lovey,' said Susie.

'Thank heaven for Sammy,' said Polly.

'And for me and Paula?' said Phoebe.

'Heaven must be thanked for all its angels,' said Polly.

'There, aren't you lucky, Daddy?' said Phoebe who, although knowing she was adopted, was a girl happy with her lot. 'You've got two angels in me and Paula.'

'You bet I'm happy, pet,' said Sammy, 'but I've still got to watch the firm's overheads.'

Chapter Eighteen

Sunday morning.

The Fat Man wasn't at church. Church wasn't his style, nor were sermons. Sermons were all about loving thy neighbour, and he didn't go in for the impossible.

He was thinking about the poncy Adams family.

I ain't finished yet, he told himself. I'll get 'em one way or another. I'll cripple the lot.

Now that's an idea.

Accidents do happen.

I need a clever bloke, one that don't go to church and couldn't care less about his neighbours.

No, I ain't finished yet. On the other hand, I don't want any accidents that point at me. So who's clever enough to arrange clueless accidents? There's got to be someone.

It was a little past two in the afternoon when Jenny, wearing a short blue skirt with a light creamy shirt, addressed her ball on the first tee. Jimmy was wearing trousers because shorts were barred in the clubhouse, and he had hopes of enjoying a pot of tea with Jenny at the end of their round. He watched the graceful movements of her body as she drove off. The ball flew away.

'Good shot,' he said.

'Go to it,' said Jenny, 'and look here, having told me about your lesson with the pro, you'd better follow my drive with a scorcher of your own, or I'll tear you limb from limb.'

'Believe me, Miss Osborne,' said Jimmy, 'I'm against coming off this course in bits and pieces.'

He teed up. He addressed the ball, his nerves frankly taut. He reached high with his club and executed his swing. Smack!

'Great Barnaby Bill,' said Jenny, 'that's a genuine scorcher. Play you for five bob, then.'

'I'll take the bet,' said Jimmy, chest a bit puffed up with pride.

He played a good first hole, including a nifty putt, and claimed a half with Jenny. Jenny said he ought to be giving her a stroke on the long holes, seeing she was only a girl. Jimmy said that only a girl was a dis-informative term. Further, she was experienced, and he wasn't. Jenny, going to the second tee with him, said experienced at what?

'I'm talking about golf,' said Jimmy, 'what are you talking about?'

'I'm vague about that,' said Jenny. 'All right, no strokes, just a straightforward game for five bob.'

She hit another scorching drive. Jimmy followed with a fairly decent one, and then his game fell to pieces. Jenny groaned with anguish, sighed with pity, and delivered some broadsides.

'You're all over the place with your swing, you dummy.'

'I'm all over the place with everything,' said Jimmy.

A little later. 'Stop bending your knees, you wretched man, and stop trying to hit the ball to God's heaven.'

'Be nice to it, you mean?' said Jimmy. 'That little white devil?' He'd topped it and it had travelled a mere three yards.

'Get rhythmic,' said Jenny.

'Rhythmic, right,' said Jimmy. 'Come on, rhythmic, where are you.' He swung. The ball galloped and bumped for about the length of a cricket pitch. 'Rhythmic failed me,' he said.

'Never mind, keep going,' said Jenny. 'You're a trier, anyway.'

He had a horrible time as a trier in a deep bunker, one of the few on the course. What made it horrible was that one attempt was such a clumsy miss that he lost his balance and fell over. Jenny shrieked with laughter.

'You're amused?' said Jimmy, flat on his back in the sand. 'I'm not. I'm livid.'

'I'm not surprised,' said Jenny. 'You've forgotten all the pro taught you.'

'I haven't forgotten it,' said Jimmy, climbing to his feet, 'I've just got human failings.'

'Haven't we all?' said Jenny. 'Never mind, it's great to be out here. It feels like miles and miles from the madding crowd.'

True. The views were vastly panoramic, the sky a clear blue, the sea a hazy blue, the course full of gentle sandhills covered with green, and the shades of green were varied, light or mild or deep. Here and there, other golfers were visible. Jimmy felt that none of them could be as hopeless as he was.

However, he was a little better over the second half of the course, but in the end there was no denying the fact that generally his round had been another disaster.

'I think I'll go in for bowls,' he said on the last green.

'Bowls, why bowls?' asked Jenny, golden-brown.

'It's the game old people play,' said Jimmy, 'and I feel as old as any of 'em. Ninety, in fact.'

'Well, cheer up, you don't look it,' said Jenny.

'I owe you five bob,' said Jimmy, and paid her.

'Fair?' said Jenny.

'Fair,' said Jimmy. 'Can we get a pot of tea and a slice of cake in the clubhouse?'

'You can,' said Jenny, looking at her watch, 'but I have to dash as soon as I've handed in my bag of clubs. Me and my lovely lot are driving to Newquay for dinner this evening, and I need a bath before I put my glad rags on.'

'Dash away, then, I'll hand your bag in for you,' said Jimmy.

'Good-oh, you're a sport,' said Jenny.

'Thanks for the round,' said Jimmy. 'I think I'll look at it as an education and forget what it did to my self-respect.'

'If your self-respect feels wounded and I spot you on the beach tomorrow, I'll find a bandage for it,' said Jenny. 'Bye now, and thanks for handing my clubs in.' She gave him the bag and departed.

'That's it,' said Jimmy to both bags, 'that's my last time on a golf course. I think I'll take up knitting. After all, what am I if not an old woman?'

'Knitting?' said Susie over a quickly prepared supper of cold pork, sauté potatoes and a salad. No-one asked that she and Polly should use up hours of their holiday by spending unlimited time cooking. 'Knitting?'

Jimmy explained.

Sammy said something had got to be done about falling down on a job. Golf isn't a job, said Susie. Sammy said that wasn't the point. The point was that their younger son was making a charlie of himself in the presence of a proud and haughty female girl.

'Proud and haughty?' said Paula, giggling.

Sammy said that was what she would look like to suffering Jimmy, so what could be done about it? Jimmy said if anybody tried to do anything, he'd jump on them.

'What would you do, Boots?' asked Sammy.

'What would I do if I were in Jimmy's shoes?' said Boots. 'Nothing.'

'Nothing?' said Sammy.

'Jimmy's himself,' said Boots, 'he'll stand or fall by that.'

'Quite right, old sport,' said Polly, 'Jimmy doesn't need to mount a white horse and slay dragons to impress the young lady.'

'Right, Aunt Polly, I'm standing or falling,' said Jimmy. He let a grin escape. 'Mind, I think I've already fallen. Flat on my bottom in a bunker.'

'Help, that's serious,' said Susie.

'Crikey,' said Paula, 'what a palaver over a girl.'

'But we're girls,' said Phoebe. She was prepared, even at only twelve, to defend what she knew her dad would call the valuability of girls.

'Yes, but we're not soppy,' said Paula, 'and Jimmy's girl must be soppy if she's–' She thought. 'Yes, if she's playing hard to get.'

'Who said that?' asked Boots.

'Me,' responded Paula.

'Where'd you get it from?' asked Boots.

'From a play on the radio,' said Paula.

'What's everyone talking about?' whispered Gemma to James.

'Don't ask me,' said James, 'it's not about sandcastles.'

Simply, of course, the families being what they were, close-knit, Jimmy's problem with his golf and the photogenic young lady was everyone's, even Polly's. Polly, the one-time giddy flapper and Bright Young Thing, had metamorphosed into a complete Adams.

As far as Jimmy was concerned, the collective interest was irrelevant, but he bore it good-naturedly, even though his personal interest in stunning Jenny Osborne was no light thing. Blow me over, he thought, I think I'm hooked, and I didn't get that from any radio play.

Monday morning.

Paul, back from his week's holiday, arrived at his little office in the Labour Party's Walworth headquarters at the same time as Miss Lulu Saunders. She was wearing a brown beret, and with her curtains of hair and her glasses she looked not unlike Greta Garbo, the Swedish film star who wanted to be alone, except that Garbo was fair and her glasses were dark.

Lulu, her long dress a muddy brown, said, 'Hello, there we are, then. Had a good holiday?'

'Very good,' said Paul, brown-faced. 'Look here, Saunders, didn't I tell you to get your hair styled and make this place look pretty?'

'And didn't I tell you to grow a moustache?' said Lulu. 'You haven't. Wouldn't or couldn't, I suppose. Anyway, don't be personal about my hair. Or bossy.'

'Put some curlers in it every night for a week,' said Paul. 'Now, any crises?'

'Plenty,' said Lulu. 'All taken care of. Like one lippy bloke who came in binding about your leaflets. Pack of lies, he said. Asked who wrote them. The secretary, I said. So he wanted to know where you were. So that he could tread on you and dump you in a dustcart. Couldn't find you, so he started on me. I conked him a oner. He left with a split lip.'

'What was he?' asked Paul. 'A Young Conservative?'

'No, a drunk,' said Lulu. 'I hope you don't drink.'

'I'd get dehydrated if I didn't,' said Paul, opening the mail. 'You can die of that.'

'I don't include tea or water,' said Lulu.

'Kind of you,' said Paul. 'Any more cases like the drunk?'

'Loud cases,' said Lulu. 'Such as what the hell are the Young Socialists doing that's useful. Things like that. I coped.'

'How?' asked Paul.

'Calmed them down,' said Lulu. 'My

soothing touch is well known.'

'Who to?'

'Me and the beneficiaries,' said Lulu. 'All last week's letters have been answered. You've come back to a tidy desk.'

'My gratitude is enormous,' said Paul, reading a letter.

'Think nothing of it,' said Lulu. 'Told you I was brilliant. I've been jotting down ideas for the next leaflet. And suggestions. I think they're an improvement.'

'On whose?' asked Paul.

'Yours,' said Lulu.

Paul took that like a bloke who knew there were times when the last word belonged to one's opponent, or the crosstalk would go on for ever. So he gave Lulu best and changed tack.

'By the way, include some punchy slogans in your notes for the next leaflet. Winston Churchill's roaring like a lion again on behalf of the Tory opposition. He can see next year's election as a chance to be Prime Minister again.'

'Holy ghosts,' said Lulu, 'what a disaster. He'll bomb the Iron Curtain and start a nuclear war.'

'I don't think my grandmother will let him do that.'

'Your grandmother?' said Lulu, taking her jottings out of her desk drawer. 'I'd like to believe that.'

'You can,' said Paul. 'Now, about a simple slogan? I quote. "Keep the Tories out." Make it repetitive, and in bold caps, to be slipped in at regular intervals. I'll look over your ideas and suggestions sometime this week.'

'Hardly necessary,' said Lulu, and began to pore over her jottings, while Paul went through the mail and made marginal notes where required. He smiled when he opened one letter from an enthusiast and found it contained a five-pound cheque for the group's funds. There was a request for the donation to be used to start an independent fund, that of equipping every Young Socialist with the Red Flag. The signature was that of H.R. Trevalyan, the address The Lodge, Kennington Park Road, Kennington. The handwriting was neat enough to be that of a woman, and the name struck a faint chord in Paul. Now where had he heard it before?

'Lulu,' he said, 'does the name Trevalyan ring a bell for you?'

'No bells,' said Lulu.

'We've got a letter from someone of that

name, wishing us good luck and enclosing a donation of five quid,' said Paul.

'Well, hooray,' said Lulu. 'But you're interrupting my thoughts.'

'The donation is for the purpose of buying Red Flags for our members,' said Paul.

'Waste of money,' said Lulu. 'We can always raid the offices of the *Daily Worker* and snaffle all the Red Flags we want.'

'Borrow,' said Paul.

'No good being squeamish,' said Lulu. 'Can't afford tea-party stuff. Iron hand, that's the thing to turn the country into an efficient Socialist state. Socialist Republic, in fact.'

'And what happens to our revered monarchs?' asked Paul.

'Give 'em a pension and a country cottage in Tooting,' said Lulu.

'Leaving out that Tooting's not in the country,' said Paul, 'you wouldn't suggest saving the cost of a pension and a cottage by guillotining them, would you?'

'We'll get Buckingham Palace and Windsor Castle,' said Lulu. 'Don't want blood as well.'

'Would that be where the iron hand gets squeamish?' asked Paul.

'Is that a sample of your unequalled wit?'

countered Lulu, horn-rimmed spectacles perched on the end of her nose. 'It's pathetic. And you're still interrupting my thoughts.'

My own thoughts, said Paul to himself, make me wonder if her Socialist Republic will arrive in time to do away with all honours and squash the prospect of my grandparents becoming Sir Edwin and Lady Finch.

'Well, Madame Robespierre,' he said, 'you can put your thoughts in your desk after lunch. We're going to see H.R. Trevalyan, the writer of this letter and the sender of this cheque. It's a Kennington address, and I think the writer's a woman. I'd like to meet her, find out who she is and if she's prepared to be a regular donor. We can do with all the funds we can get.'

'Good idea, a person-to-person talk,' said Lulu. 'Very practical. You need me with you?'

'Bring your brilliance along and put it to work on her chequebook,' said Paul. 'And make the coffee in half an hour.'

'Your turn, not mine,' said Lulu. 'I made it every day last week, and the tea as well.'

'For yourself,' said Paul.

'It's still your turn,' said Lulu.

'I take responsibilities, you take orders,' said Paul. 'Or I'll chop your head off.'

'You'll whatter?'

'Use my iron hand,' said Paul. 'I'm not squeamish.'

Lulu tried a sardonic laugh. It spluttered.

And she made the coffee.

Chapter Nineteen

Boots and Polly were in the sea with the twins, staying in safe waters. Susie and Sammy were looking after belongings within the shelter of one of the many little coves of the bay. Paula and Phoebe were splashing about with teenagers, and Jimmy, having had a prolonged swim, was sitting close to the sea, letting his swimming trunks dry in the sun. The tide was out, the sandhills of Doom Bar emerging in the distance.

'Hello.' Jaunty Jenny appeared in one of her RAF shirts, and her white shorts. Both items looked freshly laundered, and the young lady herself looked a charmer, her round white straw hat on the back of her head, the slipped top buttons of her shirt making her very appealing to the eye.

'Top of the morning to you,' said Jimmy.

'Same to you,' said Jenny, and sat down beside him. 'I can't stay long, we're going yachting off Rock again in an hour.' With the tide out, Rock could be reached by trekking over the sand.

'Your father's yacht?' said Jimmy.

'The same,' said Jenny, observing him out of thoughtful eyes. 'You're going to ask questions?'

'Yes, how do your friends like your beach hat?'

'That's a question?' said Jenny, and laughed.

'Is your father's yacht large?'

'It's his pride and joy,' said Jenny, 'but he wasn't born with it in his mouth, like a silver spoon, so to speak. He started out as an office boy with a City firm of stockbrokers at about ten bob a week, but by the time the war began he was the senior partner.'

'He's a smart old dad?' said Jimmy.

Jenny said smart enough, and that as he belonged to a City Territorial unit he saw service during the war, even though he was old when it started. Jimmy asked how old, and Jenny said thirty-nine.

'That's old?' said Jimmy.

Jenny said old enough to give her mother fits about him going off to fight Hitler's gruesome lot, but he came home in the end with medals and the rank of major, so how about that as a self-made success? Jimmy said he liked it, it was a prime example of what initiative could do for a bloke.

'Listen,' said Jenny, 'what's your initiative doing that you're only selling shirts and things?'

'I'm like your dad, I'm starting at the bottom,' said Jimmy.

'At your age?' said Jenny.

'What age is that?' asked Jimmy.

'You're about twenty, aren't you?'

'Yes, about.'

'And you're at the bottom still?'

'Any comments?' said Jimmy.

'Yes, that's ridiculous,' said Jenny.

'Like my golf,' said Jimmy, and Jenny laughed again. 'Where are you staying, by the way?' he asked.

'Oh, Barry and the rest of us rowdy lot are at the St Moritz Hotel, Trebetherick,' she said. 'Well, it saves us having to do our own cooking and make our own beds. My parents and my brother and sister are in a cottage at Rock, so that they can stay close to the yacht. My mother loves sailing as much as my father.'

Jimmy asked if all her friends were working. Jenny said no, they were all at the art college in Kingston. She was there herself, doing fashion designing. That was what she wanted to be, she said, a fashion designer or an assistant to an established one.

'Good luck,' said Jimmy.

'What do you hope to be?' asked Jenny.

'Happy,' said Jimmy.

'Don't we all?' said Jenny.

'D'you play your golf at weekends?'

'There's a club not far from our home in Surrey,' said Jenny. 'I'm a member, my father pays the fees, but women aren't encouraged to use the course on Saturdays or Sundays, except after five o'clock. Stuffy old buffers explode if they spot a skirt before that time. Of course, our fees are on a reduced scale, but that's not the point. The principle's old hat and unfair. You wouldn't explode, would you, if you saw me hitting a ball before five o'clock?'

'I wouldn't be there,' said Jimmy.

'Don't dodge the question,' said Jenny. 'Let's say if you were there.'

'I'd ask for a few useful tips,' said Jimmy. 'I don't believe in stuffy old buffers, and I do believe in the right of skirts to be seen everywhere in moderation.'

'What d'you mean, in moderation?' Jenny seemed tickled.

'Well, perhaps I meant not quite everywhere,' said Jimmy. 'On a golf course, yes, and on a bus or a tram, but not on a football pitch or a rugby field. That wouldn't do, you'd get a broken leg.'

'Idiot,' said Jenny. 'By the way, would you like Fiona's phone number?'

'Fiona?'

'Yes, the one who thinks you're a sweetie.'

'I haven't seen her lately.'

'No, well, Roger's making sure you don't,' said Jenny.

'Good old Roger,' said Jimmy. 'And who's Barry?'

'A close friend with ambition and a high pulse rate,' said Jenny.

'I had a high pulse rate when I was sixteen,' said Jimmy.

'Because of some ravishing young schoolgirl?'

'No, because of tonsillitis,' said Jimmy. 'I didn't know any ravishing schoolgirls. They were all demons, with daggers between their teeth while they lay in wait for simple blokes like me.'

'I'll pass on simple,' said Jenny, 'but I will ask, what were the daggers for?'

'Cutting off our trouser braces,' said Jimmy.

'Kill me some more,' said Jenny.

'Oh, they just liked to see our trousers drop and flop,' said Jimmy.

'You don't think I believe that, do you?' said Jenny.

'I didn't believe it myself when it first happened,' said Jimmy. 'That is, not until I saw my trousers down to my ankles, and a hundred female demons doing a shrieking war dance around me.'

'Jimmy, you're a terrible liar.'

'I'm doing my best,' said Jimmy.

Jenny's friends appeared in the near distance at that moment. They hailed her, and she came to her feet. Jimmy unfolded himself and stood up.

'I'd ask you to join us,' she said, 'but Barry would probably heave you overboard.'

'He's your personal bloke?' said Jimmy.

'I told you, a close friend,' said Jenny. 'Bye, and enjoy your day.'

'You too,' said Jimmy. He stood watching as she joined her group to begin her walk with them to Rock by way of the beach. One of the girls turned and gave him a wave.

Fiona, he supposed, and he returned her friendly gesture.

On they went, a laughing group.

Lovely girl, he thought. Much more natural and forthcoming than when he met her for the first time in the store.

Out on the blue sea white-sailed yachts and dinghies skimmed about. Out of the water and onto the beach came Aunt Polly, Uncle Boots and the growing twins.

Aunt Polly. Over fifty, wasn't she? Who'd know it, who'd even think it? That swimsuit, that figure, that silky walk. She looks as if she's modelling beachwear for a fashion magazine. And what a witty, likeable woman she was. No wonder Uncle Boots turned to her when he lost Aunt Emily, although it did cause uneasy ripples in the family.

Jimmy remembered that when he was twelve, he'd asked his mum with all the gaucherie of an adolescent why Aunt Polly hadn't married a lord instead of Uncle Boots. And his mum had said because Uncle Boots is her kind of man. Well, what's Aunt Polly's kind of man? Uncle Boots, said Susie. Crikey, said Jimmy to that, what a daft answer, it's uninformative. And Susie asked him where he got words like that from. From Uncle Boots, he said. There you are, then, said Susie, Uncle Boots is a man for all people, young, old and in between. And especially for your Aunt Polly.

He understood perfectly now, watching them as they advanced over the shining wet sands, their irrepressible twins skipping ahead. They were talking, and holding hands, Boots and Polly. Holding hands. At their age. I know something, thought Jimmy. They're still lovers.

Up they came, the lovers and their twins.

'Where's your lady fair, Jimmy?' asked Polly.

'Gone to Rock to sail a boat, I hope and trust that boat can float,' said Jimmy.

'Crumbs, was that a poem?' asked Gemma.

'Of a kind,' said Boots, the firm healthy look of his body belying his age. 'An entertaining kind. Jimmy has his share of talent.'

'So has his lady fair,' said Polly. She smiled at Jimmy. 'We spotted you talking to her.'

'Yes, lovely girl,' said Jimmy. 'Come on, kids, I'll help this time with a sandcastle.'

Gemma and James scampered over the beach with him.

'I think Jimmy's acquired a crush,' said Polly.

'I haven't met the young lady, I've only seen her from afar,' said Boots, 'but all the same, I feel I can compliment him on his taste.'

'Isn't that a little patronizing?' said Polly.

'It wasn't meant to be,' said Boots.

'I'm very fond of Jimmy, and all our young people,' said Polly.

'So you should be,' said Boots, 'you're the mother of two of them.'

'I still feel their conception was a miracle,' said Polly, musing on that.

'Aside from the Virgin Mary, miracles do sometimes happen to a special kind of woman,' said Boots.

'I wonder, did my fairy godmother wave her magic wand?' murmured Polly.

'No, I waved mine, in a manner of speaking,' said Boots, 'and hers isn't the same as mine, in any case.'

Holidaymakers turned their heads to look at a slender woman in a white swimsuit emitting peals of laughter.

And Polly wondered exactly how many more exhilarating years she and Boots would share.

Behind them, Paula and Phoebe came running, everyone making for where Susie and Sammy were opening up the usual mid-morning snack of flask coffee and Cornish jam doughnuts.

Still exploring the waters and the hills of the English Lake District, Tommy and Vi's daughter Bess found herself much more compatible with the exuberance of her university friends. She was able to resist making comparisons between their never-failing high, noisy spirits and the mature nuances of the American man, Jeremy Passmore. He lingered in her mind, which gave her moments of quietness.

'Penny for 'em, Bess.'

That request came to her ears more than once, when one friend or another noted her absorption in her own thoughts.

'Oh, they're nothing earth-shaking.'

But they were thoughts of a kind she hadn't had before, simply because they concerned a man who made her com-panions seem just a little adolescent. Would he really get in touch with her? Or would he merely drop her a line to say he had finally gone home to Chicago? She really could not imagine he would stay on indefinitely in the UK, when America was booming and the UK, still broke, was in the doldrums.

Bess was always honest with herself, just

as Tommy, her father was. She frankly hoped she would see Jeremy again.

Jeremy, at the moment, was back working as the efficient manager of a large dairy farm that also had acres of land devoted to the cultivation of fruit and vegetables. Kent, after all, as he had found out, was the garden of England.

Chapter Twenty

Earlier that day, on the broad, tram-lined thoroughfare of Kennington Park Road, Paul and Lulu found The Lodge, an old three-storeyed Victorian house standing by itself. Paul knocked. The door was opened by a little old lady in a white lace cap, a white blouse with a starched lace collar, and a black skirt. Her eyes were bright, although surrounded by crow's feet, her cheeks as round and rosy as apples.

'Good morning, madam,' said Paul.

'Good morning, young man,' she said.

'Would you be Mrs Trevalyan?' asked Paul.

'Would be?' She twinkled. 'I am.'

'I've had a letter from you, I'm–'

'Well, come in, come in,' she said, 'don't stand on the doorstep, there's a draught. Bring the young lady in with you.'

'Thanks,' said Paul.

He and Lulu stepped into the hall, Mrs Trevalyan closed the door and ushered them into her living room. The windows overlooked the main road and its moving pictures of trams, buses and pedestrians. The room itself was full of old-fashioned mahogany furniture, the upholstery of dark brown leather stuffed with horsehair. Pot plants sprouted African violets. The several pictures decorating the walls were all oil-painted portraits of women with either Victorian or Edwardian hairstyles.

'Sit down, sit down,' twinkled Mrs Trevalyan, and Lulu seated herself on a sofa. Paul joined her, glancing at the portraits as he sat down. The little old lady perched herself on the edge of an armchair. 'Now,' she said, 'why have you called, mmm? Mmm?'

'I'm Paul Adams, secretary of the South London Young Socialists, and this is my assistant, Miss Lulu Saunders. We received a letter from you, Mrs Trevalyan, a very nice letter–'

'What? What? Mmm?'

'A letter.' Paul kept looking at one of the portraits.

'What letter?' Mrs Trevalyan was briskly enquiring.

'Wishing good luck to our organization and its aims, and enclosing a very welcome cheque towards our funds,' said Paul.

'Eh? Eh?'

'We're grateful for your generosity,' said Lulu.

'Cheque, you said, young man?' Mrs Trevalyan's bright eyes sharpened. 'Show me the letter.'

Paul extracted it from his inside jacket pocket. Mrs Trevalyan twinkled quickly to her feet, took it from him, opened it up and scanned it.

'Something wrong, Mrs Trevalyan?' said Lulu, on her best behaviour.

'What? Mmm? Yes.'

'There is something wrong?' said Paul.

'I didn't write this letter, but I know who did,' said Mrs Trevalyan. 'Let me see the cheque.'

'Here it is.' Paul handed it to her. She scanned that too with a sharp eye. She murmured something.

'I didn't catch that,' said Lulu.

'Hussy,' said Mrs Trevalyan.

'Pardon?' said Lulu.

'Not you. My granddaughter.' Mrs Trevalyan crossed in quick, sprightly fashion to the door, opened it and called. 'Henrietta!' The name travelled upwards like the shrill cry of a seabird. There was no response. 'Henrietta!' This time there was a response.

'You want me, Granny?'

'Come down here this minute.'

'Yes, Granny. Coming.'

Down she came, the granddaughter.

'In here, you hussy,' said Mrs Trevalyan, and a very pleasant-looking young lady, a brown-eyed brunette, entered the room. In a light summer dress of pale lemon, her demeanour and expression were so demure that hussy was written all over her.

Seeing Lulu and Paul, she said, 'Oh, hello, you're new.'

Paul came to his feet.

'Henrietta,' said Mrs Trevalyan, 'this is – oh, bother it, I've forgotten your names. Never mind, this is my granddaughter Henrietta.'

Paul offered a smile.

'I'm Paul Adams, and this young lady is Miss Saunders. We're from the Young Socialists–'

'Oh, how thrilling,' said Henrietta in a

little burst of delight. 'How do you do? I'm a heart and soul Socialist.' She took Paul's hand, squeezed it and looked into his eyes. Yuk, she's syrupy, thought Lulu. 'Lovely to meet you, I adore campaigners for the cause of the workers.'

'Poppycock,' said Mrs Trevalyan. 'Now, you hussy, what's the meaning of this?' She brandished the letter. 'And this?' She held the cheque under Henrietta's eyes.

'Oh, so sorry, Granny,' said Henrietta, 'I forgot to mention it to you.'

'You forgot to mention you'd forged my name?' said Mrs Trevalyan. 'A likely story.'

'Well, Granny dear, you weren't at home at the time—'

'Poppycock, you hear?'

'Ever so, ever so sorry,' said Henrietta, and glanced at Paul and offered a winsome smile. 'I'm absent-minded sometimes, you know.'

'Absent-minded, my glass eye,' said Mrs Trevalyan. She uttered a little chuckle. 'That's if I had a glass eye. Which reminds me, dear old Percy Beresford had one. The poor man lost his good one in a tussle with a truncheon when he was trying to shield Emmeline from a police charge in Downing Street.'

'Emmeline?' said Paul, and looked at the particular portrait yet again. 'Got it,' he said, 'that's Mrs Pankhurst, Mrs Emmeline Pankhurst.'

'The great pioneer of the suffragette movement?' said Lulu.

'Oh, its leader and its champion,' said Henrietta. 'You know something about her?' She put the question to Paul.

'I know she's part of the historical annals of the Labour Party,' said Paul.

'Rubbish,' said Mrs Trevalyan. 'There was no such thing as a decent Labour Party in her day. If you try to claim her, I'll take my umbrella to you. Where is it, Henrietta?'

'In the hallstand receptacle, Granny dear,' said Henrietta.

'Besides,' said Granny dear, 'Emmeline couldn't stand the Labour fellows bleating about the lot of the working classes. Let me tell you, young man, it was their women's lot that needed looking at. Yes, my word, it did and still does, for the working classes still keep their wives chained to their kitchen sinks. Disgraceful.'

'Well, really,' said Lulu, prickling. 'Don't you know why? Other classes employ servants. The working classes can't afford to. And probably wouldn't, anyway. Like me, they don't believe in menials.'

'Piffle,' said Mrs Trevalyan. Then, 'Henrietta, who is this young woman?'

'I've really no idea,' said Henrietta.

'Miss Saunders is my assistant,' said Paul, 'I'm the secretary of the South London Young Socialists.'

'Are you really?' Henrietta's eyes glowed. 'I'm thrilled to meet you. I'm devoted to Socialism.'

'A likely story,' said Mrs Trevalyan. 'It's just one more of your fanciful fads. I won't have it, you hear me, miss?'

'Granny, it's not a fad to believe in the benefits of Socialism,' said Henrietta sweetly.

'Total Socialism?' said Paul, and Henrietta gave him a winning smile.

'Yes, of course,' she said.

'You share that belief with Lulu,' said Paul.

'Lulu?' said Mrs Trevalyan. 'Never heard of her. Who is she, a belly dancer? Disgraceful, and a reprehensible slur on womanhood.'

'I'm Lulu,' said Miss Saunders.

'A belly dancer?' Mrs Trevalyan quivered. 'You need correction, my girl. Henrietta, fetch my umbrella.'

'Miss Saunders is a visitor, a guest, Granny,' said Henrietta.

'Rubbish,' said her grandmother. 'You know very well I'd never invite a belly dancer to tea. Are we having tea?'

'Of course, in a while,' said Henrietta. 'Do sit down, Paul, and my grandmother will be delighted to talk to you about her idol, Mrs Pankhurst, and the suffragettes. You sit down too, Granny.'

Paul and Lulu were virtually locked in. Paul minded not at all. Lulu had the fidgets. Henrietta, looking sweetly happy with events, seated herself on the other side of Paul, her dress coyly hitched.

Mrs Trevalyan treated her audience to tales of her time as a suffragette and as one of Mrs Pankhurst's umbrella-wielding bodyguards. It was dear Emmeline who put women on the march towards equality and the vote, she said, but my, what battles they had to fight, and what suffering they had to endure each time they were arrested and sentenced by whiskery old reactionary magistrates to a term in prison. When they went on hunger strike, odious police doctors force-fed them, scarring their human dignity. As for the politicians, they were all devious men, of course, promising much but doing little. She interrupted herself to ask Paul if he was devious in his politics.

'You wouldn't expect me to say yes, would you?' said Paul.

'That, young man, is a devious reply,' said Mrs Trevalyan.

'You bet it is,' said Lulu under her breath.

'Oh, we must give him the benefit of the doubt, Granny,' said Henrietta.

'Mmm? What?' said the little old lady, looking as bright as a button. 'Well, he's a fine-looking young man, of course, but looks can be deceptive.'

'Have a banana,' said Lulu, also under her breath.

'It's a pleasure to have him visit,' said Henrietta.

'Yerk,' muttered Lulu.

'What's this belly dancer saying, Henrietta?' asked Mrs Trevalyan.

'I really don't know,' said Henrietta, lightly hip-to-hip with the fine-looking young man.

I'm going to be sick, thought Lulu, but sat bravely through more anecdotal reminiscences relating to hair-raising episodes in the doughty suffragettes' campaign to secure votes for women.

'Granny loves reliving the years when the

suffragettes were at war with politicians,' said Henrietta.

'These portraits,' said Paul, 'are they all of suffragettes?'

'Yes, and aren't they splendid?' said Mrs Trevalyan. 'My late husband painted them. Of course, when war broke out against Germany in 1914, dear Emmeline immediately called a halt to our campaign and instructed us to support the Government unreservedly, on the grounds that of all men the Prussians were the chief enemies of women's emancipation.' She stopped to wrinkle her brow. 'Half a mo',' she said, 'wasn't there something about a cheque?'

'Oh, we're past all that, Granny,' said Henrietta.

'No, we're not,' said Granny. 'You hussy, you forged my name. You and your hare-brained enthusiasms will ruin me. What was the last one, mmm? I know, a home for tramps, and that cost me a year's interest on some of my investments. You saucy girl, fetch my umbrella.'

'If I fetched your chequebook instead, perhaps you'd sign one yourself for our Young Socialists,' said Henrietta. 'We can't let Paul go away with nothing, Granny dear.'

'Paul?' said Granny dear. 'Is he hare-brained too? Are you?' The question arrived sharply in Paul's ear.

'I can truthfully say no,' he replied, and Henrietta smiled at him and crossed her knees. 'In fact, it would cause me pain if I had to say yes.'

Poor bloke, he's mesmerized by that girl's tarty legs, thought Lulu.

But she said, 'We do need funds. To help the Labour Party win the next election. And to keep Churchill and the Tories out.'

'Churchill? Winston Churchill?' said Mrs Trevalyan. 'Goodness gracious me, what do belly dancers know about Churchill? Of course, he could be as devious as Asquith and Lloyd George regarding votes for women, but when the world needed the right kind of leader to fight Hitler, he proved to be a lion. Keep him out? I won't have it.'

'Come on, Granny dear, be a darling,' said Henrietta. 'We can tear the other cheque up.'

'I've a good mind to disown you,' said Granny dear, but a little chuckle made its mark, and she looked at Paul. 'You must forgive Henrietta, young man. She lost her parents years ago, and has lived with me ever since. Alas that I failed to cure her addiction to fanciful ideas. My, my, young people today, so wild. How much money is it that you need?'

'How kind,' said Lulu. 'Would you be offended if we say as much as you can spare?'

'It's not to be spent on anything to do with the Labour Party,' said the dear lady.

'Just the young people who want to see good government,' said Paul.

'Splendid,' said Henrietta.

'Can I afford ten pounds, Henrietta?' asked Mrs Trevalyan.

'Easily,' said Henrietta.

'Where's the tea? I thought we were having tea.'

'I'll get Annie to bring in the tray,' said Henrietta.

'With the carrot cake.'

Paul and Lulu spent more time there, Mrs Trevalyan chatting away over tea and cake, Henrietta bringing her back to the present whenever she wandered too deeply into the past, and addressing Paul winsomely from time to time. She was seated in an armchair opposite him at that stage, and Paul, who had a young man's natural appreciation of what his Uncle Sammy referred to as a female girl, which meant feminine, wasn't unresponsive.

Sick-making, thought Lulu.

When she and Paul finally left, Paul had a cheque for ten pounds, made out to him personally, and an invitation to call again.

'You can give the money to Mr Churchill, if you like,' said Mrs Trevalyan, twinkling a smile.

'I'll use it to the best advantage, you can be sure,' said Paul. 'Goodbye.'

'Mmm? Oh, yes, goodbye, young man. And goodbye, young lady.'

'Happy to have met you,' said Lulu.

'Do give up belly dancing,' said Mrs Trevalyan, 'it's demeaning. And don't forget who won the vote for you.'

'Goodbye,' smiled Henrietta, fluttering lashes at Paul.

On their way back to the Walworth Road, Lulu said, 'I'm sick.'

'Too much carrot cake?' said Paul, striding manfully.

'Not that kind of sick,' said Lulu, long dress whipping and rustling as she kept pace with him. 'Yerk, that sugary Henrietta. All over you. And you grinning at her. Like a besotted monkey.'

'Still, the fund's richer by ten quid,' said Paul.

'You prostituted yourself,' said Lulu.

'Good as.'

'You showed a lot of brilliance,' said Paul.

'Could you believe that old girl? Me a belly dancer?'

'I'll believe it when I see it,' said Paul. 'How about during lunchtime in the office tomorrow?'

'Do what?'

'Have you got the right kind of costume?' asked Paul.

'How would you like a hole in your head?'

'Not much,' said Paul. 'Look, I'm only telling you I've never seen a belly dancer perform.'

'Oh, really?' said Lulu. 'Bloody hard luck, mate.'

'Tuppence in the swear box when we get back,' said Paul.

'Ha ha,' said Lulu. 'By the way, why doesn't your dad contribute to the funds?'

'My dad is dead against Socialism. He's a confirmed capitalist.'

'God, imagine having a capitalist father,' said Lulu, daughter of a doughty if somewhat dogmatic Socialist MP. 'Imagine having to live with the fact.'

'Fortunately,' said Paul, 'my dad's a good old dad, if a bit old-fashioned.'

'Old-fashioned means standing still,' said

Lulu. 'Wait till we get a Socialist Republic. That'll wake him up.'

'I don't think you're in a very good mood,' said Paul.

'No wonder,' said Lulu. 'Would you like to be called a belly dancer? By a crazy old has-been?'

'Not the thing for a bloke,' said Paul. 'Our bellies aren't as picturesque as yours. But I don't see Mrs Trevalyan as a crazy old has-been.'

'All right, so she gave us ten quid,' said Lulu. 'Are you going to butter her up for more?'

'No,' said Paul, striding down Penton Place and noting the run-down look of the terraced houses. Everything in the country needed a facelift, and Prime Minister Attlee needed millions of extra oof from the already burdened taxpayers. 'No, I'm not.'

'Why not?' asked Lulu, her ankle-length dress an inconvenient handicap around her fast-moving legs. 'Yes, why not?'

'Because she's a sweet old girl who's not in favour of our aims,' said Paul. 'The ten quid's enough. If I call again, it'll just be to say hello to her.'

'To say hello to Henrietta and her tarty dress, you mean,' said Lulu.

'Should we be unkind about a girl who's just helped to swell our funds?' asked Paul.

'She was nearly on your lap, you weakling,' said Lulu.

'No sauce, Saunders,' said Paul, 'and no Socialist Republic, either. It sounds Marxist to me.'

'True Socialism does have a Marxist flavour,' said Lulu.

'Don't tell our voters that, or they'll bring Churchill and his Conservatives back,' said Paul.

'I'll plant bombs if that comes about,' said Lulu.

'Guy Fawkes tried that, and you know what happened to him,' said Paul. 'Cheer up, Lulu, we've enjoyed an entertaining afternoon.'

'Leave me out,' said Lulu. 'And listen. You're walking my legs off.'

'I'm not to know that, am I?' said Paul. 'I can't see 'em.'

'Bloody hard luck again,' said Lulu.

'That's another tuppence in the swear box,' said Paul.

Lulu stopped. Outside the open front door of a house she uttered a tight little scream. At once, a woman hurried out.

'Here, what's that young man doing to yer,

275

love?' she asked.

'Killing me,' said Lulu.

'Oh, gawd help us, what's he killing you with?'

'A phantom umbrella,' said Lulu.

Paul laughed and resumed walking. Lulu, hitching her dress, dashed after him.

'Come on, don't hang about,' he said, 'there are still some letters to type.'

'I'm resigning,' said Lulu.

But she didn't.

Chapter Twenty-One

The foxes turned up again that night, but not with their cubs. The young ones had been driven off to find their own territory. And the fat lambs had gone. The dog fox and its vixen prowled around the high wire fence enclosing the chicken run and the roosting houses. Red tongues dripped saliva as the smell of plump hens reached their sensitive noses.

They moved close to begin digging a tunnel, their teeth primed to bite off the head of every chicken. In their movement they crossed the line of an electric eye fashioned by Matthew with the help of Jonathan, and on came the glaring flood-lights. At the same time a howl like that of an Irish banshee shattered the silence. That device was the exclusive brainchild of Matthew, an electrical wizard.

The foxes fled.

The howl lasted only five seconds. But it brought Matthew and Rosie awake.

'They're out there, those foxes,' said Rosie.

'Not now,' said Matthew. 'Right now, I'll wager they're still running.'

'Are you going down to take a look?' asked Rosie, too cosy to want to get out of bed with him.

'I don't fancy showing a lack of confidence in that contraption of mine,' said Matthew. 'So I'm staying here, but since we're awake, how about a cuddle?'

'Nice of you to ask,' murmured Rosie. 'Yes, very nice, old boy.'

'Don't mention it,' said her old boy, not noted, however, for failing sinews.

That same night, the hideous dream of the revolting Belsen concentration camp fashioned its nightmare once more for Boots. It fashioned the skeletal inmates, the naked carcases of the dead ones, and the starkly emaciated faces of the dying. It brought into being the black hollows that were the suffering eyes of starving Jews, and it pictured the ugly images of brutalizing SS guards.

At its most virulent stage, with the cold eyes of Himmler's murderous camp officers boring into his very soul, the nightmare woke Boots. He lay there beside Polly, silently swearing at that which he knew was afflicting many American and British soldiers, disgusting dreams of all they had encountered when the Allies were over-running the western regions of Germany.

The Nuremberg trials had resulted in the execution of Germany's major war criminals, but had encompassed relatively few of Himmler's depraved SS men. And women too. Women. Could any ideology be worse than that which had turned even women into sadists?

Women.

Something was at the back of his mind, something he instinctively felt he needed to know. It might have transmitted its message if it had been capable of penetrating the cloud that fogged his head, a cloud thick with the horrendous greyness of Belsen. His mind made its effort, but failed and turned to Germany.

Germany. The country that had been ravaged by war and the forces of retribution was slowly recovering from overwhelming defeat. The Four Powers, America, Britain, France and Russia, occupied Berlin. The Russian sector, an uninspiring area, was jealously guarded by Stalin's Communists. Last year Soviet Russia's leader had attempted to blockade the city, prompting immediate action by America and Britain in the form of an air lift that dropped regular supplies of food to the starving Berliners. In the end, it forced dictator Stalin to lift the blockade.

The German people had paid the price for accepting a dictator of their own, a dangerous and despotic fanatic. Except for a few courageous men and women, none had lifted a finger to save the Jews.

Men and women. Ours and theirs, thought Boots. Thank God for ours, and thank Him for all those I call my own, from Chinese Lady and Edwin Finch down to the youngest, Emma and Jonathan's infant daughter.

For Emily who had gone.

For the twins.

And for Polly, their living and breathing mother.

He smiled at himself for his indulgence of sentiment, but it had calmed him, and he turned over and went back to sleep.

Wednesday morning.

'Hello, Jimmy!' Jenny, passing along the edge of the tide with her friends, called her greeting.

Jimmy, in the water with his sisters, raised his voice in response.

'Top of the morning to you!'

Jenny waved and went on with the group. Fiona turned her head.

'Enjoy your day, Jimmy!'

'Ta muchly,' called Jimmy.

He heard Jenny laugh, and he heard them all singing as they went on their way to climb Brea Hill.

'Crikey, those girls, Jimmy, they're teasing you,' said Phoebe.

'I'll work out some way of having my own back,' said Jimmy, thinking it didn't make for holiday rapture when a stunning girl was so wrapped up in the activities of her group that she hardly knew he was alive. Well, it amounted to that, which didn't do a lot for his male ego.

What about carrying her off to Land's End? There were some wild views of the heaving Atlantic from Land's End, and some spectacular cliff walks. No, she'd push him over the edge for abducting her.

'Blow that,' he said.

'Blow what?' said Paula, splashing close.

'My pathetic brainbox.'

'Dad's got a brainbox,' said Paula, 'but you couldn't call it pathetic.'

'Mine needs a doctor,' said Jimmy.

'Why?' asked Phoebe.

'It's falling apart,' said Jimmy. 'Come on, race you and Paula over a hundred-yard sprint. Give you both ten yards start. Loser's a wally.'

'Crikey,' said Phoebe, when the race in the sea had been won and lost, 'fancy Jimmy being the wally.'

'It's made my day,' said Jimmy.

On top of Brea Hill a little later, a number of young people were celebrating their victorious climb. The triumph of one of the girls was clearly evident. She was waving her white straw hat.

'You can't see him from here, can you?'

said Fiona, a giddy blonde.

'Can't see who?' said Jenny.

'The sweetie,' said Fiona.

Barry, a close friend to Jenny, with ambitions of becoming a lot closer, poked his nose in.

'Who's a sweetie?' he asked.

'Me, of course,' said Fiona.

'And who's my Jenny waving to with her hat, I wonder?' asked Barry.

'My audience down below,' said his close friend, 'and I'm not your Jenny.'

'I'm giving it time,' said Barry, working at the task of acquiring a winning personality.

They stood there, all of them, bronzed by the sun, surveying the expansive, colourful view with the clear unclouded eyes of young gods and goddesses poised on the highest slope of Olympus.

The place in the inner haunts of Soho was smoky and fuggy, of course. It deigned to call itself the Smokers Club, and had a licence for booze. It was fairly full this evening with members and their friends. Most members looked like shifty geezers, and most of their friends looked like furtive hangers-on. All seemed to prefer fug to the twinkling lights of the West End, where the post-war resuscitation of cinema, theatre and pub life was encouraging the nightly arrival of swarming revellers. The Windmill Theatre, famous for never having closed all through the war, was staging its revues of scantily clad or totally unclad girls and stand-up comedians. The stand-up comedians had a hard time. 'Get off, Charlie! Bring on the crumpet!'

In the Smokers Club, the Fat Man was sitting at a corner table, and making the table top look about the size of a saucer. In case anyone thought of lifting his wallet, or thumping him with a sandbag to get the shirt off his back, so to speak, he had Large Lump sitting with him. And outside were Rollo and the two other bodyguards. An honest man couldn't be too careful in this part of Soho. Nor could the Fat Man.

'He's here, y'know, guv,' whispered Large Lump, whose slightly punctured backside was feeling better.

'I do know,' gurgled Fat Man.

'Well, ain't yer going over to talk to him?'

'No, I bloody well ain't. I'm the mountain, and the mountain don't go to Mahomet.'

'That ain't his business name, guv. He's the Parson.'

'Don't keep telling me what I already

know,' said Fat Man. 'Drink your cocoa.'

Large Lump swallowed a couple of mouthfuls of dark beer. Fat Man sipped a Scotch, his eyes, peering through podgy framework, fixed on a man in the opposite corner, a thin man, with a black bowler tipped on the back of his black-haired head, and eyes like black diamonds. He had a slim cigar between his lips, and was playing dominoes with a bulky geezer as hairy as a gorilla. It looked a lot, all that fur, but was sometimes useful in camouflaging a guilty look. On the other hand, it was inconveniently in the way whenever he was trying to let innocence shine through.

The thin man ignored the glances from across the way. He chewed on his cigar, let the smoke curl upwards to join what was already hanging close to the yellowed ceiling, and concentrated on his dominoes.

'He ain't in no partic'lar hurry,' growled Large Lump.

'Nor am I,' said Fat Man, his over-burdened chair creaking a bit. 'That is, as far as he's concerned.'

'Still, I'm starting to feel sorry I recommended him,' said Large Lump. 'It ain't too polite, taking no notice of you.'

'Don't fidget, drink your cocoa,' said Fat

Man, afflicted by oncoming perspiration in the stuffy heat of the place. Its atmosphere was one of dubious deals being done. No-one was sitting with a straight back. Heads and shoulders were bent, and the smoke of black market cigarettes formed drifting clouds around them. A shifty geezer suddenly became argumentative with a furtive hanger-on, and clouted him. At once, the bouncer appeared, a Hercules. He didn't stop the fight. He waited until they were both at each other's throats on the floor, and blood was visible. He then dragged them up, and carried them out, one under each arm. No-one present took a great deal of notice. There was too much going on in the way of whispered business.

The dominoes game ended. The thin man got up and crossed the floor. He sat down at the Fat Man's table.

'You're Mr Ford?' he said. He spoke without, apparently, moving his lips. It kept what was left of the cigar in place.

'Right.'

'I'm the Parson.'

'So I believe.' Fat Man studied his prospective helper. 'You officiate at funerals.'

'Indirectly.'

'I'm not looking for a funeral.'

'You'll get one eventually. We all will.'

'I'm not looking for my funeral, or anyone else's,' said Fat Man. 'Just an injurious job on a certain party.'

'Ah.' The Parson's coal-black eyes glinted. 'How injurious?'

'Crippling.'

'That's pretty injurious.'

'You can do it?' said Fat Man.

'It'll be a come-down.' The words were still arriving without any real movement of the lips. 'Usually I do fatally injurious.'

'Forget that. It ain't my line. I want a hospital case, not a mortuary stiff.'

'I get you. Hospital case. Artificial leg, say?'

'That I like the sound of,' said Fat Man.

'Me too,' said Large Lump.

'Running the certain party down with a car could do it,' said the Parson. 'But you can't always guarantee the right result. Your certain party might end up a funeral case, after all.'

'Mr Ford said he don't want that,' interjected Large Lump.

'I heard him,' said the Parson.

'I'll take your orders, gents.' A bloke from the bar materialized, with a tray.

'Shove off, Willy,' said the Parson, 'we're busy discussing imports.'

Willy dematerialized into the fog.

'Well?' said Fat Man, now sweaty.

'We can do business,' said the Parson, shifting his bowler about. 'You give me name and details, and I'll work out the method.'

'There's three certain parties, three brothers,' said Fat Man. 'Any one of them will do.'

'I like options,' said the Parson. 'Concerning which, an arm would do instead of a leg?'

'Either,' said Fat Man, and the rest of the discussion was conducted in whispers. It ended with the Fat Man slipping a piece of paper to the Parson. The writing on it, however, wasn't his own. He avoided carelessness.

'Just let me know when it's done,' he said.

'There's the fee, of course,' said the Parson. 'And the advance. In oners.'

'Fifty,' said Fat Man.

'That's the advance? Good, you've got a deal.'

'Don't push me,' said Fat Man. 'Fifty's the fee, a pony's the advance.'

'Now you haven't got a deal,' said the Parson, and finally removed his cigar, a mere butt, and squashed it in the ashtray. Still without moving his lips, he said, 'And I'm off to the pictures to see Grace Moore in *One Night of Love*. I like a nice romantic story.'

'Hold on,' said Fat Man.

'Did I hear a hundred?' said the Parson.

'No, you bleedin' didn't, not from me,' said Fat Man.

'Pity.' The Parson began to rise.

'All right, a hundred.'

'Fair enough. Pass the advance. In oners.'

That done and the deal settled, the Parson disappeared.

'You can't stop some of 'em being greedy, guv,' said Large Lump.

'Finish your cocoa and let's get out of here,' said Fat Man. 'I'm bloody cooking.'

'I've finished it, guv,' said Large Lump. 'You offering me another pint?'

'Not here. Get up and help me out of this chair. It's stuck to my backside.'

Chapter Twenty-Two

The two families took the ferry from Rock to Padstow on Thursday morning. They had a mere two days left of the holiday, and it was the accepted thing to buy little gifts for their kin. Padstow was the place. Padstow was still quaint and unspoiled, its few gift shops offering Cornish pottery and little items made of the mineral serpentine, indigenous to the county.

The twins and the girls, of course, had been promised ice-cream cornets. The ferry carried them all across the estuary, and they landed at the harbour. There they saw the fishing boats, the boats that had sometimes sneaked out during the war to brave the German menace that had cut down fishing all over the seas of Europe.

The families wandered around the harbour walls, watched fishermen repairing nets, and Boots and Polly let the twins know they couldn't go for a ride on any of the boats.

'But I could do fishing,' said James.

'And I could catch shrimps,' said Gemma. And after a moment, 'Not crabs. They've got huge claws.'

'I bet you'd both get all smelly,' said Paula.

'Fishing's not smelly,' said James.

'The boats are,' said Paula. 'They're bound to be.'

James took the bull by the horns and called down to a fisherman.

'Mister? Mister?'

'I be here, young 'un.'

'Your boat's not smelly, is it?'

'Well, I be a tiddly bit that way myself at times,' said the ruddy-faced fisherman, 'but they old boat, she be smelling as sweet as my old lady's roses.'

'There, it's not smelly,' said James to Paula.

'Well, something is,' said Paula, 'there's a fishy smell all over the place.'

'It's not me,' said Phoebe.

'Nor me,' said Gemma. 'Nor Mummy, is it, Daddy?'

'Very unlikely,' said Boots. 'I equate your mother with the roses of the fisherman's wife.'

'It's the harbour,' said Susie, 'the tide's out.'

'That's a relief,' said Sammy, 'everyone was beginning to look at me.'

'Shall we do the shops?' said Polly.

'Let's do the shops,' said Susie.

'Kids,' said Sammy, 'we're going to do the shops.'

'Shops? Oh, hell,' said young James.

'Oh, dear,' said Polly.

'You're not supposed to say things like that,' said Gemma to her brother.

'Where'd you get it from?' asked Paula.

'From Dad,' said James. 'And Mum.'

'Black mark for both of you, Aunt Polly,' said Jimmy.

'We're still going to do the shops,' said Susie.

Half an hour later, they were all dispersed, some in some shops, some in others. Jimmy was looking at a little serpentine brooch, thinking of Aunt Lizzy, who had an old-fashioned liking for brooches.

'Hello.'

He turned. A blonde girl, wearing a thin yellow sweater and saucily brief dark blue shorts, was smiling at him. He recognized her, while noting the sweater did wonders for her bosom.

'You're Fiona,' he said.

'You're Jimmy.'

'First time we've met in a shop.'

'Fantastic,' said Fiona.

'Think so?' said Jimmy. 'What're you doing in Padstow?'

'Looking it over with the girls. The fellers have all gone fishing for mackerel. You can catch any amount in these waters. They've gone with a boatman, just for five bob each.'

'What will they do with what they catch?' asked Jimmy, who'd gone out last year with

Sammy and Boots on just such an excursion.

'Give it to the hotel kitchen, and they'll put mackerel on the menu,' said Fiona, 'but who wants to talk about fish?'

'Fishermen?' suggested Jimmy.

'Funny man,' said Fiona. 'Where d'you live?'

'South London,' said Jimmy, and blonde Fiona wrinkled her nose.

'That's a long way from Epsom,' she said.

'Why does Epsom get a mention?' asked Jimmy.

'It's where I live,' said Fiona.

'And where they run the Derby,' said Jimmy.

'Who wants to talk about horses?' said Fiona.

'Jockeys?' suggested Jimmy.

Fiona giggled.

'I think I like you,' she said.

'Well, I'm sure you're very likeable yourself,' said Jimmy.

'So there you are,' said someone from the open door of the gift shop, and in came Jenny and two other girls, Jenny in her RAF blue top, a short skirt and her round straw hat. 'What's the idea, giving us the slip?' she asked Fiona.

'I'm innocent,' said Fiona.

'Tell me another,' said Jenny. 'That's Jimmy you're talking to. Hello, Jimmy, are you having an assignation with Fiona?'

'Just a chat,' said Jimmy.

'Sweet,' said one of the other girls. Chloe.

Boots appeared in the doorway.

'Jimmy, we're off to the ice-cream parlour,' he said.

The girls turned and saw a tall, tanned man in a white cotton shirt, with light summer slacks of blue draping his long legs, a smile touching his fine mouth.

'Oh, right,' said Jimmy, 'I've been temporarily delayed.'

'I see four good reasons for the delay,' said Boots, and Chloe positively sighed at how appealing he was.

'Are you Jimmy's father?' asked Jenny.

'His uncle,' said Boots.

'What a spoilsport,' said Matilda, 'he didn't tell us he had an uncle like you. I'm Matilda, that's Jenny, that's Chloe, and she's Fiona.'

'I'm impressed,' smiled Boots. 'You'll excuse us?'

'So long, girls,' said Jimmy, and he and Boots left, pointing themselves in the direction of ice cream.

'Well, would you believe?' said Chloe.

'What a darling man,' said Matilda.

'I could live in an Arabian tent with him,' said Chloe.

'You'd get sand in your filmy Arabian pantaloons,' said Jenny.

'Still, wasn't he gorgeous?' said Fiona. 'How old d'you think he is, Jenny?'

'Old enough for Chloe,' said Jenny, and her laugh arrived, putting the sparkle into her eyes.

'It's my pleasure to ask if any of you young ladies be going to buy something,' said the shop proprietor.

The young ladies vanished.

In Paul's office, Lulu was typing out her list of ideas and suggestions for the next propaganda leaflet.

'Ratification, yes, good,' she said. 'Brilliant, in fact.'

Paul was replying to letters, scribbling down his answers for Lulu to type.

'How did ratification get into your notes?' he asked.

Lulu looked up from her typewriter, pushed her spectacles back and said, 'Not in yet. Thinking about it.'

'Unthink it,' said Paul. 'Leave it out. Keep

the facts simple.'

'What's wrong with "the ratification of proposed legislations for the nationalization of merchant shipping"?'

'There's no proposed legislation for that,' said Paul, 'and in any case, our leaflets are for the people of Walworth, not for Old Etonians who live around Buckingham Palace.'

'Get you,' said Lulu. 'It's up to us to help educate the people of Walworth.'

'Ratification of proposed legislation won't educate them,' said Paul, 'it'll make them use the leaflets for wrapping up potato peel and dumping same in their dustbins.'

'You're a trial to me,' said Lulu, her horn-rimmed specs glowering at him. She was wearing a white blouse, buttoned up to the neck, and a long black skirt which, seen through the kneehole of her desk, draped her legs and fully covered them. Paul was beginning to wonder if she was knock-kneed or bandy. Or if she had any tent pegs. He grinned. 'What's funny?' demanded Lulu.

'Why do you dress like that?' he asked.

'Helps men to keep their minds on my political career,' said Lulu. 'Listen. How about this for a final slogan? "Support a Socialist Republic."'

'That's a slogan for a Labour Party

pamphlet, is it?'

'Brilliant, would you say?'

'Barmy,' said Paul. Someone knocked on the door. Another visitor, he thought. They'd had two this morning. A young couple enquiring about membership. Both now had membership cards, at the cost to each of ten bob. 'Come in.'

The door opened and in came Henrietta Trevalyan, looking very pleasant indeed in a white dress trimmed with navy blue, and a cute little navy blue hat.

'Hope I'm not interrupting,' she said, 'but as I was passing I thought I'd look in, and someone told me this was your office.'

'You're very welcome,' said Paul, rising.

Lulu growled, good as.

'Hello, Miss Saunders,' said Henrietta.

'Close the door when you leave,' muttered Lulu.

'Pardon? I didn't catch that.'

'I said what nice weather we're having.'

'Yes, isn't it lovely?' said Henrietta, and fluttered a winsome smile at Paul. 'So this is where you do your heroic work for the Young Socialists.'

'I'm no hero,' said Paul.

'Too right you're not,' said Lulu under her breath.

'But you're working against the odds, Paul,' said Henrietta.

'Oh, I think the odds will be in our favour,' said Paul, 'I'm confident the Labour Party will be voted in again come the election.'

'Due as much to the efforts of lovely young men like you as to boring ministers,' said Henrietta.

I'm going to be sick for real this time, thought Lulu, I really am.

'I think you're overstating the case,' said Paul.

'No, I'm sure I'm not,' said Henrietta. 'One realizes that although we lost so many fine men in the beastly war against beastly Hitler, we now have young men just as fine taking their places. It thrills me.'

'Where's the sick bucket?' said Lulu under her breath.

'What's the reason for all these compliments, Miss Trevalyan?' asked Paul.

'Oh, simple admiration for your devotion to your work,' said Henrietta. 'And do call me Henrietta. Look, it's just about lunchtime, and I'd like to talk to you. Would you come and have lunch with me somewhere?'

'So that we can talk?' said Paul.

'Lovely,' said Henrietta.

'Hope the food chokes both of you,' muttered Lulu.

'Excuse me, Miss Saunders?' said Henrietta.

'Enjoy your lunch,' said Lulu who, although not yet nineteen, was already formidable.

Paul usually ate lunch in the office. Vi, his mum, supplied him with sandwiches and something like a couple of apples, or a salad with apple pie to follow. He had sandwiches today.

'Right, shall we go, then?' he said to Henrietta.

'How nice,' said Henrietta.

Paul left with her, but was back almost at once. He took a lunchbox from out of a desk drawer, and placed it on Lulu's desk.

'Have my sandwiches as well as your own,' he said. 'See you later. Look after the shop while I'm away.'

'It'll be smashed up by the time you get back,' said Lulu, specs steaming.

'Tck, tck,' said Paul, and out he went again.

Lulu sat glowering for a couple of minutes. Then she got up, crossed to the front of his desk and hitched her skirt and slip high, disclosing a perfect pair of legs in imitation silk stockings. She aimed a ferocious kick at his chair with the hard point of her right shoe. The chair crashed. A leg fell off.

'Good,' she breathed. 'Bloody brilliant, in fact.'

She followed that by placing his lunchbox on the floor and jumping on it until it was a mashed wreck.

She felt a bit better then.

Over a salad lunch, Henrietta talked. Paul suspected she had a notion to include him in one of her pet projects. And so it proved. After some minutes of chatting him up, she came to the point and said she would simply love it if he would help her set up a home for lonely old maiden ladies.

'Er, what?' he said.

Henrietta assured him there were more than a few such ladies living in a declining state, and that she had an option on a large house for renting in a road off Brixton Hill, with lots of room and a nice garden with two apple trees. Paul said who'd believe it, apple trees in Brixton. He asked who was going to pay the rent. Oh, Granny will see to that, said Henrietta. Does she know she will? Not yet, said Henrietta, but I'll talk her into it, she's got oodles of lolly. Giving lonely old maiden ladies a home where they could be jolly good company for each other would touch her heart. And I suppose she could have some of the apples, said Paul. There, I was sure you'd be practical, said Henrietta. Do say you'll join forces with me.

Paul said his work for the Young Socialists wouldn't leave him much time. But think how rewarding it would be, said Henrietta. Paul said he didn't know much about old maiden ladies. There weren't any in his family, he said, and how rewarding are they, anyway? Oh, satisfaction at making them happy will be very rewarding, said Henrietta, and couldn't you spare a little time in the evening, and a little more at weekends? Touching his foot under the table and fluttering her eyelashes, she said they could do a lot together at weekends.

Blimey, thought Paul, what does a lot mean? A lot of what?

'What will the work entail?' he asked.

'Oh, doing the place up, painting and decorating and all that,' said Henrietta. 'Granny, of course, will pay for the paint. Oh, and the furniture.'

'Does she know she will?' asked Paul.

'Not yet,' said Henrietta. 'I wanted to have this talk with you first.'

'I'll have to think about it,' said Paul.

'Oh, do think in a positive way,' said Henrietta, 'I'd be heartbroken if I couldn't have your support.'

'I'll think about it, I promise,' said Paul.

'It's been a lovely lunch,' said Henrietta, again playing footsie with him.

'Rewarding,' said Paul.

When he got back to the office, he found he couldn't sit down. His chair had a leg off.

'Well, Mother O'Reilly, look at this,' he said.

'Your chair?' said Lulu. 'Yes, it fell over. I heard it. Hard luck. Oh, and I gave your lunchbox to a visitor. Unemployed and starving. Victim of uncaring Tory governments.'

'What I want to know is how the chair leg fell off,' said Paul.

'Rotten workmanship in a capitalist furniture factory,' said Lulu. 'Well, that's my theory.'

'It's not mine,' said Paul, and regarded her under lowering brows, so to speak. Lulu's specs shone with innocence. 'You hussy, where's my umbrella?'

'What's your beef?' said Lulu.

'Dark suspicion,' said Paul. 'It's going to lead me to tanning you.'

'You lay just one finger on me and I'll sue you,' said Lulu. 'Enjoy your lunch with the winsome witch, did you?'

'Charming girl,' said Paul.

'Ugh,' said Lulu.

'Get your hair styled,' said Paul, and went to borrow or purloin a spare chair from somewhere.

One day, thought Lulu, I really will bash a hole in his head.

Chapter Twenty-Three

Friday, the last full day in Cornwall for the families. They spent it on Daymer beach, the favourite playground for many holiday-makers in this part of North Cornwall. Paula and Phoebe took the twins and their nets to look for shrimps in the pools among the rocks. Sammy and Susie went strolling over the expansive sands. Polly and Boots sat in the sun.

Jimmy, going for a swim, met Jenny going for a swim. She was following her group into the sea, but she stopped to say hello to Jimmy.

'You look as if your holiday's doing you good,' she said.

'Now you've made me worry about how I looked before,' said Jimmy.

'Oh, before, you looked like a well-dressed shirt salesman with an impertinent line of chat specially thought out to slay your lady customers,' said Jenny. 'It tickled me.'

'I thought it put your nose in the air,' said Jimmy.

Jenny's laugh gurgled about.

'That was my line of defence,' she said. 'Why do men chat up every girl they meet?'

'Well, they hope that one day one girl will fall for it,' said Jimmy.

'You've got a wicked tongue,' said Jenny.

'You've got lovely hair,' said Jimmy. Her dark hair was full of springy clusters, dry from salt, sun and sea breezes.

'Well, thanks, Jimmy.'

'My pleasure.'

'When does your holiday end?'

'We're going home tomorrow.'

'Tomorrow?' Jenny looked surprised. 'But we've got another week. We always have three weeks and a bit. The bit takes care of two days of travel here and back.'

'Do the eight of you travel in your own bus?'

'No, four in one car, four in another. Tomorrow, you said?'

'Yes,' said Jimmy, 'tomorrow we're homeward bound.'

'Oh, well,' said Jenny. 'Listen, your uncle, who is he?'

'My uncle,' said Jimmy.

'Fathead,' said Jenny. 'No, is he someone distinguished and important? Only Chloe's got a terrible crush on him.'

'Barmy,' said Jimmy. 'She only saw him for about five seconds.'

'In those five seconds, Chloe went ga-ga,' said Jenny.

'Ga-ga about what she thinks is distinguished importance?' said Jimmy.

'No, we all thought he looked impressive,' said Jenny.

'Well, tell Chloe he's old enough to be her grandfather,' said Jimmy.

'He doesn't look it,' said Jenny, her tightly fitting blue swimsuit streamlining her ups and downs. 'And it won't make any difference to Chloe. She's cross-eyed and wandering.'

'She's rollicking about in the water right now,' said Jimmy.

'Oh, she's a fighter,' said Jenny. 'What's your uncle's name?'

'Boots.'

'Boots? Boots? That's absurd.'

'It's a nickname pinned on him as an infant,' said Jimmy, 'and it's stuck ever since. He doesn't mind.'

'What's his real name?'

'Robert Adams.'

'I'll tell Chloe,' said Jenny, 'I think she'd like to send him a Valentine card.'

'I advise against that,' said Jimmy, 'or his wife, my Aunt Polly, will track her down and chuck her off the top of Tower Bridge.'

Jenny rippled with laughter.

'Jimmy, you're a wag,' she said.

A head popped up high out of the sea and a shout issued forth.

'Hey, come on, Jenny!'

'That's Barry,' said Jimmy.

'That's Barry,' echoed Jenny. 'Well, I don't suppose we'll see each other again, unless you'll be down here next year. Be good. Lots of luck. Bye, now.'

'Send me a Valentine card,' said Jimmy.

She laughed again, and away she went to splash through the shallows.

Jimmy looked up at the blue heavens.

'Thanks very much,' he said, 'you've been a great help, I don't think.'

Susie, far away on the other side of Brea Hill, was enjoying her stroll with Sammy.

'By the way,' she said, 'something's happening to our Jimmy.'

'He's shaving?' said Sammy.

'He's been shaving for a year, you goof,' said Susie.

'Well, perhaps I meant is he growing a beard?' said Sammy. 'Tell him not to, or his grandma will come after him with her scissors. You know what she thinks about bearded men. They're either bandits or Bolsheviks. Might I ask, incidental like, where you get goof from?'

'From our American daughter-in-law Patsy,' said Susie.

'Americans use a funny kind of language,' said Sammy.

'Not as funny as our kind, like corblimey, how's your father,' said Susie. 'Sammy love, I think Jimmy's been struck by lightning.'

'Don't I know it,' said Sammy, 'he walked into a door at the cottage yesterday. That's serious.'

'It's that girl we've seen him talking to,' said Susie, 'the one he played golf with.'

'Looks a bit of all right to me,' said Sammy.

'You don't say a bit of all right about a girl

that makes our Jimmy walk into doors,' said Susie.

'How can we help?' asked Sammy, his sandals and Susie's in his hands, their bare feet treading wet sand.

'If that means you're thinking of interfering, Sammy Adams, think again,' said Susie. 'Let Jimmy work things out for himself.'

'Might I point out, Mrs Adams, that I was only going to suggest inviting her to Sunday tea?' said Sammy.

'That's up to Jimmy,' said Susie.

'I feel for him,' said Sammy. 'I mean, I had a hard time meself with you, didn't I.'

'That's a laugh,' said Susie, 'you spent years backing off and driving me dotty. Still, you came to your senses in the end. Just as well, or I'd have finished you off with my dad's chopper.'

'Well, I'm glad you didn't, Susie, or me business would've died an early death, and the profits likewise. Susie, what d'you think, has it been a good marriage, me and you?'

'Sammy love, a lot better than if it had been me and someone else.'

'I'll buy you a fur coat come winter,' said Sammy.

'I don't want a fur coat,' said Susie. 'I've

got everything I ever needed. Except something that would make this day last for ever.'

Saturday morning.

Jenny knocked on the door of a cottage in Daymer Lane. A woman in an apron answered.

'Oh, good morning,' said Jenny, 'I'm looking for Jimmy Adams.'

'Oh, he went off with the families early on,' said the woman. 'I'm Mrs Boddy, I do the clearing up and cleaning for them on the day they go, like last year, m'dear. They always leave early.'

'Blow that,' said Jenny.

It was a long drive home for the families. The twins tumbled into bed soon after arrival. Paula and Phoebe tucked down soon after nine, Jimmy at ten. Sammy and Susie retired five minutes later. Boots and Polly sat up for a while, sharing an old-fashioned pot of night-time tea, something Polly would have eschewed in her pre-marriage days.

They flopped when they were eventually in bed.

Boots had a dream, the same one. Belsen. Corpses, faces, eyes. Faces. One face out of many. It woke him up.

'Jesus Christ,' he whispered.

Polly stayed asleep.

Sunday morning.

The twins, refreshed, consumed a rattling good breakfast. With Flossie on holiday, Polly, not the world's greatest or most enthusiastic cook, could at least produce happy-looking eggs and bacon, and what Boots called classy toast. The large three-pound jar of marmalade was a present from Susie, who always made her own, from Seville oranges. She'd missed out during the war, but Sevilles were now being imported.

'Daddy,' said Gemma, 'what we going to do today?'

'Laze about,' said Boots.

'Well,' said Gemma, 'I don't think much of that. Can't we get some sand and make castles in the garden?'

'Can't we dig a hole and make a pond to swim in?' said James. 'I'm prepared,' he said grandly, 'to do my bit.'

'And I've got my seaside spade,' said

Gemma. 'Daddy,' she said generously, 'you could use that. I could just watch. I don't mind just watching.'

'Just watching?' said James. 'Well, can you believe that?'

'Shall we dig a hole, Polly?' asked Boots.

'Such decisions, old bean, I cheerfully leave to you,' said Polly. 'I'll cut some gladioli for the house.'

'I'll help Mummy,' said Gemma.

'Right, then,' said Boots. 'James can start digging the hole, and I'll help him after I've attended to some of the letters that were waiting for us yesterday. We'll fill the hole with water from the hose. If it runs away, we'll use the hole to plant a flowering shrub. I'll show you where you can start digging, young 'un.'

'It's got to be a big hole,' said James.

'So-so,' said Boots.

Later, when James was digging and Gemma was watching, Boots had a word with Polly.

'Polly, you remember the Nuremberg trials?'

'Will I ever forget?' said Polly. They had spent a day there.

'You remember the film that included scenes at Belsen, with some of the camp guards in evidence?'

'Once again, will I ever forget?' said Polly.

'When I was there in '45, I looked into the faces of most of the guards. Women as well as men.'

'You told me of that well before we went to the trials,' said Polly. 'What's on your mind?'

Boots said most of the men and women guards avoided being looked in the eye, that all of them had suddenly been made aware of their infamy by the arrival of British troops. There was one man, however, an SS officer, who refused to accept that the extermination of Jews was any kind of crime. He'd been sent by Himmler to arrange for all surviving inmates to be finished off before any Allied troops turned up. He was too late, and that alone bothered him. He looked me in the eye, said Boots, without showing any signs of remorse whatever. All that has played on your mind since it happened, said Polly, but is there something new?

'There's the fact that one of the women guards, a handsome bitch, was the only guard to meet my eye,' said Boots. 'I saw no remorse, no guilt, just contempt for what I represented, an enemy of her ideology, the ideology of Himmler.'

'Did you hang her?' asked Polly.

'I made her and all the other guards, and Himmler's unrepentant messenger, a Major Kirsten, bury the mounds of dead and clean up the filth of the camp before being taken to prison and to Nuremberg,' said Boots. 'Now, Polly, how did that one woman escape Nuremberg?'

'Did she escape?' said Polly. 'If so, how do you know she did?'

'She's here,' said Boots.

'Here?' said Polly.

'In London,' said Boots.

'You're losing me, old soldier,' said Polly.

'I'll help you catch up with me,' said Boots. 'I saw her.'

Polly stared at him, at his deep grey eyes, the left one as clear as the right, yet almost blind. Years and years ago, during the first battle of the Somme in 1916, the searing flash of an exploding German grenade had blinded him. An operation in 1920 had returned full sight to his right eye. His left had remained permanently damaged, but only the slightly lazy action of the lid betrayed that. Polly kept a subconsciously caring watch on his sound eye.

'Boots, you saw her?'

'Yes, and of all places, in the East Street

market of Walworth on the day Sammy and I took his girls and the twins there. The twins and the girls were with me at old Ma Earnshaw's stall, and this woman was a little way off. She'd changed, of course, she looked like a nicely dressed housewife. I gave her only a brief glance, and although her features didn't clearly register, I had a faint idea there was something familiar about her. It didn't stay with me. We moved on and she took her place at the stall. The kids saw her again later on, and pointed her out to me. Again, nothing important registered, not until I had that dream again last night. Her face and her eyes – she had the blue eyes that Himmler regarded as true Aryan – surged into the dream. I woke up, and I knew then that I'd seen her that day in the market.'

'Ye gods,' said Polly, 'so what are you going to do?'

'Find her,' said Boots. 'I owe it to the poor murdered inmates of Belsen.'

Polly noted then that the grey of his eyes was touched by the hint of blue steel. That happened whenever his tolerance was shattered by the vicious, the unspeakable or that which posed a dangerous threat to the family. She wondered if the SS woman had glimpsed that steel when Boots, as Colonel Adams, had come face to face with her and looked her in the eye. Polly hoped she had, for if Boots did find her she would know her time had come.

'Go hunting, old love,' she said, 'I'll be right beside you.'

Chapter Twenty-Four

Monday morning.

Lulu was ten minutes late arriving for work. She found Paul in argument with a beefy woman from the publicity department of the collective grass roots of the Party. The woman was known as Blunderbuss Beryl on account of her tendency to deliver booming broadsides at opposition newspaper editors for allowing unadulterated tripe about Clement Attlee's government to appear in their rags. She wasn't averse to rushing off to Fleet Street and demanding to see an editor in person. And person to person she was almost always bigger and louder. Some editors locked themselves in when told she was in their building.

The argument she was having with Paul was not only verbal. It was also physical in that she had hold of two legs of a chair, Paul was gripping the back of it with both hands, and a violent tug-of-war was taking place.

'Let go, you squirt!' she roared. A Young Socialist official was small fry to her. 'This is my chair and you pinched it, you young bugger. Let go, you hear?'

'This chair,' hollered Paul, 'was spare and unoccupied at the time I chanced on it, and by the old and true working-class principle that possession is nine points of the law, I'm claiming it.'

'Working-class principle my Aunt Fanny, let go!' Blunderbuss Beryl yanked. Paul yanked.

Lulu looked on, specs glinting with happiness. There was no way that that smarty-pants was going to get the better of Blunderbuss Beryl. It was said that in 1946 she'd demolished the entire editorial staff of the *Daily Mail*, and that when the corpses came to and found they were actually still alive, they emigrated to Australia, that being as far from her as they could get. Only a story, of course, but it was typical of her reputation.

'I'm getting cross!' shouted Paul. He must have been cross. Like his dad and his uncles, he never resorted to bawling. This was a first-timer. 'This chair's mine!'

'You saucy pipsqueak, let go!' Blunderbuss Beryl yanked mightily. Paul let go. Back she staggered and her abundant bottom cannoned against the wall. Every cushioned spring in her body quivered. But she was made of sterner stuff than to yell for the law. She waited until all her springs had settled down, then said, 'So this is how you treat a defenceless woman, is it, Adams? And in front of another one, eh?'

Lulu tried looking the part.

'You've got me there,' said Paul.

'I've got you all right,' said Blunderbuss Beryl, keeping hold of the chair. 'You're finished, you'll be out by the end of this week, and you'll be lucky to escape a charge of assault.' A quiver returned to her bottom. 'And I'm not sure battery didn't take place as well. Yes, you're finished, and I'll see that Miss Saunders takes your place. Miss Saunders, open this door.'

Lulu opened it and Blunderbuss Beryl departed, with the chair. Lulu closed the door.

'Exit Boadicea with her chariot,' said Paul.

'You weren't at your best,' said Lulu. 'What a clown. Ought to know better than to pick a fight with her. You're going to lose your job.'

'I'll find another,' said Paul, cooled down. 'I'd like to stay in politics. I'll try for a job in the Commons, as assistant to the assistant of an MP's parliamentary secretary. Yes, good idea. MP George Brown might be the answer. He went to the same school as one of my uncles, West Square.'

'You've got an uncle called West Square?' said Lulu, wearing what Paul thought could double for a brown tent. 'Mercy me, can you Adam-and-Eve it?'

'West Square's a school in St George's Road, you dolly,' said Paul. 'Look, there's a maintenance bloke somewhere in this building. I'm going to find him and borrow some tools that'll help me fix back the leg on that broken chair. Be a good girl and open the mail for me while I'm gone. Put any applications for membership in the relevant tray. OK?'

'Will do,' said Lulu.

At mid-morning, Mrs Kloytski was in the East Street market, buying apples and cabbages from Ma Earnshaw, and having a friendly little conversation with her.

'Ah, I think many people know you, Mrs Earnshaw,' she said. 'You have many customers.'

'So I have, ducky,' said Ma, selecting the kind of cabbages she knew the Polish woman liked. Good solid crisp ones. 'And so I should, I been running this here stall for more years than I care to remember.'

'I wonder,' said Mrs Kloytski, 'do you know if anyone has been asking about me?'

'Didn't you ask me that there same question before, like?' said Ma.

'Well, you see, I lost sight of my brother when he was taken from Warsaw by the Germans to work in one of their factories–'

'Gawd help us, them devils of 'Itler's,' expostulated Ma in a compulsive paddy, 'when they weren't killing people or dropping bombs on them, they were making slaves of 'em.'

'Ah, but some survived, and I am always hoping my brother did, yes,' said Mrs Kloytski. 'I am also hoping he will find out I have come to England with my husband. Then perhaps one day he will reach London and ask people questions about me. Perhaps he will even reach this market and ask people here. No-one has asked you about me, Mrs Earnshaw, no?'

'Well, I did tell you last week no-one has,' said Ma.

'Ah, how sad,' said Mrs Kloytski.

'Still, you never know,' said Ma, 'so keep yer pecker up, eh?'

'Excuse me?'

'Don't get downhearted, ducky.'

'I see, yes.' Mrs Kloytski smiled. 'Ah, wait, if anyone should ask, please let me know quickly. I will pay if you send a boy with the message.'

'All right, dearie,' said Ma.

Mrs Kloytski paid for the apples and cabbages and left. A few minutes later, Ma thought, well, she didn't say where she lived. I'm sure it's Wansey Street, where Cassie Brown lives, but what number? Still, I don't expect her brother to come asking. If he ain't dead, I'll be more than surprised. Them Nazis left a lot more people dead than alive. Oh, well, it's all over now, praise the Lord, and I ain't one to keep on about it.

That evening, Lulu left her flat in Walworth to call on her parents at their home in Kennington. Her dad was there, not at some political function, and she had a long chat with him.

The following morning, Blunderbuss Beryl took a phone call from Mr Saunders, the constituency's MP.

'Look here,' he said, 'I believe you've had words with our Young Socialists secretary, Paul Adams.'

'The squirt pinched my office chair.'

'You've got it back?'

'You bet I've got it back, after a lot of sauce, impertinence and too much bloody heave-ho, and I'm arranging for Adams to be replaced.'

'Don't do that.'

'Mr Saunders—'

'Don't do it.'

'But your daughter can have the job.'

'My daughter doesn't want the job under those kind of circumstances.'

'Listen, Mr Saunders, I'm objecting to this conversation.'

'Object all you like, there's two sides to any argument unless the other bloke's a Tory. Adams keeps the job. He's good at it, he's increasing the membership week by week, and every member is a guaranteed Labour Party voter. That's all, thanks. Good morning.'

Mr Saunders didn't inform Paul of this. Lulu had said she'd disown him if he did.

What happened was that one of Blunder-buss Beryl's hunched underlings brought a scrawled note down to Paul.

'You're reprieved, but don't do it again.' It was signed by Beryl.

'Look at that,' said Paul, handing the note to Lulu, who read it.

'Lucky old ratbag, aren't you?' she said.

'Blunderbuss must have bumped into my fairy godmother,' said Paul.

'Don't suppose your fairy godmother thought much of that,' said Lulu, presently revising the list of members.

'Much of what?' asked Paul.

'Being bumped into by half a ton of plum duff,' said Lulu.

Paul yelled with laughter.

'Lulu, you made a funny,' he said.

'Pardon me, I'm sure,' said Lulu.

'There'll be quite a few letters for you to type this afternoon,' said Paul.

'Give 'em to your fairy godmother,' said Lulu. 'I'll still be busy.' Paul let that go. A minute later, she said, 'By the way, you never told me what tarty Henrietta talked to you about.'

'Oh, some project concerning a home for lonely old maiden ladies,' said Paul.

'Oh, my word, dearie me, how sweet,' said

Lulu. 'And what help will you give?'

'Well, for a start,' said Paul, 'she thinks we could do a lot together at weekends.'

'Not for the old ladies. No, I bet not. The mind boggles.'

'At what?'

'At what you'll look like on Monday mornings.'

'Lulu, you're in form today,' said Paul. 'Listen, I've got a letter here from a Left-wing church deacon. He wants me to join him on a soapbox at Speakers Corner one Sunday and address the crowd on Jesus as the first Socialist.'

'The mind boggles,' muttered Lulu, and used a savage blue pencil to cross out the name of a defector who hadn't and wouldn't renew his subscription. The soft lead broke.

'The invitation doesn't include her,' said Paul.

'Weekends do. Sundays are a part of every weekend.'

It was lunchtime when Ma Earnshaw turned to serve her next customer, a man who had been waiting in the background until the stall was clear, when he made a quick approach.

'Hello again, Ma,' he said.

'Well, if it ain't yerself again, Boots dearie,' said Ma. 'It's a real pleasure. I hear about the family from Cassie Brown now and then, here and there, like. What can I get yer, love?'

'First, you remember when I brought Sammy's girls and my twins to see you?' said Boots.

'Lovely surprise, that was,' said Ma.

'After we left, you served a woman, a blonde woman. D'you remember that too?'

'Course I do. She's one of me Polish customers, Mrs Kloytski,' said Ma. 'She buys a lot of apples, spuds and cabbages, which she said last week she makes sauerkraut with. I dunno why them Poles eat stuff like that, and have names like that.'

'D'you know where she lives?' asked Boots.

'Here, wait a tick,' said Ma, 'that's a bit odd. I mean, she's been on at me lately about people asking after her. Only yesterday she said her lost brother might just come looking for her. You ain't her lost brother, are yer, Boots? She said to let her know quick if anyone at all asked after her. I didn't think you'd be one.'

Lost brother my elbow, thought Boots. There's a woman who's been on the run, and still has something to worry about, even though she's parked herself in London with her husband.

'I need to find her, Ma,' he said. 'I can't explain right now. Simply, do you know where she lives?'

'I'm pretty sure it's Wansey Street, but I don't know what number,' said Ma. 'But yer family friends, Cassie and Freddy Brown, they live in Wansey Street.'

A customer arrived.

'Good enough, Ma,' said Boots.

'Can I serve yer something now?' asked Ma.

'Here's two quid,' said Boots, fishing the notes out of his wallet. 'Make up a box of fruit and let the Salvation Army have it for one of their hostels.'

'I'll do that,' said Ma. 'You're a good bloke, Boots, you always was, and a gent as well. Mind, you've got me wondering about Mrs–'

But Boots was away through the market crowds, and Ma turned to her customer.

Cassie, answering the knock on her front door, found Boots on her step. Cassie, fond of the Adams family, was particularly fond of Boots and his younger brother Sammy.

'Well, look who's here,' she said, her smile

rich with pleasure, a decorated apron over her turquoise blue dress. 'Boots, you look as if you've been in the sun for ages.'

'Cornish holiday, and hello to you, Cassie,' said Boots. He had a soft spot for Cassie, wife of Susie's brother Freddy. Thirty-three now, she still projected a hint of teasing mischief, the kind that had driven Freddy dotty during their growing years together. 'How are you?'

'Hot,' said Cassie, 'I'm ironing yesterday's washing, and that's hot all right in August. Still, Freddy does like his nicely ironed shirts. You'll come in, won't you, Boots? Muffin and Lewis are out with friends.'

'Thanks,' said Boots, stepping in. Cassie closed the door and took him into the front room which, like most front rooms in Walworth, was still known as the parlour. Boots noted the clean, tidy look of the room and the obvious use of furniture polish. On the piano stood a large framed photograph of Cassie and Freddy on their wedding day. On the window ledge were pots of African violets in flower. Boots could recognize any parlour that knew the care and attention of a Walworth housewife.

'Would you like a cup of coffee, Boots, and something to eat?' asked Cassie. It was lunchtime, and she was going to do a light meal for herself and the children in fifteen minutes.

'Thank you, Cassie, but no,' said Boots, 'I'll catch a pub sandwich and a beer a little later. But it's good to see you, Cassie, and I know Freddy's doing well at the store.'

'Oh, you and Sammy gave him a nice job there, Boots,' said Cassie.

'Freddy's always given of his best for the firm,' said Boots, and came to the point of his call. 'Cassie, do you have a neighbour called Mrs Kloytski?'

'Not half I do,' said Cassie, 'but I'm not sure I like her. The blessed woman's got a fancy for Freddy, and her at her age. She must be all of ten years older.'

'What's the number of her house?' asked Boots.

'Twenty-three,' said Cassie. 'A few doors down, next to Mr and Mrs Hobday. And you've got me curious. She's Polish, Boots, and so's her husband. And he's a cool one all right for a Pole.'

'Cool?' said Boots.

'As handsome as Cary Grant,' said Cassie, 'and ever so friendly, only when he smiles it's not like a real smile. It's sort of cool and his eyes look right through you. Mrs

Kloytski now, when she smiles she kind of embraces you. She's always smiling at Freddy and trying to get her bosom closer to his chest. Freddy says he's going to undo her buttons one day and see what all the fuss is about.' Cassie laughed. 'He'd do it too, he came out of Burma a lot tougher, Boots, only he knows I'd hit him with a saucepan if he did.'

'Seeing what all the fuss is about could call the lady's bluff,' smiled Boots.

'Give her a thrill, more like,' said Cassie. 'When I was talking to my dad about her, he said she was probably what was known as a voluptuous woman. Well, you should have heard what my mum said to that, including telling him she wasn't going to have those kind of words used in her house, especially in front of an innocent daughter. Me, the innocent daughter, Boots.' Cassie laughed again.

'Innocent daughters, Cassie, grow up like the rest of us, but I'm never sure if some fathers wouldn't prefer them to stay young and innocent for ever,' said Boots.

'Is that what you'd prefer for Gemma?' asked Rosie.

'Shouldn't we all allow our children to choose their own way of life?' said Boots.

'But we've got to give them some guidance,' said Cassie.

'Yes, so we have,' said Boots, and spent a few moments reflecting on that which was foremost in his mind. The woman and her husband, both said to be Polish. If her husband really was Polish, did he know she wasn't? As a Pole he should know. 'This woman Mrs Kloytski, what's her husband's job, Cassie?'

'Oh, he works mostly at home, writing articles for a Polish newspaper, and going up to town to meet other Poles,' said Cassie. 'He's got a phone. Freddy's arranging for us to have one, which I said wasn't before time. Boots, I'm just bursting with curiosity.'

'Well, don't go off bang, Cassie,' said Boots, 'none of us want to lose you. Hang on for a while, and then perhaps some news will come your way and satisfy your curiosity. Thanks for your time and our chat. I must go now.'

'Boots, it's been lovely seeing you,' said Cassie, 'and all the best to Polly and the twins.'

'Come and have Sunday tea with us, you and Freddy and your children,' said Boots. 'I'll ask Polly to get in touch with you about the date.'

'Boots, we'd love that,' said Cassie, and tingled when he gave her a goodbye kiss.

Farther along the street, Mr and Mrs Kloytski were eating lunch, a large dish of sauerkraut being the mainstay.

Boots, on his way to the Walworth Road and a pub, suddenly thought about the sauerkraut that Ma Earnshaw had mentioned. Did Poles like it as much as Germans did?

Chapter Twenty-Five

Mrs Rachel Goodman, a forty-seven-year-old widow, was as well preserved as Susie and Polly. A strikingly beautiful Jewess in her younger years, lush in her vivid looks, she had avoided the traditional foods that were so appealing to her race, but could be fattening. She had a decided horror of being called fat by Sammy. Not that he would in bald terms, not Sammy, the dear man. He'd make do with something like, 'Hello, Rachel me old lollipop, you've been eating well lately, I see.'

No-one knew that since the age of fifteen

she had been in love with Sammy the irrepressible, or that only her affection for and her dutiful attitude towards her gentle-mannered father would have prevented her converting to the Christian faith if Sammy had asked her to marry him. Sammy, however, had never thought of subverting her faith, and so she did the dutiful thing and married Benjamin Goodman, an up-and-coming bookmaker and a fine man in many ways. She had lost him when he died of a heart attack during the war. She put that down to the time when, as an ARP warden, he had entered a bombed house during a German air raid in an attempt to bring out a trapped woman. The trembling house fell on him, and on the woman and another warden. Both Benjamin's legs had been broken. Rachel was sure the shock, the stress, and the painful road to recovery had weakened his heart.

He had been gone now for several years, leaving her to take care of their two daughters and her widowed father. Her father, ageing but enduring, was still with her. Rebecca, her elder daughter, a university graduate, worked in the research department of an international chemical company in Manchester, where one of the managers, Joseph Symonds, was doing his best to interest her in a wedding ceremony at the city's main synagogue.

Leah, her younger daughter and such a sweet girl, had done something that delighted Rachel. She had married Edward, the younger son of Sammy's sister Lizzy, thus allowing Rachel to relate to the extensive Adams family. Rachel, despite the strict tenets of her religion, was enduringly close in every way to this Christian family, to its attitudes, its customs and its patently old-fashioned values. She had a warm affection for Sammy's mother and her many descendants and in-laws. Further, she and Boots's wife, the once madcap Polly, had always hit a high note together.

Rachel had been Sammy's business manager during the latter years of the war, a position she happily relinquished back to Boots when he returned. She was now the secretary of all three companies, Adams Enterprises, Adams Fashions and Adams Properties, and her salary gave her immense pleasure, even if Sammy sometimes said, 'You sure we're not paying you twice too much, Rachel?'

Sammy was the driving power of the business, its engine, but Boots, she knew, was the mastermind of its stability. Sammy periodically came up with great ideas, and laid them before Boots and herself with the flourish of finality. But Boots, in his casual but subtle way, would offer a few comments, and those comments would govern the outcome. Rachel loved her job and adored all that Sammy and Boots meant to her working life.

Boots was back after an extended lunch hour. Rachel thought that he and Sammy, so tanned and fit after their time in Cornwall, could put many a Hollywood star in the shade. But I'll admit it, I'm biased, she told herself. She put her head into Boots's office.

'Maggie Collier's been after you,' she said, entering. Maggie Collier was chief buyer of women's clothes for Coates, who had a store in the West End and branches all over South England. Maggie Collier was the post-war replacement for Harriet de Vere, who had suffered treacherously from weak knees whenever face to face with Boots. Rachel suspected the same weakness was afflicting Maggie.

'Rachel,' said Boots, regarding desk paperwork absently, 'suppose we throw the lady at Sammy?'

'She'll bounce back in your direction,' said Rachel. 'My life, aren't you ashamed at what you still do to perfectly respectable women?'

'If I did do it, God knows how they'd rearrange their respectability,' said Boots. 'What's Maggie Collier after besides me?'

'Somehow,' said Rachel, 'she's got wind of the fact that we're on course for manufacturing a glorious amount of nylon stockings. And we are now that the machine's installed and Tommy has it working like Frankenstein with six arms. Maggie wants to contract totally.'

'I suspect that,' said Boots.

'You're right,' said Rachel. 'She wants Coates to have the lot.'

'Ring Tommy,' said Boots. 'Ask him to estimate the output. Then ring Maggie and offer half the total. Tell her, of course, that it's the lot.'

'I should put my head on Maggie's block?' said Rachel. 'It's your head she wants, on her West End necklace.'

'Favour me,' said Boots, who knew that if he spoke to the lady himself he'd get invited to a three-hour lunch.

'I'll do it for you, Boots,' said Rachel, 'and risk the bruises.'

Later, when Rachel had survived her

phone conversation with Maggie Collier, Boots was talking to Sammy.

'You want what?' said Sammy.

'Immediately our day here is over, I want you and Tommy to come to Walworth with me,' said Boots. 'I've phoned Tommy and he's leaving the factory early to be here by five thirty. In a case like this, three can operate more effectively than one.'

'What case you talking about?' asked Sammy, up to his ears in property-speculation figures on paper.

Boots said that at Belsen he came face to face with the men and women SS guards, and that one woman in particular attracted his attention by way of her cold, contempt-uous defiance and total lack of remorse. She was supposed to have ended up at Nurem-berg, to be tried, along with all concen-tration-camp guards, as a war criminal. That hadn't happened. She'd obviously escaped, as some other known war criminals had, and was living in Wansey Street, posing as the Polish wife of a Polish man.

'Wansey Street?' said Sammy. 'Not next door to Cassie and Freddy, for Christ's sake?'

'Not far from them,' said Boots.

'Send the police round,' said Sammy.

'Sammy lad,' said Boots, 'it's my personal job, something I owe to myself and the victims of Belsen and Himmler.'

'Funny thing, I never did go much on Himmler,' said Sammy. 'Always looked like Monday's leavings to me. Well, a sort of leftover from a dog's dinner. Lucky we had a fortnight in Cornwall and had our muscles toned up. I mean, has this female got muscles of her own and is she handy with her coal hammer?'

'You can expect that,' said Boots.

'Well, I don't usually like laying hands on a female,' said Sammy, 'but as it won't be in business hours and it's personal to you, I'll come along. I'll ring Susie and tell her I'll be delayed a bit. Has Tommy phoned Vi?'

'He said he would, and I've spoken to Polly. I fancy, Sammy, that we're all going to be delayed a bit.'

Polly had responded to Boots's phone call by saying she had a fat chance of being right behind him if he was sneaking off without her. Sorry, Polly old love, said Boots, but you look after the twins and I'll look after Mrs Kloytski. Take care, said Polly, we don't give a damn what happens to Himmler's filthy vixen, but you're our Rock of Ages.

That evening, Mr and Mrs Kloytski heard a knock on their front door.

'I'll go,' said Kloytski.

'See who it is before you let them in,' said Mrs Kloytski.

'Of course,' said Kloytski. Arriving at the door, he put his right eye to the spyhole. He stiffened, alerted and retreated. 'God damn it,' he hissed, 'it's the English swine himself, the one we knew as Colonel Adams, and he's not alone. I glimpsed other men.'

'There, I told you he could have recognized me that day in the market,' breathed Mrs Kloytski. 'Don't let them in.'

'I'm not an idiot,' said Kloytski as the knock was repeated.

'What shall we do?'

'Stay quiet until we're sure he's gone,' said Kloytski, 'then do some packing and depart as soon as it's dark.'

'What if he fetches the police and they force an entry?'

'At the sound of the first blow, we'll have to slip out through the back,' said Kloytski. Again the knocker thumped.

'Into the back yard that's hemmed in by other back yards?' said Mrs Kloytski.

'We'll turn them into an escape route somehow,' said Kloytski.

They waited. There were no more knocks. Kloytski took another look through the spyhole. He saw nothing. He went into the parlour, and made a cautious survey through net curtains. The street was empty.

At that moment, Boots, Tommy and Sammy were with Cassie and Freddy, with Boots doing the talking. Subsequently, Tommy called on Mr and Mrs Hobday.

Thirty minutes later, when Kloytski and his wife were upstairs hurriedly packing, their knocker sounded again.

'They're back,' said Kloytski.

'I'll take a look,' said Mrs Kloytski. She descended the stairs quietly, Kloytski following. Through the spyhole she saw Cassie, a neighbour with a very attractive and decidedly masculine husband. 'It's only Cassie,' she said, and opened the door.

'Oh, hello, Mrs Kloytski,' said Cassie, a dish in her hand, 'I've brought you some–'

Figures materialized at speed from the step next door. Kloytski turned in the narrow hall and bolted for the kitchen as Boots and Sammy, rushing past Cassie, landed on the mat to confront the paralysed blonde woman. Sammy took a brief look at her, saw the staring blue eyes, then went after the man.

Boots closed the door. Cassie, pulse jumping, went back to her house to tell Freddy she had played the part that Boots had asked of her.

'I've seen you before,' said Boots to the blonde woman. 'At Belsen.'

Kloytski was unlocking the back door. Except on the occasions when he or his wife needed to put something into the dustbin, it was always kept locked, even though it only opened onto a back yard. All back doors could be vulnerable.

Opening this one, with the sound of pursuit at his back, he tensed himself for a dash to the wall and a leap over it. Out he went. Tommy, who had climbed the wall from the Hobdays' yard, was waiting for whoever emerged. Seeing it was a tall, arresting man who could obviously look after himself, Tommy delivered a thumping punch to his stomach. The man let out an agonized gasp, doubled up and collapsed.

'Sorry about that,' said Tommy, 'but I had orders.'

Out came Sammy. He looked down at the writhing man.

'What's he fussing about?' he asked.

'Search me,' said Tommy, 'I just gave him a tap, that was all.'

'Is he the Polish gent?'

'I suppose so,' said Tommy, 'but Boots said not to do fairy dances with him.'

The writhing man was mouthing audible imprecations.

'Dear, dear,' said Sammy, shaking his head, 'I don't know what language he's using, but I do know Chinese Lady wouldn't like it. Let's wrap him up. Boots said to.'

'Now and again,' said Tommy, 'Boots will keep playing God.'

Boots had the woman in her parlour now. Her face was white, but her blue eyes were full of the fire of hatred.

'You're German,' said Boots.

'Yes, I am German,' she hissed, 'and better than any of your women. The English? Pah!' She spat. 'Wait, only wait, and Germany will rise again and this time do what our race was born for, become masters of the world.'

'Unfortunately,' said Boots, 'you don't have the right knack of empire-building, only a talent for exterminating people.'

Sammy and Tommy appeared, with their prize, whose wrists were lashed behind him, his face livid, his strangely expressionless eyes bulging. Boots looked at him. Recognition arrived at once. God Almighty, thought Boots, he escaped Nuremberg too.

'Well, I'm damned,' he said, 'Major Kirsten of Himmler's SS, I believe.'

This was the man sent by Himmler to arrange the despatch of all surviving inmates at Belsen.

'And you,' said ex-Major Kirsten between grinding teeth, 'are the most cursed of men.'

'I'll have you know,' said Tommy, 'that you're talking to my family's Lord-I-Am. So watch yourself, mister, or you'll get struck by thunder and lightning.'

Boots used the captives' phone to put a call through to Scotland Yard, and was connected to the Special Branch. Three plain-clothes men arrived no less than thirty minutes later, to take charge of prisoners and to carry out an intensive search of the house. After which Erich Kirsten and Hanna Friedler, once of Himmler's SS, were taken away for a thorough investigation into their background.

Boots and his brothers thanked the Hobdays, as well as Cassie and Freddy, for their invaluable help, then departed homewards.

'Tommy,' said Vi, wide-eyed, 'I don't believe it.'

'I know how you feel, Vi,' said Tommy. 'You and me, we live quiet lives, except when Chinese Lady is chasing me over something I shouldn't have said or done. We're not used to sensations, but if anyone can surprise us, it's Boots. Would you credit he could pick out a woman in the Walworth market and convince himself she was one of Belsen's bitches?'

'I don't know what to say about it all,' said Vi, 'and I should think Cassie and Freddy were a bit struck dumb, weren't they?'

'Freddy offered to lend his muscle,' said Tommy, 'but Boots said it would be enough if Cassie could trick the Polish geezer or his missus into opening their door.'

'I still can't believe what happened,' said Vi.

'Vi, me girl,' said Tommy, 'you can believe my every word. Boots, Sammy and yours truly copped 'em, and some blokes from Scotland Yard took 'em away.'

'They really were Germans?' said Vi.

'They admitted it once they were copped, and blowed if they didn't brag about it,' said Tommy. 'Tell you what, Vi, Cassie was as chirpy as a summer cricket that Scotland Yard took 'em away. She said Freddy was safe now from that voluptuous woman.'

'What?' said Vi.

'Voluptuous.' Tommy grinned. 'Came out with it just like that.'

'Oh, help, and what did Freddy do when she said it?' asked Vi.

'Fell about,' said Tommy.

'Sammy, don't you ever do anything like that again,' said Susie. 'Suppose they'd had pistols or machine guns, did you think of that?'

'Well, no, Susie–'

'If I'd known exactly what you and Tommy and Boots were going to do when you phoned,' said Susie, 'I'd have stopped you.'

'Now, now, Susie, it was–'

'Suicide, good as,' said Susie.

'Well, you know, Susie, when Boots acts the sergeant major–'

'Yes, I know, you and Tommy behave like he's got you on parade,' said Susie. 'Wait till I next speak to him. I may adore him as my brother-in-law, but that won't stop me giving him a headache.'

'Susie,' said Sammy, 'how many times have I told you you're not supposed to adore him? Blimey, each time you say it, I can't believe me own ears.'

'Oh, dear, what a shame,' said Susie. 'Now

tell me more about what happened, I've never heard anything more thrilling.'

'Women,' sighed Sammy.

The twins had long been in bed by the time Boots arrived home. Polly, on hearing all the details, shook her head at him. However well one knew him for what his mother called his airy-fairy ways, one would have thought he would at least have shown some reaction to the events in Walworth, even if only a slight flush of triumph. But no, the steely light had gone, and he was as much at peace with his world as ever. He had done what he was determined to, and in doing so had discovered that the man living with the woman was a cold-blooded SS officer first encountered at Belsen.

'You old fraud,' she said, 'you enjoyed it all.'

'A slight measure of satisfaction,' said Boots.

'Dear God, a what?' said Polly. They were in their modernized kitchen, the preserve of their maid Flossie until six each day, except at weekends. Boots was eating a tomato salad covered with curling flakes of shredded cheese, a glass of his favourite dark ale beside his plate. The salad, he'd said, was all he wanted. Polly, sitting opposite him, had her elbows on the table, chin cupped in her hands. 'A slight measure of satisfaction?' she said.

'You could say so, Polly.'

'Objection,' said Polly. 'It's like describing an earthquake as a slight upheaval.'

'Hardly.'

'The comparison's fair,' said Polly.

'Well, all over now,' said Boots.

'Oh, just another little hiccup, would you say?'

'Tommy did an excellent job on Kirsten,' said Boots, swallowing a mouthful of ale.

'You've already told me that.'

'Well, it was worth a second mention,' said Boots.

'You airy-fairy old dog,' said Polly, 'you've laid a couple of German war criminals low and you're behaving as if you've just been shopping for a new tie.'

'Do I need a new tie?' asked Boots.

'You never seem to need anything,' said Polly.

'That, Polly, is because I have everything any reasonable man could want,' said Boots. 'Most of all I have you and the twins.'

Polly's eyes actually turned misty. That was so like him. Ever since the end of the calamitous war of the trenches and the return of his sight, he had been grateful for being alive. No wonder Emily had been fierce in keeping him to herself. Emily the spitfire, with her thin face and peaky nose, but glorious auburn hair and expressive green eyes. What had been her thoughts when she was dying from the shattering blast of the bomb? That she was leaving him, losing him? Perhaps nature had been merciful enough to smother any coherent thoughts.

'Boots?'

'Well, Polly?'

'I'm grateful too for being alive.'

'Polly dear girl, we're two of a kind,' said Boots. 'By the way, I've invited Cassie, Freddy and their children to Sunday tea sometime. Will you get in touch with her and set the date?'

'Sunday tea, Sunday tea,' said Polly. 'Well, that's putting everything back to normal, isn't it?'

'Normal?' said Boots. 'Sunday tea with visitors is supposed to be special in this family.'

'Bless us all,' said Polly.

Chapter Twenty-Six

Bess Adams was home from her holiday in the Lake District. Sammy and Susie were delighted to have her with them for a few weeks before she went back to Bristol University. She was quite willing to tell them of her encounter with Jeremy Passmore from Chicago, and did so at length. He was, she said, a very nice man. That made Susie look at her with interest.

'Very nice, Bess?' she said.

'Yes, and not at all like a noisy cowboy,' said Bess.

'Wait a minute, isn't Chicago in America?' asked Sammy.

'Yes, of course it is,' said Paula.

'Unless it's slipped a bit,' said Jimmy.

'You mean he's an American?' said Sammy.

'Daddy, yes, if he comes from Chicago,' said Phoebe.

'Unless it's slipped into Canada,' said Jimmy.

'Funnycuts,' said Paula.

'Half a mo',' said Sammy, 'we've already got one American in the family. Our Patsy. But she comes from Boston. Chicago, well, I don't know. Doesn't Al Capone live there?'

'Crikey, we don't know any Al Capone,' said Phoebe.

'And we're not likely to,' said Bess. 'He's a long-dead gangster. And I think our dad is jumping the gun.'

'I'm doing a bit of natural presuming if this bloke Jerry has made an impression,' said Sammy.

'Presuming is still out of order,' said Bess. 'And it's Jeremy, not Jerry. Listen, everyone, I don't even know if I'll see him again.'

'But, Bess love,' said Susie, 'you did say he promised to contact you.'

'I also said he was thinking of going back to Chicago,' said Bess.

'He won't if he's got any sense,' said Sammy. 'Al Capone might be dead, but the place is still full of bootleggers.'

'Sammy, all that was over years ago,' said Susie.

'Before some of us were born,' said Jimmy.

'Yes, their President repealed the act,' said Paula, 'and their pubs opened up again.'

'Who's giving us this information?' asked Sammy.

'Paula,' said Phoebe, 'she's good at geography.'

'You mean modern American history,' said Bess.

'Yes, that as well,' said Phoebe.

'I accept the compliment,' said Paula grandly. 'Bess, what's he like, this American? Anything like Clark Gable?'

'Not really,' said Bess, 'and I think we've talked enough about him. Let's just say I met him, and that I might or I might not meet him again.'

'Wait till Patsy knows he's American,' said Paula.

'But Chicago, I ask you,' said Sammy. 'Don't they gun each other down there?'

'No, that's in Dodge City,' said Jimmy.

'Have I heard of Dodge City?' asked Sammy.

'The American Wild West,' said Jimmy.

'Why's it called Dodge City?' asked Susie.

'Because it's where hot lead flies around, and you're stone dead if you don't dodge it,' said Jimmy.

'What a feeble joke,' said Paula.

Jimmy smiled and thought of stunning Jenny Osborne in her RAF shirt. There was nothing feeble about Jenny.

The interrogation of Erich Kirsten and Hanna Friedler by British Security representatives was slowly grinding on.

The Parson was busy taking his time. He had Sammy and Boots under observation, noting their daily business routine, their prompt arrival at their Camberwell Green offices above a ready-to-wear clothes shop, their lunchtime emergence in the direction of a pub opposite, and their further emergence at the end of their day. Each had a car parked a little way from the premises. The spot fronting the shop seemed to be reserved for a small delivery van, which occupied it from time to time.

A car job could be injurious right enough, but there was no way of guaranteeing the right result, which was required to be an arm or a leg. And guns were noisy. He never used a gun. In any case, guns left clues, such as the bullets. He contrived fatal accidents, like death by unfortunate drowning.

He lay in bed one night thinking about the right kind of method. He had a woman he visited, but no wife. In his particular line of business, a professional couldn't afford to live day in, day out, with a wife without her getting to know too much. And wives tried to do conversion jobs on husbands.

A picture entered his mind, that of the two brothers leaving at the end of the day. They used an entrance at one side of the shop, and always stood there together talking for a few moments before separating. Four trousered legs all in a row, four knees all in a row.

Got it. A bolt from the blue. That would smash any knee and leave the leg permanently crippled. It might even take the leg right off from the knee downwards.

That's it, I'll use Little Blaster. Little Blaster's bolt went right through a certain gent a year ago, making retrieval kid's play, and the law still wasn't sure what had made a fatal hole in his chest.

The phone rang in Sammy and Susie's house one morning. Sammy and Jimmy were at work, Susie was out shopping, and Bess, who had been home three days, had taken Paula and Phoebe up to town before the young girls went back to school. And Susie's daily help was on holiday with her family.

The ringing phone went unanswered.

It rang again half an hour later, but to no effect.

That evening, Susie answered the ringing phone.

'Hello?'

'Hello, would that be the home of Bess Adams?' said a man's voice.

'Yes, I'm her mother,' said Susie.

'Oh, good evening, Mrs Adams, I'm Dan Passmore down in Tenterden, Kent, and I'm phoning on behalf of my American nephew, name of Jeremy.'

'Oh, we've heard of Jeremy,' said Susie, 'he and Bess met in the Lake District.'

'So they did, yes,' said Dan Passmore, 'and Jeremy reckoned Bess might be coming home from there about now.'

'She's been home three days,' said Susie.

'Could I talk to her? Jeremy hoped to reach her on the phone this morning. He tried twice, but there was no reply.'

'Oh, so sorry,' said Susie, 'she was up in town with her sisters and the rest of us were out.'

'Ah. Right. Well, I'd be obliged if you'd tell her Jeremy's had to go home to Chicago, his father being seriously ill.'

'Oh, I'm really sorry,' said Susie. 'Please hold on, and I'll call her so that you can talk to her yourself.'

'Much obliged, Mrs Adams.'

Bess, called to the phone, spoke to Jeremy's English uncle, who said he was pleasured to talk to her. He repeated what he'd said to Susie, that Jeremy had had to go home to Chicago on account of his father being seriously ill. He'd received a cable from his sister, asking him to return as soon as possible. He was actually flying from London Airport this evening.

'Flying?' said Bess.

'He always said that when he did go back home, he'd sail in the old *Queen Mary*, but now that he's got to get there in a hurry, he's going by plane. Anyway, I promised him I'd do what I could to let you know, and to give you his best wishes.'

'Well, thank you, Mr Passmore, and I do hope his father will recover,' said Bess.

'I'm sure we all hope so. Otherwise, Jeremy says his mother will probably want him to step into his father's shoes. He says he's a farmer now, not a packaging expert. That's his father's business, packaging. Well, I'm glad I've been able to let you know about all this, Miss Adams, and I daresay Jeremy will write to you. He spoke very highly of you.'

'Thank you, Mr Passmore, we all like being spoken highly of, don't we?' said Bess.

'Don't we and all,' said Dan Passmore. 'Goodbye, now.'

'Goodbye,' said Bess.

Over supper, of course, the family wanted to know what Bess thought of the unexpected news. Bess reminded them that she'd said she might or might not see Jeremy again, and that was still the position. It was the same with cousin Alice, she said. Alice's admirer, Sergeant Fergus MacAllister, was soldiering in Malaya as a regular, and Alice might or might not see him again.

'Hold on a bit, Bess,' said Sammy, 'don't let's suggest he might get–' He coughed. 'Well, a soldier's funeral.'

'Of course I'm not suggesting anything like that, Dad,' said Bess, 'only that you never know where the Army will take him next.'

'When do we get to see Alice?' asked Paula.

'Yes, we don't hardly ever see her,' said Phoebe.

'We saw her when she was home with Aunt Vi and Uncle Tommy for two weeks in July,' said Jimmy.

'Crumbs, that's not much,' said Phoebe.

'Well, I'm keeping my fingers crossed for her and Fergus, and for Jeremy,' said Susie.

'I hope Jeremy's plane knows where it's going,' said Sammy, 'and that it don't land him in Dodge City.'

The BOAC post-war airliner, carrying Jeremy among its passengers, was just taking off for New York, an all-night flight.

The Parson was driving an old jalopy. It could play up a bit, but was on its best behaviour as he motored across the junction at Camberwell Green and parked outside the pub opposite the Adams shop and offices. The time was just after five.

He was wearing a cap with a large soft peak. Beside him on the passenger seat was a square cardboard box. The pub wasn't yet open for evening business, and there were few pedestrians on this side of Denmark Hill. On his right he could expect the occasional passing bus or tram, that was all. He lifted the lid of the box and took a loving peek at Little Blaster, a sleek modern version of a crossbow, conveniently compact in its size and deadly in the velocity of its bolt.

He watched. He saw the parked cars of the brothers. The van was absent from its spot, giving him a clear view of the shop, to the left of which was the door leading to the stairs up to the offices. Well, even if the van did show up, it blocked only the lower view of the shop window. He took the crossbow out of its box, placed it on his lap and gave it a caress. It was already loaded, the bolt in place.

He was neither nervous nor sweating. He was a professional, with a job to do for a lovely hundred smackers. He waited and watched.

At five thirty, he was very much on the alert, the crossbow in his hands but hidden by the door. The window was wound down. A bus passed, completely blocking his view for a few seconds. The door to the office stairs opened the moment the bus passed, spilling the usual office workers, most of whom were girls. There were a couple of blokes who looked like pale-faced book-keepers, and following on, a lush-looking matronly woman. The Parson had seen them all during his watching briefs.

A minute or so elapsed, and then out came the two brothers, clear in the evening sunlight. The Parson lifted his crippling weapon, drew the bow back to his full extent, fixed it, and sighted on the two men. There they were, side by side, talking as usual.

He sighted on Sammy's right knee, and

silently swore as the van arrived, hiding the target for a moment before edging into its place. Committed, he confirmed his sighting and fired. His trigger action coincided with the unexpected. The van backed. Its driver, ex-Corporal Mitchell of the West Kents, an NCO in Boots's platoon at the first Battle of the Somme, exploded verbally as something tore into the offside of his vehicle, blasted through it, and buried itself low down in the nearside.

'What the bloody hell and gorblimey Amy...?' He turned, saw a ragged gaping hole in one side of the van, and a wicked-looking steel bolt quivering where it had jammed itself in the other side. 'Blind me, who done that?'

Boots and Sammy were at his driving window, rapping on it. He wound it down.

'Mitch, you all right?' said Sammy.

'Me van ain't, it's been hit by a bleedin' lump of iron,' bawled Mitch. Pedestrians were coming up and gaping.

Boots took a quick look at the embedded bolt, then turned. Across the road was a dirty old Morris, and the driver was trying to start the engine. The engine, however, was having none of it. It was coughing and stuttering on a contrary note of refusal. The capped driver kept trying. Boots saw him shoot a quick glance at the injured van. The engine fired then, and he was away. For once, however, the Parson was careless, due to the galling realization that he'd been thwarted by an idiot van driver. Boots saw the car angle out from the kerbside into the path of an oncoming bus. The full weight of the nearside front wheel of the bus crashed into the side of the car. Savaged metal shrieked and the crippled car turned over. The bus pulled up, and a couple of pedestrians some way back stood paralysed and gaping. Boots shot across the road at speed, Sammy following. They were the first to reach the car, lying on its side. Its driver, tipped from his seat, was a crumpled and unconscious heap. Jammed against the passenger door by his hips was a steel crossbow, plainly visible. Boots wrenched at the offside door. It refused to budge.

The shocked bus driver, down from his vehicle, said, 'I swear I had no chance of not hitting him.'

'Any of your passengers would confirm that,' said Boots, relieved that there had been no explosion, although he could detect the smell of leaking petrol. Mitch had joined him and Sammy, and a crowd was gathering, but staying well clear in case the leaking petrol ignited. Despite that risk, men were offering to help right the car and get the unconscious man out. The bus driver said best not to do that, in case it shook up the poor bloke and made any broken bones worse. Nor could anyone be certain that both doors weren't jammed.

'If you see what I mean,' he said to Boots.

'Knock the pub landlord up, Sammy, and use his phone to call an ambulance,' said Boots. The pub door opened at that point, and out came the landlord to investigate. He returned to his pub only moments later to use his phone. From the direction of Camberwell Green, two policemen were hurrying.

An ambulance from nearby King's College Hospital arrived in quick time, and a fire engine also turned up, its crew speedily doing all that was necessary to eliminate the risk of fire, and to right the car and prise open the doors. The ambulance crew effected careful removal of the driver and stretchered him.

The Parson, now semi-conscious, was carried off to the hospital. The police, curious, took charge of the crossbow.

'Do we say anything about what happened

to the van, Boots?' asked Sammy.

'Not here,' said Boots, and they crossed the road, where Mitch, having returned to the van, had his head inside it and was examining the ragged hole on one side and the embedded bolt on the other.

'You reporting this?' he asked Boots.

'Take it home, Mitch, remove that bolt and bring the van back here tomorrow morning,' said Boots.

Mitch didn't argue. He had a long-standing respect for Boots, his one-time sergeant.

Boots, walking with Sammy to their cars, said, 'You realize, do you, that if the van hadn't been in the way, the crossbow bolt would have hit one of us?'

'I ain't exactly short of savvy, y'know,' said Sammy.

'Granted,' said Boots, standing beside his car with Sammy. 'So who was that character, and what's he got against us?'

'I'm working on it mindfully,' said Sammy.

'So am I,' said Boots. He smiled. 'I'm mindfully buzzing.'

'Are you thinking what I'm thinking?' asked Sammy.

'I'm thinking we know only one son of a gun who wishes we hadn't been born,' said Boots.

'The Fat Man?' said Sammy.

'He's taken a few knocks from us lately,' said Boots.

'If he hired that geezer to blow holes in us, he still hasn't learned his lesson,' said Sammy.

'If you consider the angle of his aim, that bolt would have smashed into your legs or mine,' said Boots.

'I got to be grateful it wasn't one of our heads?' said Sammy.

'We'll pay a visit to the patient in a day or two,' said Boots.

'And take him a bunch of flowers and a bag of grapes?' said Sammy.

'We'll ask him a few questions,' said Boots.

'Now you're talking, me old soldier,' said Sammy. 'How about if we borrowed an old-fashioned rack from the Tower of London? Could we smuggle it in?'

'It's doubtful,' said Boots.

'Susie's not going to like this new bit of skullduggery,' said Sammy.

'Don't tell her,' said Boots.

'You're not going to tell Polly?' said Sammy.

'Perhaps,' said Boots. 'Say sometime next year.'

Chapter Twenty-Seven

'Hello, what've we got here?' asked Paul the following morning. Lulu had just arrived in her beret, a white blouse and a dark brown skirt. The skirt was actually short, its hemline only two inches below her knees.

'You've got something to say?' said Lulu, removing her beret, her spectacles giving him a suspicious look between the hanging curtains of her black hair.

'Not half,' said Paul. 'It's the first time ever.'

'Go on, kill me, then, the first time ever for what?'

'For seeing your legs,' said Paul.

'That's an event, is it?' said Lulu.

'It's sensational,' said Paul.

'I've said it before, and I'll say it again,' remarked Lulu. 'You're pathetic.'

'I wish I knew why you've been hiding legs like yours,' said Paul. 'They'd win prizes.'

'God help the starving workers,' said Lulu. 'That's if you're going to make a silly song and dance about my skirt.'

361

'Nothing to do with starving workers,' said Paul, opening the morning's mail. 'They're not starving, in any case, Prime Minister Attlee, Aneurin Bevan, Herbert Morrison and MPs like your own father have got the Welfare State looking after them. We'll mention that in our next propaganda leaflet. The current one's at the printers, and should be here in a couple of days. Um, where was I?'

'Oh, just in the middle of one of your barmy dialogues about my person,' said Lulu, seating herself at her desk. Conscious of the kneehole, she treated the hem of her skirt to several tugs to make sure it covered as much as possible.

'I'm not looking,' said Paul.

'Be your age,' said Lulu. 'What do I care if you're looking or not?' That remark relegated her skirt-tugging to the inconsequential. 'You flatter yourself.'

'There's a letter here from the headmaster of the grammar school in Camberwell,' said Paul. 'He wants to know if we can send a couple of Young Socialists, good speakers, to take part in a debate, Socialism is Beneficial to the Country.'

'Grammar schools ought to be abolished,' said Lulu. 'They turn out middle-class snobs.'

'I'm one of them,' said Paul. 'And so's George Brown, a cabinet minister. Here, hold on, lovey, you went to a grammar school yourself. It says so on your file.'

'I didn't go.' Lulu was huffy. 'I was sent. By my mother. One is helpless at the age of eleven. But I fought being turned into a snob.'

'Made a belligerent of you instead,' said Paul.

'Well, good,' said Lulu, cleaning out the clogged ribbon ink from her typewriter's letter faces. 'It'll help me knock spots off the opposition. Get me elected eventually. You can put me down for that debate. As a supporter of the motion. I'll show 'em.'

'The boys will like that,' said Paul.

'Not if they're toffee-nosed young Tories,' said Lulu.

'Oh, I get you, yes,' said Paul. 'I thought you meant you'd wear a short skirt.'

'I don't know why I stay in this job,' said Lulu. 'You kill me ten times a day.'

She had another sickening time later on that day, when Henrietta Trevalyan reappeared mid-afternoon. She was gushingly profuse about interrupting Paul, but said she was desperate to know if he'd made up his mind about joining forces with her in establishing a home for lonely old maids. Paul said it was a pleasure to see her, and begged her to accept his most profound apologies for not having come to a decision yet. (Lulu ground her teeth.) The cause was a noble one, said Paul, worthy of very serious thought, and his admiration for Henrietta as its guiding light was total. He said. (Lulu gagged.) Henrietta said she dearly hoped his admiration would lead him to her side in the venture. (Yes, thought Lulu, come into my parlour, said the spider.)

Paul said he'd still like to give it more thought. Meanwhile, would Henrietta like to stay for a cup of tea? Henrietta would. Paul said Lulu was just going to make a pot. Nothing of the kind, said Lulu, it's your turn. OK, I'll make it, said Paul, and went to the kitchen. Henrietta went with him.

When they returned, with the tray, the pot, three cups and enough biscuits for three, Lulu was sure Henrietta looked as if she'd been kissed. Or was it the other way about? Either way, Lulu felt it was time to throw up.

She went home to her flat in a bitter mood, and would have kicked the cat if she'd had one.

'Tommy, Dad's getting poorly,' said Vi, when her husband arrived home that evening. Her dad, known to all the Adams generations as good old Uncle Tom, was seventy-six. A sufferer from bronchitis, he was failing in health and presently confined by doctor's orders to his bed. His wife, Aunt Victoria, was frankly worried about him.

'Don't worry, Vi, he'll pull through,' said Tommy.

'You bet he will,' said Paul with a young man's cheerful conviction.

'He looked ever so pale and drawn when I was with him this afternoon,' said Vi.

'If it was serious, they'd have him in hospital,' said Tommy. 'He's not running a temperature, is he?'

'It's a bit high,' said Vi, 'but he's not feverish, and he says he'll be up in a day or so to pick some runner beans and some of his first leeks.'

'Good sign, that,' said Tommy. 'I'll pop round and have a chat with him myself this evening.'

'I'll come with you,' said Paul.

'Yes, buck him up with a talk on the Labour Party,' said Tommy.

'He votes Liberal,' said Vi.

'I know,' said Tommy, 'so a talk about the

Labour Party will get him up and fighting.'

'Anything to help,' said Paul.

'That won't be any help,' said Vi, 'so don't try it, my lad.'

Uncle Tom was very happy to see his son-in-law and grandson, and Aunt Victoria was touched. She was all for Uncle Tom being cheered up. It was as good as medicine, she said. And certainly, Uncle Tom did buck up, without having to listen to any talk on the achievements of the Labour Party.

The following morning, Lulu turned up in a sweater and trousers. Paul raised tub-thumping objections.

'Off with 'em,' he said, after denouncing them as a garment for horsy Tory women.

'Do what?' said Lulu.

'Off with 'em.'

'Oh, yes? Keen to see my knickers, are you?'

'Go home, take 'em off, and come back wearing a skirt.'

'Who'd you think you are? William the Conqueror? Well, I'm no Saxon starveling. So drop dead, Willy.'

'Whose trousers are they, anyway? Your dad's?'

'Tell me, go on, why should they be my dad's?'

'On you, they look baggy.'

'Baggy?'

'Believe me,' said Paul. 'Well, you've got very nice hips and those trousers are too wide in the thereabouts.'

'You cretin,' said Lulu. 'I'll smash your chair up again in a minute. Have you made an inspection of my hips?'

'Yes, very nice they are too,' said Paul. 'Rounded but not bulky. Graceful, rather. Pity about the trousers, but all right, wear them for today. Just don't let me catch sight of them tomorrow. Now let's do some work before a deputation of Young Socialists from Crampton Street arrives to demand a demonstration in favour of supporting Soviet Russia's beef with America. Mind, that'll be never-ending. Stalin's always beefing about America.'

'So he should,' said Lulu. 'America's criminally capitalistic. And listen, Napoleon. What I choose to wear is my business. Not yours.'

'You arrive in trousers tomorrow,' said Paul, 'and I'll do the job myself of yanking them off you.'

'Ha ha,' said Lulu.

However, she was wearing a skirt the following morning, plus a fixed expression that suggested any untoward comments from Paul would put his life in danger.

Paul, noting the signs, said, 'Good morning, Miss Saunders, happy to see you.'

'Yourself, you look a little better than you did yesterday,' said Lulu.

'How did I look yesterday?'

'As if tarty Henrietta had half-eaten you the night before.'

'I didn't see her the night before.'

'Really? I thought you must have made a date with her while you were doing a lot together in the kitchen.'

'In the kitchen,' said Paul, 'I was telling her I didn't really have time to help her with her lonely old maids.'

'Oh, you managed to be a bit manly instead of a bit limp, did you?' said Lulu, and sat down at her desk. Paul showed a little grin. Well, the kneehole of the desk presented its view of a fine pair of feminine legs, and he had nothing in common with an unappreciative lump of wood. 'Are you giving an impression of the Cheshire cat from *Alice in Wonderland?*' asked Lulu.

'Pardon?' said Paul. 'No, never mind, the new leaflets are in, so we'll patrol Walworth

Road today and hand 'em out.'

'You and I will?' said Lulu.

'We could do a lot together in Walworth Road, even if only for an hour or two,' said Paul.

Lulu chucked an eraser at him.

Boots made a phone call to the *South London Press* from his office. This excellent local paper had covered the traffic incident at Camberwell Green, and some obliging reporter on the news desk answered Boots's enquiry as to the name of the injured car driver.

'George Wheeler.'

'Thanks,' said Boots, and rang King's College Hospital. He asked reception how Mr George Wheeler was.

'Are you a relative, or a friend?'

'A friend.'

'Then you probably know he has a broken right shoulder, fractured ribs and a broken right leg.'

'Grim for poor old George,' said Boots, 'but it could have been worse, and it usually is when you argue with a bus. What's his condition like?'

'Low but stable.'

'So he's not up to receiving visitors yet?'

'Give him two or three more days.'

'Thank you.'

Boots let Sammy know they couldn't call on the patient yet.

Rosie and Emma were packaging eggs in a converted stable. The stable, close to the large cottage, had always been incorporated in the freehold of the latter.

The packed eggs, eight hundred of them and fresh that day, would be collected for distribution to London restaurants.

The phone, on an extension from the cottage, rang its tune. Rosie picked it up.

'Surrey Downs Poultry Farm.'

'That you, Rosie? Major Gorringe here. Now look here, Rosie old girl, what the devil's going off there at night? Sounds like a dervish with his arse on fire.'

'It's an alarm system,' said Rosie. Gilbert Gorringe, a retired Army major, was a neighbour, hearty, bluff, and no nonsense. 'To frighten off foxes.'

'Foxes my Aunt Fanny. It's putting the wind up Mildred.' Mildred was his wife. 'Fell out of the bloody bed when it went off last night. I thought Matt was going to shoot the bushy-tails.'

'He and Jonathan have tried, I assure you,'

said Rosie.

'What, what? Missed 'em, did they? Well, I'm coming over myself with my pea-shooter.'

'You're very welcome, Major,' said Rosie, 'but it's rare for us to see them by day.'

'I'll bring Wellington. He'll sniff 'em out.' Wellington was his Yorkshire terrier. 'I'll be there in ten minutes. Where are Matt and Jonathan?'

'Delivering laying hens to customers in Westerham,' said Rosie.

'Right, Rosie. Leave it to me, and I'll blast the backsides off those blankety-blank perishers,' said Major Gorringe.

He arrived as promised, a large, red-faced man, square of shoulders and ramrod of back. He put his head into the egg-packing chamber.

'Hello,' said Rosie.

'Hello,' said Emma, her infant daughter toddling about.

'Good morning, ladies, that's the stuff, you both look splendid,' said Major Gorringe. 'Won't interrupt you, I just want to know I've got your official permission to do my shooting on your land, Rosie.'

'Go ahead, Major,' said Rosie, dressed, like Emma, in a white smock.

'Right. Now, where's that bloody dog? Wellington?' He roared the name. Wellington responded with an excited bark, and off went the major, gun under his arm.

He was away for an hour and a half, during which time Rosie and Emma heard the periodic crack of his rifle.

'He's enjoying himself,' said Emma.

'He's probably ordering the foxes to stand to attention before he pulls the trigger,' said Rosie.

'Well, people do say Mrs Gorringe has to stand to attention for morning inspection,' said Emma.

'Do we believe that?' smiled Rosie, placing eggs in a shaped fibre tray that held two dozen.

'It's credible to me,' said Emma, one eye on little Jessie, the other on eggs.

'He's a character,' said Rosie.

When Major Gorringe returned, he presented himself smartly to Rosie and Emma.

'Good sortie, ladies. Wellington sniffed 'em out, got 'em running in front of my shooter. Bagged a full quartet, two dog foxes and two vixens. All flea-ridden, by God. I'll ring Doug Paterson of East Surrey Hounds and get him to pick up the carcases to feed to his pack. I'll be obliged if you'll inform Matt and Jonathan, and hope your alarm won't put the wind up Mildred from now on.'

'Matt and Jonathan will be delighted at the news,' said Rosie.

'I'm thrilled and relieved,' said Emma.

'Don't mention it,' said the major. 'Damn good hunting for me and Wellington. Hrrmph, your chick's just fallen on her botty, Emma. Stand her to attention. Good morning, ladies.'

Matthew, on hearing of Major Gorringe's success in despatching four foxes, said he'd let the alarm stay on this night, just to make sure.

It was only an hour after dark that the floodlight blazed and the banshee sound howled. Matthew woke up cursing, Major Gorringe woke up swearing, and Mrs Gorringe, waking up shrieking, fell out of bed. Major Gorringe helped her up and stood her to attention.

In the cottage, Matthew said, 'Damn my shirt tails, Rosie, either the major missed our pair or they've risen from the dead.'

'From what we know about that pair,' said Rosie, 'I'll opt for risen from the dead. And they'll burrow under the wire one night when they get used to the floodlight and the howl.'

Chapter Twenty-Eight

Chinese Lady said, 'I don't know, time just seems to be running away, Edwin.'

'It does run faster, Maisie, when one has turned sixty,' said Mr Finch.

'Oh, lor',' said Chinese Lady, 'in no time at all I'll be Lady Finch, and I still won't know how to talk to my neighbours and old friends.'

'You'll manage, my dear, just as you've managed everything else of a problematical kind,' said Mr Finch, who had received official confirmation of the honour being accorded him.

'Well,' said Chinese Lady, 'I'm not sure about problem – what was the word, Edwin?'

'Problematical,' said Mr Finch.

'I can't remember anything like that happening to me,' said Chinese Lady. 'What I do remember is Sammy giving me head-aches every time he went out of my front door in Walworth. Well, I never knew what he was going to get up to.'

'What he got up to, Maisie, turned out to be notable,' said Mr Finch.

'Yes, lining his pocket,' said Chinese Lady. 'That boy and his liking for money just wasn't respectable. Edwin, I won't have to do any curtseying at Buckingham Palace, will I?'

'No, Maisie, none, you'll be shown to a seat and you'll only be required to observe the ceremony.'

'That's a mercy,' said Chinese Lady. 'Would you like a cup of tea, Edwin?'

'Thank you, Maisie, very much,' said the understanding Mr Finch.

'What the hell's happening with the Parson?' growled Mr Ben Ford, the Fat Man.

'I ain't heard from him meself,' said Large Lump.

'Well, shift yourself,' said Fat Man. 'Rat off to Soho and ask questions. Find out what his official monicker is, and where he lives.'

'Asking about official monickers in Soho, guv, ain't supposed to be too healthy,' said Large Lump.

'Take the back-up with you,' wheezed Fat Man. 'Do a bit of eye-gouging if you have to. I want to know where the Parson's got to with me fifty nickers. If he's on his way to

Australia, I've been done to a turn, and I ain't going to like it.'

'Guv, I got recommendations about him being honest, didn't I?' said Large Lump.

'If honesty with my fifty oners is on the way to Australia,' said Fat Man, 'I'll dock your bleedin' wages. So shove off to Soho and start asking. I want to know why Sammy Adams, or his brother Boots, ain't crippled yet. Then there's Tommy Adams. Is he still walking about uncrippled? Get moving.'

Off went Large Lump, leaving the Fat Man to brood on the dishonesty of people these days. You couldn't trust anyone. What with that and the continuing downtrend in the prices of scrap metal, and cocky bleedin' Sammy Adams, he'd be better off emigrating to the Isle of Wight.

A little parcel, registered for safe delivery, arrived for Bess. Opening it, she discovered a slim volume of poems by William Wordsworth, and a greeting from Jeremy Passmore on the flyleaf.

'To Bess, a delightful companion for some happy hours on one of Wordsworth's little islands on Lake Windermere, August 1949. With every good wish. Jeremy.'

There was also a brief covering letter from

Mr Dan Passmore.

'Dear Miss Adams, I'm enclosing a book Jeremy handed to me just before he left, asking me to send it on to you, which I felt I must do. And I'd like to say it was a pleasure talking to you on the phone. Yours sincerely, Dan Passmore.'

Bess, delighted with the book, acknowledged its receipt in a letter of thanks.

'Well, isn't it nice?' said Susie, leafing through the book. 'It's poems. Sammy, look.'

Sammy took his turn to glance through the volume.

'Always being busy trying to earn a bit of the ready for me dear old ma,' he said, 'I never had much time for reading books, Bess.'

'Oh, rotten hard luck, Dad,' said Bess.

'And I only know one poem,' said Sammy.

'Which one is that?' asked Jimmy.

'Well, let's see,' said Sammy, and quoted.

*"A merchant of London put his profit
Into a Cheapside safe deposit,
But very sad to say,
On a heartbreaking day,
The Germans dropped bombs and he lost it."'*

'He ought to have put it in his old socks,

like you did, Dad,' said Paula.

'Daddy, you don't still do that, do you?' said Phoebe.

'No, not much,' said Sammy. 'Anyway, this book of poems shows this feller Jeremy has got a soft spot for our Bess.'

'Romantic,' said Paula.

'Is she blushing?' asked Phoebe.

'I can't see any signs,' said Jimmy.

'You can all stop looking,' said Bess.

'But she's supposed to blush, isn't she?' said Phoebe, giggling.

'She might have, a hundred years ago,' said Jimmy.

'Don't be soppy,' said Paula. 'Mum, did you blush when Dad did things that showed he had a soft spot for you?'

'What things?' asked Jimmy.

'I'm innocent,' said Sammy. 'I was then, and I am now.'

'But didn't you ever send Mum a Valentine card before you were married?' asked Paula.

'Valentine cards cost money,' said Susie, 'tuppence each at least. But you can forget about him being innocent. He actually gave me some fancy undies for a Christmas present once.'

'Undies, Mum?' said Bess. 'Before you were married, and in those days?'

'Yes, would you believe?' said Susie.

'Dad, you saucy old thing,' said Paula.

'Mummy, what did you do?' asked Phoebe.

'Blushed,' said Susie. 'I was the innocent one, not your dad.'

The morning after he'd been sent to Soho on an enquiry job, Large Lump reported to the Fat Man that he'd had no joy.

'You standing there like the Rock of Gibraltar with nothing good coming out of your concrete?' gurgled Fat Man.

'Well, I did me best, guv, with me back-up standing by,' said Large Lump. 'We stayed there till gone midnight, asking around all the time, but no-one invited me to sit down and put me ear to his cakehole. I got to tell yer, guv, that I'm short on information for yer, like.'

'You're bleedin' useless,' yelled Fat Man out of his blubber.

'Hold hard, guv,' said Large Lump, 'I showed me knuckledusters, didn't I? And me intentions if nobody spoke up. And I trod on more'n one foot. But I never met such a gorblimey kiss-my-elbow lot. Mind, I did say you don't make no friends, asking around in a place like that.'

Fat Man began a wheezing rumble of discontent, mainly to the effect that no-one on his payroll was earning his dibs, that he'd be better off hiring bob-a-job Boy Scouts. Large Lump mumbled something about he didn't like listening to ingratitude.

'Eh? Eh?' Fat Man's squeezed eyeballs turned a bit red.

'Well, I ask yer reasonable, guv, where's any Boy Scout that's got enough muscle to do yer shop collections? Ain't we always done them reg'lar rounds of the shops that's got contracts with you for protection, and ain't we always brought back the correct monthly commission?'

'I ain't denying that, am I?' rasped Fat Man. 'But who was it that recommended the Parson, and who's sloped off with me fifty quid? The bloody Parson.'

'I ask yer, guv, did anyone tell me he wasn't honest?' said Large Lump plaintively. 'No-one, me word of honour. That reminds me, just as we was leaving last night, some geezer did come up and whisper to try the 'ospitals.'

'Hospitals?'

'Course, it ain't what you call inform-ation–'

'I call it that, you charlie. Start trying.'

'You think he's having an operation, guv?'

'That whispering geezer was probably telling you he's been done over for another dishonest contract,' growled Fat Man. 'So start visiting.'

'Visiting?'

'Hospitals.'

'But we don't know his monicker.'

'But you can recognize him, can't you? Try the accident cases wards. Start now, you and the others, while I take some aspirin.'

The receptionist at King's College Hospital perked up when two impressive-looking gentlemen arrived to ask if they could see a certain patient.

'Which one?'

'Mr George Wheeler,' said Boots.

'Last week's car crash victim, poor old George,' said Sammy.

'You're relatives?'

'Friends,' said Boots. 'How is he?'

The receptionist consulted notes.

'Better than he was, you'll be pleased to know, and now able to receive visitors. But visiting times are evenings or Sunday afternoons.'

'Ah,' said Boots, and gave the lady a smile. 'It's afternoon now.'

'Yes, sir, Thursday afternoon.'

'The only afternoon we can manage,' said Boots.

'Well, as you're the first visitors he's had, perhaps Sister Phillips will stretch a point.'

Sister Phillips, looking crisp, starched and hygienic, crumpled a little when trying to cope with Sammy's blue eyes and Boots's whimsical comment that visitors out of hours could sometimes be better for a patient than visitors at all hours. She attempted to point out that visitors at all hours were never permitted under the hospital's strictly necessary regulations, but lost the thread of it halfway through.

'...never permitted – oh, well, perhaps as you are Mr Wheeler's first visitors, apart from the police who came yesterday to ask him about the accident, I believe, we can make an exception.'

'How very kind,' said Boots.

'Much obliged,' said Sammy.

Sister Phillips took them to the surgical ward of this internationally famous hospital, now a vital unit of the National Health Service, in which all treatment was free, if one ignored wage deductions imposed on the masses.

The Parson, all done up in plaster and bandages, was awake when Boots and

Sammy entered the ward in company with Sister Phillips. If his bones had suffered, his eyes hadn't. They blinked rapidly.

'Here are two visitors to see you, Mr Wheeler,' said Sister Phillips. 'No longer than twenty minutes now,' she said to Boots. 'And don't excite him.' She turned to go, then said, 'Or make him laugh.'

'I promise you, it'll only be a quiet, friendly chat,' said Boots, and she left them to it.

The Parson, caged up in his bed, followed the movements of his visitors out of quick eyes as they sat down, Boots on the right of his bed, Sammy on the left.

'Yes, sit down,' he said, 'I'm at home to visitors today. Would it be inquisitive of me to ask who you are?'

With other patients looking on, Boots leaned forward and said very quietly, 'I think you know who we are.'

'Flanagan and Allen?' The man, Boots and Sammy both noted, spoke without moving his lips, or so it seemed.

'What we'd like to know ourselves,' said Sammy, just as quietly, 'is why you tried to puncture us.'

'With a very nasty crossbow bolt,' said Boots.

'You're joking, of course,' said the Parson.

'I wish you wouldn't, not with the kind of ribs I've got. Didn't I hear the ward sister tell you not to make me laugh?'

'Well, let me put it very seriously,' said Boots. 'Either you tell us something we believe, or we'll hit you with a hammer. Show him, Sammy.'

Sammy opened up one side of his jacket to reveal a hammer, its handle tucked inside an unbuttoned section of his waist. He gave the Parson just a brief eyeful of the iron head.

'That's serious?' said the Parson. 'In here in front of my fellow sufferers?'

'It's your party, tosh,' said Sammy, 'we're only here to help you enjoy it. Tell him, Boots.'

'Pleasure,' said Boots. 'Yesterday, the police asked you about the crossbow, of course?'

'How'd you know that?'

'Mind your own business,' said Sammy.

'What I object to about the police,' said the Parson, 'is their nosiness. Even if a bloke was only in possession of a penknife, they'd want to know if he only used it for sharpening pencils. As I explained to them yesterday in the middle of all my pain, I bought it for my dear old dad, a retired Sunday School teacher. It's the kind of thing he likes to play with, being in his dotage, poor old chap.'

'Well, you'll get the hammer one way or another, either here or the day you're discharged,' said Boots, the dialogue still very quiet to avoid the straining ears throughout the ward. 'We'll be waiting, front and back, or some of our men will, and you'll be taken back into the hospital with both legs broken. That, Mr Wheeler, is no joke, it's seriously serious.'

'It strikes me as being grievous bodily harm, which is against the law,' said the Parson, quick eyes still going from one to the other.

'There's an option,' said Boots. 'It's either the hammer or telling the police about the bolt that ended up stuck in the van, but which was intended for one of us.'

'I don't like one or the other,' said the Parson. 'One's going to aggravate my injuries, and the other's going to make the coppers ask me more questions.'

'So tell us something we'll believe,' said Boots, 'such as why you targeted us, and who paid you to.'

'I don't like that, either,' said the Parson. 'It's asking me to go against my principles, and that'll make me ill. I can't afford to be ill as well as injured.'

'Go to reception, Sammy,' said Boots, 'and ask if you can telephone the police.'

'Now wait a minute,' said the Parson, 'I'm not saying I can't put up with being ill.'

'So stop mucking us about,' said Sammy, 'we're busy and we ain't got all day to listen to excuses.'

'Personally, I've got nothing against you gents,' said the Parson.

'So who has?' asked Sammy.

The Parson's quick optics met Boots's unblinking grey eyes, and what he saw there didn't soothe the ache in his broken bones.

'A certain party who wanted a disabling job done on one of you. Nothing fatal, on my oath, just an arm or a leg. You want a name?'

'That's all,' said Boots, 'just a name.'

The Parson sighed.

'Ben Ford,' he said, without moving his lips, or so it seemed.

Boots and Sammy met Sister Phillips in the corridor on their way out.

'You left our patient happy, I hope,' she smiled.

'Happy, but not delirious,' said Boots.

'On account of his suffering ribs,' said Sammy.

'Simple happiness is a pleasure to come by,' said Boots.

'Yes,' said Sister Phillips, her starched front crumpling again, 'yes, indeed, Mr Adams.'

'Thanks once more for making our visit an exception to the rule,' said Boots. 'Goodbye.'

'Do come again,' said Sister Phillips, and watched them as they left, two delightful gentlemen.

It was lunchtime for Lulu and Paul at the Labour Party's Walworth headquarters, and as usual they were eating it in the office.

'Let's see,' said Paul, tucking into a dressed salad prepared by his mum, 'I don't think you've told me how you got on in supporting the motion "Socialism is Beneficial to the Country" at that grammar school yesterday evening.'

'Why weren't you there instead of the Young Socialist you paired me with?'

'I abstained, I had a date,' said Paul.

'With tarty Henrietta?'

'With an old friend.'

'Female, of course,' said Lulu, her expressive horn-rimmed specs reflecting sorrow for anyone who put social relationships before the excitement of politics.

'She wore a very nice frock,' said Paul. 'So how did you get on?'

'Crushed the opposition, and carried the motion,' said Lulu.

'With the assembly hall full of toffee-nosed grammar school pupils whose parents probably all vote Conservative?'

'My support for the motion was brilliant,' said Lulu.

'What were you wearing?'

'Clothes,' said Lulu, 'I'm against debating in the altogether.'

'You wore a sweater and skirt, say?' suggested Paul.

'A dress,' said Lulu, munching an apple.

'Pretty?'

'What's that got to do with politics? Aspiring women politicians in pretties don't get taken seriously.'

'Lulu, you're still a girl,' said Paul.

'Piffle,' said Lulu.

'At only eighteen,' said Paul, 'you've got years yet before you need to be taken seriously.'

'Listen to you, Methuselah,' said Lulu. 'You're nineteen, aren't you?'

'Going on for twenty,' said Paul.

'You like to be taken seriously, don't you?'

'Certainly,' said Paul. 'I'm a senior official of the Young Socialists. Everything sacred would fall apart if I let the members treat me as an Aunt Sally.'

'Oh, really?' said Lulu. 'Well, the same goes for me. True Socialism means equality. So put that in your in tray.'

'Equality doesn't mean you should wear your father's trousers,' said Paul.

'I don't, and I'm not,' said Lulu, presently clad in a light brown jumper and a dark brown skirt, quite attractive stockings gracing her legs. Somehow, she was coming round to letting her legs be seen.

'Anyway, congratulations on crushing the opposition in the debate,' said Paul. 'Did any reward come out of it?'

'A bunch of flowers,' said Lulu.

'Pretty?' said Paul.

'What?'

'Pretty flowers?'

'I'm going to say something to you,' said Lulu.

'Such as?'

'Get your head examined.'

Paul laughed. The phone rang. He answered it.

'Hello, Paul.'

'Hello, Henrietta.'

Lulu growled.

But Paul avoided making a date. He was wary of Henrietta Trevalyan. He had an idea that one of her permanent fads was collecting poodles. He didn't go in for being that kind of bloke. His lifestyle was one which instinctively adhered to Grandma Finch's values.

Somehow, in some way, Chinese Lady's own lifestyle, based on respectable behaviour, had had its effect on her extensive family, from her sons and daughter downwards. No-one stepped out of line. Everyone consciously or subconsciously felt she was looking over his or her shoulder. Boots was the exception. He had had his moments with a woman ambulance driver and his love affair with Eloise's French mother. But that had been during the Great War, in Northern France, when Chinese Lady wasn't close enough to look over his shoulder.

Polly was waiting for someone to break the chains in these years following the war against Hitler. It had been a war that made old-fashioned conventions look archaic, and gave many women ideas about new horizons.

Yes, someone in the family would kick over the traces one day.

Chapter Twenty-Nine

The twins had had their bath, had come down for their Ovaltine, and after saying goodnight to their mother, were now being taken up to their beds by Boots. He was telling the immortalized story of Don Quixote.

'You might not believe this, kids, but he then charged the windmill.'

'Charged it?' said Gemma.

'Courageously and with determination,' said Boots.

'Crikey,' said Gemma, as they reached the landing.

'I know what happened next,' said James.

'Tell, then,' said Gemma.

'He fell off his horse,' said James. 'Well, I mean, a windmill.'

'Yes, but he didn't actually think it was,' said Gemma.

'Barmy,' said James.

'A valiant eccentric,' said Boots, and saw Gemma to her bed. He tucked her in. She looked up at him, her dark sienna hair soft and curling, her eyes already dreamy.

'Daddy, you're ever so nice,' she said.

'Well, I'm glad you think so, poppet,' he said, and kissed her nose. A little giggle escaped her, followed by a soft sigh of cosy content.

Boots then went to James's room. James, tucked up, delivered himself in manly fashion.

'Well, goodnight, Pa.'

'Goodnight, young 'un.'

'A windmill, I ask you,' murmured James, and closed his eyes.

On his way downstairs, Boots wondered, and certainly not for the first time, why life had favoured him so much. To have known his years with Emily, Rosie, Tim and Eloise, was as much as any man deserved. To now have Polly, Gemma and James, was richer than the icing on any cake.

Polly's educated tones interrupted his reflections.

'Something's going on, you old warhorse.'

'Just Don Quixote and the windmill, Polly.'

'Not that,' said Polly, knees curled up on the plush velvet of a settee, 'something quite different.'

'Such as?' said Boots.

'How do I know?' said Polly. 'You haven't

392

told me. But something is going on.'

'Is it?' said Boots, looking forward to listening to a radio talk by Lieutenant-General Sir Brian Horrocks, the cavalier wartime Commander of the British 30 Corps. Boots had been with the corps all through the Normandy campaign and its momentous advance into Germany itself. A reasonable man did not bring the war home with him, but it had its moments that could still stir the memory. A talk by Sir Brian was bound to be one of them. 'Is your intuition at work, Polly?'

'Intuition my Sunday bonnet,' said Polly. 'I know you, and I know when you're up to something. Out with it, or I'll come and bite you.'

'Bless the woman,' murmured Boots.

'Procrastination will get you nowhere,' said Polly. 'Watch my teeth.' She showed them, moistly white between modestly carmined lips.

'Excellent,' said Boots, 'who's your dentist?'

'My toothbrush,' said Polly. 'Oh, come on, old love, what's going on?'

'The fact is,' said Boots, 'after the incidents relating to the bales of nylon, I didn't think I needed to alarm you over something else that was a bit murky.'

'Alarm me?' said Polly. 'The only alarm I'd feel would be for the opposition, so come on, Geronimo, who's trying to set fire to your wigwam this time?'

'Same old cowboy,' said Boots, and told her in detail about the man in the car who had fired a crossbow bolt at himself and Sammy, and how Mitch, in putting the van into reverse at the critical moment, had taken the full impact.

'Oh, my God,' said Polly, 'now I am alarmed. And aghast.'

'Yes, not exactly pleasant,' said Boots, and told of the car's collision with a bus, the sight he had of a crossbow, the hospitalization of the driver, and the visit that resulted in extracting information and the name of what one could call the prime suspect. Ben Ford.

'Him again?' said Polly. 'The Fat Man? Get him here and I'll lynch him. Or will you and Sammy do it?'

'I think we'll send him a letter,' said Boots.

'A letter?' said Polly. 'A letter? The man's Public Enemy Number One. Phone the police.'

'Calling in the police will mean turning keen business rivalry into war,' said Boots.

'Very messy.'

'If it's not messy war already, I'm a mountain goat,' said Polly.

'We'll settle for a letter,' said Boots.

'Can I trust you to make that effective?' asked Polly.

'We'll see,' said Boots.

Polly gave him a searching look. It was no surprise to find not the slightest sign of a man worried. His lurking smile surfaced, and his lazy left eye performed a slow wink. That told her that what he had in mind for Mr Ben Ford wasn't likely to make the Fat Man think Christmas had come.

Polly smiled.

'Go get him, Geronimo,' she said.

The following day, ex-Corporal Mitchell broke his journey to the firm's shop in Oxford Street by parking the van near the Elephant and Castle. It was an area devastated by German bombers, and development had begun by way of levelling ugly sites. Mitch entered the building in which the Fat Man's offices were situated. He announced himself to a heavy, the man called Rollo.

Rollo, who, in company with Large Lump, had so far failed to find any hospital that had admitted the Parson, spoke to the Fat Man half a minute later.

'A bloke to see you, guv,' he said.

'What bloke?'

'Says he's got an important letter for you, and that he's got to deliver it personal.'

'Who is he?'

'Just some elderly geezer.'

'Let's have him in, then.'

Mitch was admitted. He'd been in this place before, years ago, and he recognized the Fat Man at once, a barrel of lard squashed into his padded chair, a large geezer standing beside the desk.

'Morning to yer, Mr Ford,' said old soldier Mitch.

'You've got a letter for me?'

'You bet,' said Mitch, and drew a stout brown envelope out of his jacket pocket. 'It's from Mr Adams.'

'Oh, is it, eh? Which one?'

'Mr Adams senior, Mr Robert Adams.'

'The one called Boots?' Fat Man's face contorted, and his voice emerged to sound a bit like a suet pudding fighting for survival in a sea of dumplings. 'Boots, you're telling me?'

'The same,' said Mitch and placed the letter on the desk. Its brown envelope seemed heavy. Large Lump, guarding his boss, watched as the Fat Man picked it up, weighed it in his hand and shot Mitch a suspicious glance.

'It won't bite, I promise yer,' said Mitch.

'You'll be bleedin' dead if it does,' said Fat Man, and ripped the envelope. A steel bolt fell out and hit the desk with a dull thud. 'What the hell...?'

'I said so,' remarked Mitch, 'I said it wouldn't bite, didn't I?'

Fat Man extracted a folded sheet of note-paper. He read the message it contained.

'Your man's in King's College Hospital. You'll join him any time between now and next week, with a bolt like this one in your belly unless you move far far away. You can believe this. Robert Adams.'

Fat Man positively paled and his huge girth seemed to shrink like a leaking balloon. He knew Boots all too well and he remembered the two young men who had made mincemeat of his heavies, and done Sparky over. They were more than capable of doing himself over. Suddenly, Fat Man recognized the unpalatable fact that life for him was plainly dangerous.

'Hospital?' he croaked.

'A bloke name of George Wheeler,' said

Mitch. ''Orrible geezer. See that bolt, Mr Ford? He fired it from a crossbow at me employers outside their offices at Camberwell Green. Missed. Then he had an accident that put him in King's College Hospital. Nasty, it was. He won't be out too quick. That's all. Good morning to yer, Mr Ford.'

Mitch left, leaving Large Lump and Rollo gaping and the Fat Man sagging.

'Well, I ain't never heard anyone sauce yer like that before, guv,' said Large Lump. 'You going to make plans to do a real heavy job, say with extra back-up?'

'And end up in that bleedin' hospital?' wheezed Fat Man. 'No, I ain't. I'm emigrating.'

'Emigrating?' said Large Lump. 'Where to?'

'Bloody Australia, where else?' bawled Fat Man. 'But first, you shove off to that hospital and get my fifty quid back from the Parson, real monicker George Wheeler.'

Lulu and Paul were in Walworth Road, near the East Street market, handing out leaflets to passersby. The weather had turned cloudy and cool, and Lulu was in a thick, shaggy brown jumper and one of her long skirts. She offered a leaflet to a buxom woman carrying an umbrella to cope with the threat of rain. The woman took it, walked on, stopped, read the leaflet and brought it back.

'Here, what d'you give me this rubbish for?' she said.

'To let you see the Labour Party needs your vote,' said Lulu.

'Well, they ain't getting it,' said the woman belligerently, 'and I hope they ain't getting yourn, either.'

'The Labour Party–'

'I don't want no cheek,' said the woman. 'What's this bit about keeping Churchill out?'

'It's–'

'It don't even call him Mr Churchill,' said the woman accusingly. 'Where's your manners?'

'We don't consider–'

'I'm admiring of Mr Churchill,' said the woman, 'and so's me old man, bless his whiskers.'

'Many people don't share–'

'Well, they ought to,' said the woman. 'How many leaflets you got there?'

'A bundle, and–'

'I'll take the lot,' said the woman.

'You're not getting them,' said Lulu.

'Give 'em here, so's I can make a bonfire

of them in me back yard,' said the woman.

'Now look here, missus–'

'I'll learn yer,' said the woman, and swung her umbrella.

Lulu ducked, and up came Paul, together with several gawpers.

'What's the trouble?' asked Paul.

The buxom woman, seeing that he too held a bundle of leaflets, cracked him over the head with her umbrella.

'Vote for Mr Churchill!' she yelled.

'Sorry you're not one of us, lady,' said Paul. He took Lulu by the arm and pulled her away, crossing the road with her.

'D'you mind not dragging me?' said Lulu.

'And d'you mind not upsetting people?' said Paul.

'Well, that's choice, I must say,' said Lulu. 'What a silly old biddy. Didn't give me a chance to put more than two words together. How's your fat head? Did she raise a bump?'

'It's not damaged,' said Paul. 'Come on, it's lunchtime, and I'll treat you to a meal in the pie and mash shop in the market.'

'Pie and mash?' said Lulu. 'Now you're talking. And I'm not proud. Pride's a sin. Tories have got a surplus. My father grew up on pie and mash. Pity he didn't eat more greens. Then he'd have had more brains.

Brains get you to Prime Minister level. Still, he's on the Honest Joe level. That gets him a steady following.'

'Is that a speech or a large helping of unsolicited information?' asked Paul as they made their way to the market.

'All of us should receive information gratefully,' said Lulu. 'It helps our education.' She handed out a leaflet to a stallholder as they entered the market. The stallholder promptly used it to wrap up a bunch of spring onions for a customer.

'He wasn't grateful,' said Paul. 'Still, that kind of gesture educates us in one thing. How to take rebuffs to our bosoms and fight discouragement.'

'I don't know about your bosom,' said Lulu, 'but leave mine out of it.'

'Just a figure of speech,' said Paul, and took her into the old-established pie and mash shop, where in very short time they were sitting down to a nourishing meal, along with people who, like Lulu's dad, seemed to have grown up very sturdily on this popular Walworth fare. If the UK was still in the doldrums, the market wasn't. The noise of hustle and bustle penetrated the shop in cheerful fashion, and there was a regular intake of buoyant customers buying hot pies to take away.

'Ta for treat,' said Lulu when she and Paul were making their way back to their office, 'I enjoyed it. I suppose you could be a worse old fusspot.'

'You're music to my ears,' said Paul, and handed a leaflet to an approaching bloke, who took one look at it and thrust it back, planting it on Paul's waistcoat.

'Keep it, mate, light yer fire with it,' he said, and went on like a man who'd enjoyed a satisfying moment.

Lulu's specs reflected joy.

'There, that's one in the eye for your bosom,' she said, and laughed.

Paul grinned.

'Just another educating rebuff,' he said.

Boots wanted to know something, and asked Mr Finch to do him a favour. Mr Finch knew how much he owed Boots for never breathing a word about his German origins. Lately, he had been wondering if the time had come to give Chinese Lady all the facts of his life, but he felt too many years had passed, and so he eventually came to the conclusion that here was a definite case where it was better to let sleeping dogs lie. That meant, as far as Chinese Lady and her family were concerned, that he would take his deepest secrets to the grave with him, for he also knew Boots would ensure they stayed buried.

The British Secret Service had all the facts on his file, of course, but he had their word that on his death the file would be destroyed.

He did Boots the requested favour. He went to Whitehall, where old colleagues still not of retiring age greeted him in their pleasantly civilized way.

That evening, while Chinese Lady was entertaining two old friends from Walworth, he called on Boots and Polly to tell them what had happened to Erich Kirsten and Hanna Friedler, once of Himmler's notorious SS. Their long interrogation had produced amazing results. Yes, they had both escaped during their escorted journey from Belsen to Nuremberg. Knowing they were listed by British security forces, they decided to avoid the risk of being recaptured and turned east with the intention of making their way into Austria where, at its border with Italy, they could make contact with couriers of an SS escape route and secure new identity papers in Rome.

They did manage to reach Austria, but south of Vienna their luck ran out. They were picked up by Russians and ended up in Moscow, to be interrogated by Stalin's secret police. Here came a fundamental change in their outlook, a change that had occurred in General von Paulus, the captured Commander of the German Sixth Army at Stalingrad. They were brainwashed very successfully, and they turned their coats, as he had, in the induced belief that Stalin and his Russians had proved superior in both war and ideology to Hitler and his Germans. They became agents for Stalin's KGB, and agreed to form a cell in London with documents identifying them as Poles who had served with the Free Polish Army.

During the final stages of their interrogation by the British, they came up with the names of people recruited by them to serve the cause of Soviet Russia. Hanna Friedler had played the traditional siren's part in this, and so had a hidden camera.

'So there you are,' said Mr Finch at the end of his recounting.

'Dear God, what a pair of frightful stinkers,' said Polly, 'with a disgusting record as cold-blooded executioners of Jewish women and children.'

'So what's going to happen to them now?' asked Boots.

'Whitehall can't quite make up its mind whether to hand them over to the Russians, who'd certainly execute them, or to make use of them,' said Mr Finch.

'What's wrong with hanging them from some stark tree on some blasted heath?' said Polly.

Mr Finch said, 'Polly my dear, in my retirement I'm not privy to the innermost corridors of Whitehall.'

'Edwin old sport,' said Polly, who at least knew his government work had been with British Intelligence, 'you're not going to be knighted for having been a mere tiddler.'

'I think I was able to infer a new attitude is developing,' said Mr Finch. 'That of making use of some war criminals, instead of extraditing them to Nuremberg. I think America is already doing so. Not publicly, of course.'

'If Erich Kirsten and Hanna Friedler are going to escape trial and execution,' said Boots, 'I smell political perfidy.'

'On the other hand,' said Mr Finch, 'much of what they divulged was in return for – um – favours, although no promises were made.'

'Which probably still means they won't be hanged,' said Boots.

'We'll have to wait and see, Boots,' said Mr Finch.

Chapter Thirty

The Labour government secured the passing of an act that gave the workers a statutory five-day week, thus enabling them to enjoy a full weekend break.

One Saturday morning, Sammy and Susie's elder son Daniel was high on a ladder at the back of his house in Kestrel Avenue, off Herne Hill, south of Denmark Hill. He was fixing a gutter support, driving in a new bolt as a replacement for a broken one. At the foot of the ladder stood his wife Patsy, and nearby was their little daughter, Arabella. Patsy had one foot on the bottom rung of the ladder to keep it steady.

'Daniel, I don't like you being so high up,' she said. Daniel was outlined by the sky. 'Hey, did you hear me?'

'Sure I heard you,' said Daniel, banging away. 'But if I were lower down, I'd be hammering this bolt into the wrong bit of the wall.'

'Oh, very funny,' said Patsy, considered by the family to be much the best thing that had ever happened to Daniel. 'Wisecracks are out while you're all the way up there. The ladder's gotten trembles.'

'Cuddle it,' said Daniel.

'Oh, sure, I grew up cuddling ladders,' said Patsy. 'Daniel, come down.'

Little Arabella, nineteen months old, piped, 'Daddy.'

'There, Arabella's telling you to come down,' said Patsy. Although she was just as adventurous as Daniel, she simply didn't like to see him high up in the sky.

Daniel gave the bolt one last blow from the hammer, drove it fully home, and inspected it. Satisfied, he slid down the ladder athletically, which made Patsy give a little shriek. But he arrived quite safely.

However, she shook her finger at him.

'Daniel Adams, don't you ever do that again, d'you hear? It's showing off and it's dangerous.'

'But, Patsy, you wanted me down, so I thought I'd do it the quick way,' said Daniel.

'Don't give me any uppity talk,' said Patsy.

Daniel looked at her. There she was, his Patsy, seen against the colourful background of the garden, which she sometimes called their back yard. Excitable, larky and lovely, an all-American girl, dark-haired and bright-eyed, Patsy was a free spirit with no inhibitions. Their attractive house, centrally heated, was their very own, given to them as a wedding present by his mum and dad. His dad had also made him joint manager of the property company with cousin Tim, husband of blind Felicity.

'Right, Patsy, I won't do it again.'

'Arabella and I simply don't want you to break your neck,' said Patsy.

'Daddy,' said little Arabella again.

Daniel put the hammer aside and picked her up, cuddling her like a warm bundle of soft treasures.

'You charmer,' he said, and she put her arms around his neck. 'That's my little cheesecake. By the way, Patsy, did you know my sister Bess found an American bloke up in the English Lakes?'

'My stars,' said Patsy, 'was he lost, then?'

'Dad didn't say so when he told me. His name's Jeremy Passmore, and he comes from Chicago. Dad wondered if you knew him.'

'Well, sure, I know everyone in Chicago, don't I?' said Patsy.

'Is that a statement of fact?' asked Daniel, slightly smothered by his warm armful of infant girlhood.

'Listen to him,' said Patsy, rolling her eyes.

'What a barmy bloke.'

'That's colloquial English,' said Daniel.

'It's true,' said Patsy. 'Well, gee whiz, how would I know everyone in Chicago?'

'Dad's a bit concerned about Chicago bootleggers, like Al Capone,' said Daniel.

Patsy yelled with laughter.

'Your dad's like you,' she said through a potpourri of mixed gurgles, 'a hoot. Bootleggers went out with dinosaurs.'

'I told him that, in so many words,' said Daniel, 'but he still thinks Bess's American guy is risking it a bit. He's in Chicago at the moment, visiting his sick father.'

'Tell your pa to keep smiling,' said Patsy. 'Bess's find in the English Lakes won't get gunned down.'

'No, of course not,' said Daniel, giving Arabella a kiss on her little nose. 'Well, not unless one dinosaur disinters itself.'

'Daniel?' said Patsy.

'Yes, Patsy?'

'You're cute,' said Patsy.

At his home, in his bed, lovable old Uncle Tom, Vi's dad, contracted pneumonia and passed away at the age of seventy-six.

Aunt Victoria was stricken. Vi and Tommy did their best to console her. Vi resorted to the comforting value of providing her with a nice cup of hot tea.

'Thank you, Vi,' she said. 'Your dad was a good man, a good husband.'

'Yes, Mum, I know,' said Vi huskily.

'I can't help thinking I wasn't always as patient with him as I should have been,' said the sad widow.

'Oh, he had his funny ways,' said Vi, 'but he understood you.'

'Yes, of course he did,' said Tommy.

'But I never properly listened to him.'

'Mum, he told me only two days ago that he had a good life with you,' said Vi. 'I think he wanted everyone to know that, I think he knew by then that he wasn't going to get better.'

Boots arrived at that point. Chinese Lady was still sitting at the bedside of the dead man, a distant cousin. The doctor, still present and waiting for an ambulance to arrive while filling in a death certificate, assured Boots there had been no real suffering. Boots regarded the face of death, the peaceful face of a man who had known hardship and the trials of life. He thought of Elsie Chivers who, lamenting her mistakes, had also found peace in death.

'Goodbye, old chap,' he said, and went

downstairs to offer his own consolations to Aunt Victoria. Listening to her expressing mournful self-reproach, he said, 'There isn't one of us who can claim to be perfect, or anywhere near it. Don't we all wish there were words we'd never spoken, or tempers we'd never given in to? Think about the fact that whenever Tom needed you, you were always there. That, old girl, is your greatest consolation.'

'Thank you, Boots, you're so kind,' said Aunt Victoria.

'Tommy and I, we'll see to all the arrangements,' said Boots.

'Of course,' said Tommy.

Boots whispered, 'Give her a brandy, Tommy, if there is any.' There was.

If there was one thing the Adams family disliked to confront, it was a funeral of one of their own. In Chinese Lady's time since her marriage to Corporal Daniel Adams, there had been only two deaths and one funeral. A soldier's rites were accorded her husband, blown to pieces near the Khyber Pass. It was her daughter-in-law Emily who had had a funeral.

Now there was a second funeral, Uncle Tom's. Even though only a distant cousin, he was still one of the family, as Aunt Victoria was.

Everyone had hated burying Emily, and no-one liked the sight of Uncle Tom's coffin being lowered into his grave. It occurred to Polly that this extraordinary family either expected its members to live for ever, or thought they should by right. She murmured so to Susie.

'You mean by wish,' whispered Susie. 'Well, I don't ever want to lose Sammy, and I know he never wants to lose me. Who'd send his shirts to the laundry?'

Which made Polly think of Boots's shirts, the shirts he wore so well. God, if I ever lost him, I'd jump off London Bridge.

Ashes to ashes, dust to dust.

Silently the family watched Uncle Tom laid to rest.

Someone, deft and noiseless as a cat stalking a mouse, broke into the 'safe' house in which two suspected war criminals were under protective guard. Without disturbing the custodians, he injected a sleeping woman with poison that killed her in brief seconds. And he did the same to a sleeping man in the adjoining room. None of the four guards detected a sound or a movement.

412

'A KGB agent, undoubtedly,' said a security chief. 'Ah, well, it's solved a problem for us. The Russians knew too much for us to make double agents of them.'

Mr Finch, having been discreetly informed of the swift and sudden demise of Erich Kirsten and Hanna Friedler, phoned Boots.

'I can believe a KGB agent found his way into the house and into two bedrooms without alerting the night guard or waking up either Kirsten or the woman?' said Boots.

'It seems so, but there'll be an inquiry, of course,' said Mr Finch.

'Not in an open court, I imagine,' said Boots.

'It's how some things have to be done, Boots.'

'Well, the extinction of those two animals goes some way to satisfying me,' said Boots, 'but I fancy their victims would have preferred to see them slowly hanged.'

'It's a preference many of us understand,' said Mr Finch.

'Edwin old friend,' said Boots, 'do me another favour. Send a Christmas card to that KGB agent via the Soviet Embassy.'

'We've no idea of his name,' said Mr Finch.

'Address it "To whom it may concern",' said Boots.

Mr Finch smiled as he put the phone down.

December, the week before Christmas.

The firm's Walworth store was stacked with Yuletide lines, and everything was illuminated by Christmas lights. Manager Freddy Brown and his assistants, Jimmy and Ruby, were busy.

In came a girl, cosily wrapped up in a maroon coat with a black fur collar, and wearing a woollen hat with a bobble. She spotted Jimmy, and spent time inspecting goods until he was finished with a customer. Then she advanced at a brisk walk.

'Excuse me,' she said, 'I'm looking for– Well, I never, it's you, Jimmy.'

'Half a mo,' said Jimmy, giving his eyes a treat, 'I think that's you, Jenny.'

Gorgeous Jenny Osborne looked as colourful as Christmas itself, her face glowing, eyes sparkling.

'Where have you been all this time?' she asked.

'Working,' said Jimmy, 'and don't give me

any lip, such as all this time.'

'But you might at least have sent me a card,' said Jenny.

'I might if you'd given me your address,' said Jimmy.

'Didn't I, then?' said Jenny. 'But I did call to give you a snapshot of myself on the beach the morning you left. A fat lot of good that was. Your charlady told me you'd all departed at the crack of dawn, you rotter.'

'Have you come here just to get my goat?' asked Jimmy.

'No, as if I would,' said Jenny. 'I've come to buy two more RAF shirts. I hope you've still got some in stock. If you haven't, I'll do you to death.'

'That's what you've come for, shirts?' said Jimmy. 'I'm chuffed, I don't think. Shirts, she says.'

'And to make sure I was served by you,' said Jenny. 'I want all your attention.'

'You can have my last farthing as well,' said Jimmy.

'Really? Jimmy, that's sweet. Is it all right to give me your undivided attention? I mean, are you terribly busy?'

'Not at the moment, not personally,' said Jimmy. There were just two customers, apart from Jenny, and Freddy and Ruby were attending to them. 'How's Barry?'

'He's fallen for a Siamese art student, thank goodness,' said Jenny. 'Look, I've got tickets for a jolly pantomime at the Kingston rep theatre for the second Saturday in January. I love pantomimes. Jimmy, would you like to call for me and take me?'

'Er?'

'Well, would you?'

'Do what?'

'Oh, come on, Jimmy, don't go gaga on me,' said Jenny.

'What's happening?' asked Jimmy.

'It was happening all the time at Daymer Bay,' said Jenny, 'and I should have known it. I've thought about you lots. Have you thought about me?'

'Only in a hopeless way.'

'Well, my word, think positive, can't you?' said Jenny.

Jimmy cast a look at Freddy and Ruby. They were still busy.

'I have to ask,' he said, 'exactly why d'you want me and not one of your close friends to take you to this show?'

'Because you're a sweetie, and I want us to see more of each other,' said Jenny.

'I saw a lot of you in your swimsuit,' said Jimmy. 'Talk about moments of joy.'

Jenny laughed, and Jimmy thought, as he had on other occasions, how it made her look sparkling.

'Jimmy, you're my kind,' she said. 'You'll call for me at seven, say, if I give you my address?'

'Not half,' said Jimmy, 'and if the snapshot you mentioned is one of you in your swimsuit, or your shirt and shorts, let me have that too.'

'Well, congratulations, Jimmy, that really is positive,' said Jenny.

'My pleasure,' said Jimmy. 'Now, this way to the shirts.'

'Silly man,' said Jenny, 'I didn't really come for any shirts, I came to see you.'

'You're making my day,' said Jimmy, a little light-headed. 'After all, I can sell shirts any old time.'

In came customers.

Jenny dug into her handbag, extracted a beach snapshot of herself in her shirt and shorts, and gave it to Jimmy. Her address and phone number were on the back.

'There you are,' she said. She glanced at the new customers. 'I'll have to push off now, I suppose, but Happy Christmas, Jimmy.'

'Happy Christmas, Jenny, and may all your days be sunny, as the dandelion said to the daffodil. "Look who's talking," said the daffodil.'

Jenny was laughing on her way out.

A little later, Freddy asked Jimmy if he'd let a customer escape without buying anything.

'Which customer?' asked Jimmy.

'The peachy young lady,' said Freddy.

'Oh, she just wanted to tell me the time,' said Jimmy.

'The time?' said Ruby.

'Yes, seven o'clock on the second Saturday in January,' said Jimmy.

'Sounds promising,' said Freddy, whose happy-go-lucky nature had taken a savage beating during the Burma campaign against the insufferable and inhuman Japs. His return home to Cassie and his children had restored a large amount of his cheerful appreciation of life. 'Ought to be an entertaining evening, Jimmy, considering her high-class looks.'

'Yes, where'd you find her?' asked Ruby.

'On a beach,' said Jimmy.

'Have I seen her before?' asked Ruby. 'She seems familiar.'

'Not with me,' said Jimmy, 'she's a well brought up girl.'

'Gertcha,' said Ruby.

Jimmy smiled. He was on a high.

Later that day, with the art college students on vacation, Jenny met her friend Fiona.

'Did you see him?' asked Fiona.

'Yes, I saw him.'

'What a sweetie,' said Fiona.

'Yes, isn't he?'

'I could eat him,' said Fiona.

'Well, hard luck, Fiona ducky, you're not eating Jimmy,' said Jenny, 'he's reserved.'

'He's got a girlfriend?' said Fiona.

'Yes, me,' said Jenny.

Chapter Thirty-One

Matthew and Jonathan set a trap that night, a cold and crisp night, very much like that which, according to legend, King Wenceslaus and his page had endured about a thousand years ago. The trap was formed by a large spread of stout rope netting, fixed very lightly halfway up the hedge and fanning out from there to the ground. When the foxes frisked through, they'd bring the netting down on top of them the moment they nosed into it.

Well, that was the idea, and it had its humanitarian aspect in that it would inflict no pain. Trapped, the foxes could be cleanly shot.

'Think they'll fall for it?' Jonathan had said.

'We'll tempt the perishers,' said Matthew, 'we'll rub meat grease all over the netting. The smell of that will reach their noses far quicker than our smell.'

The banshee had been switched off during recent days on account of a bellowing phone call from Major Gorringe to the effect that the blankety-blank contraption had caused Mildred to fall out of bed again and bruise her rear end. The consequent silence of the banshee had resulted in the foxes getting to the wire fence and taking no notice when the floodlight came on. They'd dug deep. Jonathan had filled in the hole, but he knew that next time they'd dig deeper and be in among the hundreds of roosting hens.

Now, Matthew and Jonathan were waiting not far from the netting. They themselves could smell the meaty odour. It was strong enough to kill their human smell, for sure.

At about eight o'clock, the hedge lightly rustled to the influx of furry bodies.

Matthew and Jonathan tensed. The rustles were just audible, and so was the swish of the netting as it fell. Matthew was up and rushing, Jonathan following. Matthew had a torch, and they each had a rifle. The netting was emitting frantic little scuffles. On went the torch to illuminate the captives.

'Well, blast my damned braces,' breathed Matthew. 'Look what we've caught, Jonathan.'

Jonathan, arriving, looked at what was showing in the bright light of the torch.

'Bloody rabbits,' he said.

'Six of 'em,' said Matthew, 'two old bucks and four plump does.'

'When did rabbits start liking meat?' said Jonathan.

'About five minutes ago, so it seems,' said Matthew.

'D'you fancy rabbit pie?' asked Jonathan.

'It'll make a change from scrambled eggs and roast chicken,' said Matthew. 'But not for six days in a row. We'll skin a couple for Mildred Gorringe, as recompense for her bruised bum. And we'll rig the netting up again, for the foxes.'

'Leave a card inside it, wishing 'em a merry Christmas,' said Jonathan.

The rigging stayed up all night, but it

didn't catch anything. However, there were hordes of ants digging into the smeared meat grease and carrying it off.

Bess received an American Christmas card from Jeremy, airmailed from Chicago. He had penned the following greeting.

'Happy Christmas, Bess, many regrets that I'm two thousand miles-plus from you, but my father has died and I've problems to solve. All the same, I intend to keep my promise to see you, so don't go away. Jeremy.'

Christmas Eve, and the afternoon atmosphere at the Labour Party's Walworth headquarters was festive. No-one could say that since the victorious election in 1945, Prime Minister Attlee's government had failed the people with its measures. There were still problems, mainly with the economy, but the headquarters' workers felt entitled to enjoy some Christmas cheer.

Lulu, however, had her head down. She'd finished typing letters and was now engaged in what had become her favourite occupation, the devising of catchy slogans. Her spectacles were on the end of her nose, her rich black hair hanging, her lips pursed, and her legs a visual brightness below the hem of her skirt. Her concentration represented an earnest disregard of the noises of partying in the building.

Paul came in, a glass of beer in one hand, and a bottle of cider in the other.

'Lulu,' he said, 'what're you doing?'

'Working,' said Lulu.

'Go easy,' said Paul, 'it's Christmas Eve. There's free food and drink in the main office, as well as a large amount of mistletoe.'

'All that's for adolescents,' said Lulu. 'I'm a woman of serious application. To my career.'

'I've told you, you're still a girl,' said Paul, 'and serious application at your age will make your hair fall out. Now, would you like a glass of cider? Or a cupful if we can't find a glass?'

'Thank you, but not yet,' said Lulu. 'Listen. How's this for a New Year slogan? "Workers! Rise up! Make sure we are still the masters!"'

'Where'd you get that from?' asked Paul.

Lulu reminded him that Sir Hartley Shawcross, a member of Britain's prosecution team at the original Nuremberg trials, and now the Labour government's Attorney-General, had made a famous declaration about the victorious Socialists in 1946. He'd said, 'We are the masters at the moment, and not only at the moment, but for a very long time to come.'

Paul said he wasn't sure he liked that kind of declaration. It sounded as if the Labour Party had the power and inclination to flog anybody who upset it. Like Winston Churchill, for instance. As leader of the opposition, he was always tearing strips off Labour's ministers.

'It wouldn't be very popular, Lulu, even with a whole lot of Labour voters, flogging Winston Churchill.'

'Are you drunk?' asked Lulu.

'Not yet,' said Paul. 'Now look here, we were elected to set up free health care, to nationalize public services and the means of productivity in certain industries, like coal-mining, and to provide social welfare benefits for the poor. We've done all that without flogging anybody. That slogan about being the masters won't do. It's not appropriate for our kind. This is the time for thinking up words of goodwill to all.'

'Blow that,' said Lulu. 'Goodwill to the Tories? Their industrialists have still got their boots on the necks of the workers. Time we executed the lot of them.'

'Lulu, you terror, I'll flog you if you don't get a bit of the Christmas spirit inside you,' said Paul, plonking the bottle of cider on her desk.

'Oh, very funny,' said Lulu.

At that moment in walked her father, the constituency's MP, a happy smile on his face, a glass of whisky keeping him company.

'What's going on, eh?' he said.

'Lulu's still working,' said Paul.

'So I see. Time you started to celebrate, Lulu. Come on.'

Lulu declared herself too busy. So her father took over in the hearty fashion of a man who didn't allow his politics to interfere with old-fashioned tradition. Five minutes later Lulu found herself in the main office, crowded with workers soaking up the party atmosphere and the free drinks. Her father gave her a glass of tonic, mildly infiltrated by gin. Paul, a grin on his face, watched as she was drawn into a celebration of Christmas. Such annual festivity she regarded as a capitalist ploy to make the country's workers feel they were being treated handsomely. She tried to say that what everyone should be celebrating was one more year of a Labour government. No-one listened. People insisted on refilling her glass.

After an hour her glasses were slightly askew, her face flushed, and the party was breaking up to allow the staff to go home early. Kisses were being given and received under hanging sprigs of mistletoe. Lulu, tipsy, was nevertheless sufficiently compos mentis to escape this kind of silly behaviour. Paul, still keeping an eye on her, followed her back to their office.

Lulu, standing at her desk and regarding it as if not sure what it was or why it was there, was swaying a bit.

'How d'you feel?' he asked.

She looked at him while pushing her specs back from the tip of her nose.

'I know you,' she said.

'Good,' said Paul. 'You can go home now.'

Her father put his head in.

'Pick you up in five minutes, Lulu, and drive you home,' he said with an understanding smile, and his head went away again.

'That'll make sure you get there,' said Paul.

'Is it Christmas?' asked Lulu.

'Christmas Eve,' said Paul.

'Invented by capitalists,' said Lulu, stumbling a little over the latter word.

'Well, never mind,' said Paul, 'have a

happy time.'

Lulu's spectacles blinked.

'You're going to give me a silly kiss,' she said.

'There's no mistletoe in here,' said Paul, 'but perhaps a kiss is called for.'

'I – oops–' Lulu emitted a hiccup. 'I wouldn't advise it.'

Paul kissed her, anyway, to show goodwill. Lulu quivered.

'There, that didn't hurt, did it?' he said.

'What a liberty,' said Lulu. Putting her arms around his neck, she kissed him back, her lips laden with gin and tonic. Her glasses fell off.

What a kiss, thought Paul. She's got hidden talent.

Her father walked in.

'Hello, hello,' he said heartily, 'is this a Christmas special?'

Lulu, her arms still around Paul's neck, said vaguely, 'Where's my specs?'

'On the floor,' said Mr Saunders.

'I think the swine kissed me,' said Lulu, slowly unwinding herself. She swayed. 'Someone hit him.'

Her father laughed. Paul picked up her spectacles. He gave them to her, and she put them on. They peered at him.

'Well?' said Paul.

'Some Christmas,' she said.

Her father took her home then.

Boots and Polly entertained a gathering of the clan on Christmas Day evening, at their large house close to Dulwich Village. One could have said it was as much a multitude as a gathering. Widowed Aunt Victoria was present, and so were Polly's father and stepmother. And so was Rachel, who, since coming to know the family, had never felt she needed to dissociate herself from Christian customs. She was, in any case, regarded as one of the family now that her daughter Leah was married to Lizzy and Ned's son Edward.

The old-fashioned party games were riotous.

Lizzy said to her daughter-in-law Leah, 'Is it too much for you?'

'Oh, no,' said Leah, 'I love it.'

Polly said to Susie, 'It'll never change.'

'Well, do we want it to?' said Susie.

'Boots doesn't,' said Polly. 'He's convinced there are too many other changes happening already.'

'Sammy says he hopes they'll be good for business.'

'That's Sammy, the old sport,' said Polly.

Rosie said to Boots, 'Same old games.'

'Same old world, Rosie.'

'Our old world?' said Rosie.

'Yes, ours,' said Boots.

Patsy said to Daniel, 'I used to think I'd never survive English Christmases.'

'I sure am chuffed you did, honey chile,' said Daniel, 'I sure am.'

'Some cowboy,' said Patsy. 'Daniel, you're cute.'

That, she knew, would rouse him. It did.

'Wait till I get you home,' he said.

'Promise?' said Patsy.

'You bet,' said Daniel.

Bobby said to Helene, 'Something on your mind?'

'Yes,' said Helene, 'I'm thinking all the English are crazy, especially at Christmas.'

'Are we?' said Bobby.

'Yes, *chéri*, and so am I,' said Helene.

Rachel said to Jimmy, 'What are you thinking about?'

'To be honest, Aunt Rachel, the second Saturday in January.'

'My life,' said Rachel, 'is that going to be special?'

'That, Aunt Rachel, is what you call in the hands of fate,' said Jimmy.

'There's a girl, is there?' said Rachel.

'Yes,' said Jimmy, 'and she's special, I can tell you that.'

Chinese Lady, sitting with Edwin, Aunt Victoria, and Sir Henry and Lady Simms, said to her husband, 'Edwin, I can't remember Christmas being as noisy as this.'

'Maisie, my dear, there are quite a few more of us now,' smiled Mr Finch.

'Well, I just hope the few more don't bring the house down,' said Chinese Lady.

At the chicken farm, the dog fox and its vixen, trapped at last by the rope netting, were biting their way through it, and hoping to run free by the time Boxing Day dawned.

Chapter Thirty-Two

New Year, 1950.

Early January.

'Back off,' said Lulu. Paul was leaning over her desk, offering her a sheet of notepaper.

'Something bothering you?' said Paul. Well

into his twentieth year, he could not claim to be as handsome as his father, but he was still personable enough to please many a fair maiden looking for a steady.

'I'm not forgetting Christmas Eve,' said Lulu, in her nineteenth year and not looking for anything but a career in politics. 'Nor that sloppy drunken kiss you gave me.'

'Oh, you remember that, do you?' said Paul. 'I thought you were too foggy with gin and tonic to remember anything.'

'Some swine laced my glass of lemonade,' said Lulu, specs glowering.

'That lemonade started off as a gin and tonic,' said Paul.

'I don't drink that stuff,' said Lulu. 'It's for the snooty wives of capitalists and Conservatives. And if you don't take that silly grin off your face, I'll do you an injury.'

'Forget going off your chump,' said Paul, 'and type this out for me, there's a good girl.' He placed the sheet of notepaper in front of her.

'I'm busy,' said Lulu.

'Doing what?'

'Typing letters.'

'You've just finished them,' said Paul.

'Have I? So I have. So you're lucky, then.' Lulu was always on her guard during their many dialogues, much as if she suspected her person was going to be taken apart and refitted. She picked up the sheet. 'What is it?'

'Agenda for the AGM of the Young Socialists' committee,' said Paul. 'When you've typed it, run off a dozen copies on the Roneo, and we'll get them posted tomorrow.'

'Your writing's grim,' said Lulu.

'So am I when I'm getting sauce,' said Paul.

'That's it, scare me silly,' said Lulu. 'Listen. We need more outdoor meetings. The kind to draw crowds. To get the populace election-minded. Or they'll forget to vote next month.'

A General Election had been fixed for February, when Prime Minister Clement Attlee and his Labour Party were hoping for the victory that would entitle them to remain in office. However, some doubts existed, due to what looked like a swing to Winston Churchill's Conservative Party. Although the promised Welfare State had been created, the economy was still shaky, and industry still lagging behind competitors. Lulu, very Left-wing, was all in favour of taxing the rich up to their eyebrows. Paul, although an opponent of capitalism, was wary of extremism. He didn't think beggaring the rich would provide the country with untold wealth. It was more likely to put the rich on the dole.

'More outdoor meetings?' he said. 'Good point, Lulu, but it's January, and not many people of Walworth and Camberwell are going to stand about listening to Young Socialists on soapboxes. They've got their chilblains to think about. Better if we organized a doorstep canvass by as many volunteers as possible. What are you doing tomorrow evening?'

'Studying,' said Lulu.

'Studying what, might I ask?'

'The life of James Keir Hardie, the first Socialist ever to be an elected MP,' said Lulu.

'Lulu, not on a Saturday evening,' said Paul.

'When's Saturday evening, then?' asked Lulu.

'Tomorrow,' said Paul.

'What's today, then? Oh, yes, Friday. But it makes no difference. I'll still be studying tomorrow.'

'Now look here,' said Paul, 'you'll get old before your time unless you go in for a bit of recreation. Haven't you been to any of these dance halls specializing in that American-imported craze, the jitterbug?'

'Six wild elephants couldn't drag me,' said Lulu. 'The jitterbug was invented by men. It gives them an excuse to chuck girls about until their knickers fall off.'

Paul laughed.

'Stronger elastic, that's the answer,' he said.

'Your sense of humour kills me,' said Lulu.

Paul regarded her with curiosity. He had moments when he thought there might just be a female girl struggling to get out, such as when she gave him a clinging smacker on Christmas Eve, but they were moments few and far between. All the same, someone ought to help her to start living.

'Well, tell you what,' he said, 'how about coming to the cinema with me, the one showing a reissue of *Pygmalion*, starring Leslie Howard as Professor Higgins, and Wendy Hiller as Eliza? It's a classic.'

'Must you think of the trivial?' said Lulu. 'At a time when the serious is raising its dark head? D'you want Churchill and his Tories to win the election? Bang goes the Welfare State if that happens. And back into the workhouses go the starving widows and

434

their children.'

'Might I point out workhouses no longer exist?' said Paul.

'The Tories would encourage the capitalists to build new ones,' said Lulu.

'You won't come to the cinema, then?' said Paul, going back to his desk.

'It's fiddling when Rome might start burning again,' said Lulu.

'You're a sad case, Lulu,' said Paul, sitting down, 'very sad. Oh, well, it's your life. Let's have some tea now, shall we?'

'Your turn,' said Lulu, putting a sheet of paper into her typewriter.

'Yours,' said Paul, 'so get on with it.'

Her specs scowled at him, but she went to the kitchen. When she brought the tea in, she said, 'Oh, all right, then.'

'All right what?' asked Paul.

'I'll come to the cinema with you.'

'Good,' said Paul, 'you'll enjoy it.'

'Listen,' she said, looking down at him, 'it's not going to be meaningful.'

'Meaningful?'

'Yes, it won't mean I'll be willing to repeat it.'

'Well, let's both live for the present,' said Paul.

'And for helping the Labour Party to get

re-elected,' said Lulu.

'Right, got you, Lulu,' said Paul.

'That makes a change,' said Lulu.

She enjoyed the film and was frank in her praise when they left the cinema. Paul said hang onto happiness. It can be a bit elusive. Lulu said she'd wait for it.

'For how long?' asked Paul, walking with her through the bright lights of London's West End.

'Until I'm an MP,' said Lulu.

'Lulu, you've got years of agony between now and then.'

'Oh, really? Well, if it gets to hurt, I'll shout.'

'I can't promise I'll be around listening,' said Paul.

'Listen, big chief,' said Lulu, 'I stand on my own feet. I'm one of this country's modern women.'

'My grandma's suspicious of modern women,' said Paul, shepherding Lulu through crowds turning out of theatres and cinemas.

'Grannies like that have their feet stuck in the past,' said Lulu. 'Is that my arm you're holding?'

'Just to keep you from being bumped,' said

Paul. 'It's not meaningful.'

'Ha ha,' said Lulu. When they reached the bus stop at Waterloo Bridge, she said, 'Have you got ideas of seeing me home?'

'No, I'm letting you stand on your own feet in case you aim a wallop at me,' said Paul, as a bus pulled up. 'But as I don't want to walk all the way to Denmark Hill, d'you mind if I share the bus with you?'

'Don't be funny,' said Lulu.

They followed several other people onto the bus. It was full downstairs, so they climbed to the upper deck, Lulu preceding Paul. She was wearing a long coat over a plain, practical winter costume, and all it gave Paul was a view of her ankles. Very trim, he thought.

The bus took them to Kennington, where she alighted. She said goodnight to Paul.

'And thanks,' she said.

'You're welcome,' said Paul.

When he arrived home, Vi, of course, asked him if he'd enjoyed his evening. He said the film was just the job. What about the young lady, said Vi, did she enjoy it too? Paul said yes, she had, though much against her will.

'Against her will?' said Vi, with Tommy hiding a grin.

'Yes, she believes that film-going is a waste of time for modern females,' said Paul.

'What a funny girl,' said Vi.

'It's what comes of being a serious Socialist,' said Tommy, 'so let that be a lesson to you, me lad.'

'Nothing wrong with serious Socialism,' said Paul, 'as long as you know you're living.'

A week later the second Saturday in January arrived, and Jimmy, given use of his dad's car, motored to Jenny's home in Wimbledon. It was close to the open spaces of Wimbledon Common, and even in the dark Jimmy could see it was a house of impressive design, standing by itself and fronted by an in-and-out gravel drive. It was five minutes after seven when he rang the bell.

Jenny herself answered the summons. Framed by the light of a handsome, oak-panelled hall, she looked as stunning as ever in a crimson dress.

'Hello,' said Jimmy.

'You're late,' said Jenny.

'Only by a few minutes,' said Jimmy, 'and it was dark all the way.'

'Never mind, I'm happy to see you,' said Jenny. 'Come in and– Wait, what's that?'

'My dad's motor,' said Jimmy.

'Oh, good show,' said Jenny. 'My father was going to drive us to the theatre and pick us up afterwards, but now we can be independent. So come and meet my family.'

Jimmy met them in a large drawing room, beautifully furnished and with an open log fire crackling and blazing. Jenny's mother was tall, well-dressed and charmingly receptive to the introduction.

'So you're Jimmy, the young man we've heard about,' she said in well-educated tones.

'Happy to meet you, Mrs Osborne,' said Jimmy, 'but should I ask if what you've heard has alarmed you?'

'I assure you, we haven't heard it's preferable to avoid you,' said the welcoming lady. 'You're the one who played golf with Jenny, aren't you?'

'I'd be grateful if we kept off golf,' said Jimmy, and that brought a smile to Mrs Osborne's face.

Mr Osborne was also tall, if a little stout and slightly bald. He was a vigorous man, however, and he shook hands firmly with Jimmy.

'Glad to meet you, young man,' he said. 'And you look to me as if you've got the physique to swing a fine club. Practice, that's all you need.'

'Be a sport, Mr Osborne,' said Jimmy, 'keep off golf.'

'I won't say a word about it myself,' said Jenny's sixteen-year-old sister, Caroline, on being introduced. Her handclasp lingered as she took in Jimmy's firm features.

'You've got my promise too,' said brother Christopher, the eldest of the offspring.

'In that case,' said Jimmy, 'you could both get to be my friends.'

'Love it,' said Caroline, 'do come again.'

'That's it, Jimmy,' said Jenny, 'time we went. Oh, and we've got our own transport, Dad. Jimmy has a car.'

'Fine,' said Mr Osborne, 'that lets me out. Glad you dropped in, Jimmy.'

'Thrilling,' said Caroline.

Once in the car, Jenny said, 'Don't let Caroline get too close, she's already wicked.'

'Well, that's great,' said Jimmy, pulling out of the drive, 'she's the first wicked girl I've met. Exactly how wicked is she?'

'On a par with Dracula,' said Jenny.

'How'd you manage to cope with your evil friend Fiona and your wicked sister?' asked Jimmy, heading for Kingston.

'With gritted teeth,' said Jenny, 'but if you

turn out to be like either of them, say swinish, I'll give up. Did you have a good Christmas?'

'We had a big fat turkey, I'll tell you that,' said Jimmy.

'Big fat ones are still hard to come by,' said Jenny.

'Oh, ours fell off the back of a lorry,' said Jimmy, 'and my dad knows the bloke who picked it up. Incidentally, what do you rate as swinish?'

'Gropers,' said Jenny.

'Grocers?'

'No, you idiot.' Jenny laughed. 'Gropers. Ugly-minded men with wandering hands, like one of the tutors at the college. You're not that kind, are you, Jimmy?'

'I can honestly say no,' said Jimmy, driving at a steady speed through lamplit roads.

'I believe you,' said Jenny, 'or I wouldn't be in this car with you. By the way, do you like pantomimes?'

'Mad about 'em,' said Jimmy, overtaking a slowcoach.

'Is that a polite lie?'

'Well, say a polite exaggeration.'

'Jimmy, you'd better like this one.'

'Well, I will, won't I? I like a pantomime. It rounds off Christmas.'

'Same here, pantomimes are fun,' said Jenny. 'Drive on, Ben Hur.'

They arrived in good time in Kingston, the county town of Surrey on the banks of the Thames, and Jimmy was able to park close to the rep theatre. He and Jenny joined a stream of people going in, and they found their seats halfway up the stalls. Up went the curtain five minutes later, the auditorium lights were dimmed and the pantomime, *Cinderella*, began.

It was a riot of fun, the Ugly Sisters, played by male comedians, as per tradition, a giggle to kids in the audience. Kids loved pantomimes, and parents gave them a yearly treat. The Prince, the character who picked up Cinderella's glass slipper as she fled the ball on the stroke of midnight, was played by a girl, also as per tradition, and commonly known as the principal boy, all very confusing to visitors from abroad. The girl in this pantomime wore sleek theatrical tights, dark blue velvet shorts, a red doublet and a plum-coloured velvet hat with a plume. Girls who played principal boys had to have very good legs and thighs, and this one certainly did. Jimmy was accordingly appreciative. Jenny gave him a dig in the ribs once or twice, to let him know she wasn't in favour of where his eyes were.

The Ugly Sisters had songs to sing, songs slightly barmy, and the audience, requested to join in, did so, the kids with great enthusiasm.

The first half ended with Cinderella fleeing the ball and leaving one glass slipper behind, and the curtain came down on the Prince clasping the slipper adoringly to his (her) chest, and Jimmy feeling there was something familiar about his (her) looks.

Along with other people, he repaired with Jenny to the refreshments bar, where he bought coffee and cake for her and the same for himself.

'Thanks, Jimmy,' she said. 'Enjoying yourself?'

'Good fun,' said Jimmy, 'and I'm thinking I've seen the principal boy before.'

'You have,' said Jenny, 'it's evil Fiona. The pantomime's being performed by a local amateur dramatic society, and she's a member.'

'Well, I must say she's got—'

'Don't say it,' said Jenny. 'You're with me, and I'll get savage if you try to make me listen to what you think of Fiona in her sexy tights.'

'Point taken,' said Jimmy. 'Anyway, you'd

look better.'

'In sexy tights?'

'That's my firm conviction.'

'What brought that on?'

'Cornwall by the sea,' said Jimmy.

'I still can't think why you're just a shop assistant,' said Jenny.

'Didn't I tell you?' said Jimmy. 'It's my first foot on the ladder leading to future prospects of enviable promise.'

'What a mouthful,' said Jenny, and Jimmy caught the smile that made her bright eyes sparkle. What a girl.

They enjoyed the second half of the performance, even more riotous than the first, and the curtain came down on the Prince (the principal boy) gathering Cinderella to his (her) bosom.

On their way out, Jimmy said, 'Do we go backstage to compliment Fiona on her performance?'

'Not likely,' said Jenny, 'I'm not letting you get a close-up of evil Fiona in her tights.'

'Oh, right,' said Jimmy.

Outside, the coldly crisp night air attacked them, and Jenny slipped her arm through Jimmy's as they walked to the car.

'Look here,' she said, 'how about a fair arrangement?'

'What's a fair arrangement?' asked Jimmy.

'Well, you've got my address and phone number, haven't you?'

'So I have,' said Jimmy.

'So when do I get yours?' asked stunning Jenny Osborne.

Which made Jimmy think a very promising friendship could develop. His Uncle Boots would have told him it also pointed to Jenny being a very modern post-war young lady, quite different from the modest violets of pre-war days.

Taking time off from the office the following Tuesday, Boots visited Southwark Cemetery, carrying two sheaves of white chrysanthemums with him, one to place on the grave of Emily, the other on another grave close by, that of Elsie Chivers, the widow of a German landowner. He had loved both women.

Emily. A woman of bright life and undiminished spirit. Elsie. A woman of gentleness and tragedy. In her brief will she had left him all that she was worth, which was the money in her bank, three hundred and twenty-one pounds. Boots thought the gesture one that placed her as a lonely woman. No close relatives, no near and dear friends. Only himself as a memory of her time in Walworth, of the days when she was in happy company with him and the family and Emily. Sunday teas. Conversation, quick sallies and constant laughter.

Elsie and Emily. Both gone, both still in his thoughts so often. He poured water from the available can into the standing metal vases, then put the sheaves of large white blooms in place. He stood for a few moments, wondering about life and death, and what it all meant, then turned and left.

Chinese Lady was thinking about the young ones, and their marriages, and their children. Lord, I just don't know how I'm going to count them all.

She mused on her years of life and her family, then spoke to her husband.

'Edwin, it won't be long now before we have to go to Buckingham Palace.'

'True, Maisie, not long,' said Mr Finch.

'Well, I hope all our family will be able to keep their heads about it,' she said, 'and I still don't know how I'm going to keep mine, or to put up with being Lady Finch for the rest of my life. Oh, lor'. Edwin?'

'Yes, my dear?'

'Where's my smelling salts?'

The publishers hope that this book has given you enjoyable reading. Large Print Books are especially designed to be as easy to see and hold as possible. If you wish a complete list of our books please ask at your local library or write directly to:

Magna Large Print Books
Magna House, Long Preston,
Skipton, North Yorkshire.
BD23 4ND

This Large Print Book, for people
who cannot read normal print,
is published under the auspices of

THE ULVERSCROFT FOUNDATION

... we hope you have enjoyed this book.
Please think for a moment about those
who have worse eyesight than you ...
and are unable to even read or enjoy
Large Print without great difficulty.

You can help them by sending a
donation, large or small, to:

**The Ulverscroft Foundation,
1, The Green, Bradgate Road,
Anstey, Leicestershire, LE7 7FU,
England.**
or request a copy of our brochure for
more details.

The Foundation will use all donations
to assist those people who are visually
impaired and need special attention
with medical research, diagnosis
and treatment.

Thank you very much for your help.